CAMELOT FALLEN

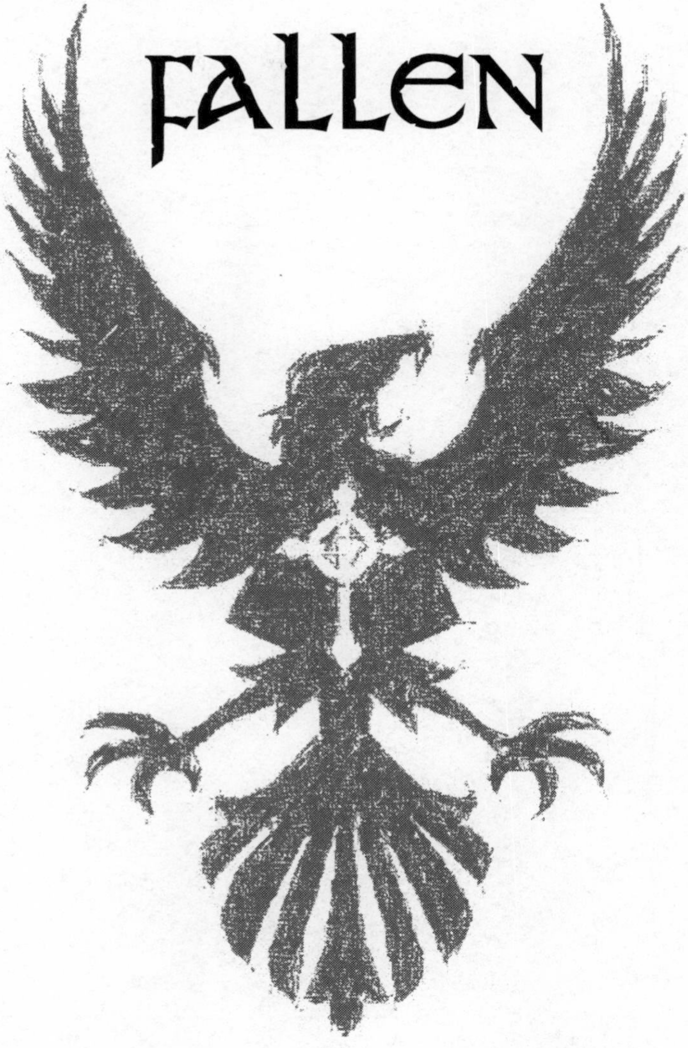

JOSHUA DARWIN

The characters and events portrayed in this book are fictitious. Any similarity to real persons, living or dead, is coincidental and not intended by the author.

ISBN: 1502913674
ISBN-13: 978-1502913678

Table of Contents

Author's Introduction

During the 17th Century, British writer John Milton wrote the epic poem *Paradise Lost*, one of the most famous literary works in the English language. However, Milton's original intent was to base his poem on the legend of King Arthur rather than the biblical Fall of Man. I've always been fascinated by this idea and have long wondered what an Arthurian epic by Milton might have been like. So I finally decided to write one myself. Now, my novel is written in prose rather than verse, and I imagine that fact will be much appreciated by modern audiences who may not have the patience or stamina to endure epic poetry. However, I can see clear similarities between the legend of King Arthur and Milton's magnum opus. Both stories are tragedies marked by an idyllic land (Camelot/Eden) beginning in perfection but eventually being lost due to the failings of mankind. Even the title of my novel, *Camelot Fallen*, is a play on *Paradise Lost*, and the savvy reader may even notice the handful of lines I adapted from Milton and placed throughout my own text.

I have also always been a lover of the Arthurian canon, specifically *The Once and Future King* by T.H. White and *Idylls of the King* by Alfred Tennyson, with both authors leaving their mark upon my writing and my imagination. The internal historicity of *Camelot Fallen*, while not strictly accurate and dotted with anachronisms, was largely drawn from my own research on the mysterious world of Post-Roman Britain as well as Geoffrey of Monmouth's pseudo-historical *Historia Regum Britanniae*. Other literary influences for this novel include *This Present Darkness* by Frank Peretti, *City of God* by Augustine of

Hippo, and the many works of C.S. Lewis, specifically *That Hideous Strength*.

I spent seven long years completing *Camelot Fallen*, and throughout the process it has been a labor of love, a challenge, an achievement, a frustration, and now... a dream ultimately realized. As we delve into this legendary world together, I'd like to leave you with a quote from Lewis himself. In a now-famous review of J.R.R. Tolkien's seminal *Lord of the Rings* trilogy, he wrote the following about the value of myths and fairy tales:

"'But why,' (some ask), 'why, if you have a serious comment to make on the real life of men, must you do it by talking about a phantasmagoric never-never land of your own?' Because, I take it, one of the main things the author wants to say is that the real life of men is of that mythical and heroic quality. One can see the principle at work in his characterization.... The imagined beings have their insides on the outside; they are visible souls. And man as a whole, Man pitted against the universe, have we seen him at all till we see that he is like a hero in a fairy tale? ...The value of myth is that it takes all the things you know and restores to them the rich significance which has been hidden by the veil of familiarity."

In the course of time, the usurping king Vortigern, to buttress the defense of the kingdom of Great Britannia which he unrighteously held, summoned warlike men from the land of Saxony and made them his allies in the kingdom. Since they were pagans and of devilish character, lusting by their nature to shed human blood, they drew many evils upon the Britons.

Presently their pride was checked for a while through the great Arthur, King of the Britons...

- from *The Legend of St. Goeznovius*, A.D. 1019

Prologue

"It happens tonight. The child must never see the light of day."

"Yes, my lord," replied the smaller creature, "You have no need to worry. All will be done just as you commanded."

"You have always been a loyal servant, Oriax," his master continued, "Do not disappoint me."

"On my life, Lord Astaroth, I will not fail."

With those final words, the one called Oriax spread his black, leathery wings and began to drift through the cool twilight air. He flew low to the ground, careful to conceal himself within the shadows, and grateful for the heavy clouds that billowed in from the north, masking the sun as it lay low in the western sky. His would be a mission of stealth and precision. Lord Astaroth had promised him the command of seven legions should he succeed, and Oriax yearned for such an opportunity. After all, how hard could it be to murder a mere infant? With his twisted mind focused on the task at hand, Oriax slithered across the wild moorland landscape and into the outskirts of Tintagel, an isolated little village nestled within the steep coastal cliffs of northern Cornwall. The rocky hills were dotted with modest thatch houses, and the cobblestone walkways were bustling with smithies, carpenters, farmers, tailors, fishermen, and all other sorts of folk on their way home for their evening meals. The landscape was brushed with patches of rough grass and heather blossoms, and in between the houses lay small square fields of oats, rye, and wheat. In the center of the town stood a great stone fortress, from whose highest tower flew a crimson banner emblazoned with the golden eagle of the Roman Empire. And within the walls of that fortress, past the gatehouse and beyond the bastions and battlements, walked the town's lord and protector, a man known in those parts as Uther Pendragon. As a stalwart Roman soldier, on most days he was a paragon of strength and leadership. But tonight he was a nervous wreck.

Uther paced anxiously through the Great Hall, breathing rapidly and chewing his fingernails. It was a dreadful habit, and his wife Igraine had scolded him for it on numerous occasions. He told himself that it was a rather childish tendency for a decorated cavalry officer, but every time he forced his hands away from his mouth, they quickly found their way back. However, on this night Igraine wasn't around to scold him. On this night she was lying in bed, sweating profusely and wailing in agony, and each time she wailed, Uther chewed his nails more vigorously. Every so often one of the servant maids would enter the Great Hall and scurry past him toward the kitchen, and he would turn his head hoping for some news – any news. But eventually the maid would emerge from the kitchen carrying a towel or a steaming kettle or something, and she would disappear back into the bedroom without uttering a single word to him. So, he went back to his fingernails.

It wasn't so much the wailing that bothered him. Uther had seen more warfare and bloodshed than he cared to remember, and by this point in his life, such sounds were almost commonplace. No, it was the source of the wailing that caused his anxiety. Igraine was delicate, frail even, and he hated to imagine her in any sort of pain. He loved her deeply and was often a bit overprotective, sometimes to the point of her annoyance. So despite his consternation, Uther had to keep telling himself to stay out of the way. The servant maids knew what they were doing. Igraine knew what she was doing as well. After all, this *was* their second child.

Uther and Igraine had been married for seven years now. They had first encountered one another after Uther was sent to an outpost in Britannia at the behest of his father, the Roman Emperor Constantinus, also called the King of the Britons. By the time Uther and his men arrived, the vast majority of the Roman legions had been evacuated from the islands and redeployed to other, more easily accessible ends of the crumbling empire. He was to remain in Britannia along with a single legion, *Legio Draconis*, with orders to repel the Saxon hordes, who had been aggressively invading from the southeast. The pagan Saxons had been brutal and merciless, burning villages to the ground, slaughtering livestock, and abducting young women for their own lustful purposes.

In the Roman fashion, Uther swiftly began recruiting indigenous Britons and Celts to assist in the military campaign. Several kings and tribal leaders joined his ranks, though not for the fading glory of Rome, but for strategic alliances in their fight against a common and previously insurmountable enemy. Despite their more primitive weaponry and armor, the natives had proven themselves to be valuable assets in battle, and with the warlords' aid and counsel, the Romano-British troops swept across the countryside, systematically driving out the occupying forces until they had been largely pushed back to their settlements on the southern coast. Before long, Saxon armies began to flee at the mere sight of Uther's battle standard – a gaping bronze dragon head followed by a long tube of red silk that billowed in the wind, forming the tail of the flying serpent. Uther's ferocity as a warrior, along with Roman standard he carried, soon earned him the title *Pendragon*, an epithet of fear and respect bestowed upon him by his enemies.

Following a series of successful campaigns, Uther and his men came upon a small Saxon raid near Ryskammel, a modest fishing village nestled along the banks of the River Alen. The small band of Celtic warriors defending the town had fought fearlessly behind their aging chieftain, but despite their best efforts, they had been no match for the formidable Saxon raiders, whose greater size and stature provided them with a distinct advantage. Fortunately, the invading forces were easily scattered by the well-trained Roman troops, and their leaders were promptly captured or killed.

When Uther first spied Igraine, she was tied to the back of an abandoned horse, bruised, weeping, and clothed in nothing but her woolen undergarments, undoubtedly claimed as a prize by one of the Saxon warriors.

One look and he was unmade.

The battle-hardened heart that beat within Uther's breast instantly melted into a deep pool of adoration, and he was then no longer the rugged, stone-faced soldier who commanded a legion of fearsome warriors. Instead, he reverted into the eager lover of his youth, full of anxiety and hope, ready and willing to trudge through Hell for a single touch of her hand.

The girl shivered in fear as she felt her bonds being cut, but by the time she opened her eyes, Uther had wrapped her in his cloak, and she felt herself being carried back to the village in a pair of strong, protective arms. When she timidly peered up at him, the big Roman officer told her that she was safe, and despite her marred features and stained clothing, Uther found himself overwhelmed by her beauty. Igraine smiled weakly, and her tears traced thin lines through the dust covering her face. Upon returning her to the village, Uther discovered that she was the town chieftain's only child, and in his gratitude, he offered Uther his daughter's hand in marriage. Igraine did not object, and the two were wed as soon as she recovered from her injuries. A few years later, Igraine gave birth to their first child, a raven-haired baby girl they named Morgana.

And now, as the birth of their second child steadily approached, Uther grew more and more nervous. He loved little Morgana with all of his heart. He truly did. But on this night he was *passionately* hoping for a boy. There is just something about a father that yearns for a son – a little version of himself that he can teach and inspire and raise to be a man. Uther daydreamed of these things until he was snapped back into reality by the growing intensity of Igraine's wailing. He could hear the servant maids speaking words of encouragement as his wife grunted and groaned and made all sorts of noises that rattled his bones with anxiety. Then suddenly, it stopped. Uther took a break from biting his nails and gazed toward the bedroom, his eyes wide open and his ears perked.

The next thing he heard was an infant crying. A grin stretched across Uther's face as he ran through the hallway, eager to meet the newest addition to his family.

* * * * *

As the last rays of daylight veiled the countryside in long shadows and the rich blue of the western sky faded into brilliant shades of orange and pink, two figures dressed in cloaks of emerald green appeared atop the rocky hills surrounding Castle Tintagel. They seemed taller than most men of the day, and their faces shone with an otherworldly glow. The old man had sharp features and a long flowing beard, but his pale blue eyes were soft and almost childlike. The woman was younger and beautiful, with fiery, flowing red hair and piercing green eyes. When she spoke, it was almost like the sound of singing.

"It is beginning," the woman whispered, "Igraine has given birth to a son."

"The boy cannot stay here," answered the old man, "Evil will hunt him, and he will never be safe unless we take him from this place. His destiny is far too important for him to be left unprotected in the care of a reckless Roman cavalry officer."

"That Roman officer is the last son of the Emperor. He may be a bit foolhardy, but his honor and courage know no bounds. He would surely make a fine father to the boy."

"Aye, that he would." The old man paused and gazed toward the horizon. He closed his eyes and breathed slowly, as if in deep thought, then continued to speak. “But his time on this earth is short. Uther will not live to see his son come of age, nor will he live to see the day his elder child gives herself over to the darkness. For the latter, at least, I count him fortunate.”

“They are coming for him,” said the woman, as she gazed down at the village below.

The old man frowned and began to speak quickly. “Go now,” he said, “Make haste to Armorica and find a suitable place for the boy. I will remain here and provide whatever defense I can.”

The woman vanished into the mountain mist, and soon the evening shadows began to fade, leaving the landscape shrouded in the darkness of night. The old man stood still and waited, looking downward at the little town nestled among the hills. The air was quiet, and the torchlight gleaming from the tiny thatch houses illuminated Tintagel like a second set of stars. Then off in the distance, the lights seemed to die away as a thick black vapor began creeping along the narrow cobblestone streets. A few villagers still wandered the town, oblivious to the darkness that swirled around their ankles. They couldn’t see the way Oriax crawled toward the castle, scraping his talons across the pavement and frothing at the mouth like a rabid animal. They couldn’t see the faint outline of the black, fibrous wings that propelled him through the icy night air. And they couldn’t see his blood-red eyes staring coldly past a face one might only imagine in the fiercest of nightmares. But the old man could see everything.

As Oriax crept through the darkness toward the castle gate, his twisted mind consumed with bloodlust, an evil smile stretched across his black, wrinkled lips. He chuckled to himself softly as he pondered how Lord Astaroth would richly reward him for this one little murder. The sheer ease of killing one so helpless filled him with hubris, and he stretched his wings and began soaring rapidly toward the fortress. All but certain that he had eluded detection, Oriax sneered confidently and lunged onward through the night sky, faster and faster, each moment growing closer to his sinister objective.

Then suddenly he felt his leathery skin being scorched and torn from his body by a towering wall of white-hot flame.

Shrieking in unfathomable pain, Oriax fell to the earth and began writhing on the ground in a smoldering heap of tar and sulfur. He slowly lifted his eyes toward the castle gate and gazed upon his assailant. There stood the old man, his green cloak transformed into a radiant white, wielding a massive sword that blazed with a blinding, ethereal fire. Slowly the old man approached him and began to speak in a booming voice that echoed through the night.

"Be gone from here, demon," he rumbled, "You have no claim on the boy."

Coughing loudly and struggling to breathe, Oriax grinned with crooked yellow teeth and snarled his response. "Don't be a fool, Ambrosius. You of all people should know that more will come after me, and they'll keep coming until the child is dead. Lord Astaroth will *not* let this mission fail."

"If Astaroth is looking for a fight, he knows where to find me," answered the old man as he raised the enormous sword above his head, "Now, return to the Abyss!" And before Oriax could scream, the flaming sword came crashing down from above and his charred body dissipated into wisps of black vapor.

The old man stood still for a moment, surveying the surrounding landscape before concealing his sword within the folds of his cloak. No sooner had he done so than the brilliance faded from his face and his garments returned to their original deep green hue. The creature had called him Ambrosius, the name by which he was known in the Unseen Realm. However, he had many other names in many other times and places, as is often the case when one has lived so long. As it happened, in this time and place, he was most commonly known as Merlyn.

* * * * *

Uther's face beamed with unfettered joy. He sat cradling his newborn baby in a large wooden chair next to the bed where Igraine lay exhausted. Every so often he looked away from the child and gazed lovingly at his wife, and Igraine looked back with a weary but tender smile. She had done it. She had given him a son, and he couldn't be happier.

"How are you feeling, love?" Uther asked softly.

"Exhausted but content," answered Igraine, "Even more so since you're here now."

"Well, I'll be right by your side all night long. The entire Roman Legion couldn't drag me away."

Uther reached over and gently brushed a few strands of his wife's chestnut-brown hair away from her damp forehead. She sighed and closed her eyes, quickly drifting off into a deep and much needed sleep. Little Morgana sat next to her father, staring at her new brother and jabbering away like a typical, curious toddler. Uther smiled and looked down once again at the baby boy resting in his arms.

"You will be called Arthur," he said.

* * * * *

Screams of agony echoed throughout the cavern as the messenger felt a jagged blade tear through his belly. A rivulet of black mist leaked from the wound for a few short moments before he wheezed a final breath and his scaly remains withered into dust.

At the other end of the blade was the clawed hand of Lord Astaroth, demon prince of the land called Britannia – or *Logres*, as it was known by the ancients. He stood still for a moment, allowing the last remnants of black, crumbly ash to fall from his sword before returning it to the scabbard that dangled from his belt. Astaroth was immense – nearly eight feet tall and as thick as an oak, with pale, cadaverous skin stretched tightly over an intimidating physique. His royal robes, heavy and festooned with crows' feathers, hung loosely from his shoulders as he peered about the room with rage seething behind his ghostly, colorless eyes. He had just received word of Oriax' failure.

"Where is Naberius?" Astaroth growled, his thunderous voice echoing loudly throughout the murky cave.

The small horde of creatures that knelt before him remained silent and cowered away in fear, terrified of meeting the same fate as the lowly little messenger. Ever so slowly, a gaunt, spindly figure from the back of the crowd stood up and began inching his way forward. He kept his head lowered as he reached the center of the cavern, finally kneeling down at the feet of his dark master. "I am here, my lord," he said quietly.

Naberius the Deceiver certainly lacked the threatening physical presence of the prince, but he was no less dreadful to behold. His gangly frame was covered from top to bottom in a thick coat of grey fur, which, together with his long snout and pointed ears, gave him a rather lupine appearance. The hairs themselves were sharp and pointed, more akin to the quills of a porcupine, and they grew thick and bristly along his spine. In his right hand he carried a gnarled wooden staff adorned with a variety of talismans and crystals, and with his left hand he pulled back the hood of his tattered cloak, revealing watery, yellow eyes sunken deep within his gruesome visage.

"How m-m-may I serve you, Lord Astaroth?" he stuttered.

"Quit your sniveling, you pathetic little imp," Astaroth answered, "Show me some backbone or you'll feel my blade."

"Forgive me, my lord," Naberius said as he stood and straightened his posture, attempting to feign confidence while his knees continued to shake.

"As you are now aware, Oriax has failed me. The child still lives, and apparently Ambrosius, that doddering old fool, is now determined to protect him from our advances. Therefore, we must alter our strategy. Tell me, Naberius, how fares your influence over the human traitor?"

"He is like clay in my hands, lord. The man cares nothing for friendship or loyalty or honor. As long as I continue to dangle the promise of power a few inches from his face, he will follow me without question like a mule in pursuit of a carrot."

"Excellent," Astaroth replied, "Summon him at once. If we cannot kill the boy then we'll crush his spirit. No matter what he gains from the guidance of Ambrosius, the boy will crumble when he learns the fate of his family. Tell the traitor to deal with Pendragon, but leave the rest to me. I have my own plans for the mother and her innocent little girl."

BOOK ONE: RISE

"GOD JUDGED IT BETTER TO BRING GOOD OUT OF EVIL THAN TO SUFFER NO EVIL TO EXIST."

- AUGUSTINE OF HIPPO

A Strange Visitor

The sun had only just risen in Dinan, a small, hillside village crowded onto the shores of the River Rance in northern Armorica. Fishermen sat in the tall grass along the shores of the river hoping to catch their breakfast, while farmers gathered their tools and yoked their cattle in preparation for a long day of harvesting. The village priest waited outside his modest stone chapel, giving thanks for the new day and offering blessings to passersby. A brood of chickens that seemed to have broken loose from their enclosure wandered aimlessly up the side of a nearby hill, where a small, abandoned fort sat in a state of disrepair. The city walls, built centuries before by Julius Caesar to protect the Roman settlements against marauding Gallic tribes, were little more than ruins now, having long-since crumbled into elongated piles of indistinct grey stones. The town itself was primarily populated by displaced Britons who had fled their homeland after the Saxon invasions, as well as a contingent of retired Roman soldiers, hoping to put their violent exploits behind them and live out their days in peace.

But there was little peace to be found on *this* morning. Midway up the hillside on the western shore of the river, the dawning sunlight peered through the windows of a stone-built blacksmith's shop, revealing the silhouettes of two men whose noisy commotion had already become responsible for waking half the town. The elder blacksmith was shouting at the top of his lungs, but the young apprentice could barely hear him over the metallic *clang* of a hammer pounding a pair of red-hot horseshoes against a large, iron anvil.

"Dash it all, lad!" yelled the blacksmith, "Stop that infernal hammering for a moment and listen! How can you possibly hear me over all that racket?"

"I've heard it all before, Uncle," the boy responded, "In fact, I hear it almost daily! This entire village knows how much you loathe King Vortigern and the Saxons."

Indeed, the blacksmith's rancor was common knowledge among the townsfolk. And while most of the immigrant citizens of Dinan shared his distaste for the self-proclaimed king of their native Britannia, few shared the blacksmith's passion or his vengeful spirit. After escaping from life under Vortigern's thumb, many had grown apathetic and simply chose to ignore his ongoing acts of petty tyranny, instead focusing on their crops, their cattle, and the large flagons of mead served nightly at the local tavern.

On this particular morning, the blacksmith's anger stemmed from a piece of news he had received the previous evening from a traveling merchant: The Saxon army was marching north toward Hadrian's Wall, preparing to invade Caledonia. Evidently Vortigern sought to expand his power even further.

"Don't you dare refer to that usurper as *king*!" the blacksmith continued, "He's a knave and a traitor to all Britons. *You* ought to know that more than most after what that beast and his pack of mercenaries did to your parents!"

The boy didn't reply. For a moment he stood in silence, allowing his right hand, which held the heavy cross-peen hammer, to fall lifelessly to his side. He opened his mouth as if to say something, but then he abruptly turned away and went back to his work on the horseshoes.

In that moment, the blacksmith knew he had gone too far. The fervor fell from his face and his posture slumped with remorse as he laid a hand on the boy's shoulder. "Forgive me, son," he said quietly, "I let my anger get the best of me."

"It's alright, Uncle. No harm done."

"You're doing a fine job," said the blacksmith as he walked toward the door, "In fact, you may just be good enough to put me out of business one of these days!" The boy looked up and smiled, and the blacksmith gave him a firm but comforting slap on the back. "Now let me see if your old aunt has some breakfast ready for us."

He watched his uncle leave the forge and then heard the stout man's booming voice further disrupt the calm of the early morning as he shouted down the road, "Vivienne! Where's the bleedin' food then, woman?"

The boy laughed to himself. Despite his uncle's temper and blustering flashes of tactlessness, the blacksmith was a good man. A soft heart beat beneath his gruff exterior, and more often than not, a mischievous smile was hiding behind his bushy black moustache. The boy was only a toddler when his parents died, and unable to bear children themselves, his Uncle Bors and Aunt Vivienne had taken him in and raised him as their own. He barely remembered his parents now, but on numerous occasions he had been told the story of their tragic demise.

According to his uncle, the pagan Saxons had been attempting to invade Britannia for generations, but had largely been held at bay by the Roman garrisons stationed throughout the island. The last great Roman leader in Britannia, a brave general called Uther Pendragon, had all but driven the Saxons from the land before his premature death. People say that he contracted a mysterious illness, growing ever more sickly and weak until he could no longer lift his sword, and finally breathed his last fourteen years ago on Christmas Day.

In the chaos that followed, a warlord named Vortigern, previously one of Uther's most important allies, took command of the Romano-British forces and vowed to restore peace. He married Igraine, Uther's widow, and proclaimed himself High King of the Britons, ordering a massive castle built on Badon Hill near the town of Bath in eastern Dumnonia. Initially, Vortigern enjoyed almost universal goodwill from his subjects. The Saxon raids abruptly ceased, and it seemed that this new king had magically returned order to the land. However, the apparent Saxon withdrawal turned out to be nothing but a ruse, and Vortigern soon betrayed his people by allowing the pagan hordes to overrun Britannia in return for the use of their military might and loyalty to his despotic rule.

In the midst of Vortigern's deception, some say that a group of Roman soldiers still loyal to Uther took his body away from Britannia, so his grave would not be desecrated by the Saxons, and buried him somewhere in Armorica in a tomb marked only by his ancestral sword. There were even those who believed that Uther would return one day, reclaim his sword, and save Britannia from Vortigern and the murderous Saxons. The boy believed those legends through and through, with a faith unhindered by the bitterness of reality, hoping that the death of his parents might one day be avenged.

His father, Ban, had been the lord of a farming town called Benoic, and as one of many nobles who remained loyal to Uther, he became part of an early rebellion against Vortigern. Unable to contend with the massive Saxon army on the field of battle, the nobles sent a message to the high king, detailing their grievances and pleading with him to remember his people and his heritage. Under the guise of truce, Hengist, the Saxon general, lured Ban and the other rebel lords to an abandoned church, penitently promising to bring their complaints to the king. But instead, their throats were cut and the church was slowly burned to the ground. In time, the bloody event came to be known as the Night of the Long Knives. Vortigern then sent his warriors to burn the nearby villages and slaughter the rebels' wives and children as a warning to all those who might defy his rule. But the boy's mother, Elaine, had somehow managed to escape the carnage. To this day, he retained vague memories of being awoken in the dark of night and bundling up with his mother on the back of an aging horse, fleeing to the coast in hopes of crossing over into Armorica. Having preserved for her son what little food and water she carried, Elaine had managed to reach her sister's home in Dinan before succumbing to starvation and exhaustion. Slumping over on her horse, she died before she could even tell Bors and Vivienne the boy's name. They decided to call him Lancelot.

Over the years he grew tall and strong, towering over the other boys his age and able to easily beat any one of them in a wrestling match. He could probably beat most of the adult men in town as well, but would never be so bold as to make the claim publicly. His arms and back had become broad and muscular from the hours each day he spent in the forge, and the sunny blonde hair of his childhood had darkened with time, producing an unkempt, sandy-brown mane that required the boy to constantly brush loose strands away from his eyes.

Now here he stood, on the brink of manhood, pounding horseshoes into shape while pondering his lost childhood and the family who had been cruelly taken from him. And yet, having never really known his parents, the boy remained intellectually able to comprehend an innate sense of loss, but found himself incapable of fully experiencing the searing pain that comes from losing those closest to you. In his mind, he had always had a family. Furthermore, he had never really been much of a sentimentalist.

One day I'll be a great warrior, the boy thought to himself. *My enemies will fall before the power of my sword, and I'll put an end to all this madness. My conquests will become legendary, and people everywhere will know who I am. As for those Saxon dogs – they will hear my name and cower in fear. And one day, when the Pendragon returns to Britannia to reclaim his throne, he'll ask me to lead his army, and we'll fight side-by-side to set our homeland free!*

No, not a sentimentalist. But *certainly* a romantic.

With a surge of enthusiasm, the young apprentice leapt away from his work at the anvil and began slashing and thrusting into the air with his cross-peen hammer, imagining himself to be a valiant soldier clad in a chainmail hauberk, vanquishing scores of enemy soldiers.

"YAH!" he shouted at his invisible foes while swinging the hammer wildly, "Run and hide, Saxons! Or the last thing you see on this earth will be the point of my sword! You are no match for the mighty Lancelot!"

And with those words he lifted the hammer over his head and swung it downward, dealing a blow of defeat to his imaginary opponent and accidentally knocking over a large wooden barrel, thus causing a heap of iron slag to spill all over the floor of the blacksmith shop.

The boy froze, quickly surveying the results of his carelessness. He allowed the hammer to fall from his hand and then retrieved a large straw-bristled broom from the corner of the shop, scurrying back to the slag heap in a desperate attempt to clean up the mess he'd made before his uncle returned. Knowing full well that he would be soundly scolded for fooling around on the job, the young apprentice swept furiously, coughing as he kicked up clouds of black dust made from tiny bits of stone, glass, and unused iron ore. *This was going far too slowly.* He stopped sweeping and looked around frantically for some other tool that might accelerate his efforts, and spying the coal shovel near the bloomery furnace, he dropped the broom and began running to the other end of the shop. But as he ran past the front door, it swung open and struck him soundly in the forehead, knocking him to the floor with a loud thud.

The boy lay flat on his back, terribly disoriented and with a dagger of pain throbbing through his skull. Was he bleeding? He gingerly slid his hand between the floor and the back of his head, fully expecting his hair to be a wet and sticky mess. No, thank goodness, there was no blood. But what was he doing down here anyway? Oh yes, the front door hit him while he was running to fetch the coal shovel. *Oh hell, the slag heap!* Uncle Bors was going to *kill* him.

As the boy came to his senses, he rubbed his eyes and gazed up at the open doorway, nervously expecting to see the bulky frame of the blacksmith staring down at him in displeasure. But instead, he saw a strange old man.

The visitor wore a dingy, dark-green cloak and a wide-brimmed hat, and he carried a gnarled walking staff with a little grey owl perched on top. His beard hung down almost to the ground, and the tangled hair at the end was covered with dirt, leaves, and thistles. Actually, he looked like a vagrant. The old man glanced around the shop, apparently searching for the blacksmith, until he looked down and saw the dust-covered boy staring up at him from just behind the door.

"Hello, Lancelot," he said.

The boy searched his mind, struggling to remember whether he had met this person before. The old man obviously knew *him*. Confused and still a little woozy from being hit by the door, he stumbled to his feet and managed a rather bewildered reply.

"Um, hello. Good morning, sir. Um... can I help you?"

"You've grown a great deal since I last saw you," replied the old man, "Although, I suppose it *has* been a long time. I do have such a difficulty keeping track of the passage of time, you know. At least, in the way *you* perceive time."

While the old man was talking, the little grey owl who had been perched on his walking staff abruptly flew up into the air, fluttered around for a few moments, and then sat back down on the top of his wide-brimmed hat, promptly falling asleep. Lancelot found this all very curious and had no idea what the old man was talking about. But finally regaining his composure, he brushed a few strands of hair away from his face and attempted to make some sense out of his current situation.

"Are you looking for the blacksmith, sir?"

“Looking? Well, at this moment I’m not looking for *anyone*, really. As a matter of fact, my boy, when I first walked through the door I was looking for *you*. But now, since I have obviously located you, I am looking no longer.”

He must be mad, thought Lancelot. But still, he seemed harmless enough.

“I’m sorry, sir, but do I know you?” he asked.

“No, my boy. But I know *you*,” said the old man, who suddenly grew very serious. The playful grin he had worn since entering the shop fell from his face, and his clear blue eyes seemed to stare directly into the boy’s battered soul.

“I know about the terrible murder of your father,” he continued with a hint of sadness in his voice, “You never really had a chance to know him, of course. But you do look very much like he did, and you have every bit of his confidence and spirit. I also know about your mother’s sacrifice in saving your life and bringing you to this place. She loved you more than you will ever know. But most importantly, I know the fire that burns within you, hotter than the pit of any blacksmith’s furnace. You dream of glory and adventure, yes. But more than anything, my boy, you seek justice for those who have taken everything from you and your countrymen.”

Lancelot stood aghast, unable to move or speak. Who was this eccentric old man who seemed to know his innermost thoughts? Soon his shock turned to amazement, and then his amazement turned to fear.

“W-w-who are you?” he asked timidly.

“Don’t be afraid,” the old man replied, “I’m not here to hurt you. Just think of me as a messenger. I came here to bring you good news, and to entrust you with an important task.”

“W-what do you require of me, sir?” Lancelot asked. At this point, he could not even imagine saying no.

"I hear that you've become quite skilled working at the forge, my boy. Indeed, your uncle is certainly a fine teacher. But if you're to fight in the rebellion against Vortigern one day, you're going to need more than a blacksmith's hammer to wield in battle." Reaching into his cloak, the old man produced a small, handwritten note scribbled on a piece of vellum. "On this parchment, I have written the instructions for the forging of Damascus steel, a material which may be used to construct a sword that is tougher, sharper, and more durable than any weapon brandished by the Saxons."

Lancelot reached out and took the hand-scrawled instructions from the old man's bony fingers. He glanced at them briefly, still incredulous at what was happening to him. *Surely this must be a dream*, he thought.

"You're not dreaming," said the old man.

Once again, Lancelot was speechless. He just stood and stared, his eyes wide and unblinking and his mouth gaping open like a codfish, wondering whether this old man was some kind of fortune teller or sorcerer or even a demon in disguise. The old man smiled at him and chuckled softly, obviously amused by something, and then headed back toward the door.

"Remember, my boy," he said, "be diligent and watchful. I'll return when the time is right."

The old man turned to leave, and Lancelot continued to stare blankly and silently, watching him duck down so that the little owl sitting atop his hat would pass under the doorframe. Then suddenly, the puzzled apprentice snapped out of his entranced state and had a brief moment of clarity.

"Wait, sir!" he called out, "You mentioned before that you also bear good news!"

The old man stopped and turned back.

"Ah yes, I almost forgot," he said, "You see, you never asked me who is meant to *lead* this rebellion of which I spoke.

Honestly, I'm surprised your curiosity didn't inspire you to ask sooner. You really must pay closer attention. Anyway, let it be known that the Pendragon is returning. Prepare yourself, my boy, for justice will reign again."

And with those final words, the old man vanished, as if his presence had been nothing more than an illusion.

Lancelot searched inside and out, but he was unable to find any sign of the old man – not even footprints in the dewy grass. However, he did notice that the floor of the shop was now spotless. Somehow, the iron slag he had spilled earlier had miraculously been returned to the wooden barrel, almost as if the whole mess had never happened.

Path of the Wicked

"The Lord is my shepherd; I shall not want," Morgana prayed, "He maketh me to lie down in green pastures, He leadeth me beside the still waters, He restoreth my soul."

The young woman was kneeling on the cold, stone floor of her room beside her large feather bed, which, in point of fact, had recently become severely disheveled.

"And yea, though I walk through the valley of the shadow of death, I will fear no evil, for Thou art with me," she continued, "Thy rod and Thy staff they comfort me. Surely goodness and mercy shall follow me all the days of my life, and I will dwell in the house of the Lord forever."

It was a prayer she uttered frequently. But over time, repetition of this simple passage from the Psalms had become more of a ritual than anything else. In fact, the words had long since lost much of their meaning for her, especially the part about "goodness and mercy." After all, her life had hardly been filled with such blessings. Having spent far more time dragging herself through the valley of the shadow of death, she often wondered if God were even listening.

After finishing with a rather half-hearted *amen*, Morgana stood and straightened her long, black hair and smoothed out her dress as she prepared to leave her bedroom and make her way down to the Great Hall, where a hot supper was already waiting. Turning and gazing at her reflection in the ornate, full-length mirror in the corner of the room, she realized her face was still noticeably red and cursed quietly, scolding herself for such emotional weakness. Wiping a few remaining tears from her cheeks, she took a deep breath, sighed, and slowly walked through her door into the torch-lit hallway.

It was quite a long walk to the Great Hall, and her soft leather shoes made a faint, shuffling sound as she wandered alone through the now deserted corridors. Everyone else had certainly begun eating by now. Her mother hated it when she arrived late to the table and often chastised her on such occasions, but Morgana was long past caring. In truth, she no longer cared about much of anything. Over the years she had grown numb to the difficulties of her everyday life, including the frequent unwelcome visits by her stepfather, the king, as well as the infuriating indifference of her mother, who seemed to be either blind to the goings-on in her own home or else unwilling to deal with the horrors of reality.

As she sauntered through the torch-lit hallways, Morgana allowed her mind to return to the nagging doubts and burning questions that had been plaguing her thoughts with increasing regularity. She wondered almost daily how a loving God could allow such pain and injustice in the world. She wondered why a cruel, abusive tyrant like Vortigern was permitted to rule anyone or anything. But mostly, she wondered why her true father had been so unfairly taken from her.

Although he had died of some unknown illness when she was still very young, those few short years with her father left Morgana with a pocketful of faint memories that she clung to like a warm blanket. In fact, if she closed her eyes and concentrated hard enough, she could still see his cheerful smile and almost hear his deep, soothing voice gently singing her to sleep. When Morgana was young she would beg her mother for stories about her father, but her requests were never granted. Ever since Vortigern arrived, even speaking the name of Uther Pendragon had become forbidden.

Morgana quickened her pace. Despite her usual lack of appetite, she was beginning to feel weak and knew that she needed to eat soon in order to avoid passing out in the middle of an empty hallway. Finally approaching the Great Hall, she was greeted with the savory aroma of roasted venison as well as the objectionable caterwauling of King Vortigern, who yet again was angrily railing at one of his war ministers in the middle of their evening meal.

"Driven back, Wulfric?" she heard him bellow, *"Bested by those primeval Pictish savages?* Tell me, how is it that you dare to even stand before me in such abject failure?" Vortigern gulped down the last of his wine and then angrily hurled his goblet to the ground, allowing the ornate bronze cup to bounce and rattle loudly across the floor.

"Sir, they may seem primitive," answered the Saxon general, "but their numbers far surpass our own. Perhaps if you granted me more men..."

"Silence, you insolent fool!" the king snapped back, "I'll hear no more of your pitiful excuses. Do not attempt to pass the blame for your failures onto *me*. I've given you more than enough men to defeat those painted animals from the north, and thus far you have proven yourself to be both spineless and incompetent! You are hereby relieved of your command, Wulfric. Now get out of my sight!"

For a moment the general stood firm in defiance, having briefly considered screaming in Vortigern's face and then burying a sword up to the hilt in his large, protruding belly. But the presence of two heavily armed guards at his back strongly urged Wulfric to reconsider, and he eventually left the Great Hall quietly, with an unquenched anger bubbling up almost visibly beneath his skin.

Once the general was out of earshot, Vortigern turned to one of his guards and said calmly, "He can no longer be trusted. I want him dead by morning."

It was a command that Morgana had heard her stepfather utter many times before. Despite her lack of knowledge about this condemned Saxon general, she knew that the next time she saw his face, it would be contorted in anguish, staring into nothingness as his severed head sat impaled atop a sharpened wooden pike. It would be a warning. Under Vortigern's rule, brutality had become commonplace, human life had become dispensable, and virtue had been cast aside in favor of his unquenchable thirst for power and domination. As inhuman as it may seem, the death of a man like Wulfric hardly mattered under such circumstances. The king expected absolute loyalty from his subjects and absolute victory on his battlefields. And he accepted nothing less.

After Vortigern regained his calm and sat down to finish his meal, Morgana quietly slipped into her usual seat at the far end of the table and began picking at a small loaf of rye bread. Her mother, Igraine, sat to the right, her once beautiful eyes now glazed over and staring off into the distance, as if lost in her own little universe. Morgana realized she would not be scolded for her lateness tonight. On some days her mother remained a strict yet compassionate disciplinarian, but with growing frequency, she was beginning to show signs of losing all connections, perhaps purposefully, to the cruel and decaying world that surrounded her.

To Morgana's left sat her only real friend in the castle, a young Saxon girl named Rowena. In contrast to Morgana's own dark hair and fair skin, Rowena was surprisingly tanned, with braided blonde hair that had turned almost white from the sun, sparkling blue eyes, and an athletic figure that revealed her training and skill in combat. It was not uncommon for Saxon women to fight alongside the men, and Hengist, Rowena's father and high commander of the Saxon forces in Britannia, had been teaching her to kill since childhood.

A pagan like most of her people, Rowena gave her worship to Woden, the head of the Germanic pantheon and the god of wisdom, magic, war, death, and victory. Although she refused to participate in the bloody animal sacrifices and occasional human sacrifices given to Woden by her father and his soldiers, Rowena prayed piously to her god almost daily at the foot of his Sacred Tree. Hengist actually believed himself to be a direct descendant of Woden, as did many Saxon rulers, and he commanded his men with matching authority. Rowena usually dismissed her father's inflated sense of self as a vain attempt to display power and strength to his men, but it also made her wonder why he continued to submit to the leadership of a manipulative little snake like Vortigern.

"The king's temper has been worse than usual lately," Rowena whispered in between bites of venison.

"He's been barging into my bed more frequently as well," Morgana said as she turned toward her friend, "God, I hate him. I can still smell the stench of his sweat on my clothes."

She glanced across the room at Vortigern as he messily consumed the remains of his dinner. His thick auburn beard was dripping with sloshed wine, and bits of partially chewed venison flew from his gaping mouth as he spoke. He wore a gaudy, silk-fringed tunic with gold embroidery that was now dingy with neglect, and his oversized gut was flecked with breadcrumbs and greasy morsels of meat. *What a pompous, malevolent wretch*, thought Morgana.

"You have to tell your mother," Rowena interjected quietly, "She needs to know that this is happening."

"Oh, she knows, she knows," said Morgana, "But she doesn't care. Or if she does, she no longer has the ability to express any sort of passion or indignation. Honestly, I think she's completely lost touch."

"She *has* been rather like an empty shell lately, hasn't she?" With a tinge of sadness, Rowena peered over at Igraine, now only a shadow of her former self.

"I think he beats her sometimes."

"Why do you say that?"

"I've seen bruises," Morgana answered, "Once I was helping her dress and I noticed that the entire left side of her back was discolored and swollen. When I asked about it she made up some ridiculous story about falling off of her horse, but I could tell she was lying. She's the best rider I know."

"That's terrible," Rowena sighed.

"Honestly, I think this whole country would be much better off if some upstart peasant would just run him through and put the rest of us out of our misery."

* * * * *

Just south of the castle lay the town of Bath, which the Romans had called *Aquae Sulis*. It had been named for the naturally occurring thermal springs that welled up in the nearby hills surrounding the River Avon. The ancient Celts had built a shrine to one of their pagan goddesses at the hot springs, and later the invading Romans had claimed the shine for one of their own deities. However, after the rise of Christianity in the Roman Empire and its influential spread throughout Western Europe, the shrine was largely abandoned by the locals and it soon fell into disrepair and ruin. Following the Saxon invasions, the battle-scarred walls of many of the bathhouses were systematically torn down and their stones used to repair more vital parts of the town, leaving the once stately Roman structures to be further demolished through plunder and erosion. Now all but forsaken, the bathhouses rested in the silence of apathy. No one came here anymore, especially on a cold, wet, miserable night like tonight.

No one, of course, except the two young men who were now trudging separately through the drizzling rain. Originally they had chosen to discuss their plans at a private table at the local tavern, allowing commotion made by the crowd of patrons to mask their clandestine conversation. But their nerves had gotten the best of them, and they quickly decided to brave the elements and adjourn to a place where there was almost no chance of being overheard. After all, one couldn't be too careful when it came to matters of sedition.

Heavy storm clouds cloaked the moonlight, veiling the landscape in a blanket of darkness, and the light mist of rain that fell began to thicken into a heavy downpour as the young men finally drew near to their meeting place. Entering the pitch black of the main bathhouse, two cloaked figures approached one another with swords drawn.

"The king is dead," said one.

"Long live the king," answered the second.

They both breathed a sigh of relief. Having thus confirmed their identities to one another, the two men sheathed their swords and sat down on the soggy ground, huddling together beneath the scant remains of a roof, which provided them only a modicum of shelter from the rain. It was several minutes before one of them finally spoke.

"So how do we begin?"

"It certainly can't be anything big or abrupt. We'll have to work slowly and discreetly so we have time to build alliances and raise an army large enough to make some difference. Otherwise this whole enterprise is all for naught."

"Exactly. Being hasty and forthright is what doomed the first rebellion just after that miserable serpent took the throne. If I remember correctly, they were all locked in a church and burned to death when they dared to make their voices heard. We have to keep this quiet."

"Do you know anyone else we can trust?"

"I know a few good men in Bristol with axes to grind. They ought to jump at the chance to get involved. And although it's still a secret to the general public, I've also heard that there's a small movement beginning in Gloucester."

"That's a good place to start – casting out our nets."

"My father has business in Bristol next week, so I should be able to get things moving there without much notice."

"Perfect. And once we've got our legs underneath us, we should send some men down to Armorica to recruit there as well. It's full of retired Roman soldiers and Britons who were displaced by that God-forsaken traitor."

"What are *you* going to do then?"

"Believe it or not, I'm going to try to work my way inside. Maybe I can steal a little useful information or even plant some seeds of discontent in the ranks."

"That sounds like suicide to me."

"You forget, Bedivere, that I am one-half Saxon. My mother taught me both their customs and their language. I even look the part, so I don't think I'll have much difficulty blending in. The real problem will be getting out in one piece."

"I still think you're insane."

"Maybe. But no more so than any other poor soul who decides to join this starry-eyed rabble of ours. Hell, even if we're successful we may end up dead."

"Truer words were never spoken."

"Do you even think we have a chance?"

"You *know* what I think."

"I assume that means you're still clinging to that rubbish legend about Pendragon somehow coming back and leading us all to conquest and glory. You know, Bedivere, sometimes I envy your romantic sense of optimism."

"I prefer to think of it as *faith*."

"Well, I suppose we're going to need all the faith we can get right now." He paused for a moment and then stood to leave.

"It's getting late. You know what to do. Let's meet here again in a month and we'll discuss our progress."

"Go with God, Gawain."

"You too. Goodnight. And keep yourself alive."

Might for Right

Lancelot sat on the edge of his bed and stared down at the wrinkled scrap of paper in his hands. Replaying the old man's cryptic words in his mind, the young blacksmith attempted to envision the magnificent sword he had agreed to create. It had been a rather slow week down at the shop, and he would have begun work on the project days ago if not for one small detail. He couldn't read.

He furrowed his brow with bewilderment. The old man seemed to have known everything else about him. Did he not also know that a youth of Lancelot's station would never have been given the opportunity of a formal education? His aunt and uncle had taught him well enough, of course. He learned right from wrong, a little history, and the tricks of his trade, but he still remained a simple laborer. As such, the old man's written specifications remained undeciphered.

It had been nearly two weeks since that mysterious day at the blacksmith's shop, and Lancelot still hadn't told a soul about the strange visitor's unusual request.

He had briefly considered telling his uncle about the whole experience, but he quickly reconsidered upon the realization that doing so would only result in one of two probable outcomes. Most likely, Uncle Bors would think his apprentice had lost his mind and would dismiss him out of hand with that jolly, boisterous laugh of his. However, if the old blacksmith actually believed his fantastic tale, all hell would surely break loose. If a man such as Uncle Bors – one so full of vehemence and zeal – were led to believe that Vortigern would soon be challenged and replaced by a just and honorable king, the lovable old coot would probably strap on a sword and nearly drown himself trying to swim across the British Channel in a desperate attempt to join in the fray. He would end up running through the streets screaming at the top of his lungs about vengeance and a final day of reckoning, leaving streaks of pandemonium in his wake.

No, he would not tell his uncle about the old man. Not yet, anyway. But he would *have* to tell Arthur. If anyone could ever understand this mess, it would be him.

Like Lancelot, Arthur was an orphan. He lived in a small monastery on the other side of town under the care of Ector, an aging Roman soldier who had become something of a holy man after the untimely death of his wife. Ector also had a son of his own, Kay, who was a few years older than Arthur but seldom acted like it. He spent most of his time hunting in the nearby woods and using his pet falcon to terrify local children for his own amusement. Arthur, on the other hand, was a thinker. Ector had taught him to read and write, not just in his native Breton language, but also in Frankish, Greek, and Latin, which meant that his nose was almost always buried in a book. Like most monks, Ector made his living as a scribe, creating handcrafted copies of literary works, mainly Jerome's Latin translation of the Bible, for various patrons. As such, Arthur had access to centuries of history, fiction, and philosophy. He had read Plato and Herodotus, Sophocles and Homer, Virgil and Cicero, and of course the Holy Scriptures. Lancelot recalled that as of late, he had been raving about the writings of some Berber theologian named Augustine.

As daylight stretched her glowing fingers over the eastern horizon, Lancelot scurried down the cobblestone roads of Dinan toward the monastery, hoping to receive some much-needed assistance from his literate friend. He passed by the tavern and the cobbler's workshop, weaving through throngs of eager street merchants peddling all sorts of goods, from hats and wool jerkins, to mounds of fresh fish and plucked chickens, to little vials of herbal medicine concocted by the local apothecary. The noisy crowds began to dwindle on the outskirts of town, and approaching his destination, Lancelot immediately spied Arthur walking about in the garden, reading out loud to himself from a large, leather-bound book.

"Two cities have been formed by two loves," he read, seemingly oblivious to Lancelot's presence, *"The earthly by the love of self, even to the contempt of God; and the heavenly by the love of God, even to the contempt of self. The former, in a word, glories in itself, the latter in the Lord. The one lifts up its head in its own glory; the other says to its God, 'Thou art my glory, and the lifter up of mine head.'"*

"Sounds like an interesting read," blurted Lancelot.

Startled by the interruption, Arthur jumped and nearly dropped the heavy volume, fumbling with it for a moment before clasping it securely against his chest, which caused him to lose his balance and finally tumble over into a freshly tilled bed of turnips. With his trousers significantly muddied by the wet soil, Arthur clutched the book tightly and looked up to see his smiling friend staring down at him.

"Sorry about that," Lancelot said, holding back his laughter, "I didn't mean to spook you."

"How about a little warning next time, huh?" Arthur replied with a grin, "Perhaps a tap on the shoulder or something? What if my book had fallen into the mud?"

"I don't know, you were pretty engrossed in your reading. You might not have noticed even if a stampede of horses had crashed into the monastery bell tower."

Lancelot stretched out his hand and Arthur took it, pulling himself up so the two boys were standing toe to toe. "I suppose you have me there," Arthur said as he righted himself and brushed a few patches of dirt from his clothes. Back on his feet, he stood nearly six inches shorter than Lancelot, but only because the young blacksmith was so uncommonly tall.

"Why were you reading to yourself out loud, anyway?"

"I find it helpful when I have to translate something from Latin," Arthur answered, "Otherwise I tend to get a bit befuddled. Oh, and in response to your earlier statement, yes, it is a *very* interesting book."

"More theology from that Augustine fellow?"

"Augustine of Hippo. He was a bishop from North Africa who converted from his old dualist beliefs and became a great Christian philosopher. I already read all about his youth and conversion in another book he called *Confessions*. But in this one, Augustine presents all of human history as a conflict between what he calls the City of Man and the City of God, with the latter term giving the book its title."

"I suppose his City of God is probably Rome," Lancelot mused, "I wonder where he'd place the City of Man."

"Actually, it's not meant literally," said Arthur, "He uses those terms to illustrate the differences between people who fix their eyes on Heaven and those who remain focused on the transitory, material pleasures of this world. For instance, here's a passage that might remind you of that usurper who sits on the British throne." Arthur flipped through the smooth vellum pages until he found what he sought: *"The good man, though a slave, is free; the wicked, though he reigns, is a slave, and not the slave of a single man, but – what is worse – the slave of as many masters as he has vices."*

Lancelot furrowed his brow. "So Vortigern is really a *slave*?" he asked incredulously, "Maybe Augustine should go relay that message to him. It would save all of *us* a lot of trouble."

"If only life were that easy," Arthur laughed, "Sorry, I won't bother you with any more this theology business. What did you come to see me about, anyway?"

"Well, it's funny you should mention Vortigern." Lancelot paused and looked over his shoulders warily. "I think we should talk about this inside. There are a lot of people roaming about this morning, and you never know who's listening."

At Lancelot's urging, the boys made their way through the garden and into the front room of the monastery. In truth, it was really just a house, but long ago Ector had removed most of the superfluous fineries, added a bell tower and a chapel, and hung a large iron cross from the front door, leading the townspeople to *assume* that it was a monastery. Ector wasn't even an actual monk. He dressed and acted like one, but he had never been officially ordained into any specific monastic order. Regardless, Ector still considered this place to be holy ground. He always said that God wasn't concerned with buildings or titles or ceremonies, but only what was in the heart.

Upon entering, the boys spied Ector sitting hunched over a small oak desk on the far side of the room, immersed in his transcription of Homer's *Odyssey* in the original Greek. The old soldier certainly didn't look like a typical man of the cloth, as his strong, battle-hardened physique was still visible underneath the heavy, brown, hooded cloak that was draped over his expansive shoulders. His balding head was bare, and his short grey beard was neatly trimmed, as always. A faint musty smell lingered in the room, which was filled with manuscripts, leather hides for binding, tenuously stacked piles of parchment and vellum, and small glass bottles full of fresh hawthorn ink. Ector greeted the young men without looking up.

"Good morning boys," he said, "Lancelot, it's a pleasure to see you again. I pray all is well with you and your uncle."

"Yes, sir," Lancelot answered, "Uncle Bors and Aunt Vivienne are both in good health. They send their best."

"Well then, you may give them my thanks. I do apologize for not being a more attentive host, but as you can see, I'm right in the middle of Odysseus' voyage to the underworld. I couldn't possibly tear myself away now. Oh, that reminds me – Arthur, did you finish your work in the garden like I asked or did you spend the whole morning reading again?"

Arthur looked around sheepishly. "It *was* Augustine, sir. Hardly a waste of time in my opinion."

"Qui congregat in messe filius sapiens est qui autem stertit aestate filius confusionis," Ector replied.

Frowning as if he had just lost a debate, Arthur looked down at the floor and muttered, "Yes, sir. I'm sorry for neglecting my chores. I'll have the gardening finished by the end of the day."

"That's a good lad," said Ector, "Now I must return to my writing. A pleasant day to you, boys."

Arthur nodded to his adoptive father and then turned and grabbed Lancelot by the arm, pulling him up the stairs and into his own room. After closing the door he let out a sigh. "It's always unpleasant to be proven wrong," he said, "but it's far *more* unpleasant when you're proven wrong in Latin."

"What did he say?" asked Lancelot.

"He was quoting from the Old Testament – the book of Proverbs. *He that gathers in the harvest is a wise son, but he that sleeps in the summer is the son of confusion."*

Lancelot smiled at Ector's clever Biblical jab and began trying to think of a witty retort, but before he could speak, Kay rudely barged into the room. "What's this, then?" the older, red-haired boy bellowed, "The book worm has been skipping out on his chores again? Well, we'll just have to teach him a lesson!" Kay had been out hunting and was still carrying the arrow-pierced body of a wild boar over his shoulder. He thrust the dead boar face-first toward Arthur, then began to move the beast's mouth as if it were talking.

"Reading books is for sissies!" snorted Kay in his best boar voice, "Finish your chores or I'll bite your fingers off!"

"Kay, you lunatic!" shouted Arthur, "Get out of here with that thing! You're going to get blood and fur everywhere!"

His protests fell on deaf ears. Lancelot was soon doubled over with laughter as he watched Kay chase Arthur around the room with the dead animal in his arms, issuing bizarre threats that might be made by a boar, such as "I'll bury my tusks in your hide!" and "I'm going to eat all your turnips!" After a while, Kay apparently decided he had tormented Arthur long enough and headed for the door.

"Just remember," Kay said with mock-seriousness, "He who does his gardening work gets fresh vegetables for dinner, but he who reads books gets attacked by talking pigs!"

Arthur reared back and hurled a shoe at his obnoxious step-brother, but it bounced off the door as Kay left the room and ran back down the stairs laughing.

"What an insufferable fool," Arthur grumbled.

Lancelot, however, found the entire situation hilariously absurd, and he struggled to hold back a tide of laughter while Arthur continued to complain about Kay's unwelcome intrusion. After ranting and raving for a while, Arthur stopped short and admonished himself for the outburst, humbly reciting the scripture about loving one's enemies.

At that moment, Lancelot remembered his original purpose for visiting Arthur, and he eagerly retrieved the old man's handwritten note from his pocket. Now free to unleash his excitement, Lancelot began rapidly recounting his remarkable story. He told Arthur about spilling the iron slag and being struck by the door, about the strange old man and his little grey owl, and about the visitor's almost otherworldly knowledge of his life. Lastly, he repeated the old man's cryptic request, along with his promise that a new king was coming.

"...and then, just before he vanished, he looked at me and said, 'Prepare yourself, for justice will reign again.'"

Arthur sat quietly for a moment, having clearly forgotten all about Kay. "If that old man was telling you the truth," he finally said, "then it sounds as if there may already be a rebellion brewing to overthrow Vortigern. Frankly, I don't know quite how to feel about that."

"You don't know how to feel about it?" Lancelot exclaimed, rising up in shock and anger, "You must be joking! It's the best thing that could possibly happen!"

"Is it?" Arthur replied, "Vortigern is certainly a brutal and corrupt tyrant, but I also wonder whether we, as mere men, have the authority to challenge those whom God has ordained. After all, all of life *is* within His hands. Kingdoms rise and fall, but God's will remains forever. I mean, David refused to kill Saul, despite his sins and many faults as king. So the question we have to ask ourselves is whether insurrection is defensible. Is there such a thing as just war?"

"For goodness sake, Arthur, try to think of it in simpler terms. A father who harms his children would rightfully be arrested and prevented from committing murder! It's no different with kings or queens."

"Yes, but does the responsibility for *dispensing* that justice belong to God or to man? To what extent does God use us to carry out His will here on earth?"

"I don't know," Lancelot grumbled in frustration, "but if a rebellion does come, then I certainly hope He uses *me*."

Arthur nodded slowly and ran his fingers through his stringy brown hair. "Hopefully God will use all of us, no matter what," he said. An awkward hush then fell over the room until Arthur finally broke the silence. "Can I see the note?"

Lancelot handed him the scrap of paper on which the old man had written his instructions. After reading for several minutes, Arthur leapt to his feet and gasped. His face turned white and his jaw dropped in amazement.

"What's wrong?" Lancelot asked, "You look like you've just seen a ghost."

"There's another message here… and I think it's for *me*."

"What? What are you talking about?"

Arthur walked over to Lancelot and pointed out several lines of writing on the scrap of paper. "Look," he said, "most of this stuff is just instructions and specifications on how to forge this Damascus steel you mentioned. But look down here at the bottom. He's written something else in Latin – a passage from *City of God*. It's from the beginning of the book, but I must have just read over it before without even thinking."

"Well, what does it say?" asked Lancelot anxiously.

Arthur read the passage once again to be sure he had translated it correctly. *"They who have waged war in obedience to the divine command, or in conformity with His laws, have represented in their persons the public justice or the wisdom of government, and in this capacity have put to death wicked men; such persons have by no means violated the commandment, Thou shalt not kill."*

Again, Arthur fell silent. For what seemed like an eternity, Lancelot leaned forward and stared at him with anticipation, waiting for some sort of additional commentary or explanation. Lancelot was certainly no simpleton, but this heavy theological writing was a bit over his head. Finally he could wait no longer. "So what does it mean?" he asked.

Arthur looked up at his friend and smiled. "It means might *can* be used for right, Lancelot."

He turned back to the old man's note, reading through it again slowly and carefully, assuring himself that what he had just seen was real. "This is just astonishing," Arthur continued, "A strange old man appears out of nowhere, and he somehow knows everything about you. Then he gives you this note that he presumably *knows* you can't read."

"Forcing me to bring the note to you," added Lancelot.

"Right! And amazingly, we discover a quote at the end of it from the very book I've been reading! Lancelot, something *big* is going on here."

Neither of the boys knew quite what to say. They both just stared in awe at the scrap of paper until Arthur leaned over and whispered, "Hey, do you believe in angels?"

Lady of Avalon

Arthur and Lancelot spent the remainder of the morning on their hands and knees in the large vegetable garden outside the monastery, finishing the chores Arthur had promised Ector he would complete by the end of the day. Fortunately, an extra pair of hands had lightened the workload considerably, and the boys were nearly finished by lunchtime.

To pass the hours while they harvested baskets full of carrots, turnips, onions, and cabbage, the boys continued their conversation, debating the true nature and intentions of the mysterious old man and his enigmatic request. As the initial excitement of the situation waned, they began to wonder if such a person could be trusted. Indeed, how *had* he known so many things about Lancelot's past? Didn't the old man say that he had been watching him since childhood? Perhaps he was sick in the head – or even dangerous. And how had he disappeared into thin air? Was he a simple magician, fooling the gullible with tricks and illusions? Was he a warlock or a powerful wizard? Was he an angel or a demon?

"And who is this so-called king he told you is coming?" asked Arthur, "We know nothing about him! I don't recall ever hearing about Uther Pendragon having a son, so how can we be sure this new king would be any better than Vortigern? For all we know, he could be a bumbling crackpot!"

"You know what we should do," Lancelot said, "We should go out to the woods and try to find the Lady of the Lake. I bet she'd have some answers."

Arthur furrowed his brow. "The Lady of the Lake? Come now, Lancelot. That's just an old superstition." The words of the educated young man were dripping with skepticism.

"No, she's real!" Lancelot retorted, "My uncle says he's seen her several times, and I'm pretty sure I've seen her as well. Do you remember a few years ago when my horse got spooked and I fell into that ravine and broke my leg?"

"Of course," Arthur replied.

"Well, I was lying there for hours, hoping someone would find me and help me out, but no one came. I guess I passed out eventually, but I have this vague memory of being pulled out of the ravine and carried home by... well, *someone*. All I know is that when I finally woke up, I was in my own bed and my wounds had been dressed. And even though it wasn't much more than a flash of light, I had this image etched on my mind – a glowing face framed by fiery, flowing red hair."

"And you believe that was her? I must admit, it all sounds a bit fantastic, but then again, so does everything else today. What do you think she is, anyway?"

"Well, people say that she's an angel or a fairie or a water nymph or some other kind of supernatural being. Either way, I think she just might be able to help us."

Despite his doubts, Arthur ultimately agreed to accompany Lancelot on a quest into Brocéliande Forest to search for the mythical Lady of the Lake. So after a hearty meal of fresh pork from Kay's boar, the boys bid farewell to Ector and set out on their journey. The forest itself was about an hour's walk to the northeast of the village, following the path of the river, and it was filled with extremely old broadleaf trees, primarily large oaks and beeches. It tended to rain there a great deal, with the weather conditions often changing quickly from bright and sunny skies to violent thunderstorms and then back again just as suddenly. The age of the ancient forest, as well as its unusual climate patterns, lead many locals to believe it was either enchanted or haunted by evil spirits.

At the center of the forest sat the Lake of Diana, which had been named long ago by the Romans in honor of one of their pagan deities. According to their theology, Diana was the goddess of the moon and hunting, as well as the protector of children and childbirth, and she was said to dwell on high mountains or in sacred woods. Arthur thought that such beliefs probably led to the contemporary legends about this *Lady of the Lake* figure, but he refrained from expressing this sentiment to Lancelot, who had obviously become a full-fledged believer. Of course, if the Lady of the Lake were indeed real, then it's possible that the Romans could have seen her themselves and understandably mistaken her for their beloved goddess. *It was possible*, thought Arthur, *but entirely implausible*.

They walked gingerly, tracing the winding path of the River Rance toward the woods and chatting casually about books and blacksmithing, food and family, and the surprisingly pleasant weather they were fortunate enough to enjoy. It was warm, dry, and breezy, without even a hint of storm clouds – at least for the time being – so they took off their shoes and strolled through the shallow water and bulrush reeds that filled the riverbanks. It wasn't long before they could see Brocéliande Forest up ahead, with its immense, primordial trees forming a dense green canopy above the grassy undergrowth.

Just as the boys were approaching the outer groves of the forest, they heard a loud rustling coming from the trees beyond. At first they dismissed it and continued their conversation, but as the sound grew closer, they both realized that whatever was out there was far too large to be a deer or a rabbit. Neither of them had thought to bring a weapon along, and in fear of meeting a hungry bear or something worse, the boys quickly retrieved handfuls of smooth, hard stones from the nearby riverbed to hurl at their adversary.

"Remember," warned Lancelot, "Don't let it know you're afraid. We can't allow it to scare us, or it'll attack."

"I suppose that means *running* is out of the question," Arthur replied as he nervously cocked his arm back, stone in hand, ready to face whatever emerged from the forest.

The rustling grew louder and closer until they could actually see the movement of the trees in front of them. With muscles tightened and jaws clenched in anticipation of the beast's imminent arrival, they remained still as statues, ready to react to the first sign of danger. Finally, a deafening noise broke through the silence, echoing through the woods and causing both boys to nearly jump out of their skin.

"AH-CHOO!!!"

It wasn't a bear. The thunderous sneeze had come from a middle-aged man on a horse, who was evidently experiencing an allergy attack as he rode forth from the forest. He was tall and painfully thin, with a scraggly head of hair and a long grey moustache drooping lazily below his chin. His aging palfrey seemed both exhausted and bored, yet the man himself sat upright with excellent posture, his head held high and his chest protruding triumphantly as if he were returning home from some victorious battle. He had a large sword strapped to his back that seemed entirely too big for such a slight man to handle, and as he approached the boys – who were now feeling particularly foolish – he raised his right hand in greeting.

"Hello, lads!" the man exclaimed, "Beautiful day, eh?"

Having fully prepared themselves for fighting and perhaps dying in hand-to-hand combat with a large, ferocious animal, the boys were not at all equipped to reply. They simply stared at each other blankly until Arthur eventually got his wits about him and stuttered a response.

"Umm... yes, sir. It certainly *is* a beautiful day."

"Yes, lovely, lovely," the man continued, "Say, do you lads happen to know of any maidens in need of rescuing?"

"No, sir," answered Arthur, "I can't say that we do."

"Oh, dash it all. Well, it appears that this journey has been a colossal waste of time. I suppose I'll just... oh, bother, where are my manners? I've entirely forgotten to introduce myself! My name is Pellinore – gentleman, equestrian, courtly lover, and faithful servant of the true king, Uther Pendragon."

Lancelot's ears perked up at the mention of Uther's name. He pushed his way past Arthur and stood as close as he could get to the aging soldier, blue eyes sparkling with excitement.

"Excuse me, sir," Lancelot asked eagerly, "But did you really serve under Uther Pendragon?"

"Of course, young man," said Pellinore, "He was the finest man I ever knew, and it was the greatest honor of my life to fight at his side. Oh, I had so many glorious adventures in those days – battling the Saxons, hunting the White Dragon, saving damsels in distress... speaking of which, do you lads happen to know of any maidens in need of rescuing?"

"You already asked us that, sir," Lancelot answered.

"Did I? Well what did you say in response?"

"Sorry, sir. We don't know of any. But we can try to let you know if we hear anything," said Arthur, clearly amused by the man's absentmindedness.

"Oh, dash it all. It's been nearly fifteen years since Uther was killed and that treacherous, beef-witted canker-blossom took his throne, and I *still* can't find any adventures fit for a man of my stature! Perhaps I should just go home."

Arthur was about to mention that the whole of Britannia remained trapped under Vortigern's tyrannical thumb and that the Saxon raiders had been cruel and oppressive to *countless* maidens, but he decided it was best to keep quiet, not wanting to be rude by making an elder look ridiculous.

"Pellinore, sir," interrupted Lancelot, "Did I hear you say that Uther was *killed?* I was always told that he died slowly due to some mysterious illness."

"Ah yes, lads," he said, "That's exactly what they *want* you to think. But I know the *truth*."

A sly grin stretched across Pellinore's face and he leaned down toward the boys, his voice falling to a whisper.

"You see, Uther Pendragon was *murdered*, and the culprit was none other than Vortigern himself, the king's one time ally. Every day, that swag-bellied miscreant put a tiny amount of poison in Uther's meals so it would go unnoticed. As the weeks wore on, the king grew sicker and sicker, but no one knew why. Eventually his body succumbed to the poison, and Vortigern was able to steal both his wife and his kingdom."

Arthur frowned. "But sir, if you knew all this, why did you do nothing to stop it from happening?"

"I tried, lad, I tried!" Pellinore exclaimed, "After I caught Vortigern in the act, I set out immediately to tell the king, but that villainous knave came with his men and had me locked in the dungeon! He somehow convinced Uther I had gone mad, and I remained imprisoned for years. By the time I escaped, it was far too late. Vortigern had won."

"So you fled here," said Lancelot.

"Yes, but it hasn't done much good," Pellinore continued, "Most people down *here* think I'm mad as well. Honestly, it's a fine thanks I get for roaming the countryside at my own expense, looking for quests to take and wrongs to right, never asking for *anything* in return – well, except for a nice mince pie now and then. I do *love* mince pies. And I know I've made some innocent little mistakes here and there, but I can hardly be held accountable for hurling an old woman into a pond when I have it on good authority that she's a witch! I mean, how was I supposed to know she was the priest's mother? And you know something else – a donkey can look an *awful* lot like a dragon in a certain light! I'm not the only one who thinks so! What about you, boys? You don't think I'm crazy, do you?"

Arthur and Lancelot looked back and forth at one another, speechless, completely bewildered, and struggling to maintain their composure after Pellinore's bizarre tirade. He certainly seemed like a pleasant man, but he also seemed to be as mad as a March hare. Finally, Arthur spoke.

"You know, sir, now that I think of it, I do believe I heard several maidens in distress a few miles south of here. Yes, I'm certain that I heard them begging for a valiant warrior to come and rescue them."

"Well then, why didn't you say so before?" cried Pellinore, "There isn't a moment to waste!" He quickly pulled the massive sword off his back and held it aloft, but the weight proved to be too much for the frail old soldier and he fell forward, tumbling off his horse and into the river.

"No harm done, no harm done!" he exclaimed as trudged up the riverbank and climbed back onto his horse, who still appeared to be incredibly bored, "I must leave you now, for I am needed elsewhere. Good day, lads. Oh, and you may want to find some shelter from this rain."

As Pellinore galloped off into the distance to rescue the nonexistent maidens Arthur had mentioned, the boys realized that they were now caught in the midst of a sudden downpour. They picked up their shoes and rushed into Brocéliande Forest, hoping that the wooded canopy would provide some measure of protection from the watery deluge.

Once within the shelter of the forest, the boys found their surroundings to be surprisingly dry. The stifling humidity brought on by the storm had somehow not followed behind them, thus the woodland air remained crisp and cool, making them feel as if they had stepped into another world. The tree covering overhead was evidently dense enough to block out all but a few sparse drops of rain, and so they sat and rested for a moment atop a pair of large, flat rocks and put their shoes back on before pressing ahead toward the Lake of Diana.

As Arthur and Lancelot continued their journey, they began to take notice of the breathtaking beauty surrounding them. The sunlight breaking through the trees left behind intricate patterns of green light that filled each clearing with a heavenly radiance, and a soft, sweet smell wafted through the forest air, leaving them feeling strangely invigorated. The few scattered raindrops that had managed to trickle through the thick canopy above fell to the ground and rested gently upon flowers, twigs, and grass, shimmering like beads of glass whenever the sun reached them. Dry leaves crunched pleasantly beneath the boys' feet as they ambled on, satisfied by the sheer loveliness of their surroundings. An intoxicating feeling washed over them, and they soon understood why so many people believed the forest was enchanted. After exhausting all commentary on this captivating sensation, their conversation soon turned to their peculiar encounter with Sir Pellinore.

"How about that old horseman, eh? What an eccentric person," said Arthur, who was staring at the ground in front of him, attempting to catch a brightly colored frog that he had been tracking for some time now.

"Oh, he's a raving loon," Lancelot replied as he wiped strands of damp hair away from his eyes, "But do you think he was telling the truth about Pendragon?"

"I'm not sure," said Arthur, making an unsuccessful grasp for the elusive frog, "On one hand, his story about the poison certainly *sounds* like something Vortigern would have done. On the other hand, the man is obviously a bit daft."

"I suppose so, but I would still like to trust him. Can you believe that he..."

Lancelot stopped short. Both boys silently turned their heads, honing their ears toward of the grove of trees just behind them. It was another rustling sound. But this time, they knew better than to blame the noise on a bear.

"Sir? Pellinore?" called Arthur, "Is that you?"

There was no answer. Arthur called out again.

"Pellinore? Are you following us?"

Still no answer. As the rustling continued to grow louder, the boys soon began to wonder if this time it really *was* a bear, rummaging for food and tracking their scent through the forest.

And then they found out for sure. All of a sudden, the rustling stopped and a thunderous roar rolled forth from the grove of trees. Their faces now white with terror, Arthur and Lancelot turned and began to run toward the Lake of Diana as fast as their legs could carry them, hoping to hide themselves beneath the murky water. The snapping of branches and whooshing of leaves behind them indicated that the beast had emerged from the grove to give chase – *and was gaining fast*. Lancelot's long legs propelled him forward at a lightning pace, but Arthur lagged behind, unable to keep up with his taller friend. Sheer adrenaline provided him with an added burst of speed, but the monster's crashing footsteps still grew closer, threatening to overtake him.

"Oh God, please don't let me die!" Arthur cried out to the heavens as he ran for his life through the brambly undergrowth. Out of morbid curiosity, he peeked over his left shoulder, hoping to catch a quick glimpse of the ferocious creature that would surely seal his fate. But much to his surprise, instead of seeing a half-ton beast covered in thick brown fur, he saw a gangly young man with red hair and large ears.

It was Kay.

Arthur turned his head and glared with disdain at his oaf of a step-brother, who had apparently been following them the entire day, biding his time in anticipation of the perfect prank.

Arthur was about to give Kay a piece of his mind, but with his head twisted around, he couldn't see where he was going and tripped on a protruding tree root while still running at full speed. Arthur gasped as his momentum threw him into the air, and he soon came crashing down to the ground, cracking his head against a rock and finally rolling flaccidly into the lake.

By this time, Lancelot had looked back as well and realized that they had been duped. Backtracking from the far side of the water, he rushed up and grabbed Kay by the front of his tunic.

"What on earth is wrong with you?" Lancelot yelled, "You and your stupid antics might have just killed him!"

"I-I'm sorry, I didn't mean to hurt anyone," stammered Kay, "I was only trying to scare you two. I-I-I just wanted..."

"Stop blathering and go get some help!" shouted Lancelot.

"But what are you going to..."

"Go NOW!"

Kay ran off through the woods and was soon out of sight, though in the distance, Lancelot could still hear him muttering over and over again, *"I didn't mean to hurt anyone...I didn't mean to hurt anyone..."*

Lancelot turned and gazed out at the lake, but there were no signs of Arthur – no body floating near the shore, no bubbles of air rising to the surface, not even a single ripple in the dark water. However, just as he was about to dive in and attempt a desperate search for his wounded friend, Lancelot noticed a small spot out in the middle of the lake that had begun to bubble and foam, almost as if it were coming to a boil. A low, rumbling sound emanated from within the raging froth, and then a lithe, humanlike shape slowly began to emerge from the depths. *The Lady of the Lake!*

She was strikingly beautiful. Her long red hair blew gently in the wind, ebbing and flowing like rolling waves, and her emerald eyes sparkled like sunbeams on the water. A glistening gown of deep green samite was draped softly over her body, and her skin, as fair as porcelain, glowed as if some ethereal light were being generated from within. Arthur's body hung lifelessly from her arms, yet she walked without urgency toward the shoreline, rising higher until the soles of her bare feet rested delicately on the surface of the water.

Lancelot stared in awe as the Lady of the Lake gently placed Arthur on the soft, moist ground among the reeds near the water's edge. He had a large bump on his forehead and didn't seem to be breathing. But as the woman looked over at Lancelot and smiled, a warm feeling washed over him, and a soft, soothing voice whispered to his heart that everything would be all right. Kneeling over Arthur's pale, lifeless body, she leaned down and kissed him delicately on his forehead, and almost immediately, the color returned to his face and the sweet forest air began to refill his lungs.

"He is hurt," she said, "but he will fully recover. Fear not, Lancelot. Your friend is alive. Now we must let him sleep."

Arthur's countenance had changed so drastically in a few short moments that Lancelot could scarcely believe his eyes. A face that once appeared to be locked in the pallor of death now seemed to be growing in both vitality and strength, being supernaturally rejuvenated by a deep, peaceful slumber. In his shock and amazement, Lancelot struggled to speak.

"You... you're the..."

"I am Nimue," she said. Her voice was like a melody.

"Thank you," Lancelot finally managed to say, "Thank you so much for saving my friend."

"No, young man, thank *you*," she replied, "I have been your silent guardian these many years, Lancelot. I watched over your mother as she gave her life to save you, and I have watched over you every day since you took your first step. I will even watch over you as a man – a powerful warrior, and a loyal friend. And believe me when I say that you will do far more than I to serve Arthur over these coming years."

"But how can you know such things?"

"The passage of time here on earth is hardly a concern for the children of Avalon," Nimue answered.

Her statement stirred something in Lancelot's memory, and he suddenly recalled that the old man had told him something eerily similar. *"I do have such a difficulty keeping track of the passage of time,"* the stranger had said, *"At least, in the way you perceive time."* Lancelot remembered why he'd come.

"The old man who visited me in my uncle's shop," he said, "Can he be trusted? Are his intentions good or evil?"

"His name is Merlyn," replied Nimue, "and he bears you no ill will. Listen to him, Lancelot. Forge the sword. Your destiny is greater than you can possibly imagine."

As she finished speaking, Kay returned with Pellinore in tow. He had found the old soldier attempting to rescue a small girl from her own pet cat, who he was convinced had become possessed by Satan. Despite the man's odd behavior, Kay was desperate and thought he could be of some use, plus the girl and her cat were both glad to be rid of him.

"I've brought help!" called Kay, "Did you find Arthur?"

"Actually," said Lancelot with a smile, "*She* did."

But when he turned back to introduce Arthur's angelic rescuer to Kay and Pellinore, she had vanished. And no trace remained but a gentle ripple on the surface of the lake.

A House Built on Sand

It was Christmas morning, and the castle was bustling with merriment, music, and life. It seemed as if the holiday season had brought out the best in everyone, including Morgana, whose warm smile and cheery disposition provided a welcome respite from her typically morose demeanor. Even Igraine had temporarily broken free from the vacant emotional detachment that ruled her on most days, and she had spent much of the past week carefully decorating the Great Hall with candles, holly wreaths, and brightly colored tapestries.

Morgana had awoken earlier than normal, unable to sleep and overwhelmed with excitement in anticipation of the day's festivities. Throughout the morning and afternoon, the servants would all be busy in the kitchen, working diligently to prepare the sumptuous Christmas feast that she so eagerly awaited throughout the year. It would begin with warm gingerbread and candied fruits, followed by assorted cheeses, bacon with mustard, and savory mince pies. The centerpiece would be a massive roast goose, stuffed with quinces and sour apples and bathed in a rich sauce of sage, parsley, and onion. Then after the meal they would all huddle up together next to a roaring fire, sipping hot mulled wine and enjoying a dessert of sweet Christmas plum pudding.

As Morgana wandered through the castle, humming a little tune to herself and dreaming of the forthcoming feast, she chanced upon a group of servants – most of them a few years younger than she – rehearsing their yearly reenactment of the

Nativity. The eldest boy, who appeared to be playing Joseph, was acting as a director, feeding lines to the others and ordering them to various positions around their makeshift stage. He seemed to be growing a bit exasperated with one of the younger actors, a small boy playing a shepherd, who was unable to correctly repeat the line, "Behold, the Angel of the Lord!" with any measure of consistency. The older boy kept making the line shorter and shorter in order to help the younger one with his memorization, until it had finally been whittled down to a succinct, "Look!" Further chaos was caused by the fact that the various animals in the stable where the Christ child lay were being played by the castle dogs, who were far more interested in sniffing one another and searching for scraps of food than pretending to be sheep and donkeys. After taking a moment to enjoy the simple humor of the situation, Morgana chuckled to herself and continued on her way.

She initially set out for Rowena's room, hoping to spend Christmas day with her closest friend, but Morgana quickly remembered that Rowena would be out in the forest with the rest of her Saxon family, celebrating their pagan Yule festival in honor of the winter solstice. Rowena had told her about it once, and honestly, the whole thing seemed rather odd. Apparently, December 25 marked the first day of the Saxon calendar, and they would venture out into the woods and dance and make blood sacrifices to their mother goddesses, praying for the fertility of the land during the coming year. They would also celebrate the Wild Hunt, a supposedly supernatural journey across the heavens, with the god Woden leading a band of phantasmal huntsmen after some mythic beast.

It certainly sounded a bit far-fetched, but then again, so did the idea of a baby being born to a virgin, or the idea of magi following a moving star around the desert. Indeed, Morgana knew that she hardly had the right to criticize Rowena's beliefs when she so often questioned her own. But today she wasn't concerned with such things. Today she thought only of the celebration, the feast, and the presents, and as a result, she was absolutely overflowing with delight.

Since Rowena was otherwise engaged, Morgana decided to visit her mother, who seemed to be happier now than she'd been in years. Perhaps her change in mood was simply due to the cheer of the holiday season, but Morgana suspected that her mother's newfound joy actually resulted from the fact that Vortigern had been away for the past several weeks, leading yet another campaign against the Picts in Caledonia. He had already ordered the execution of three unsuccessful generals before finally deciding to just handle the situation himself, and it had now been nearly a month since Vortigern stormed out of the castle in full battle regalia, vowing not to return without the head of Drest, the Pictish king. Much like her mother, Morgana took great pleasure in her stepfather's absence, and she prayed daily that his war in the north would drag on as long as possible. Sometimes she even prayed for his death.

The morning sunlight poured through the hallway windows as Morgana approached her mother's room. She raised her hand to knock, but before she could do so, the door swung open and Igraine emerged abruptly from her bed chamber, elaborately dressed and apparently quite agitated.

"Oh, good morning, Morgana," said Igraine, "You startled me. You really mustn't loiter around outside my room like that. Have you eaten breakfast yet? My goodness, dear, what are you still doing in your dressing gown? The bishop will be here at any moment, and we must all look our best! Quickly!"

Before Morgana could utter a word, Igraine grabbed her by the hand and began hurriedly pulling her down the hallway and back toward her own bedroom. Needless to say, Morgana had no clue what her mother was talking about.

"Whatever do you mean, mother? What bishop?"

"Dear, I'm certain I told you. Bishop Germanus is coming to visit this morning. This is his second journey through Britannia to combat the threat of the Pelagians, and I offered to let him spend Christmas with us."

The Pelagians were a Christian sect that had been making waves in the church for a number of years. Morgana didn't know exactly what they believed, but she had heard a little about them, and she knew they rejected the doctrine of Original Sin and claimed that mankind was responsible for its own salvation. Germanus and another Gallic bishop had come to Britannia many years ago and had confronted the Pelagian clergy at a huge public meeting, eventually defeating them after a long and heated theological debate. Some say that Germanus then traveled around the country healing the sick and performing other miracles, including a tale that he warded off an entire army of Pictish raiders by baptizing the British troops and ordering them all to shout "Hallelujah!" in unison. Just the idea that Bishop Germanus may have subdued an army of Picts with one word while Vortigern had failed so miserably to win a single victory against them filled Morgana with a smug sense of satisfaction. Perhaps she would enjoy this visit.

* * * * *

As it happened, Igraine's frantic rush to make everyone presentable had been slightly premature. Bishop Germanus arrived at the castle shortly before lunchtime, several hours after Morgana had swiftly dressed at her mother's urging, and much to Morgana's surprise, he didn't look much like an ordinary bishop. She was used to seeing clergymen wearing either colorful, ornate robes – often bright red and lined with fur – or drab hooded cloaks tied modestly around the waist with a bit of rope. She was used to their mannerisms being either pompous and preening, like overstuffed peacocks drunk on their own self-satisfaction, or meek and lowly, too deep in penitence to even lift their faces.

But this man was different.

He rode up to the castle gate on a large black stallion, then dismounted and threw back his cloak, revealing the well-worn leather armor that covered his torso on most days. The symbol of the Roman Empire, a golden eagle, now heavily tarnished with age, was emblazoned across his chest, and a Gallic infantry sword hung loosely from a loop on his belt. His hair was shaved into the typical clergy tonsure, and a grey goatee rested neatly upon his chin. He carried himself with confidence but not with arrogance, and when Igraine opened the door, he greeted the women with a warm smile and a gentlemanly bow.

"Good day, ladies," said Germanus with a twinkle in his eye, "and a happy Christmas to you both."

"We are honored by your presence, Excellency," Igraine replied, and she and Morgana each knelt in reverence.

"Oh, do stand up, Madame," Germanus laughed as he took Igraine's hand and led her to her feet, "I'm only a man. You and your daughter need only kneel before *God*. And don't bother with this 'Excellency' business either. Just call me Germanus. Or *Bishop* Germanus if it makes you more comfortable."

"Certainly, Excel... I mean, *Bishop Germanus*. Please come in and make yourself at home. If you'll allow me to take your cloak, one of the servants will bring in your belongings and lead your horse to the stable. We also have a room prepared for you where you are welcome to change your clothes."

Germanus smiled and thanked Igraine profusely, and then one of the servants led him to his room where he was given the opportunity to remove his armor and put on clean clothing. A hot bath was also prepared for him, allowing him to cleanse the dust of the road from his weary body.

He emerged from his room about an hour later, happy and refreshed, wearing a simple white linen robe with a deep blue stole draped over his shoulders. Igraine had busied herself in the kitchen, supervising the preparation of the Christmas feast, so Germanus sought out Morgana, who was seated next to the fire reading from a thick, leather-bound tome.

"What are you reading, child?" asked Germanus as he sat down next to the raven-haired young woman.

"It's Herodotus, sir," she replied, "His histories. I've been learning about the Spartan King Leonidas and his suicidal stand against the massive Persian army at Thermopylae."

"Suicidal, eh?" Germanus said with a sly grin, "Is that the way you see it? I've always thought he was quite noble."

"I mean no disrespect, Bishop Germanus, but Leonidas had a wife and a child back home in Sparta. It seems to me that he should have just *surrendered* to the Persians. It would have saved his life and the lives of his soldiers. And his son would not have been forced to grow up without a father."

Morgana's voice cracked slightly with her last few words, and Germanus could clearly sense that she had been personally affected by the ancient tale. He knew she wasn't thinking of Leonidas, but of her own father, Uther Pendragon, a man he had known and respected in his younger years.

"You know, Morgana, the Holy Scriptures tell us that the willingness of a man to lay down his own life for others is the greatest form of love. I've always thought King Leonidas was very brave for sacrificing himself in order to help stave off the Persian invasion of his homeland. If you think about it, Christ did the same thing when he allowed himself to be crucified for the sins of humanity. In both cases, a king laid down his life in order to save those he loved."

With those few words, Morgana's typically stoic exterior softened and her eyes began to glisten with moisture. There was something about this man that made her feel *safe* – free to let down her guard and express her deepest doubts and fears. They had only just met, and yet she felt as if she had known him for ages. So she looked up into the friendly face of the bishop and prepared to bare her soul.

"But what about *my* father?" Morgana asked softly as a single tear ran down her cheek, "He didn't die to save *anyone*. He was taken away from us pointlessly, only for a... for a *far lesser man* to take his place. If God loves us so much, Bishop Germanus, then why does He allow such evil?"

Germanus sat quietly for a moment, contemplating how to word his response. He had been asked similar questions on countless occasions by countless hurting individuals, and he knew the correct theological answer. However, despite his extensive knowledge, it was never easy to express such difficult truth to one so tormented by pain and loss.

"My child," he began, "we live in a corrupted, fallen world. Ever since our first parents were cast out of the Garden of Eden, the sin of mankind has resulted in suffering. God loves us more than we could ever fathom. But He also gave us free will, since without freedom there can be no loving relationship between the Creator and His creation. Evil exists because mankind is free to make moral choices. Now, I don't know why your father had to die, but I do know that your Heavenly Father is watching over you, and He has a plan for all things."

The room grew still with silence. Neither Morgana nor the bishop spoke another word for what seemed like an eternity. Finally, hoping for some kind of response, Germanus gently placed his hand on the young woman's cheek and wiped away her tears. Her dark eyes looked sad, and they seemed to be hiding a deep, lingering pain that went far beyond the loss of a father. The moment Morgana felt the bishop's tender touch, something broke inside of her and she lost all control. Her emotional walls collapsed, leaving her no choice but to fall weeping into his warm, comforting embrace. All at once, this stranger became a father to her, and she surrendered herself to his loving arms. The young woman, so prematurely aged with grief, once again became the little girl, hiding in the shelter of a love she had not felt for ages – a love that hibernated in the depths of her memory, struggling to escape from the often impenetrable darkness within.

Germanus brushed Morgana's hair away from her face, and she forced herself to smile meekly. He then placed a small but beautifully decorated book into her shaking hands.

"This is a prayer book, Morgana," he said, "also known as a book of hours. It's filled with prayers, psalms, and other texts, and it's always been of use to me whenever I doubt my faith. I'd like you to have it for a Christmas present."

Never looking directly into the eyes of the kindly bishop, Morgana whispered a tentative, "Thank you," and then abruptly changed the subject.

* * * * *

The Christmas feast that night was splendid. The bishop opened with an eloquent prayer, thanking God for the gift of His blessed Son, and then all those in attendance ate and drank until they felt like they would pop. The Nativity play put on by the servant children was cute and delightful, although they all got a good laugh when one of the castle dogs felt the need to relieve himself all over one of the Wise Men. When it came time to exchange presents, Morgana received a gorgeous, deep crimson dress from her mother, lined in white ermine and embroidered with gold along the hems, and then they spent the remainder of the evening telling funny stories and laughing themselves silly. Morgana was particularly surprised at how witty Bishop Germanus turned out to be, as he regaled them with elaborate, hilarious tales from his journeys throughout Gaul and Britannia. Even more surprising was the serendipitous presence of Morgana's Saxon friend, Rowena.

She had arrived at the feast just as they were finishing off the gingerbread and candied fruits. There were flecks of blood on her dress, although she appeared to be uninjured, and her clear blue eyes looked sullen and troubled. When she sat down next to Morgana, she said that she had left the Yule festival, sickened with her father and his soldiers as they danced about in a drunken stupor, wantonly slaughtering animals and painting their bodies with the spilled blood, hollering at the heavens for

Woden to make them stronger and more virile. Apparently the celebration had grown steadily worse over the past few years, and she had finally reached her breaking point. *In what way did such senseless revelry honor the gods?* Rowena had asked. After eating her fill, she ended up spending a large part of the evening in deep conversation with Bishop Germanus.

The Great Hall was filled with laughter and singing as the festivities continued well past midnight. Germanus was the first to excuse himself, informing everyone that the celebration had been absolutely wonderful, and the company unforgettable, but that he was far too exhausted to carry on. Rowena returned to her quarters soon afterward, followed by Igraine and then Morgana, who stayed up jovially chatting with the servants until after they had cleared the table and left for bed themselves.

Upon returning to her bedroom, Morgana was still too excited to sleep. She eagerly unwrapped the crimson dress that Igraine had given to her and tried it on, grinning from ear to ear as she posed in front of her full-length mirror. She let her slender fingers gently brush against the soft ermine lining, then twirled and watched the elegant silk fabric as it swished around her ankles, making her feel both beautiful and loved. Gradually it dawned on Morgana that for the first time in ages, she was genuinely happy. Perhaps Bishop Germanus was right. Perhaps God really did love her and was watching over her. Perhaps her mother had finally regained her lost smile. Perhaps Vortigern had finally been taken away from them for good. Still floating on a cloud of joy, she playfully winked at herself in the mirror and said aloud, “Well, Morgana, don’t you look ravishing.”

And then a voice from behind her answered, “Yes, my dear, you certainly do.”

Morgana’s eyes popped wide open as she froze in terror. She looked into the mirror at the open doorway and there she saw Vortigern, still dressed in his dirty, iron armor and clutching his spear – an old, blood-stained Roman *pilum* that the king had carried for as long as she could remember. *He had returned*.

Morgana didn't move a muscle as he slowly approached her, finally setting his weapon aside and resting his large, rough hands on her delicate shoulders.

"I've been away at war for a long time now," he hissed, "Over a month surrounded by no one but foul-smelling Saxon soldiers. And I've greatly desired the scent of a woman."

Morgana cringed as Vortigern lifted a lock of her smooth, dark hair to his nose and inhaled. He groaned with satisfaction and then grabbed her by the arms, turning her around to face him. He was obviously drunk, and the stench of his breath made her want to vomit.

"Now then, let's get those ugly rags off of you, and you can show your king how much you missed him."

Choking down her fear, Morgana managed to work up enough courage to respond, silently praying that God would save her from this nightmare.

"P-p-please leave," she stammered, desperately hoping for some kind of divine intervention. For a few moments the room was silent. She looked up at Vortigern pleadingly, and he stared back with unbridled lust burning behind his eyes.

"Leave?" he asked furiously, *"Leave?"*

Then he reared back and slapped her hard across the face, sending her sprawling onto the floor.

"How dare you reject your king!" he shouted, "I am lord of this land and lord of this castle! And all that dwell here belong to me, including *you*, you little witch!"

With those final words, Vortigern picked her up and angrily tossed her onto the bed. Then he proceeded to remove her new silk dress by ripping it to shreds with his bare hands.

As the king continued with his vicious assault on her body, Morgana simply lay there, looking down at the tattered pieces of her Christmas gift, sobbing quietly.

* * * * *

Unseen by human eyes, two wraithlike figures stood by, watching the scene unfold with devilish delight. The first was gaunt and twisted, covered from snout to tail with bristly grey fur, and he smiled wickedly as he whispered lies into Vortigern's ear, filling his soul with inhuman malevolence. The second was immense and terrifying, his royal robes adorned with pitch black feathers that seemed to absorb all light. He approached Morgana's frail, violated body and dug his talons deep into her skull, speaking to her softly as she wept.

"God doesn't love you, my child," he sneered, "That narcissistic tyrant has *never* cared about you. He doesn't even know your name. But the sad truth is that even if he *did* care, he wouldn't be able to help you. He doesn't have that kind of power – not the power *I'm* offering to you."

The dark figures continued their manipulation deep into the night, until eventually Vortigern left and Morgana fell into a dreamless sleep. The next morning when the servants came to clean her bedroom, Morgana was gone, but they noticed a strange, black item near her fireplace. It was the beautiful little prayer book Bishop Germanus had given to her. It had been tossed into the fire and burned beyond all recognition.

The Sword in the Stone

The blade hissed and steamed as Lancelot plunged it into a large quenching barrel near the bloomery furnace, cooling the red-hot Damascus steel after it had been tempered a sufficient number of times to render the weapon strong and sharp while keeping the body flexible so that it would bend rather than break during combat. He had spent much of his free time for the better part of three years forging, grinding, and hardening the blade, until at last he had achieved perfection. Once the temperature of the steel waned enough for him to handle it freely, the young blacksmith carefully attached the grip, guard, and pommel he had painstakingly constructed from polished bone and leather, accented with a gleaming copper alloy.

Finally finished, Lancelot propped the magnificent sword up against the wall and stepped back a few feet to admire his handiwork – *his masterpiece*. The weapon was truly a sight to behold. It was made in the Celtic style, with the bone-crafted hilt carved into the fearsome form of a roaring lion. The blade itself had been pattern-welded from numerous layers of steel, then twisted and folded upon itself countless times, resulting in a banding pattern reminiscent of flowing water. It was light enough to be wielded with one hand, yet strong enough to cleave a man in two. He decided to call the sword *Arondight*, an ancient name meaning "adorned with great strength," which Arthur had etched for him across the hand guard.

The work had progressed slowly at first, since Lancelot had very little time to spare outside of his normal duties in the blacksmith's shop. He had also never forged Damascus steel before, but using Merlyn's detailed instructions – transcribed by Arthur, of course – he soon learned how to properly heat and cool the tough, shatter-resistant metal so that it could be formed into the proper shape. Eventually, Uncle Bors began spending more and more time away from the shop, partly due to Lancelot's growing skill and talent, and partly due to his own failing health after decades of inhaling smoke and charcoal dust. Although somewhat distraught by the cause of his uncle's increased absence, Lancelot cherished his new-found freedom and was thus able to devote more time to finishing his task.

Now, standing in awe of all he had accomplished, Lancelot began to imagine the man for whom he would brandish this sword on the field of battle – the prophesied king who would rise up and lead his people out of oppression and darkness. He would be strong and bold, riding forth with righteous vengeance on the back of a snow white destrier, his armor flashing in the sunlight and flames of justice blazing behind his eyes. Lancelot dreamed of one day taking up arms and following this king into battle, striking fear into the hearts of the barbaric, pagan hordes that had overrun his native land and ending Vortigern's cruel and tyrannical reign forever. It would be a day of liberty and triumph. It would be the dawn of a new era. It would be the second coming of the Pendragon.

Lancelot was abruptly awakened from his daydream by a loud knock on the front door of the blacksmith's shop. Coming to his senses, he rubbed his eyes and ran his fingers through his shaggy, sandy-brown hair and then quickly retrieved a large, woolen blanket to hide his sword from public view.

"Just a moment!" he shouted toward the entrance, "I'll be right there!" After carefully wrapping the blanket around the marvelous weapon, Lancelot walked back to the door, loosened the bolt lock, and swung it open wide.

There stood the old man with the long, white beard. He carried the same gnarled walking stick and wore the same dingy, green cloak as he had three years ago when Lancelot saw him last. His little grey owl looked older and barely moved, but he remained perched atop the old man's wide-brimmed hat. Lancelot then remembered his parting words: *Be diligent and watchful. I'll return when the time is right.*

"Hello, my boy," said the old man, "You've done well."

At first, Lancelot was unsure of how to respond. He should have been anticipating the return of the old man – Nimue had said his name was *Merlyn* – but now that they were face to face, he found himself speechless. *What was he to do now? Just take up arms and follow this stranger to the gates of Vortigern's castle? And where was the foretold king? Had his promised rebellion already begun without acclaim or fanfare? Or was he still in hiding, waiting for the right moment to reveal himself to the world?* No matter what happened next, Lancelot was determined to have his questions answered.

"You've grown into a fine young man," Merlyn continued, "How long has it been? Forty-five, fifty years?"

"It's only been three years, sir," Lancelot replied quizzically, "After *fifty* years my hair would be as white as yours."

"Oh yes, quite right, quite right. I hope you'll excuse me for my disorientation, but I always have trouble relating to those who are forced to live within the constraints of *time*. You see, I myself have journeyed thousands of years into the future and even further into the past. Technically, I'm still there. Well, no, that's not quite accurate. I was never truly *there*, just as I am not truly *here* at this moment… I mean, not in the way that *you* happen to be *here*. Do you follow me?"

"No, sir. Not in the least," he responded, a blank expression upon his soot-covered face.

"Well, my boy, you must understand that you perceive my presence only because I am allowing you to do so, but I actually dwell in another plane of existence, which is merely overlapping with your own. But that is neither here nor there, as they say. Regardless, time is not linear for me, Lancelot. I can see and experience yesterday, today, and tomorrow all in the same instant. For example, as I stand and talk to you now, I am also witnessing man's discovery of fire, the crossing of the Red Sea by Moses and the Hebrews, the coronation of Queen Victoria, and the invention of the very first automobile!"

"What's an *automobile*?"

"Nothing, nothing. Forget about it," Merlyn said sheepishly, and then he abruptly changed the subject, "I've been watching over you, Lancelot, and I applaud you for completing your task faithfully. But now that you have prepared your sword, you must next prepare your heart. Soon the new king will rise, and he will need you more than you know."

Lancelot furrowed his brow. He found the old man's final statement a bit confusing, but since it was far less confusing than those which preceded it, he shrugged his shoulders and allowed the bewilderment to pass.

Harkening back to the original subject of their conversation, Lancelot reached behind the quenching barrel and retrieved Arondight, still wrapped in the woolen blanket, and uncovered it to present his finely-crafted steel creation to Merlyn. He waited in anticipation, watching the old man carefully in an attempt to gauge his reaction, but Merlyn simply stood there and smiled in approval, without even a hint of astonishment or enthusiasm on his face. It was almost as if he had already seen the weapon several times before and had no reason to be surprised by its brilliance.

"Magnificent," said Merlyn, "The old Romans would have claimed it was the work of Vulcan himself."

"Thank you, sir," Lancelot replied, grinning brightly at the old man's compliment.

"Tell me, young blacksmith, what made you decide to forge this sword? Why did you follow the cryptic instructions of a strange man whom you had never met? Was it fear, or faith, or was it simply a pretext for acting on your own desires?"

Lancelot pondered for a moment, deeply grateful for a question that he at least understood, and then offered Merlyn his honest reply.

"I must admit that all three played a part in my decision, sir. I was certainly afraid of you at first, and I secretly dreaded what a man of your... *talents* might do if I were to refuse. I also developed a sense of faith – mostly due to conversations with my friend Arthur and my encounter with the lady Nimue. But as for my own desires, while I have always dreamed of possessing a weapon such as this, my deepest longing is to witness the return of the true king. So in all sincerity, I believed because I *wanted* to believe – because I *needed* to believe that all hope is not lost, and that though the road ahead is cloaked in darkness, the morning sun still rises."

"And when the dawn breaks," Merlyn replied with a smile, "will you accept the new day as it is and follow faithfully, or will you instead pine for that which you *wish* it to be?"

"I'm afraid I don't fully understand the question, sir," said Lancelot, "But whenever and however the Pendragon comes, I will follow him to the ends of the earth."

"I'll remember you said that," the old man smirked, and then he turned and walked briskly through the front door of the blacksmith shop, out into the crisp, cool air of late afternoon.

Lancelot's jaw dropped and he froze in astonishment as Merlyn abruptly disappeared from sight. *Is that all? Am I to be given nothing more than a few obscure statements to satiate my curiosity? What of the rebellion? What of the new king?* Renewing his determination, the young blacksmith burst through the door and onto the narrow cobblestone road, fully prepared to give chase if need be.

Once he spotted Merlyn, Lancelot found it exceedingly peculiar that the old man was already much farther down the road than anyone would have expected. Although he appeared to be walking, plodding along slowly and leaning against his wooden staff, even a younger man – such as himself – running in full sprint would not have been able to cover that amount of ground in such a short period of time. But then again, Lancelot had already seen enough peculiarities thus far, so one more hardly unnerved him.

Perhaps Merlyn has created this distance between us for a reason. Perhaps he wishes to be pursued, but not overtaken. With this seed of an idea in mind, Lancelot decided to follow on foot, keeping to the shadows and moving only fast enough to maintain eye contact with the old man's silhouette, occasionally ducking behind trees to avoid detection.

He must have followed Merlyn for miles before the old man turned away from the main road and began to descend into a dark, wooded valley, long overgrown with vines and brambles. Now wishing he had brought his sword along to cut through this unruly mess of vegetation, Lancelot did his best to remain untangled and avoid the thorns, still keeping a watchful eye on Merlyn as he delved deeper into the thicket.

Suddenly, Lancelot tripped and fell over something hard and flat. He cursed quietly to himself and then sat up in the underbrush, rubbing his wounded shin and searching for the cause of his misfortune. He had expected to find a large rock or a tree stump, but instead, he found what appeared to be a gravestone. It was badly cracked and moss covered, and the inscription had been worn off by the elements, but it was clearly a burial marker. As Lancelot stood up and looked around, he saw several other stones and realized that he was standing in a cemetery – a very old and long forgotten cemetery.

Quickly recognizing that he had lost track of Merlyn, Lancelot began to survey his surroundings, eventually spotting the old man about 100 feet away near a small grove of trees. He was seated atop a large oak stump and was speaking to someone, but the shadows cast by the setting sun made any positive identification next to impossible. Lancelot slowly crept closer until he could hear their conversation clearly.

"Your origins are not as humble as you may think, my boy," he heard Merlyn say, "You see, your grandfather was a powerful Roman general named Constantinus who led a legion of soldiers in protecting Britannia from the Saxon invasions. In recognition of his success, his men hailed him as Emperor of Rome and the Britons proclaimed him their king. And after his death in battle, your father, a man known to most as Uther Pendragon, took his place and led Britannia to victory against the pagan hordes."

"You mean to tell me, sir," said the other figure, "that I am really the son of Uther Pendragon, King of the Britons?"

"When you were born," Merlyn continued, "dark forces sought you out, intending to slay you in the cradle, in hopes that you would never be able to ascend to the throne. So I revealed myself to your father and warned him of the danger you faced, and he reluctantly allowed me to take you away so you could be watched over and protected until the proper time. While your mother and sister were led to believe that you had perished in infancy, I left you in the care of a kindly monk, safe on holy ground. Within his monastery, you were beyond the reach of those agents of evil who still yearn for your destruction."

Hidden within the surrounding brush, Lancelot swiftly clamped his hands over his mouth to keep from shouting. Did Merlyn really say that this particular young man, the son of Uther Pendragon, the heir to the throne of Britannia, had been raised by a monk in a local monastery? Could it be *him*? The voice *had* sounded rather familiar. Lancelot attempted to calm himself, listening closely in anticipation of Merlyn's next words.

"You were christened Arturus Riothamus, the one and only son of Uther and Igraine. You are the true and rightful king of Britannia. You, Arthur, are the next Pendragon."

At that moment the blinding sun finally ducked beneath the horizon, and Lancelot was able to clearly see the familiar face of his best friend. The revelation caused him to drop to his knees in shock. After all, how could this be? Arthur was certainly an intelligent and honorable young man, but he hadn't so much as lifted a sword a day in his life! How on earth could this scrawny bibliophile have what it takes to lead a defiant assault against the entire Saxon army? Lancelot began to feel sick.

* * * * *

Meanwhile, Arthur was caught in a state of shock himself. He stared at Merlyn in silence, his eyes open wide and his mouth gaping wide like a codfish, unable to believe such an outrageous tale. Despite the fact that Arthur had never known much about his own ancestry, he found the idea that he was a prophesied king destined to save Britannia from darkness a bit hard to swallow. Therefore, as a logical, studious young man, he decided to ask the old man for some evidence.

"I don't mean to be rude, sir," he began, "but the story you've just told me *is* rather fantastic. Do you happen to have any proof of your claims?"

"Your father thought you might ask me that very question one day," Merlyn replied, "So before he died, he decided to leave you a sign. Come and see."

Pushing aside a thick tangle of withered vines, Merlyn revealed a large, square stone with Latin inscriptions covering each face. Many of them were weathered and difficult to read, but Arthur was able to make out the phrase *Rex Brittonum* – "King of the Britons." A Roman sword, called a *spatha,* had been thrust into the top face of the stone, and on its blade were inscribed the words *Legio Draconis,* indicating that the sword's owner had been a member of the fabled Dragon Legion, a band of Roman soldiers charged with protecting Britannia from the barbarian invasions. It was the sword of Uther Pendragon.

"This is your father's tomb," said Merlyn, "He was brought here and buried in secret by those of his men who remained loyal to Rome, hoping to keep his body safe from desecration by Vortigern and the Saxon hordes. They left his legionnaire sword here as a marker and a sign of honor, but thanks to Uther's foresight, it will now serve a greater purpose."

Arthur moved closer to the tomb and examined the sword carefully. It was dirty and tarnished with age and exposure, but as he rubbed away the grime, he discovered another Latin phrase written upon the hilt. The tiny letters were jagged and uneven, clearly etched by a man who lacked skill in metalwork. But despite the amateur nature of the engraving, the meaning of the words was all too clear:

DILECTO FILIVS MEO ARTVRVS

"To Arthur, my beloved son."

It was Uther Pendragon's last will and testament – the sole means by which a great man would pass down his legacy. As Arthur read the inscription over and over again, the truth crashed down upon him like a hammering tidal wave, robbing him of breath and nearly knocking him to the ground. With his hands shaking uncontrollably and tears streaming down his face, Arthur reached out timidly and grasped the handle of his father's sword. He took a deep breath and gathered his resolve, then clenched his teeth, gripped the sword with both hands, and pulled with all his might.

But it refused to budge.

Again and again he tried, struggling to extract the sword from the gravestone until he was red in the face and sweating profusely. Finally Arthur bent down with his hands on his knees, desperate to catch his breath, utterly defeated.

"It's no use, Merlyn," he whimpered, "It cannot be moved. Perhaps I am not worthy of so great a birthright."

But Merlyn simply smiled and put his hand beneath Arthur's chin, lifting the young man's eyes to meet his own. Arthur had not yet been this close to him. He smelled of peat moss and wet leaves, as if somehow he had been birthed by the forest itself, but there was something deeper than mere comfort in his steady gaze – something both dangerous and protective, something fierce and gentle all at once.

"Stand up, my boy," said the old man, "Dry your tears. The inheritance you await cannot be claimed through strength of arms. Not by might, nor by power, but by the spirit of the Lord are great deeds accomplished."

With Merlyn's words fresh on his mind, Arthur wiped his face on his sleeve and composed himself, standing tall and gazing up to the heavens. He closed his eyes and his lips began to move, mouthing a prayer whose substance was known only to God and himself. He reached out slowly and touched the hilt of the sword with his outstretched fingers, then suddenly felt a supernatural strength begin to course through his body. Alive with newfound energy, he grasped the handle and pulled, and the Roman sword slipped loose from the stone like a hot knife sliding through softened butter. Arthur opened his eyes and stared in awe at the weapon he held in his hands, and then he turned and looked at Merlyn, grinning with satisfaction.

"Come, Arthur," Merlyn chuckled as he wrapped his long arm around the young man's shoulders, "We have a great many things to discuss."

* * * * *

Lancelot watched from a distance as Arthur and Merlyn talked late into the night. But when they finally picked up their belongings and began to leave, the old man turned his head and stared in Lancelot's direction, catching his eye for only the briefest moment. Startled at being discovered, Lancelot leapt to his feet and rushed back toward the blacksmith's shop. But before he was completely out of sight, he looked back and saw Merlyn, who was smiling at him knowingly.

Descent Into Darkness

It was an unseasonably warm spring afternoon, yet a soft, cool breeze was rustling past the tall grass and flowering shrubs that filled the rolling moorland landscape. Rowena closed her eyes and savored the feeling of the sun on her face and the wind blowing through her waist-length blonde locks, then she looked to the sky and thanked God for the unfathomable beauty of His creation. Once again, she had ventured out to visit Igraine at her final resting place. Drinking in the beauty all around her, Rowena hoped the queen had found the peace and solace in death of which she had been so deprived in life.

Her suicide was both gruesome and heartbreaking, but not entirely unexpected. For several weeks, Igraine had been more depressed and sullen than usual, locking herself in her room and refusing to eat or bathe. She had given strict orders that she was not to be disturbed for any reason, but eventually the scent of death emanating from beneath her bedroom door became unmistakable.

When the servants finally forced their way into her room, they discovered Igraine hanging from a makeshift noose tied to the rafters. She was naked, and large purple bruises covered her slender legs and emaciated torso. She had obviously been badly beaten, which was not surprising to anyone familiar with Vortigern's wrath. Blood had begun to pool at her feet, causing them to look discolored and swollen. Her large brown eyes, at one time her most alluring feature, now stared lifelessly into oblivion, with tears of pain and desperation still lingering on her smooth, porcelain skin.

No one dared to speak of Igraine's death in the presence of the king, whose feigned sorrow was both obvious and odious to all those who dwelt within the castle walls. Vortigern had even sunk to using his supposed need for human comfort to openly proposition nearly every young maiden in sight.

A funeral for the queen was expected to be held on the Sunday following her death, and conversation around the castle soon began to revolve around the question of whether or not Morgana would be in attendance. However, after the young woman's mysterious disappearance on the day after Christmas nearly three years ago, no one had heard even the faintest rumor of her whereabouts. She had vanished in the dark of night without speaking to a soul, and apparently without taking so much as a change of clothing along with her. Some believed she was dead – abducted and killed by some unknown assailant, while others suspected that she may have escaped to Armorica like so many others fleeing the king's tyranny.

Although Vortigern had always been egotistical and cruel, most would agree that he grew discernibly worse after Morgana departed. His temper became far more volatile, and he would fly into a blinding rage over the slightest irritation. And without Morgana around to satisfy his more carnal impulses, he had taken more of his anger out on Igraine, whose willingness to end her own life now revealed the sheer depth of his torment. Of course, Vortigern's continued failure to fully subdue the Picts in Caledonia only fanned the flames of his fury.

On the night Morgana left, Vortigern had returned from battle in triumph, with the severed head of Drest, the Pictish king, impaled atop his bloody spear. But before long, he received word that the Picts had appointed a new king, a fierce warrior named Talorc, and it became clear that his provocation had served only to awaken a sleeping giant. Now, instead of simply defending their homeland from invasion, the Picts had begun actively raiding Saxon and British outposts south of Hadrian's Wall. Moreover, rumors were beginning to spread of a rebellion brewing among the native Britons, and Vortigern began living in fear that some charismatic leader might one day rise up and unite his enemies against him.

With the king's mind completely preoccupied by strategies for protecting his realm from incursion and revolt, the lavish funeral that was anticipated for Igraine never came to pass. Instead, the queen was interred quickly and quietly, denied the benefit of a proper Christian burial. Due to the unsavory nature of her death, her head was severed and her body was burned before being placed in the ground, in accordance with the widespread superstitions regarding victims of suicide.

Hengist, the Saxon commander and Rowena's father, had suggested this form of burial himself, claiming that mutilation of the corpse would prevent Igraine, dishonored as she was, from returning to the earth as an undead *revenant* or a succubus. But Rowena found the whole idea sickening and offensive, and she took it upon herself to plant wildflowers near the burial site, hoping to restore at least a modicum of dignity to the deceased queen. More than a month after Igraine's tragic death, Rowena still visited her daily, praying for her tortured soul and tending to the snow-white blossoms surrounding her grave.

On this particular warm, spring afternoon, Rowena had just completed her prayers when she opened her eyes and noticed a long shadow on the ground ahead, apparently cast by someone standing directly behind her. Startled, she turned to identify her guest and saw young woman, about her age, wearing a long gown made from white linen. Her skin was as smooth and fair as polished ivory, and flowing hair fell over her delicate shoulders in silky, jet-black tresses.

Morgana!

Despite the passage of time, Rowena easily recognized her long-lost friend, and she leapt to her feet, wrapping her arms around her in a joyful embrace. But when her affection was not returned, Rowena remembered where they were standing and stepped back, lowering her head in respect for the dead.

"You've been away for a long time," she whispered.

"How did it happen?" Morgana replied stoically, without bothering to address her mysterious years of absence.

"The queen... she took her own life," Rowena answered.

She waited silently for the grim news to envelop Morgana, expecting her eyes to well up with tears of sorrow and anguish. But the young woman showed no discernible emotion – almost as if she had completely lost the ability to feel.

"I'm so sorry, Morgana," Rowena continued, "I know the two of you had your differences, but she was still your mother. I know you always loved her."

"Did I?" Morgana snapped back, "Did *anyone?* That sadistic piece of excrement who dares to call himself 'king' beat and abused her relentlessly, and I did *nothing.* I just stood by and watched it happen. Vortigern may have driven my mother to suicide, but her blood is on *my* hands as well."

"Don't say that, Morgana! It wasn't your fault! You were a victim, too. Just like her. And... and just like *me*."

Morgana's eyes flashed with shock and confusion, almost as if she had been awakened from a long slumber. She stepped closer to Rowena, tenderly brushing her fingers against the Saxon girl's sun-kissed face. "Tell me," Morgana said. Then after a few moments of uneasy silence, Rowena took a long, deep breath and began her story.

"After your mother's death, rumors began to swirl around the castle about whether the king would remarry. He certainly had his way with any of the servant maids that caught his fancy, but you and I both know that he was expected to eventually choose a new queen. As for me, I had felt his leering eyes upon my body on several occasions, but he never made any outright advances – that is, until my father got involved."

"Hengist?" Morgana blurted, "I always assumed that his aspirations rose no higher than victory on the battlefield and drunkenness in the tavern."

"Perhaps all his time spent with Vortigern has taught him ambition," said Rowena, "Either way, he became obsessed with the idea of joining me to the king, with hopes that he could breed the Saxon race into the royal bloodline."

"And you refused?"

"I told both my father and Vortigern that I had no desire to marry or to become queen, but neither man seemed to take my rejection seriously. They aren't terribly concerned with the *marriage* aspect anyway. My father only wants a royal heir, and Vortigern... well, you *know* what he wants."

Rowena's voice cracked as she struggled to continue. She bowed her head and took hold of a small iron cross that was hanging from a chain around her neck – a simple act that seemingly renewed her inner strength.

"And so the king came to my bedroom and took from me that which is most precious," Rowena said softly as a single tear rolled down her cheek. She looked back at Morgana for some gesture of sympathy, but instead, all she saw was disgust.

Seemingly oblivious to her friend's disturbing tale, Morgana was intently staring at the iron cross Rowena held clenched in her trembling hand. Her expression was a mixture of confusion and abhorrence, and she quickly pushed Rowena's hand aside in order to get a better look at the tiny object.

"Why are you wearing this?" Morgana sneered, "I thought you worshiped the *Saxon* gods, not this delusional carpenter!"

"I have been a follower of Christ for over two years now," Rowena replied, taken aback and somewhat offended by the raven-haired girl's thinly veiled insult, "I became appalled and disillusioned by the selfishness, vanity, and complete disregard for innocent life displayed by my father and his men during their sacrifices to Woden. But on the night you left, at the Christmas feast, Bishop Germanus told me of another way. He described a God who desires to *give* rather than to receive, a God of love and mercy who is all-knowing and ever present."

"And was your god present when Vortigern forced himself upon you? Was he loving and merciful *then*?"

"Pardon me, Morgana," said Rowena, now puzzled beyond belief, "but I thought He was *your* God too."

"Not anymore," Morgana muttered angrily, "Not after he *abandoned* me. Rowena, I was abused and victimized by that pathetic excuse for a king for nearly half of my life, and your 'God of Love' did *nothing!* He either doesn't care about me in the least, or he isn't as *all-powerful* as you think."

Rowena was shocked by her friend's stark transformation. She had never seen Morgana so completely overwhelmed with bitterness and fury, and it frightened her deeply.

"It's a long, hard road," Morgana sneered, "that leads out of hell and up to the light. Well, I spent the past three years of my life crawling through hell, and eventually I just decided to stop fighting. It was then when I realized that I could make hell my *ally*. When I finally gave myself over, I tapped into a power greater than any I'd ever known – far greater than *your god*."

By now, Rowena could feel the oppressive weight of some dark presence in the surrounding air. Despite the warm, sunny weather, she began to feel deathly cold and her heart filled up with despair, almost as if all love and light had been banished from the universe. Suddenly, she was knocked off her feet as a fierce, icy wind crashed into her body, and on the ground below she saw the little white flowers she had planted for Igraine gradually wither and die. A chill shivered up her spine as she watched Morgana's eyes turn black, like a bottle of ink being spilled over the pages of an open book.

In an instant, all other consciousness seemed to vanish, and fear became her only reality. Rowena's soul begged for some form of escape, be it sleep or even death, from the suffocating wickedness that was clawing at her mind. But the light within her fought back against the encroaching darkness, and although part of her wanted to flee in horror, a spark of compassion still remained for the friend she once knew.

"What happened to you, Morgana?" she shouted over the howling wind, "What manner of evil has imprisoned your heart? I know you suffered greatly, but God would *never* abandon you! He loved you then, and He loves you now. It's never too late for forgiveness and restoration."

"Forgiveness?" Morgana hissed, "Ha! Not in *this* life! Never can true reconcilement grow where the wounds of fear and hate have pierced so deep!"

With those words, the sun grew pitch dark and a violent tempest arose, veiling the hillside in an all-consuming gloom. A bolt of lightning flashed across the sky and struck a nearby dogwood tree, splitting it in two as its flowered branches were consumed by the rapacious flames. In the midst of this rising chaos, a sinister laugh burst forth from Morgana's mouth, but the sound was deep and booming, as if it had been made by some other voice than her own. Finally, unable to contain her terror, Rowena turned and ran from the darkness as fast as her legs would carry her.

Once Rowena had vanished over the horizon, the storm subsided, the air regained its former warmth, and light began to peek through the fading clouds. Morgana's eyes returned to their typical hazel coloration, and she convulsed slightly as the menacing presence left her body.

The icy wind and dark shadows began to recede, but then seemed to gather together into a thick, swirling mass of evil, like celestial matter being consumed by a black hole. Gradually, the ominous, ethereal substance began to condense into a solid form, slowly evolving into an immense humanoid figure. The shadowy apparition soon developed distinct features, taking the shape of a tall, powerful man wearing a heavy cloak adorned with crows' feathers. A long, jagged sword was sheathed in a scabbard dangling from his belt, and in his massive arms he held a small boy, no more than two years old.

"I have brought your son to you, my dear," the man said.

"Thank you, Lord Astaroth," answered Morgana, and she bowed before him in servitude.

City of God

Relax, Arthur!" Ector shouted, "It's perfectly natural for you to tense up during combat, but you *must* make every effort to stay calm. Keep your muscles loose and regulate your breathing. If you're rigid or jittery, you're going to get yourself killed."

"Yes sir," Arthur replied as he picked himself off the ground and retrieved the wooden broom handle that Ector had given him as a substitute sword during his training.

"All right, now what you learned thus far?"

"Always draw your sword *before* you engage an enemy. Because it takes longer to draw than it does to be slain."

"Very good," said Ector, approaching Arthur for another sparring session, "Keep your body balanced so you can thrust or parry without being hit. Remember, most duels are decided and finished by the very first blow."

The teacher and student faced one another and held their mock swords ready. Arthur had already been defeated at least a dozen times today, and he was beginning to grow frustrated. So this time, before Ector seemed to have a chance to prepare himself, Arthur screamed and abruptly rushed forward, his weapon aimed at the old soldier's gut. But almost as if he had been expecting it, Ector casually stepped to the side and let Arthur stumble past him, then swatted him on the back with his broom handle, knocking him clumsily to the ground.

"Come now, Arthur, that's the oldest mistake in the book!" Ector chastised, "If you charge in recklessly, *especially* against a well-trained soldier, he will simply wait and allow you to impale yourself on his sword!"

"There's no award for second place in armed combat!" shouted Kay, who had been sitting on a nearby fencepost and laughing at Arthur's apparent ineptitude, "Either you're still standing at the end, or you're *dead*."

Arthur grumbled at Kay's annoying interjection and then rose to his knees, dusting off his clothes and stretching his aching back. "Well," he joked, "do I at least get credit for the element of surprise?"

Ector said nothing, but simply raised his mock sword again, encouraging Arthur to engage him. The younger man stood up slowly and brandished his own weapon, attempting to feign confidence in the face of his adversary after being defeated again and again. A few yards away, Merlyn leaned against his walking staff and watched with curiosity and amusement.

"Surprise can indeed be an effective tool, as can strength," Ector continued as the two men dueled, "but speed, agility, and cunning are *far* more valuable. A shrewd warrior should always be aware of his surroundings, his assets and liabilities, and those of his enemy. Take notice of the terrain beforehand, and know where the sun will be, keeping it in your opponent's eyes rather than your own. Know how your enemy fights. Is he an expert or a novice? And know your weapon – its advantages and its limitations. Is your sword light and nimble, designed for quick cuts and stabbing? Or is it slow and heavy, but capable of cleaving a body with a single stroke? Every part of your sword can be used as a weapon, including the point and edges of the blade, the hand guard, and the pommel. Finally, remember that *everyone* has a weakness."

As Ector finished lecturing, he disarmed Arthur with a swift flick of his wrist, and then thrust the end of his broom handle into the younger man's chest. Angry with himself at having lost yet another match, Arthur dropped to his knees in exhaustion, drenched in sweat and struggling to catch his breath.

"Face it, father," Kay taunted, "The book worm will *never* be a warrior. It's a lost cause."

"That's quite enough, Kay," Ector replied, calmly but sternly, "Don't forget, I may be an old man now, but even on my worst day, I could still best *you* on the field of battle. Now get out of here and finish your chores or *you'll* be the one feeling this broom handle against your hide."

Kay attempted to issue a worthy retort, but he was far too overwhelmed with embarrassment. Instead he turned as red as his own hair, and Merlyn chuckled to himself while he watched the vexing young man scamper off into the forest to chop firewood. Once Kay was out of sight, Ector reached out and took Arthur's hand, gently helping him to his feet.

"Don't despair, son. You'll learn in time. Just remember what Augustine said: *Pray as though everything depended on God, but work as though everything depended on you.* Go get some rest now. We'll try again tomorrow."

As Ector turned and headed back to the monastery, Arthur trudged slowly toward Merlyn, dragging his feet in the dirt, with his shoulders sagging and a forlorn expression on his face. After finally reaching the old man, he idly reached up and began caressing the smooth feathers on the back of the little grey owl as it sat motionless on the brim of Merlyn's hat.

"Perhaps Kay is right," Arthur sulked, "Perhaps I *am* nothing more than book worm. How could I possibly be a king?"

Merlyn frowned and furrowed his brow as he looked over at his discouraged young protégé. "You know, Arthur," he said, thoughtfully stroking his long white beard, "Ector is a wise man and you can learn a great deal from him. With his incredible literacy in history, languages, philosophy, and theology, he has taught you to be a scholar – a *fine* one at that. And with the skills he acquired during his years serving in the Roman army under

Magnus Maximus, he can *surely* teach you to be a soldier. But no mere man can teach you to be a king."

"How am I to learn then, Merlyn?"

"Take my arm and follow me," the old man answered.

Arthur did as he was told, and the very moment his fingers touched the sleeve of Merlyn's cloak, the world surrounding them seemed to melt away. Gone were the lush fields of Dinan and the humble monastery bell tower, and in their place arose massive marble statues of pagan gods and the imposing grandeur of the Circus Maximus. The soft grass beneath their feet had transformed into the dry dust of an immense, oblong race track, on which nearly a dozen chariots stood ready behind staggered gates, their drivers eagerly awaiting a signal to begin. Trumpets blared as a man appeared, dressed in a purple toga with a crown of laurels upon his head. As he ascended to the highest seat in the arena, the crowd began to shout and cheer in Latin words that Arthur easily understood. "Hail, Caesar!" they chanted in joyous unison.

Upon realizing that he was now standing directly in the path of a legion of formidable, horse-drawn juggernauts, Arthur shouted out to Merlyn and then hastily grabbed him by the hand, attempting in vain to run for safety. But Merlyn simply laughed and refused to budge.

"Have no fear, Arthur," he said assuringly, as the young man continued trying to pull him away from his apparent doom, "Although we *appear* to be standing in the middle of a chariot race in ancient Rome, in reality we are still safe in Dinan. This is only a vision. We cannot be heard or seen."

"Well, a little warning might be nice in the future!" Arthur responded breathlessly, "I'm not exactly accustomed to being dropped into the middle of supernatural visions!"

Merlyn wiped the smile from his face and looked at Arthur with a mix of remorse and confusion, lifting his wide-brimmed hat with one hand and scratching his head with the other. "I do apologize, my boy," he mumbled, "I journey so frequently between various planes of time, space, and existence, that I often forget the limitations of others. But still, you *must* admit that this is truly a sight to behold!"

As Arthur slowly regained his poise, he rubbed his eyes and began to gaze intently at the face of the man in the purple toga. He had seen that face before. It was a face he recognized from coins and statues. It was the face of a legend.

"Merlyn, am I correct in assuming that the man for whom they cheer is none other than the immortal Julius Caesar?"

"Aye, it is indeed," the old man replied, "As the Bard wrote, *he doth bestride the narrow world like a colossus."*

"Who's the Bard?" Arthur asked curiously.

"Umm, never mind," Merlyn replied. Then after a short, awkward silence, he quickly returned to the subject at hand.

"Gaius Julius Caesar," he announced, "Conqueror of Gaul, hero of the Roman people, and author of the greatest and most powerful empire this world has ever seen. Revered by his subjects, he was credited with extending civil rights throughout the Roman world, rebuilding Carthage and Corinth, reforming the tax system, and knitting together the warring factions of his territory into a strong, cohesive whole."

They watched as Caesar dropped a cloth and the starting gates swung open, sending the charioteers barreling down the enormous track. While the audience cheered, the Emperor reclined in his seat as servants dutifully fed him fresh fruit and fanned him with large palm branches.

"But after his many triumphs, statues were built for Caesar as an 'unconquered god.' His birthday was declared a public festival, and he was elevated to a state of equality with Jupiter and Mars, being given the Latin epithet *Divus Julius*. After Caesar's death, his son Octavian began referring to himself as the 'Son of God,' thus beginning the Roman cult of emperor worship and sowing seeds for the widespread persecution of Jews and Christians, which endured for over 300 years."

Arthur recalled reading about the war between the Jewish dissenters and general Vespasian, as well as the imprisonment, torture, and execution of Christians for their refusal to worship the emperor or offer sacrifices to the Roman gods. Tacitus the historian had written that during the reign of Nero, Christians were torn to pieces by wild animals, nailed to crosses, or set on fire and burned to serve as nocturnal lights.

"No matter how grand your accomplishments, Arthur, you must always remember that you are merely a man. Caesar was a brilliant leader, but he was certainly not a god, and his pride and ambition led to his demise. Truly, pride is the downfall of many men. *It was pride that changed angels into devils; it is humility that makes men as angels."*

Suddenly the scene shifted, and Arthur now found himself standing in the middle of a crowded battlefield, with armored cavalrymen carrying golden standards bearing images of Christ and the saints. Many of them wore white mantles emblazoned with red crosses, and in their midst rode a tall, imposing figure with a reddish-blonde beard and an iron crown. As he held his sword aloft and ordered his men to charge, the knights crashed down upon their opponents like a massive tidal wave, decimating all who stood in their wake.

"Who is this man, Merlyn?" Arthur asked, "He appears to be both a great Christian king *and* a skilled warrior."

"He is known as Richard the Lionheart, King of England, although he will not even be born for another 700 years. During his life, he will be admired by his people as a crusader against the Saracens and as a man of God. Both king and soldier, he is the very portrait of courage and chivalry."

"And yet, he is destined to fall. Just like Caesar."

"You're learning, my boy," Merlyn replied with a smile, "Richard will sit on the throne of England for ten long years, but will spend no more than six months at home in his own country. You see, much like the mighty Achilles, he is far too concerned with his own legacy to bother with the needs of his people. He neglects his kingdom and spends most of his days in pursuit of personal glory and conquest. And although he carries the cross into battle, he fights not for Christ but for himself. Remember, Arthur, a good king is meant to be a servant – first to the Lord God, and then to his people."

The vision then vanished almost as soon as it had come, and Arthur now stood on a new, very different kind of battlefield. Mobs of unruly men were forcing their way into a massive stone fortress, violently attacking all who stood in their way, and emerging with barrels of black powder and armfuls of what appeared to be weapons, though Arthur had never seen such things before. They were long, narrow objects, constructed from both wood and metal, and they hurled bolts of fire and thunder. Other men, who seemed to be prisoners, had broken free from the fortress and were eagerly aligning themselves with the rebellious citizens as they worked to set up makeshift barricades nearby.

"Their society was headed for collapse," said Merlyn, "The people faced widespread hunger and malnutrition, along with the near bankruptcy of the crown due an endless series of territorial and religious wars. The king, while wielding absolute power, was weak and indecisive, and he was easily manipulated by the powerful nobility. The common man longed for liberty and equality, and so began a revolution. What you are now witnessing is the first battle of that revolution, the storming of the Bastille fortress."

As Arthur and Merlyn maneuvered their way through the throngs of rioting commoners, the Bastille began to fade from sight and was replaced by a vast track of open land filled with grassy hills and flanked by forests of oak, beech, and chestnut trees. The common clothing of the rebellious townspeople changed into brightly colored uniforms of red, blue, and white, and the chaotic rabble transformed into two massive armies, which were lined up facing one another in rigid formations. The soldiers took turns, alternatively discharging their weapons as dozens of men at once fell maimed and bleeding to the ground. A short man on a white palfrey surveyed the battle from the summit of a nearby hill, shouting orders at his generals and aggressively waving his shining saber in the air.

"Do not be deceived by his small stature," Merlyn began, "The man on the hill is Napoleon Bonaparte, a brilliant general and tactician. In the ensuing chaos after the successful revolt and execution of the king, his military prowess will allow him to take absolute power, eventually restoring law and order throughout the land. He will also expand civil rights, lend his support to education and the arts, and grant religious freedom to all those within his realm."

"But the people will only succeed in trading one form of tyranny for another," said Arthur, perceptively picking up where the old man had left off, "And this Napoleon fellow will become a ruthless warmonger. Am I right, Merlyn?"

"Well done, Arthur," he replied, "Your intuition serves you well. Indeed, Napoleon *does* become a conquest-obsessed despot. He turns his country into a prison, controlled by a vast network of secret watchmen and spies, making it nearly impossible to express any sort of opinion without his approval. So you see, my boy, although the coming rebellion against King Vortigern will be both honorable and just, you must never allow yourself to become that which you despise. As you strive for justice, you must always remind yourself that in the end, the purpose of all wars must be *peace*."

Arthur nodded in agreement and watched the bloody battle continue, but he soon noticed that the world around him was changing yet again. The groves of beech trees and rolling hills soon disappeared and were replaced by massive grey buildings and stone walkways filled with curiously dressed people. The streets were lined with iron poles topped by glowing light sources of some kind, and strange metal carriages moved about without horses to pull them. Off in the distance, black smoke poured from tall, cylindrical towers, and a peculiar sort of music began blaring from a mysterious machine nearby. Arthur's mind was overflowing with questions, but before he could ask any of them, Merlyn began to speak.

"In a nation struggling to recover from the ravages of war, a young, charismatic leader will rise to power, and he will oversee one of the greatest expansions of civil improvement and industrial production in history. Employment will become near universal, and the standard of living will increase for most citizens. Indeed, the country will be revitalized, giving even the common man a newfound sense of national pride."

Before Arthur could fully survey his surroundings, he and Merlyn were suddenly whisked away into the midst of a large crowd of people, all of whom were listening intently to a man speaking from behind a podium. He was wearing some manner of uniform, adorned with various medals and insignia, including a spider-like symbol Arthur thought he recognized from his studies of ancient Greek architecture. The man had a small, narrow moustache, and his dark hair flopped to the side over one eye. Arthur couldn't understand the language the man spoke, but as he shouted and pounded his fist violently on the podium, the people watching cheered in agreement. And then, almost as if the crowd shared a common mind, they all stretched their right arms outward in unison.

"His name is Adolf Hitler," said Merlyn, his voice low and solemn, "and future generations will come to know him as one of the most evil men who ever lived. He will use nationalistic sentiment to increase his authority until he becomes an undisputed dictator. Through lies and propaganda, he will unite his people against a perceived common enemy, and then brutally execute millions whose only crime was daring to exist. And although he will be loved and respected by many of his countrymen, his reign will also be marked by hatred, oppression, and death."

"Why do you show me this, Merlyn?" Arthur asked nervously, "Do you fear that I may become such a man?"

"With his oratory skills and personal charisma, a man like Hitler could have been a force for great good amongst his people. But instead, he will use his incredible influence for selfish, vindictive means, leading the world into war and committing heinous atrocities in the name of racial superiority. No, Arthur. I know you are not such a man. But there will be those among you, allies and even friends, who will foolishly wish to exterminate all races but the Britons, to convert pagans to Christianity by force, and to extend a righteous rebellion against tyranny into an unholy mission of conquest."

A cacophony of images soon began to flood Arthur's vision. He saw legions of uniformed men marching in lock-step, raising their right arms and gazing with admiration at their mighty leader behind the podium. He saw glass windows being broken and frightened citizens being tossed into the streets while their belongings were trampled and burned. He saw battle-ravaged coastlines littered with dead bodies and severed limbs, while the nearby waters ran red with blood. And lastly, he saw the naked corpses of ghostly, emaciated men, women, and children, being dumped haphazardly into mass graves.

"Enough!" Arthur shouted, his eyes closed tight to shut out the horror, "Please, show me no more!"

"There is but one more vision for you to see, my boy," the old man replied.

Suddenly the noises of war stopped. When Arthur opened his eyes, he and Merlyn were standing at the base of a rocky hill within an arid desert landscape. A few robed commoners with thick beards and leather sandals milled about somberly, while mobs of others yelled obscenities and threw rotten food. Several large men with spears, who appeared to be Roman centurions, watched the crowds carefully as if they expected a riot to erupt at any moment.

As he studied his new surroundings, Arthur's eyes were drawn to a woman who was on her hands and knees sobbing. A younger man had wrapped her in his arms and was trying in vain to comfort her, but she simply cried out in anguish, gazing fixedly at the scene unfolding on the top of the hill.

When Arthur looked up, he saw three wooden crosses, and from each cross hung a dying man with nails hammered through his hands and feet. The man in the middle had been savagely whipped and beaten, and his flesh hung like ribbons from his broken body. A crown of thorns had been forced onto his head, sending streams of blood down his face, and a crude sign had been placed on the cross above him. Arthur could read the Latin inscription, but he already knew what it said:

IESVS NAZARENVS REX IVDÆORVM

"Jesus the Nazarene, King of the Jews"

At that moment, the man lifted his face to Heaven and pushed hard against the nails, raising his body and filling his lungs with air. "Father, forgive them," he groaned in Aramaic, "for they know not what they do."

But the crowd just watched and jeered, calling out, "If you are truly the Messiah, then save yourself!" But the man on the cross remained silent. Soon afterward, heavy black storm clouds began filling the sky, hiding the midday sun and cloaking the land in darkness. With a crash of thunder, the man on the cross lifted himself up one final time and cried, "It is finished." Then he breathed his last.

"Greater love hath no man," Merlyn said quietly as he dropped to his knees and bowed his head in reverence. Arthur followed the old man's example, kneeling down next to him and struggling to steady himself as the ground began to shake. If he remembered his readings of the Gospels, tombs were also breaking open and the Temple veil was being torn in two. After a few moments, the earthquake subsided, and Merlyn turned and placed his hand upon Arthur's shoulder.

"Do you wish to know what it truly means to be a king, Arthur?" Merlyn whispered, "Behold. *This* is a king."

Groans of the Britons

Rowena was still sore and aching when she emerged from her bedroom in the late morning hours, resolutely striding into the sun-drenched hallway with eyes sharp and head held high. She had been kneeling in earnest prayer ever since Vortigern, grinning with conquest, had gathered up his clothing and left her presence. But despite her resultant physical and emotional turmoil, she chose to walk with confidence and purpose, refusing to allow that monster to break her spirit.

On the nights when he came for her, rather than simply submitting and hoping for the liaison to end quickly, Rowena remained bold and defiant, choking back tears as she knowingly provoked the king's wrath. Additional pain was the price of her insolence, but it was a price she paid gladly as she clung tightly to the shreds of her tattered honor.

After such encounters, she often remembered a passage from the Book of Isaiah, which promised that *those who hope in the Lord shall renew their strength. They shall mount up with wings as eagles; they shall run and not be weary; they shall walk and not faint.* And although she had certainly grown weary of the abuse she endured at Vortigern's hand, Rowena somehow found the determination to carry on, as if some unseen arms were lifting her up and leading her forward, her battered soul powered by a well of strength whose source dwelt beyond all human understanding. She remembered the story of Saint Peter stepping out of the boat and walking on the water toward Jesus, sinking whenever he looked down at the raging waves and away from his Savior. *Don't look at the waves*, Rowena told herself. *Don't look at the waves.*

But mostly, she remembered Morgana.

Their terrifying reunion at Igraine's graveside had left her disturbed and shaken, but the initial fear soon gave way to empathy and sorrow for the lost friend she still loved like her own flesh and blood. Rowena now understood at least a portion of the pain Morgana had endured throughout her childhood and formative years, having unwillingly taken her place as Vortigern's favorite plaything, but unlike the raven-haired Briton princess, Rowena was raised as a warrior and thus possessed an inherent advantage when it came to matters of resilience and internal fortitude. And although the dark whispers of despair still clawed away at her mind from time to time, they were pushed back and kept at bay by the newfound faith that spread like a blazing wildfire within her heart and ignited her spirit with incomprehensible joy, however alien and contradictory such a concept may seem.

It wasn't even an emotion, *per se* – nothing like ordinary happiness or excitement, which are typically aroused by external stimuli and would be grossly improper to the point of profanity under present circumstances. Rather, it was a joy that persisted in spite of the fallen world in which she found herself, in spite of her pain and anger, in spite of her stolen innocence and wounded honor. It was a baffling joy that originated not in gifts or compliments or sunsets, but in an unwavering, supernatural, inexplicable love that held her close through the storm and would never let her go.

As she walked through the empty hallways in the calm light of morning, Rowena said another quick prayer for Morgana, holding onto the hope that the layers of ice and stone now imprisoning her friend's heart would be chipped away, that she would lay down her hatred and allow herself to experience the healing touch of this unfathomable love. After a silent *amen*, Rowena opened her eyes and surveyed her surroundings, finally noticing that the castle was nearly deserted. The corridors were usually bustling with life at this hour as soldiers mulled about, propositioning the servant girls and scrounging around for a midday meal. But instead, it was quiet as a cemetery. The only audible voices seemed to be coming from the barracks at the far end of the Great Hall, where the entirety of the Saxon army must have been gathered for some unknown purpose.

* * * * *

Blonde, thin, and growing paler by the second, the small Saxon soldier shook with terror. Vortigern glared at him accusingly, his eyes filled with contempt, and yet the nervous young man – no more than a boy, really – mustered just enough courage to stand at attention and look the king square in the face as he slowly opened his mouth to defend himself.

"I would never betray you, my lord," stammered the fretful Saxon, "I have nothing to hide."

"Don't waste my time with your pathetic lies," Vortigern spit back at him, "Your face is as white as death and you are drenched with sweat – both clear signs of panic. Only a traitor or a coward would behave in this manner! Now tell your king the truth. Why are you so afraid?"

The barracks grew eerily silent as the remainder of the assembled Saxon ranks waited in morbid anticipation for the young man's response. Like a hangman before the gallows, Vortigern paced back and forth awaiting his answer, as the footsteps of his heavy leather boots seemed to pound on the stone floor like claps of thunder. Finally sensing that his futile plea of innocence would only fall of deaf ears, the frightened soldier instead opted to beseech the king for mercy.

"Please, my lord," he wept, "I don't want to di—"

But the soldier's appeal was cut short as he felt Vortigern's spear plunging deep into his belly, severing his spinal cord as it exited through his lower back. His eyes grew wide with shock and he groaned in excruciating agony as the king cruelly twisted the iron shank and then pulled it free. His task complete, Vortigern callously turned and walked away while the young soldier's body slumped lifelessly to the floor.

"Behold the price of treason!" the king roared, holding his bloodied spear aloft for all to see. The men cheered.

Hengist, the Saxon general, silently observed the gruesome scene from the corner of the room. Vortigern had never been shy when it came to slaughtering those who failed him or were disloyal, and every man in his service knew as much. They had all seen the contorted faces of both enemies and friends as their severed heads were impaled on the wooden pikes surrounding the castle, and they all lived in fear of a similar fate. Hengist encouraged this fear, believing that it made his men stronger and more deadly. He had trained them to deny emotion and to care for nothing but the grandeur of war and the bitter taste of blood, and he hoped that their fear of Vortigern would result not in wobbly-kneed weakness, but would make them sharper and more vicious, as they prayed for a glorious death on the battlefield rather than a shameful and public execution.

"Pardon me, sire," Hengist whispered to Vortigern as the two men exited the barracks together and proceeded down the stone corridor toward the Great Hall, "but do you honestly think that sniveling boy was the traitor you seek?"

"I've no idea," the king answered, "and it doesn't matter anyway. If nothing else, he was a coward and a weakling, and I refuse to tolerate either. Regardless, the goal today was not to actually locate the traitor. It was to instill terror into any soldier who might dare defy me. But come now. I'm hungry."

The assembled Saxon soldiers remained still and listened to the receding footsteps of Vortigern and Hengist as they left to satiate their appetites. Once the king and his general were out of earshot, the soldiers broke rank and began hurling insults at the motionless corpse of their former comrade.

"It serves the traitor right!" one bellowed as he kicked and spit upon the young man's body.

"I never trusted that little whelp anyhow," said another.

"Get his filthy carcass out of here!" a third soldier shouted, "No turncoat deserves to dwell amongst *real* men!"

Gawain winced but held his tongue as he watched the other soldiers carry off the poor boy's corpse to be desecrated, doing his best not to draw any attention to himself even as his broken heart dropped like lead into his stomach. *This was his fault*. After covertly infiltrating the Saxon army, he had finally come to terms with pretending to be someone else, but the fact that he just stood idly by while an innocent young man was viciously murdered for things he himself had done made Gawain begin to question his humanity.

For nearly a year now, Gawain had managed to fit in with the full-blooded Saxon soldiers, quietly observing them at first, and then gradually immersing himself in their brotherhood as he grew more comfortable with their accents and mannerisms. He thanked God daily for his late mother, whose teachings about her Saxon heritage and language had made this intricate deception possible. And for almost nine months now, he had been secretly feeding information to his British compatriots in the growing rebellion against Vortigern's rule.

It seemed like ages ago when he first met with Bedivere on that stormy night in the ruins of the old Roman bathhouse to discuss their seditious plot. But since that time, their small, loosely organized band of British peasants had slowly learned how to disrupt and chip away at the Saxon defenses, much to the extreme annoyance of the king himself.

"Their numbers are few, their weapons primitive, and their training rudimentary," Vortigern had complained to the troops a few short days ago, "Ideally, such an insignificant force should pose no serious threat to us..."

Gawain remembered struggling to hold back laughter as he watched Vortigern grow ever more flustered and frustrated by the mounting success of the rebels, culminating in an unhinged, red-faced rant in front of the full Saxon army.

"...and yet the enemy remains!" the king had bawled like a spoiled toddler, "Our attacks on these ungrateful dogs – which *should* have been *devastating* – have been largely fruitless, as the peasants have been one step ahead of us at every turn, hiding like cowards in the shadows!"

It was that day when Vortigern began hunting for the traitor in their midst, or as he liked to say, "that sniveling insect intent on destroying my kingdom from within." In the days that followed, the king had vigorously interrogated each man, asking convoluted questions and watching their faces and posture for any sign of tension or anxiety. He had also ordered Hengist to ransack their barracks, read the letters of those few who were literate, and confiscate any material deemed to be subversive, including a few Celtic weapons that had been taken as prizes by the soldiers. The purging reached its apex with the murder of that young, frightened warrior, whose nervousness in front of Vortigern masked nothing but a simple fear of death.

Guilt-ridden and ashamed, Gawain lowered his eyes as the other men hauled the boy's lifeless body away to be sadistically brutalized. He prayed silently that God would have mercy on the young soldier and that his sacrifice, though unintended and unsung, would not be in vain. Choking back tears, Gawain also begged God's forgiveness for the blood on his hands, as he collected himself and prepared to steal away from the castle once again to provide updated tactical information to his allies in the British rebellion.

* * * * *

Having concealed herself behind a large stone pillar near the heavy double-doors leading into the barracks, Rowena craned her neck a bit and watched as the bulk of the Saxon army stampeded outside like a pack of wild dogs, intent on heartlessly desecrating the corpse of an innocent boy whose life was taken for no purpose other than intimidation. She had overheard the devious words spoken between Vortigern and her father as they walked toward the Great Hall, and she forced herself to swallow her revulsion in the face of such unabashed cruelty, instead whispering a short prayer for the soul of the deceased. However, most of her attention was focused on the single soldier who remained, standing alone in the corner of the room, seemingly lost in deep thought.

Rowena could tell that this young man was not quite normal – at least, not in comparison with his fellow soldiers. While he possessed the thick blonde hair and bulky frame common to the majority of Saxon men, his deep brown eyes lacked that spark of ferocity typically shared amongst the bloodthirsty followers of Woden. Rather, as she gazed at him as intently as possible while still avoiding detection, his eyes seemed to reveal a deep well of sadness and a longing for some faraway world beyond the realms of hope. But before long, the soldier blinked his eyes and shook his head, apparently coming to his senses, and hurried out of the barracks toward some indistinct but apparently important destination.

"You *really* ought to follow him, you know."

Rowena jumped. Had she been discovered? The male voice behind her didn't sound familiar, like that of her father or the king. It may have been another Saxon soldier, but no, it was too warm and weathered, more like a caring grandfather than a grizzled warrior. Startled and confused, Rowena turned and looked in the direction of the voice and was surprised to see a strange old man wearing a green cloak and a wide-brimmed hat sitting on the floor, his back propped up against the stone wall, gazing up at her with a mischievous smile on his wrinkled face. His long white beard was tangled with tiny twigs and thistles, and as he spoke, he absent-mindedly stroked the smooth head of a small grey owl.

"Hurry now, before you lose him," the old man continued.

Rowena looked up and spied the silhouette of the young soldier at the far end of the corridor, scurrying toward his objective and growing progressively smaller in the distance. But when she lowered her eyes back toward the old man, the space he had once occupied was empty, with the exception of a few fluffy, grey feathers littering the floor. Rowena spun around and searched in every direction, even venturing into the barracks in case the mysterious vagabond had quickly snuck inside; however, he was nowhere to be found.

She rubbed her eyes and began to believe she was seeing things. *Perhaps my empty stomach has clouded my rationality,* she thought. But then she knelt down picked up one of the little grey feathers, proving to herself that the brief encounter, despite its peculiarity, could not have been her imagination.

Standing up and gathering her resolve, Rowena began sprinting down the hallway, now desperate to catch the solitary soldier before he disappeared as well.

* * * * *

Bedivere and Maleagant had arrived on the rocky shores of Armorica two full days ago and had spent one of those days hungry and exhausted, making their way on foot until they were lucky enough to find a tavern where they were able to buy food and barter for a pair of horses.

And so it was with filled bellies and lifted spirits that they finally rode into Dinan on that foggy spring morning, banging on the doors of every cottage, ringing the bells on church towers, shouting, hollering, and making all sorts of commotion in order to draw every groggy inhabitant to the town square.

One by one they came, some curious, some angry, and others still half-asleep, stumbling along with the crowd yet having no idea where they were headed. Before long the town square was densely populated, with children perched atop their fathers' shoulders and smaller groups of citizens peering out from the upstairs windows of several nearby houses. The two strangers chose to remain on horseback, partially in order to be seen by all and partially for their own protection if the mob of townspeople should become unruly.

Bedivere was a rather slight man with a wiry build and a smooth, beardless complexion, which frequently led new acquaintances to underestimate his age by at least a few years. His hair was dark and cropped short, and he wore the simple clothing of a merchant with a chainmail hauberk fitted beneath his tunic. On his back he carried a Celtic long sword with a hilt carved from deer antler, and a small, leaf-shaped dagger hung freely from a loop on his belt. But while certainly no novice on the battlefield, his primary weapon was his golden tongue.

Maleagant, however, was not much for oratory. Almost the complete polar opposite of his companion, he was a massive, imposing man with grizzled features and a wild, unkempt mane of muddy-brown hair. He wore a clumsy hodge-podge of bronze and leather armor that appeared to have been collected from the floor of the Colosseum after a bout between two Roman gladiators, and he lugged around an enormous, two-handed war hammer, which was now weighing down his meager hackney so much that the poor horse leaned awkwardly to one side.

The two men surveyed the vast, pulsating crowd as the town square gradually filled and approached its breaking point. Once it had become clear that only a few stragglers remained, Bedivere lifted his hands in the air, calling the restless throng to silence as he prepared to speak.

"Good people of Dinan!" he proclaimed, "We come before you now on the brink of revolution! As some of you may know already, a rebellion has risen up in Britannia against the cruel usurper Vortigern and his vicious, pagan mercenaries from the far away land of Saxony. And although Aetius, the Roman governor of Gaul, has refused to come to our aid, we remain resolute and our strength grows daily! In fact, one of our men has infiltrated the ranks of the Saxon army and has been able to secretly provide us with vital information on their weaknesses, defenses, and battle plans. Most remarkably, he informed me only days ago that the daughter of their commanding general wishes to defect, renounce her people, and join our cause! So I ask you now, who else will join us? Who else wishes to reclaim the beloved homeland that was stolen from us so long ago? Who else dreams of freedom from the tyranny and oppression of this unrighteous, unworthy king? Who else is willing to take up a sword and follow us home to glory?"

Bedivere was accustomed to waiting several minutes for the cheering to die down after such passionate, rousing speeches. But on this cool, foggy morning, he heard nothing but the soft chirp of crickets in the distance.

The crowd stood by quietly, staring vacantly at the two strangers as if they were travelling apothecaries trying to sell questionable "folk remedies" made from goat's blood and stagnant bog water. After a few moments of awkward silence, the majority of the townspeople began to wander off in various directions, muttering, grumbling, and laughing to each other about their crops, the weather, and the two delusional fools who had just disturbed their breakfast. Although many of the people were still bitter about having to flee their motherland to escape the king's tyranny, the passage of time had rendered them cynical and largely indifferent the plight of those who even now remained in Britannia. Only a few brave souls stayed behind to meet with the strangers and volunteer their services for the impending war against Vortigern and the Saxons.

Arthur, along with Ector and Kay, stood near the front of the small gathering and looked about inquisitively as he attempted to discern how many of the men he knew by name. There were his foster father and step-brother, of course, both of whom seemed eager and willing to join in the fray. Over to his left was Sagramore, the dark-skinned Numidian cavalryman who once fought in the Roman army but who now earned his living tanning leather and saddling horses on the east end of town. He was a rather silent, solitary type, but still a fine man to have on one's side when things got tough. Next to him stood another former servant of Rome, a sinewy Sarmatian swordsman whose name Arthur was having trouble remembering at the moment. *Wait… his name was Palamedes. Yes, that was it.* Arthur picked out a few more familiar faces from the group, as well as several he didn't recognize, but one face was conspicuously absent. He looked high and low, scanning the entire courtyard, but there was no sign of Lancelot anywhere.

Excalibur

Glowing sparks flew through the air like a swarm of tiny fireflies as Lancelot furiously pounded the red-hot horseshoe into submission. Again and again, his heavy, cross-peen hammer clanged loudly against the iron anvil, sending shockwaves through his right arm until it was nearly numb from exertion. As the anger grew inside him, gradually bubbling to the surface like burning magma beneath the earth's crust, he finally erupted and channeled every ounce of his might into one ultimate, cathartic swing. Once the shower of sparks had cleared, Lancelot looked down and took a deep breath, dropping the hammer to the ground upon realizing that his last strike had shattered the horseshoe into several pieces.

"You know, there are far more constructive outlets for such ferocity, my boy," said a familiar voice.

"Go away, Merlyn," Lancelot muttered, not bothering to turn around and face the old man's piercing gaze, "Haven't you played enough cruel jokes for one lifetime?"

"Cruel jokes? What a dreadfully absurd idea. I have never been anything but forthright with you."

The young blacksmith spun around and glared at Merlyn, who was leaning upon his walking staff in the frame of the open doorway, his long, white beard tangled with dry leaves and his hat drooping under the trivial weight of that little grey owl.

"Come now, Merlyn. You're either joking or delusional! My father and dozens of other British lords – men with *years* of training and experience in battle – were slaughtered like sheep by those pagan savages, and yet you expect to achieve victory with naught but a rabble of commoners and a literary scholar who had never so much as *held* a sword before you arrived? Arthur is a good man – *God bless him* – and he's my friend, but he is *certainly* no war leader."

"Let me tell you a story, Lancelot," the old man replied.

"Merlyn," he sighed apathetically, "I'm really in no mood for more of your games."

"No games, my boy. No games. Only *truth*. You see, during the days of our Lord and Savior, there were many Israelites who believed that the prophesied Messiah would be an all-powerful political leader – a warrior king who would drive out their Roman rulers and achieve victory for the Jewish people, leading to an era of peace and prosperity throughout the known world. But when He came instead in the form of a humble carpenter, preaching love and forgiveness for all, including the Gentiles, many were disillusioned and believed that this *Messiah* had failed them. One of these men was Judas Iscariot, the disciple who betrayed Christ for 30 pieces of silver."

"Are you accusing me, Merlyn, of being Arthur's *Judas*?"

"No, my boy, I'm doing nothing of the sort. That particular role is destined to be filled by another."

"Then I fail to see your point," Lancelot huffed, "Christ may have come to beat swords into plowshares, but in this instance, we truly *are* at war! It isn't a metaphor for some alternate spiritual reality, but a real, *literal* war against a massive, deadly, near insurmountable army! Vortigern will *not* be brought to his knees through love and forgiveness, nor will he be impressed or dissuaded from his sinister purpose by flowing words or elegant philosophical discourses! He is a monster and a tyrant. Men such as him respond to force and force alone. Uther Pendragon knew this well when he fought like a lion against the Saxons in his day, and I expected his heir to be no different."

"Things never happen in the same way twice, Lancelot," the old man said with a knowing twinkle in his eye, "There was only ever one great flood, only one burning bush. After Jericho, never again were stone walls destroyed by trumpet blast, and no boy after King David slew a giant with a sling. Even Christ refused to copy Himself. Look at the Gospels! How many different ways did He choose to heal blind men? With one He used only words, another He smeared with mud, and He spit onto the eyes of a third!"

"But Merlyn, all my life I have *dreamed* of the Pendragon's triumphant return – of following a mighty warrior into battle and vanquishing evil with one final, crushing blow. I had *expectations*, and now they've been scattered to the wind!"

"*Curse your expectations, boy!*" Merlyn shouted, a newly kindled fire within his booming voice. His eyes flashed and his body blazed with white light, merely hinting at a deeper power that had thus far remained hidden. Never before had Lancelot seen the old man grow angry, and the force of his presence caused the blacksmith to stagger backwards and slump into a nearby chair. He did not dare argue further, for he knew that he was in the wrong and that Merlyn's anger was of a different sort than that to which he was accustomed. It was an anger without rage or violence – a righteous anger, wholly justified yet wholly controlled, which rendered it all the more terrifying.

"God is not concerned with your expectations," Merlyn said, continuing in a gentler voice as the light around him dimmed, "He is concerned with your *obedience*. And as I recall, you made a vow to follow the Pendragon 'to the ends of the earth.' I have come today to collect on that promise."

At that moment, Lancelot began to feel extremely small. He was suddenly able to see himself through the old man's eyes, and what he saw was a frightened, faithless child, selfish and blubbering as if he had been denied sweets after his evening meal. He wished that he could disappear – that he could crawl into a cave and die, if only to escape from the terrible shame he now felt within his very marrow.

"I'm sorry, sir," he whispered, "I apologize for my sinful pride and lack of faith. And though I still do not understand how we can possibly succeed in this suicidal enterprise, I will honor my vow and I will do all I can to assist Arthur... I mean, *the Pendragon*... in reclaiming his throne."

While he was speaking Lancelot's head had been bowed, and he continued to stare at the floor in silence until something happened that he did not expect.

Merlyn began to laugh.

Bemused, Lancelot lifted his eyes and saw the old man doubled over with laughter, not a mocking or derisive snicker, but a full-bellied expression of joy that seemed to flow from every vein and organ of his enormous, quaking body.

"Very well, my boy," he chuckled, "That will be good enough for now. Please, take my arm and follow me. I will show you that the morning sun may still rise for this so-called *suicidal enterprise* of yours."

Lancelot reached out and grasped the sleeve of Merlyn's cloak, and suddenly the world around him began melting away, as if the walls of the blacksmith's shop had been made from nothing but wax. The anvil and the bloomery furnace vanished from sight, and in their place appeared crude canvas tents and neatly arranged piles of bows, shields, and spears. Armed men, both young and old, wandered about the camp in groups of two or three, some discussing battle plans, others having their wounds cleaned and dressed, and still more hurriedly gnawing on handfuls of salted meat and dry bread in between their training exercises and scheduled watch duties.

"Do not worry, Lancelot, for this is merely a vision. These shadows can neither see nor hear you," Merlyn stated matter-offactly, secretly proud that he had remembered to open with such a disclaimer after his experience with Arthur.

Lancelot glanced about curiously and spotted a few familiar faces among the crude assembly of young, makeshift soldiers and aging military men. Near a small grove of beech trees he noticed Sagramore, the big Numidian horseman, adjusting the saddle on his powerful destrier and feeding the mount generous handfuls of dried oats. Palamedes the dark-eyed Sarmatian was seated nearby, polishing and sharpening his fearsome scimitar with a smooth, wet stone from the riverbed, and Ector stood in the midst of several eager youths, apparently teaching them the intricacies of swordplay. Even that brutish oaf Kay seemed to be engaged and earnest in his commitment, honing his archery skills while his shaggy red hair was ruffled by the breeze.

Having surveyed the camp, the next thing Lancelot noticed was the loud, exuberant voice of the man called Bedivere, who was standing atop an empty mead barrel and addressing the troops, showing no qualms whatsoever about Arthur's arrival and the gleeful enthusiasm that came with it.

"...and in this, our time of need, the Lord has brought to us a liberator, a leader, a *king!* The rumors are true, my friends! The heir of Pendragon has come to us at last, and I have seen the legendary sword of the *Legio Draconis* with my own eyes! So let us rally behind him and stand before our enemies with gallantry and honor, for their unholy reign is near an end!"

As Bedivere's words faded into silence, Lancelot blinked and found that he and Merlyn were now standing on a grassy hilltop with a vicious battle raging in the fields below. A contingent of Saxon warriors was bearing down upon the rag-tag band of British rebels, but much to his surprise, the rebels were apparently holding their own, even driving the pagans back from time to time. Ector and Sagramore charged into the bloody skirmish on horseback, brandishing their weapons and shouting like men possessed. Kay was crouched behind a large boulder along with several other archers, firing arrows into the Saxon infantry to provide cover for their allies. Bedivere, Palamedes, and a mammoth man swinging an iron war hammer worked the flanks, keeping the enemy boxed in and preventing their retreat. Most interestingly, Lancelot noticed a blonde-haired soldier wielding a large battle axe fighting alongside what appeared to be a young Saxon woman, though they both seemed to be on the side of the Britons.

And then his heart stopped. In the center of the mêlée, a lone warrior stood battling a horde of seax-wielding attackers, dispatching them one-by-one as if he were swatting flies. His armor was a blend of Roman and Celtic styles, with the standard chainmail hauberk augmented with steel shoulder guards, gauntlets, and greaves. His blood-soaked sword was a Roman *spatha*, and his shield bore the image of a golden eagle with a Celtic cross inscribed upon its chest. As the fighting finally wore down, the warrior sheathed his sword and removed his helmet, revealing the stringy brown hair and sparse beard of a young man Lancelot would know anywhere. It was Arthur.

"Merlyn!" Lancelot called out in shock, "I know this is only a vision, but... is it real? I mean, is this *really* happening?"

"I am revealing to you what *is*, not what might be," the old man answered, "Your eyes do not deceive you. Arthur learned well from Ector's tutelage, but those lessons only account for a portion of his skills on the battlefield. Just as Samson was given great strength when he cried out to God, Arthur's abilities do not come from within, but from above. He has been chosen, Lancelot, though many of the Britons still do not believe."

"What do you mean, Merlyn? I heard the rousing speech made before the troops by that Bedivere fellow. His faith in Arthur is unmatched!"

"Aye, it is indeed. But Bedivere is but one voice crying in the wilderness. Despite all they've seen, few others believe, and none with such intensity. Even Arthur doubts himself. He needs you, my boy. Not just as a friend, but as an ally."

* * * * *

Alone in his tent, Arthur dropped to his knees in fervent prayer and poured out his heart, still struggling to reconcile within himself numerous seemingly contradictory doctrines concerning war, violence, and regicide. Passages of scripture and the wise words of Augustine flowed chaotically through his troubled mind, and he began to identify with the story of Jacob wrestling with the angel, only this time, *he* was the one who was "contending with God."

In *City of God*, Augustine had written that "war is justified only by the injustice of an aggressor; and that injustice ought to be a source of grief to any good man, because it is human injustice." Arthur frequently turned to this particular selection, as well as others like it, in order to soothe his conscience and give his spirit rest as he attempted to rationalize the lives he had taken in battle over the past few months. But every time he allowed the theologian's words to offer him comfort, all of his old doubts and fears began rising to the surface again.

Christ's command to *love your enemies and do good to those who hate you,* His assurance during the Sermon on the Mount that peacemakers are blessed, and His admonition to Saint Peter that *all who take the sword will perish by the sword* cascaded through Arthur's thoughts and pounded against his will like waves crashing upon the rocks. However, intertwined with those arguments for pacifism were other Biblical passages, those advising that there is *a time for war and a time for peace,* those loudly proclaiming that *Yahweh is a warrior,* and those praising men such as Gideon, Samson, David, and Samuel, who conquered kingdoms, became mighty in battle, and enforced justice at the point of a sword.

The struggle in his heart seemed endless. Night after night, he begged God for assurance, but God remained silent.

In truth, Arthur's theological quandaries were not entirely to blame for his vacillation. He had originally agreed to set sail for Britannia with the other rebels after Merlyn revealed to him his true heritage and convinced him of his destiny as High King; however, this newfound confidence was not his own, and now that Merlyn was no longer by his side, Arthur found himself frightened, anxious, and lost in self-doubt. Despite his bouts of philosophical confusion, the blood on his hands mattered less to Arthur than the blood flowing in his veins, and the lingering suspicion that he could not live up to his promise – that he was nothing more than a fraud – haunted him nightly.

* * * * *

As Arthur finally drifted off into a restless slumber, Lancelot and Merlyn stood by silently, watching and listening, unseen in the corner of his tent. Once again, Lancelot began to feel small, for his meager faith had been nothing in comparison to that of his childhood friend. He had allowed fear and resentment to keep him from his vow, while Arthur had soldiered on valiantly in spite of his uncertainties and personal limitations. Truly this was the measure of courage – not being *free* from fear, but being scared to death and still striving onward.

Lancelot closed his eyes and prayed, requesting forgiveness for his own failings and strength for Arthur in his time of doubt. But when he opened his eyes, he was no longer standing in the camp of the British rebels, but in the cool shade of Brocéliande Forest, with the shores of the Lake of Diana rippling at his feet.

"Why are we here, Merlyn?" Lancelot asked, "Is this merely another vision?"

"No, my boy," said the old man, "this is very real. I have brought you to this place that you may be given a task – one that will allow you to both atone for your sins and to view but a small glimpse of the splendor that awaits."

"I will do as I am commanded," answered the blacksmith.

"Arthur was given the sword of his father, Uther Pendragon, in order to prove his heritage to others and to himself. It is the sword of a great warrior, but not the sword of a king. Now the time has come for Arthur to wield a weapon that proclaims his true destiny to all men, Briton and Saxon alike."

With those words, Merlyn turned and faced the lake, which soon began to bubble and boil with great intensity. A brilliant white light emanated from the depths, as if the morning sun had risen not upon the eastern horizon, but from beneath the turbulent facade of these murky waters. Gradually the light grew brighter until Lancelot could no longer look upon it, and he lifted his hand to shield his eyes from the naked radiance on display before him. Then a deafening roar, unlike anything he had ever heard, nearly knocked him from his feet as he covered his ears and willingly dropped to his knees, unable to stand in the presence of such unrestrained power. When the sheer ferocity of the light eventually began to wane, the same delicate figure he had seen many years ago began walking toward him upon the glassy surface of the water. Nimue's fiery red hair and samite gown, which sparkled as if it were woven with emerald thread, flowed and undulated slowly and almost musically, leading one to imagine that this woman did not simply come from the lake, but was in reality a living part of it. As she finally approached the shore, Nimue extended her slender arms and produced the most magnificent sword Lancelot had ever laid his eyes upon. The hilt bore the regal shape of a screaming eagle, wings outstretched in glorious flight and trimmed in the purest gold, with a small cross fashioned from blood-red sapphire adorning the pommel. The translucent, crystalline blade was blindingly bright, and it seemed to flash with an ethereal fire more luminous than thirty torches.

As Lancelot gazed upon the sword in awe, a thin finger of flame began inscribing words on the face of the blade in some strange, unknown language. And although he was unable to read, the words became clear to him, as if they were inscribed upon his heart as well: *For we do not wrestle against flesh and blood, but against the principalities, against the powers, against the world rulers over this present darkness, against the spiritual forces of evil in the heavenly places.*

"This is *Excalibur*," Merlyn finally announced, "It was forged in the white mountains of Avalon by servants of the Most High, and the chosen king alone may be its master. But despite its divine origin, the real power comes not from the sword itself, but from the man who brandishes it, if he be worthy. To be precise, the sword is merely a vessel, a conduit through which the qualities of a true king – love, wisdom, chivalry, valor – are channeled and honed into a force for God's glory."

Nimue then turned toward Lancelot and looked through his eyes into the hidden depths of his soul. In an instant, the young blacksmith began to feel utterly exposed, and his strength failed him as the Lady of the Lake began to speak.

"You will bear this weapon to Britannia and bestow it upon Arthur," she said, her mellifluous voice somewhere between a melody and a whisper. "He has been called upon to lead the rebel forces in one final siege against Vortigern's castle on Badon Hill, and he will need every ally that can be mustered. Before you depart, I must caution you that although this sword will be light and nimble in the hands of its owner, for all others it is a heavy burden, including yourself."

"I will send you to the outskirts of the Saxon lands," Merlyn interjected, "but the remainder of the journey must be yours and yours alone. Godspeed, my boy. Godspeed."

And before the blacksmith had time to respond, the skies flashed and he was transported to another forest, a *different* forest, with the fires of a small Saxon village glowing peacefully in the distance. *He was in Britannia!* Lancelot looked about and discovered that he was armored in leather and steel and seated atop a beautiful black courser with his own sword, Arondight, sheathed at his side, and Excalibur, weighty and burdensome, bundled securely upon his back.

Dusk had fallen, and Lancelot knew that he would have to ride throughout the night in order to reach Arthur in time. So with the reigns gripped tightly between his fists, he gathered his courage, spurred his courser into a strong gallop, and set out for Vortigern's castle, come rapture or ruin.

Mons Badonicus

Although little else could possibly be said in his favor, Vortigern certainly knew how to wage a war.

Despite several victories by the British rebels in remote skirmishes with the Saxon army and even a few larger-scale battles, the siege of a castle was a vastly different and far more complex undertaking. Battering rams, catapults, and escalade ladders had to be constructed, infiltration plans had to be concocted, and much greater manpower was required due to the heavy attrition rate of siege warfare. After three days and two nights of aggressive attempts by Arthur and his comrades, it had become crushingly clear that their war machines were weak, their infiltration plans were faulty, and their manpower was in short supply and dwindling by the hour.

"Sir, our army grows ever smaller with each passing day," Bedivere lamented, "We *must* fall back and regroup. We will never take this castle with such a meager force."

"We *will not* retreat," answered Arthur, sitting alone in his tent with his most loyal supporter, "Reinforcements will come, Bedivere. I swear it. Our most pressing need now is finding a way to break through the castle walls and draw the Saxons out into open battle. For thus far they have been content to hide within their fortress, dousing our men with boiling oil and pummeling them with boulders from the parapets. And even the small handful of soldiers who did manage to scale the walls were returned to us in pieces by the pagans' catapults."

"But we have already tried everything, sir. Our battering rams were of no use, and you have already acknowledged the tragic fate of our escalades. We have no siege towers and no knowledge of how to create Greek fire, and they are too well fortified for us to attempt starvation tactics."

"I know it appears hopeless," Arthur said, his voice strong and resolute, but his eyes distressed and weary, "but I need you to stand with me now. Most of the other men have already lost heart, and I... I can't bear for you to fall away as well."

Bedivere sat silently for a moment and stared into the face of the young man whom he would have as king. Yes, it was true that few others believed. Ector had faith, of course, and Kay was skeptical but courteous. But Gawain had his doubts, and Maleagant didn't believe in much of anything anymore. The contingent of old Roman soldiers showed loyalty and courage, and they all respected Arthur's skills on the battlefield, but most had become so jaded by a lifetime of warfare that they typically held to no higher goal than doing their duty and hopefully returning home alive. The other men he didn't know as well. He had heard whispers and rumors here and there among the ranks, but no one shared his level of devotion.

After having reassured himself, Bedivere stood up quickly, tightened his jaw, and looked Arthur dead in the eye. "Yes sir," he said with a smile, "Reinforcements will come indeed. If you'll pardon me now, I will consult with our friends at arms. Fear not. We *will* find a way to breach those walls!"

As the bright-eyed soldier left his tent, Arthur began to feel both pride and pity simultaneously. He had always been taught to value loyalty, and Bedivere was the most loyal and steadfast man he had ever met. But at the same time, his beleaguered soul was weighed down with the incessant, nagging idea that Bedivere was nothing but a deluded young man who had been naïve enough to surrender his hope to the wrong person. How had he gotten himself into this? Why had he dared to believe the ranting of an eccentric old trickster with a flair for the dramatic? Far too many men had died already due to his misguided hubris. He was simply Arthur, the scholarly orphan who lived in an old monastery and kept his nose constantly buried in books. He was no leader, and surely no king.

Unable to eat anything or to think clearly, Arthur reluctantly lay down to rest for the night, his heart being torn apart by a raging tempest of fear and doubt. He couldn't see why anyone would ever look to *him* for guidance. He couldn't see a way out of this madness other than the quiet release of death. And he couldn't see the black, ghostly figure hovering over him, digging razor-sharp talons into his skull and filling his mind with lies. The scrawny creature's coarse grey fur stood on end as he laughed sadistically to himself, saliva dripping from his hideous snout and his thick, sulfurous breath poisoning the air. Naberius the Deceiver had found his prize at last.

* * * * *

It was nearly dawn when Arthur awoke to the sound of someone attempting to enter his tent. His senses suddenly on alert, the young man slowly reached for his father's sword, pulling it from its sheath and gradually stepping toward the entrance, ready to sever the head of any Saxon warrior who might seek to murder him as he slept. Then when a brawny, chainmail-clad arm reached through the tent flap, Arthur grasped it tightly and yanked the intruder inside with all his might, pinning the arm behind him and pressing his steel blade firmly against the soldier's throat.

"Arthur, it's me!" the intruder shouted, "It's Lancelot! Would you mind putting down the sword?"

Quickly tossing his weapon to the ground, Arthur eagerly spun the captive soldier around and was greeted with the smiling face of his oldest and closest friend. Overjoyed, he threw his arms around Lancelot and laughed out loud, endlessly grateful for a warm reminder of simpler times.

"I must admit, I'm surprised that you seem so glad to see me after I deserted you in your time of need. I am sorry, Arthur. Can you forgive this prideful lout?"

"What's to forgive?" Arthur replied casually, "You were right all along. I have no business leading this rabble. This was all a fool's errand in the first place. It's high time for us to head back home to Dinan to grow fat and happy."

Arthur's grin seemed superficial and his eyes looked vacant, as if he were drunk or, worse still, as if he had lost control of his own emotions and was somehow being controlled from without by some unseen, malevolent force.

"Merlyn warned me that you had begun to doubt yourself," said Lancelot, his heart dropping with the somber realization that his friend was losing his will to fight, "but I had no idea that it would have gone this far."

"Why the devil should I be concerned with what Merlyn says? He's a doddering old liar with an impressive bag of tricks at his disposal. Nothing more."

"What has happened to you, Arthur? Have you given in to hopelessness? I *know* you, and your spirit is so much stronger than this. The man I see before me now is not the same man who left for Britannia those many months ago. It is not the man who I am prepared to offer my devotion and respect. And it is *not* the man who is worthy to wield this sword."

Then Lancelot pulled Excalibur from his back, cringing under the oppressive weight and yet summoning the strength to hold it upright, blade extended proudly toward the heavens.

* * * * *

Naberius shrieked in terror and released his grip on Arthur's mind, scurrying backward with reckless abandon and cowering like a dog in the far corner of the tent. The brilliant white light pouring forth from the angelic blade was burning his eyes and had already begun causing his leathery skin to blister and boil.

Leaping farther into the distance out of sheer self-preservation, Naberius soon discovered that the light was spreading throughout the entire rebel camp, and he watched in horror as lesser spirits of complacency, uncertainty, and despair fled for their lives like rats deserting a sinking ship. Some managed to escape from the mounting radiance while others were trapped and absorbed by it, wailing in pain as they were incinerated into nothingness, being tossed screaming back into the Abyss.

Skulking away in anger and shame, Naberius soon became filled with dread as he gradually realized the full extent of his failure. *Curse that meddling brute Ambrosius!* Victory had been within their grasp, but that dim-witted blacksmith had arrived bearing that... that *monstrosity* and spoiled everything! Lord Astaroth would not be pleased with *this*. Oh no, he would most certainly *not* be pleased.

* * * * *

Arthur was mesmerized. The shining sword felt as light as a feather and yet stronger and more powerful than any weapon, word, or conviction he had ever known. In truth, it was almost a presence unto itself, calling out to him through the darkness in a still, small voice that could be heard by no one else on earth. Slowly he turned the magnificent blade back and forth in his hands, admiring every detail, every glimmer of otherworldly brightness, while the grim despair that had held his soul captive gradually melted away like snow at sunrise. He felt as if he were just waking from a long and terrible dream – a living nightmare during which he had been trapped deep within himself, locked away like a prisoner in his own mind. And just as the scales had fallen from Saul's eyes after the blessing of Ananias, Arthur regained his sight and much more beside. The world he had known before seemed dull and grey, and all he now looked upon was richer, brighter, and saturated with colors so vibrant that it almost burned the eyes to stare at them for longer than a few moments. His newfound vision reached through time and space as well, showing him the proud faces of his mother and father at the hour of his birth, his whisking away to Armorica by the gentle hand of Nimue, and Merlyn's glorious stand against the dark spirit who sought to slay him in the cradle. Finally, he knew who he was. And more importantly, he knew what he must do.

"Thank you, Lancelot," Arthur whispered through his tears, grasping his friend and holding him close in a warm, strong embrace that signified not only gratitude and forgiveness, but brotherhood.

Then at that very moment, before the simple delight of their transformative reunion could be savored, the two were interrupted by Bedivere and Gawain, who burst into the tent in breathless excitement. Just behind them came Rowena, the young Saxon girl who had joined the rebellion after fleeing from the bestial abuse of Vortigern and her warlike father. She held tightly to Gawain's hand as he led her forward until she stood at Arthur's feet, and suddenly she was rapt in awe. The man before her – a man she had now seen and addressed on many occasions – was somehow different, changed, with a newfound majesty shining behind his eyes. Her male companions noticed as well, and all three felt strangely compelled to kneel.

"Stand up, my friends, and tell me your news!" Arthur said enthusiastically, reaching out for Rowena's hand and gently raising her to her feet. After a flurry of jumbled words about which of them would begin, Bedivere finally spoke.

"Sir, I have conversed with Gawain, and he tells me that the lady Rowena may know of a spot in which the outer walls of the castle are weaker than normal and thus may be vulnerable to penetration!"

"It's true, sir," Gawain continued eagerly, "Despite my extended infiltration of the Saxon army, I was never given knowledge of this weakness. In fact, it is my belief that *none* of the soldiers know of it! Vortigern liked to keep as many secrets as possible between himself and Hengist, his general, especially those concerning the defense of his castle. He was terrified of traitors leaking sensitive information to the outside… and with *good cause*, I might add!"

"Yes, but he *did* speak to Rowena," Bedivere interrupted, "Indeed, it seems that her cruel mistreatment by this unholy king may yet serve some purpose. Perhaps it was arrogance or merely carelessness, but he apparently jabbered on like a giddy toddler while in the bedroom."

"Alright, gentlemen, that's enough," Arthur stated firmly, although he *was* a bit amused by their rapid, explosive banter. "Perhaps we should let the lady speak for herself."

"Thank you, sir," Rowena said quietly, while sending a glare of annoyance over to Bedivere for his insensitive commentary. "On the east end of the castle, near the stone quarry on the far side of Badon Hill, there is a newly constructed gate which Vortigern had planned to use as an escape route for himself if the walls should ever be breached. The last I knew, it had not yet been reinforced, and it remains but a single layer of stone. The terrain is far too shaky and uneven for a battering ram to be effective, but if we can find another way to break through the wall, I believe our men could enter the castle undetected and take the Saxon army entirely by surprise."

Arthur stood by silently, eyes closed and head bowed, and it remained unclear to those present whether he was praying or simply processing this new information. Then abruptly his eyes popped open and he hurriedly bent down to gather up his armor and gird himself for battle.

"Assemble the men," he said to Bedivere.

"What do you mean, sir?"

"We strike now – immediately! Quick, before Vortigern has a chance to rouse his army from their slumber!"

The small assembly looked at one another in confusion, half wondering if Arthur had gone stark raving mad, but at the same time overflowing with hope and exhilaration at the thought of undertaking such a bold strategy.

"But Arthur, what about the walls?" asked Lancelot, "How will we ever breach them without a proper siege engine?"

Arthur smiled knowingly and placed his right hand upon his friend's shoulder. "Peace, Lancelot," he replied, "You leave that part to me. Now please, go help Bedivere and Gawain prepare our men for battle. Dawn is coming soon."

* * * * *

Lancelot sat atop his jet black courser, armed and ready, surveying the lines of troops that had assembled along a grassy hillside just outside their encampment. Aside from himself and a few other Britons, the mounted cavalry was largely made up of former Roman legionnaires, experienced soldiers like Ector and Sagramore who had come to Britannia looking for a new home only to be met with oppression and chaos. Kay, who had matured dramatically since joining the rebellion, had been given command of the archers and was currently inspecting his men to ensure that each quiver was filled to the brim and each bow was properly strung. The three infantry battalions were led by Gawain, Palamedes, and Tristan, a fearless Celt from Hibernia, whose deadly skill with his twin falcatas made him a force to be reckoned with in close-quarters combat. Then Maleagant, that silent soldier from Gorre whose actions on the battlefield more than compensated for his lack of words, rode up alone on a huge destrier, brandishing his war hammer with untold ferocity in his stare. Finally, Lancelot was surprised to see Pellinore, the aging, absent-minded soldier he and Arthur had met in their youth, proudly mounted next to three strapping young men whom Lancelot presumed to be his sons.

As he attempted to mentally gauge the strength of the army surrounding him, Lancelot thought of the ancient Israelites' siege against Jericho, whose walls they had destroyed by marching around the city with priests blowing on rams' horns. He also remembered Merlyn's cryptic words of warning on the matter: *Things never happen in the same way twice*. However, in the moments that followed, Lancelot was instead reminded of a different story – that of Moses descending from Mount Sinai, his face shining after he had been in the presence of God. As a matter of fact, that same image filled the minds of many of the Briton soldiers, who all fell instantly silent when Arthur finally approached.

"Brave men of Britannia!" Arthur cried out, "All of you know me, though only recently have I truly begun to know myself. My birth name was *Arturus Riothamus*, and I come before you now as the sole heir of Uther Pendragon, son of the Roman Emperor Constantinus and rightful King of the Britons. Many years ago, my father's light was extinguished by a treasonous serpent, a man who had once been his friend and ally, the same man who now sits unjustly upon his throne. Throughout this man's malevolent reign, you have been forced to live under his thumb and at the mercy of his cruel Saxon mercenaries. They have driven you from your homes, burned your churches, stolen your crops, and murdered your kin! But I swear to you now that those dark days are at an end. On this bright summer morning, we *will* breach the walls of Vortigern's castle, and I charge each of you to stand with me and fight! Fight for your homeland! Fight for your friends! Fight for your wives, your children, and the ancestors who have gone before you! But most of all, fight with the knowledge that the Lord God is always on the side of righteousness, and He will give us victory!"

A boisterous cheer echoed throughout the crisp, cool air of daybreak as Arthur lifted Excalibur on high, filling the sky with radiant light, brighter and more powerful than the rising sun. Then after a quick prayer for protection, he called upon his commanders to approach him and receive their orders.

"I want the cavalry to take position directly in front of the main castle entrance along with two infantry battalions. Tristan and Palamedes, your men will divert the attention of the Saxon army until we can penetrate the walls and open the gate from the inside. Kay, lead your archers to strategic points on the far side of Badon Hill. They will provide cover for Gawain's men as we infiltrate the castle from the rear. God help us all."

Each of the men who had been summoned then hurriedly rode back to their posts, relaying Arthur's orders and preparing their troops for battle. But before Lancelot could also return to his position with the mounted cavalry, he once again felt Arthur's hand upon his shoulder.

"Ride with me, Lancelot," he said softly, "for this will either be our greatest hour or our most grievous folly."

"Lead and I will follow," the blacksmith answered.

*****

As Arthur and Lancelot stealthily led their coursers through the nearby stone quarry, followed closely by Gawain and a large contingent of sword-bearing infantry, pikemen, and Kay's band of archers, the two friends began chatting casually about books and blacksmithing, food and family, and the surprisingly pleasant weather they were fortunate enough to enjoy. It may have been the least appropriate conversation that anyone could possibly have while preparing for siege warfare, but as they walked willingly through the long shadow of death, it did both of their hearts a great deal of good.

Finally approaching what appeared to be a recently built castle gate, partially hidden by brambles and fallen boulders, Arthur turned and signaled Gawain to stop and hold his men ready. He then dismounted and slowly made his way out of the quarry, praying that the wall was indeed unfortified and that his silent advance would go unnoticed by any Saxon guards who might be roaming the ramparts. However, just as Rowena had predicted, Vortigern's secret escape route had been left unmanned, and Arthur chuckled at the realization that this tyrant's vanity would be his undoing.

With his destiny close at hand, Arthur carefully withdrew Excalibur from its sheath and glanced back at Lancelot, smiling as he remembered Merlyn's encouragement years ago at his father's graveside: *Not by might, nor by power, but by the spirit of the Lord are great deeds accomplished.*

And in an instant, everything changed.

Mere words were not sufficient to describe the astonishing sight which Lancelot and the other Briton soldiers beheld on that warm summer morning. In the days that would follow, many would claim to have seen a man actually hurling a bolt of lightning toward Vortigern's castle, but such imagery served as an imperfect comparison at best. Regardless, only two things remained abundantly clear to everyone in the moments after Arthur called out to his Maker and plunged his mighty sword into a cleft in the mortared stone fortress.

The first was the flash of white light and the deafening sound of an explosion that shook the earth as the castle wall burst asunder, collapsed, and crumbled into dust. And the second was the sight of hundreds of Pictish warriors, their bodies tattooed with blue woad paint, as they appeared atop the crest of Badon Hill, charging fearlessly toward the startled and gloriously unprepared Saxon army.

Reinforcements had arrived.

The Pendragon Rises

Gawain did not bother to wait for a signal from Arthur. As soon as he saw that the castle walls had been breached and that the Pictish army was now rapidly descending into the fray, he gave his men the order and they charged frantically into Vortigern's fortress, each soldier hollering out a war cry and brandishing his weapon while the sleepy Saxons lumbered out of their barracks and into a chaotic whirlwind of death.

An immense cloud of grey dust that had billowed up after the destruction of the outer wall was awaiting the unsuspecting Saxon forces, and they stumbled wildly through the courtyard with burning eyes and wheezing lungs. Kay and his archers sent a deadly barrage of arrows onto the confused, flailing horde of pagan warriors, felling many as others desperately ran for cover through the murky haze. The Briton soldiers bore down upon the Saxons like hungry dogs pouncing on a slab of raw meat, excising years of subjugation and torment with every blow. Gawain himself fought more fiercely than any man, swinging his powerful battle axe with both hands and taking bittersweet pleasure in the warm catharsis that greeted its blade.

As the dust cleared, Lancelot waded through the debris and quickly located Arthur, helping him onto his horse and away from the major thrust of the attack.

"We have to get to the main gate!" Arthur shouted over the uproar of battle, "Quickly, before the Saxons have a chance to gather their wits about them and regroup!"

As it happened, Arthur's warning had come none too soon. While the first wave of Saxon warriors was being massacred as they staggered about in panic, a second wave was just emerging from the barracks, armed, furious, and thirsty for blood. Soon they were spreading in all directions, overtaking Gawain's men and engaging them in arduous combat while callously trodding upon the lifeless bodies of their fallen countrymen. Several of the soldiers also noticed the two young men on horseback and began charging toward them in a fit of rage.

"Go on, Arthur!" cried Lancelot as he drew Arondight and turned to face the rising onslaught, "I'll do what I can to guard your escape. Now ride! Get that gate open!"

Lancelot's words had barely left his mouth when he heard his courser groaning in agony and then lost his balance as the magnificent animal began to tumble to the ground with a large spear protruding from its hindquarters. Leaping from the back of the grievously wounded horse, Lancelot regained his footing and suddenly found himself surrounded by a quartet of snarling Saxon soldiers. He took a firm, defensive stance as they moved in closer, taunting, threatening, and brandishing their swords and axes in a vain attempt to intimidate the young blacksmith. Then Lancelot smiled. A peculiar blend of fear and exhilaration surged through his veins, and he held his gleaming sword ready, beckoning his enemies to step forward and taste its cold, cruel blade. Having long dreamed of a moment such as this, locked in glorious battle against incredible odds, Lancelot determined that he would savor every second.

In a flash of blood and steel, the Saxon closest to Lancelot screamed in shock as his weapon dropped to the ground, his now severed hands still holding tight to the grip. Two others then began stampeding toward him like wild bulls, but he easily averted their clumsy attack and then spun swiftly around with his sword outstretched, slashing one from behind and severing his spine at the nape of the neck. When the other turned back and charged again, Lancelot slipped a small dagger from his boot and plunged it into the Saxon's foot, painfully pinning him to the earth before burying Arondight deep in his gut.

After wiping the blood from his sword, Lancelot bent down to retrieve his dagger and then stood facing the fourth soldier, who had wisely chosen to approach this duel with far more care and consideration than his dead comrades. Slowly the two men circled one another, studying every movement and waiting patiently for the perfect moment to strike. When at last the Saxon warrior let out a shout and swung his heavy iron sword in furious assault, Lancelot deftly parried the blow and felt his opponent's blade snap and then shatter against the sturdy Damascus steel. The unexpected loss of his weapon caused the Saxon to stumble forward with great momentum until he fell and caught his throat on Lancelot's sword, inadvertently slicing it open and spilling his life onto the dusty ground.

Lancelot rose up and caught his breath, glancing down at the enemy corpses strewn about his feet and watching as the leather and fur-clad, war-painted Pictish raiders dashed about with their squarehead axes and iron broadswords, assisting the Briton army in this bloody siege against their common enemy. Exhausted from fighting yet invigorated by the thrill of battle, the young blacksmith hastened toward the Saxon lines, eager to locate their general and personally deliver justice for the death of his parents so many years ago.

* * * * *

Elsewhere, Arthur was caught in a skirmish of his own. He had reached the main castle gate without much difficulty, the bulk of the Saxon army having already made its way toward the breach in the eastern wall, but a robust force still remained stationed atop the gatehouse, watching and waiting for the Briton cavalry and remaining infantry battalions assembled outside the fortress to join in the assault. So when Arthur approached them from behind on horseback, galloping unaided into their midst with sword drawn, their attention was quickly diverted to this foolhardy rider who apparently had the gall to challenge a large portion of the castle guard alone.

"Friends!" he called out, "I am Arthur Pendragon, son and heir of the true king! Hear me now! Although you have aided Vortigern in his reign of darkness and tyranny, my feud is with *him* and not with your people. So I implore you now to leave this fortress and return to your homes. Truly, no further harm will come to you if we can agree to live in peace. However, if you choose to stay here and defend the usurper's ill-gotten throne, every one of you will surely die today."

When Arthur finished speaking, the soldiers stationed about the gatehouse stared in silence for a few moments, and then they gradually erupted into a wave of uproarious laughter.

"Who is this impudent fool?" one bellowed.

"Surely the king has named a new court jester!" chuckled another as he pointed and clutched his sides.

"How dare he threaten us!" a third warrior shouted, "that Briton scamp must be *mad* to come here alone!"

Several of the Saxon archers then drew their bows and let fly a hailstorm of arrows toward Arthur's position, filling the air with deadly iron-tipped bodkins meant to penetrate both armor and flesh. Yet when they looked down haughtily to admire their kill, the rider had disappeared, and the numerous shafts fired had pierced the earth and nothing more. Before the befuddled soldiers could discern what had happened, Arthur was upon them, riding boldly through their ranks as if he were parting the Red Sea and swinging his mighty sword like Achilles returned to life. Excalibur flashed in Arthur's hand as he tore into the Saxon forces, swiftly beheading each man he rode upon, mercifully offering a quick and mostly painless death to all those who foolishly chose to give their lives for the lying serpent occupying his father's throne. Left and right they fell, carving a pathway of casualties through the once formidable band of warriors, leading up to the summit of the gatehouse.

The younger soldiers manning the murder-holes and the kettles of boiling oil fled their positions in terror as Arthur approached, dropping their swords and running from the castle without once looking back. Then with one strike from Excalibur, Arthur broke the massive chain that held back the drawbridge and portcullis and rode his courser along the ramparts, waving his sword in the air and signaling to the bulk of the Briton army that their moment had finally come.

"The gate is open!" Bedivere cried out in excitement, "Brave men of Britannia, the gate is open! Behold Arthur as he trods upon the very walls of our enemy! He has promised us victory and it is now within our grasp! So as this new day breaks, let us join him in the fray and show the Saxon hordes our mettle! For Arthur, lads! For God and for glory!"

Swordsmen shouted and hooves pounded the earth with rolling thunder as the remaining rebel forces stormed forcefully through the castle gate. Fervent and resolute, they poured over the Saxons like a raging river, surrounding and drowning them in a sea of blood, iron, and steel. Joining together at last with the Pictish army and the first wave of British infantry, Bedivere, Maleagant, Tristan, and the others led their troops along the castle's interior walls, pushing their enemies inward and cutting off their last avenue of escape.

Arthur observed the raging battle from his perch atop the gatehouse and smiled with satisfaction, taking a moment to look heavenward and thank God for the almost certain victory that awaited them. But then a thought suddenly invaded Arthur's mind and he realized that his task was not complete. *No, not yet*. Returning Excalibur to its scabbard, he quickly dismounted and began rushing toward the castle keep, a final refuge for any king whose fortress was in danger of falling. At long last, justice would reign again. The time had come for him to face Vortigern.

* * * * *

"Behind you!" Rowena shouted to Gawain, who spun around just in time to parry a strike from a heavy Saxon blade. He dropped to a crouch beneath the weight of the blow, then pushed his way up and flung the soldier stumbling backward. Finally, with a single swing of his battle axe, Gawain severed his opponent's leg at the knee and Rowena plunged her sword into the soldier's heart. In truth, they made quite the team.

By now it seemed like ages ago when she first followed Gawain to the battlements of the castle where he fired a note-laden arrow into the forest, covertly providing information to his friends in the British rebellion. And although he had almost killed her when she revealed herself, the two soon formed a close-knit bond over their mutual heritage and common disdain for the brutal savagery of their people. That very night, Rowena was invited to flee her father's wrath and join their ranks.

When she had first arrived at camp, many of the Briton men were skeptical of Rowena's ability to fight alongside them. But now, as the day's battle wore on, their preconceived notions of this dainty little flower tripping over her skirts were proven not only false but utterly ridiculous. Rather than flitting about in a frilly dress – as pictured by *several* of her male allies – Rowena wore layers of leather and chainmail, and she moved and wielded her seax shortsword with an effortless grace that was entirely foreign to the vast majority of lumbering, boorish men. It was her vigorous display of skill on the battlefield that finally earned their silence, but it was her body count – now nearly as high as Gawain's – that earned their respect.

As they fought onward through the Saxon lines, tearing a trail through the throng of warriors leading to the barracks and the entrance of Vortigern's castle itself, Rowena began to wonder whether she would be forced to face her father before this day was over. Then before she could even express her fears to Gawain, she heard him cry out in agony and lurch forward, a small dagger lodged in flesh of his lower back. Rowena quickly looked in his direction and her blood ran cold when she heard a familiar voice in the midst of the chaos.

"My own daughter," Hengist growled, "My own flesh and blood has turned against me and joined this... *half-breed.* And yet, here she stands in my presence, unashamed of her treachery. Tell me, Rowena, now that you have killed your countrymen, will you kill your father as well?

"*You* are the traitor, father!" Rowena shouted back, "You let your lust for power transform you into a cruel monster, and you *willingly* left me to suffer Vortigern's molestation and abuse! I can no longer bear to even look at you!"

"Then look no more!" Hengist cried out in a murderous rage as he charged at his daughter with bloody blade drawn. Rowena stood firm and lifted her own sword in defense, but her father's immense strength was more than she could handle, and she fell clumsily to the ground, desperately clinging to her sword and struggling to parry blow after relentless blow. At last her arms gave out and Rowena dropped her weapon, closing her eyes and holding her breath in preparation for the final stroke.

But then the loud *clang* of metal striking metal rang out above her head, and Rowena looked up to see a large battle axe locked against the blade of her father's sword. *Gawain was still alive!* She began to plea with him to be careful, but then she unexpectedly felt a pair of strong, chainmail-clad arms around her and she turned to see Lancelot, who had been significantly wounded in the left shoulder and had apparently lost his helmet, lifting her up from the ground and pulling her a safe distance away from the battle.

"Perhaps you should be elsewhere," Lancelot said solemnly, "or at least look away. You have fought valiantly today, but I fear that such a sight may be unbearable."

"He... he is *still* my father," Rowena responded.

"I know. I promise it will be quick."

Before making her way into the barracks, Rowena took one last, tearful glance at the agonizing scene before her and said a short prayer for the soul of her father, though she knew deep within that his stone heart had long been hardened beyond all hope for salvation. *For whatsoever a man sows,* she thought, *that shall he also reap.*

Once Rowena had vanished from his sight, Lancelot turned back, pushed the throbbing pain of his shoulder wound from his mind, and tightened his grip on Arondight, urgently hurrying toward Gawain, who was now staggering backward at the sheer force of every strike from Hengist's sword.

"You're *weak*, half-breed!" the Saxon general was shouting, "You may look like us and speak our language, but you lack the killer instinct that Woden requires of his true servants! I should have known you were a turncoat from day one. But no matter, that is a mistake which can easily be remedied!"

And with one more powerful swing of his sword, Hengist swiftly disarmed Gawain, who stumbled back and dropped to the ground in pain and exhaustion. But as he raised his weapon high and prepared to deliver the fatal blow, Hengist suddenly felt his ribs crack as the cold Damascus steel of Lancelot's blade entered his chest, slicing through muscle and bone as if they were butter and exiting through his back just below the left shoulder. He dropped to his knees, frozen in shock, and let his own sword fall limply at his feet.

"That's for my father, Ban of Benoic," said Lancelot, "and all the other innocent men and women you've slaughtered."

He reached out for Gawain and helped him to his feet, then retrieved his battle axe and placed it firmly in the injured warrior's shaking hands. "Finish it," he said softly.

From within the barracks, Rowena heard cheers of triumph outside and she knew what had happened. Under normal circumstances, she would have felt as if her heart had been torn in two, reveling in the joy of victory but also cringing at the loss of her only remaining family, brutish as he may have been. Yet her mind was now far from the fate of her father as she stood motionless, doing everything in her power not to fall backward in amazement. Something... *someone* had just slipped through the next corridor. *Could it be?* Her glimpse had only lasted for a brief instant, but the image was unmistakable. She had seen a shadowy figure walking past – a woman clothed all in white with fair skin and flowing black hair.

* * * * *

Above all else, Vortigern was a coward. At least that was the way it seemed as he nervously bustled about the keep of his castle, packing trunks full of gold and fine clothing – *but mostly gold* – in preparation for his planned escape to the Saxon lands of the East. After having spent his entire reign ruling through fear, it now seemed that his enemies no longer feared him, and thus he had no idea what to do other than to flee. He could hear the angry voices of the Britons and Picts and they pounded on the barricaded castle doors, and he knew that soon they would be upon him unless he could somehow slip away unnoticed. Vortigern had never been the type of man to “go down with the ship” anyway. He was more of an opportunist. Indeed, intangible concepts such as bravery, honor, loyalty, or sacrifice had never made much sense to him, with *honor* in particular causing him the greatest deal of confusion. He never saw the profit in it. So instead of abdicating gracefully, or even taking up his sword and fighting to his last breath, he occupied himself with packing trunks full of gold.

His mind had been so occupied with this task, in fact, that he failed to notice when a raven-haired young woman entered the room and stood before him, diligently watching every spineless move he made.

“It’s astonishing that I was ever afraid of *you*.”

Startled at the sound of the young woman’s voice, Vortigern looked up to find Morgana standing in the doorway, barefoot and draped in white linen with a rather menacing-looking crow perched upon her left shoulder.

"Morgana!" Vortigern shouted in surprise, "You're alive! After you vanished in the dark of night so many years ago, most of us thought you dead!"

"Yes, *your majesty*," she answered, her words dripping with contempt, "I *was* dead. But I was given new life by someone far more powerful than *you* will ever be."

Not only did Morgana no longer fear this sniveling worm of a man, but she now failed to understand how it was possible for anyone to do so. A once terrifying, imposing figure now seemed to her almost comical as he scurried around his keep, desperate to salvage what remained of his fortune and run away like a frightened child into the arms of his mother. His thick auburn beard, now overlong, unkempt, and streaked with grey, no longer made him look brutish and untamed, but simply lazy and disheveled, like a homeless vagrant or a senile old madman. His lascivious nature and protruding gut, once symbols of his wealth and elevated social status, now only made him seem weak, like a sad, perverse glutton crippled by his inability to control his appetites for either food or women. He was a feeble, pathetic, worthless little man, and Morgana was mercifully going to put him out of his misery.

"Come now, my dear," Vortigern said, quickly remembering the dire circumstances and brandishing his old Roman spear as an unspoken warning, "You are blocking the doorway. We have to flee this place immediately!"

"Leave?" she replied mockingly, "Who said anything about leaving? I've only just arrived, and I am determined to stay here with you to the bitter end."

"Well then, you leave me no choice!" shouted Vortigern, now overcome with panic and rage, as he thrust the spear toward the young woman's chest. But Morgana didn't flinch, and with a slight wave of her hand the ancient weapon flew from Vortigern's grip and clattered loudly onto the floor.

"What sorcery is this?" he gasped, "No matter. Any power you may possess is no match for this onslaught. The castle walls have fallen and we have lost all chance at victory!"

"I did not come for victory, my king. I came for *vengeance*."

Then Vortigern watched in horror as the crow cawed loudly and flapped its wings while Morgana's already dark eyes filled up with hatred and turned as black as the pits of hell. The room grew deathly cold and an icy wind rose up out of nowhere, tearing at his skin and knocking him violently to the floor in a shaking, shivering mass of dread and cowardice.

"Oh, are you *cold*, your majesty?" Morgana snarled in a deep, gravelly voice that would make Satan himself tremble, "Let's warm things up a bit, shall we?"

With her words still hanging in the air, the flames in the nearby fireplace began to grow and churn as if they had been given a life of their own. Morgana laughed loudly as the fire rose up and began spreading around the room with writhing, serpentine fingers, igniting every piece of furniture, every wall tapestry, every shred of clothing until the entire keep had been utterly consumed by the rampaging inferno. Explosions of flame burst through each window, blowing the shutters from their hinges and sending showers of ash and debris onto stunned onlookers below. Outside of the room, throughout the long, stone hallways, and even down in the courtyard, all other sounds seemed to vanish, and the only thing anyone could hear was a bloodcurdling scream.

It was a scream that Arthur heard as well, and when he finally arrived at the entrance of Vortigern's keep, he noticed that the heavy oak door was hanging in charred splinters from its frame, and the mingled smells of smoke and burning flesh were emanating languidly from within. Curiously, the fire seemed to have died down already and had apparently left everything but the inner keep untouched. Arthur cautiously stepped inside to investigate, and abruptly his stomach turned when he spied Vortigern's smoldering corpse laying crumpled on the floor atop a massive pile of gold coins, with a large black crow greedily pecking at his eyes.

Shouts of victory rang out through the hazy warmth of day, and outside the gaping castle windows, over the eerie sizzling sound of dying flames, he could hear a choir of joyous voices begin to chant, “Hail, King Arthur! Long live the king!”

BOOK TWO: REIGN

"FAITH IS TO BELIEVE WHAT YOU DO NOT SEE; THE REWARD OF THIS FAITH IS TO SEE WHAT YOU BELIEVE."

- AUGUSTINE OF HIPPO

Calling of the Twelve

The gentle plodding of horseshoes on soggy earth accompanied the sweet sounds of rippling water and the carefree singing of sparrows, larks, and thrushes as Gareth followed the river south toward Arthur's newly built castle at Camelot. A cold spring breeze kissed his freckled face, causing him to squint in the morning sunlight and lightly ruffling his unshorn, auburn hair. He had set out from Caledonia nearly a week ago after eagerly accepting an invitation received through his father, the Pictish chieftain Talorc, to join the court of the High King on Pentecost. Since Gareth's people had fought alongside the Britons at the Battle of Badon Hill, his presence would serve to cement the new alliance between their two kingdoms.

The construction of Camelot had been one of Arthur's first and most ambitious acts as the newly crowned King of the Britons. Strategically situated between the great, ancient cities of Astolat and Lyonesse, it was meant to become a central hub in the very heart of Britannia, providing guidance, protection, and inspiration to all those who sought refuge within its walls. Upon its foundation, Arthur issued a declaration that Camelot would be a "shining city on a hill," and a beacon of light and hope throughout the entire known world. It was certainly an admirable dream, though somewhat grandiose, but it was also a dream that aroused something deep, poignant, and almost heroic within Gareth, so much so that part of him dreaded his imminent arrival for fear that the magnificent city might not live up to his lofty expectations. However, Gareth's anxiety soon melted into elation as he emerged from the grove of trees through which he had been riding and peered over a nearby hillcrest, finally catching a glimpse of the closest thing he could imagine to Heaven on earth.

Beyond the sun-drenched Camlann Fields below, perched atop a series of mighty hills rolling with lush grass and heather blossoms, stood Camelot in all its glory. Initially, Gareth had assumed that Arthur's reference to the "shining city on a hill" was merely figurative, but as he gazed upon the towering walls of white limestone shimmering in the sunlight, he was forced to revisit his preconception. Rising skyward in what appeared to be a huge oval surrounding the city, the massive walls boasted additional protection with a series of battlement-topped guardhouses, spaced at regular intervals around the perimeter. A few portions of the wall still appeared to be in the midst of construction, and Gareth watched from a distance as teams of burly stonemasons diligently hoisted large, limestone blocks back and forth along the ramparts. Though surely exhausted and drenched in sweat, these were not slaves, but free men, working arduously to pursue a shared vision of greatness.

Gareth smiled eagerly and then cautiously led his palfrey in a precipitous decent down the steep, rocky hillside, sighing with relief as he finally reached the expansive Camlann Fields, whose vast grasslands stretched out nearly to the horizon. Now safely on level ground, Gareth spurred his horse into a gallop and sped gleefully through the picturesque countryside toward the city itself, the crisp air of late spring filling his lungs with every breath. A handful of tiny hovels dotted the largely untouched landscape, and a few peasant farmers milled about nearby, grazing their livestock and gently prodding them back toward the sparkling, pebble-strewn banks of the River Alen.

A newly-paved cobblestone pathway had been constructed roughly fifty paces from the river's edge, leading to a narrow stone bridge lined with brass, torch-filled sconces. The torches had obviously not been lit, but as Gareth slowly passed over the river, he imagined them illuminating a royal procession as the king as his court journeyed out on a brisk, starlit evening.

Slowing his horse to a trot, Gareth soon ambled up a gentle incline toward the main gate, which was flanked by a pair of barbicans and several elevated archery towers. He gazed in wonder as he approached the immense oaken doors, which had been elaborately inscribed with Arthur's emblem, a soaring, golden eagle with a Celtic cross upon its chest.

"Ho, there!" called a boisterous, unseen voice from atop one of the barbicans.

"Hello!" Gareth answered, "Is anyone there?"

Then as he glanced upward, Gareth noticed a beardless young man with narrow shoulders and short, dark hair peering down at him from the battlements.

"Up here!" the young man shouted, "Welcome to Camelot! Would you mind stating your name and business?"

"I am Gareth, son of Talorc, and I have come to join the council of King Arthur on behalf of my Pictish brethren."

"Ah, Gareth! Yes, I remember now. Merlyn mentioned you were coming. Welcome! I am Bedivere, the king's marshal. Hold on a moment and I'll open the gate."

The sound of hurried footsteps loudly descending a wooden staircase echoed from within the stone barbican, then came the squealing hinges of a small door, followed by the cumbersome *thunk* of a large bolt lock being pulled free. Gareth smiled and adjusted his posture as the huge gates began to creak open, nervously readying himself to finally meet this new king he had faithfully admired from afar.

But suddenly the heavy oak doors crashed open wide and a massive, armored man riding a black destrier stormed out of the entry way, startling Gareth's own horse, who neighed wildly and lurched back on its hind legs, causing him to fly from the saddle and roll backward down the hill and into the river.

Mortified, Bedivere scurried toward the water's edge and offered Gareth his hand, quickly pulling him to dry ground and apologizing profusely for the unexpectedly rude welcome he was receiving. Meanwhile, Arthur and Lancelot came running through the gates on foot, breathing hard and desperately calling after the big man on the black horse.

"Don't do this, Maleagant!" Arthur shouted, "You've been a part of this from the beginning! Yet you desert us *now?*"

"I was part of a *rebellion!*" bellowed Maleagant, turning back to reply after angrily yanking his destrier to a halt, "My sole intent was to overthrow a tyrant! I had no desire to simply replace him with another!

"A *tyrant?*" Lancelot called back in confusion, "Hardly! Under Arthur's leadership, we have become a nation of *laws*, not of men, Maleagant. Laws that apply to *all* people, from the lowliest peasant up to the king himself! Laws meant not to enslave, but to set men free!"

"All law is slavery," the big man grumbled. Then he turned away hastily and rode into the distance, his immense silhouette growing ever smaller until it disappeared over the horizon.

Silence reigned in the minutes after Maleagant's departure. Arthur and Lancelot both stood aghast, utterly astounded by this unforeseen development; Gareth just felt awkward, wishing he could stealthily slink off somewhere; and Bedivere was far too embarrassed to attempt even a rudimentary introduction of their newly arrived guest. And so the four of them simply loitered around in front of the gatehouse for what seemed like ages, intentionally avoiding eye contact, until Arthur finally broke the stalemate and began to speak.

"Maleagant is a powerful warrior and a strong ally," he said wistfully to no one in particular, "Well, at least he *was* a strong ally until now. But it seems he never shared our vision. I blame myself for failing to perceive the darkness within him. Perhaps I was blinded by my own idealism or some misplaced need to always see the best in others. No matter. For a man such as Maleagant – one who seeks only anarchy and chaos – the field of battle is his only true home, and the strength of a sword the only law he respects. God save him."

"God save him," echoed Bedivere and Lancelot.

But Gareth remained uncomfortably silent, still standing a few feet away from the other men, soaking wet, holding tightly to the reigns of his horse, whom he had finally managed to placate, and feeling as if he had accidentally intruded upon a private conversation from which he was now unable to extricate himself. Gareth wished that he could somehow disappear, or maybe turn back time and reattempt his entrance altogether; however, Arthur eventually noticed his presence and turned to greet the anxious stranger.

"And you must be Gareth!" Arthur exclaimed, his demeanor suddenly much more jovial, "I do apologize for the mess you walked into this morning, though I'm glad you've arrived safely. We've all been waiting for you! Of course, with Maleagant's untimely desertion, our gathering will now be one man short, but I've always believed that quality is far more important than quantity. Wouldn't you agree?"

As Arthur spoke, Gareth at last began to study this man he had idolized based solely on incredible stories of questionable veracity, which he had heard secondhand from his Pictish brethren who fought at Badon Hill. Yet now that he stood before him, Arthur instead seemed rather… *ordinary*. Contrary to the legends, the king was not eight feet tall, nor did he appear to be the type of fearless, swaggering warrior who had allegedly slaughtered dozens of witches and giants during his ascent to the throne. In fact, the burly, sandy-haired warrior standing at Arthur's side fit the description Gareth had imagined far more closely than the king himself.

But Gareth was determined not to be deceived by mere appearances. Who knew what glories might hide beneath such a humble exterior? This man, after all, was still King of the Britons, and he had been the one to finally rid their land of the usurper Vortigern and his cruel Saxon hordes. So the moment Arthur finished speaking, Gareth quickly dropped to his knees and began reciting the salutation he had so carefully rehearsed on his long ride from Caledonia.

"Sire, behold Gareth, your humble servant. I bring greetings from my father, Talorc, son of Aniel, ruler of the Picts, and I kneel before you to offer tribute. On this day, I willingly grant you my service in life or death, forsaking..."

"Come now, stand up, man," Arthur interrupted as he reached down and pulled Gareth to his feet, "I may be king, but I'm not God. You will soon discover that we are all brothers here – all *equals*. No one sits at the head of my table. In fact, such a feat would be impossible! Come and see."

Arthur mounted his white courser and led Gareth inside the bright limestone walls of Camelot as Lancelot followed closely behind and Bedivere tarried a moment to bolt the massive oaken doors behind them. The cobblestone pathway that had led up to the main gate continued within, winding and meandering through orchards and farmland, with stables and thatched cottages popping up here and there throughout the grassy pastures. The pleasurable chirping of songbirds and the gentle, squishing sound of horseshoes trudging through soft, freshly plowed earth filled the morning with an air of comfortable familiarity, helping to calm Gareth's nerves as their small party ventured onward. The peasants working in the fields and tending their livestock all stopped and bowed courteously as the king passed by, though many of the younger children simply smiled brightly and waved, with one even rushing up eagerly with tiny arms outstretched. And though Gareth fully expected the child's boldness to be rewarded with a stern look from Arthur and a scolding from her father, the king instead smiled back, dismounted, and knelt down to meet her, lifting her skyward and embracing her as if she were his own. Moments later, as Gareth watched the little girl excitedly scurrying through the fields toward her parents, who were now beaming with pride, he began to realize that Arthur was in fact far from ordinary.

Before long the pastureland came to a gradual end and the cobblestone pathway widened as they approached several rows of merchant houses, meat and produce markets, smithies, and textile shops, all peddling their sundry wares to any potential customer within earshot. Gareth winced at the mingled smells of butchered meat, fresh fish piled high in the sun, steaming cauldrons of wool dyes made from roots, berries, and herbs, and the metallic smoke billowing from a nearby forge. Yet while the combination of odors was certainly pungent, its commonplace friendliness made it not altogether unpleasant.

"So tell me, Gareth," Arthur began, continuing the sociable banter that had filled most of their ride, "Why did you not join your fellow Picts in the siege of Badon Hill? I've heard tell that you're a skilled and cunning warrior."

"It was my father's will, sire," Gareth answered, "My men and I were asked to remain behind in our homeland to help protect the children and elderly while the lion's share of our warriors fought against Vortigern."

"And what of the women?" queried Arthur.

"Pardon my frankness, sire, but if a band of Saxon soldiers were to come upon any Pictish women, it would be the *Saxons* who needed additional protection."

Gareth and Arthur both chuckled lightly and carried on with their casual conversation, riding onward until they were finally within eyesight of the timber walls of the Great Hall. As great bells rang out in celebration of the Pentecost holiday, Gareth glanced up and noticed an ornate stone cathedral dedicated to Saint Stephen, with the morning sunlight illuminating the Biblical stories detailed in its intricate stained-glass windows. On one side, the windows were filled with images of Stephen preaching, his trial and theophany, and finally his stoning, as the opposite side revealed parallel images of the life, betrayal, and crucifixion of Jesus. A large, circular window above the door showed a resurrected Christ reigning in Heaven and a restored, glorified Stephen lifting his hands in adoration. It was a fitting conclusion to a tale of love and sacrifice, of persecution and martyrdom, of one man willing to die for his faith and another willing to die for the world.

Arthur was the first to dismount once they reached the Great Hall, and a group of older boys hurriedly scampered out, leading the horses to the stables to be fed and watered. Gareth would later learn that these were all orphans, taken in by Arthur to be trained as squires. Standing near the entrance to the hall was an old man with sparkling eyes and a long, flowing beard, leaning on a large walking staff and stroking the head of a little grey owl perched on his forearm.

"They're all here," the old man said with a grin.

"Thank you, Merlyn," Arthur replied, greeting him with an affectionate embrace, "You do realize that we never would have made it this far without you."

"Oh, hogwash, my boy. I merely gave you a small push in the right direction. As Augustine said, *God provides the wind, but man must raise the sails*."

Merlyn smiled and winked at the king, handing him a well-worn, leather-bound copy of Augustine's *City of God*, which he produced from beneath his cloak. He then walked past their party toward the cathedral, muttering to himself softly in some obscure language, until both his voice and his footsteps were suddenly no longer audible. Puzzled, Gareth peered over his shoulder and discovered, much to his astonishment, that the old man had vanished into thin air. Standing there frozen, wide-eyed, and speechless, Gareth's confusion only increased when the other men simply smirked at his dumbfounded expression and then erupted into a chorus of chaotic laughter.

"I *hate* it when he does that!" Lancelot chortled, "My face looked *exactly* the same my first time!"

"It never ceases to amaze me," added Bedivere, struggling mightily to catch his breath.

Eventually, Arthur reached over and gave Gareth a friendly, supportive pat on the back, managing to hold his amusement at bay long enough to reply, "Fear not, friend! Merlyn comes and goes as he pleases, usually without much regard for the laws of nature. You'll get used to it soon enough." And without another word, Arthur pulled open the door to the Great Hall, motioning Gareth to enter.

The room was large and octagonal, with dark cherry-wood walls rising up to a high, vaulted ceiling. Warmth poured from a massive fireplace, which burned and crackled on the far side of the chamber, and perched midway up each wall were small brass sconces, whose flickering torchlight filled the room with a pleasurable glow. And in the middle of the floor, resting atop a massive bearskin rug, stood a large, round table. Gareth noticed several other men already seated, and as Lancelot and Bedivere entered the room behind him, they took their places as well. Indeed, Arthur had not been speaking figuratively when he said, *No one sits at the head of my table*, for it had neither head nor foot. Even the king himself sat down in a chair that was no larger or more ornate than any other.

Intriguingly, the table appeared to be made of some type of polished stone rather than wood, and thus the light from the torches was easily reflected in its radiant luster. As a matter of fact, the entire table must have been carved from a single, enormous piece of rock, and its size and obvious weight caused Gareth to wonder how Arthur ever managed to fit it through the door, unless the room itself had been specifically built around this astonishing table. Locating an empty seat, Gareth also observed a sequence of Latin words that had been engraved in a circle around the center:

SANCTITAS • FIDELITAS • AEQVITAS • PIETAS • VERITAS

Gareth was certainly no Latin scholar, but he had gained enough basic knowledge to recognize the words for Virtue, Loyalty, Justice, Piety, and Truth.

* * * * *

Once everyone had been seated, a hearty feast of roast lamb, fresh baked bread, dry cheeses, and various stewed fruits was laid out before them, and after Arthur offered the requisite blessing, Gareth's hunger due to his long journey got the best of him and he began eating politely yet ravenously. However, despite his preliminary desire to focus solely on satiating his appetite, Gareth managed to slow down for long enough to meet and greet the other founding members of Arthur's newly christened Council of the Round Table.

Directly to his right sat Tristan, a young Celt not much older than he, with dark, shoulder-length brown hair and a long scar just above his left eye. He was rather serious and quiet, but friendly enough, and he talked at length about his love of hunting and his beautiful new wife Isolde, who was waiting for him at her family's home in nearby Lyonesse.

Kay, seated to Gareth's left, was perhaps the polar opposite of the stoic Tristan. He was jovial, garrulous, and quite loud, constantly telling crude jokes which seemed to fall flat with just about everyone except Kay himself, who always found each of his bawdy tales to be a stone riot. As the meal continued, Gareth discovered that Kay was both a highly skilled archer and Arthur's half-brother, thus he quickly understood why the redhead's oddly endearing boorishness was tolerated.

The eldest members of the council were Sagramore and Palamedes, both former Roman soldiers who had settled in Armorica after the death of their general, Magnus Maximus. Sagramore, an immense, dark-skinned Numidian from North Africa, spoke very little, but his voice was deep and resounding in a way that commanded the attention of all within earshot. Palamedes was a Sarmatian who was born far to the east in Scythia and still held to his pagan religion, which Gareth found somewhat odd based on the overtly Christian makeup of the remainder of the group. However, Gareth was familiar with his own extended Pictish family clinging to Celtic polytheism, and Palamedes was loyal, good-hearted, and told fantastic stories. The two struck up an easy rapport.

Across the table, talking loudly and often arguing amongst themselves, sat Aglovale, Lamorack, and Percival. They were the sons of Pellinore, an aging, absent-minded Briton who had once served under Uther Pendragon. All three young men clearly held their father in great esteem, having joined Arthur's council as a sort of tribute his legacy, hoping to carry on the torch he had passed. Percival, the youngest, seemed especially eager, as he deftly avoided the mostly tedious, often humorous bickering with which his two siblings were constantly engaged, and instead spent much of his time listening attentively to Gawain, whose elaborate tales of battle and espionage had him absolutely rapt with fascination.

Indeed, Gareth also found Gawain particularly intriguing, mainly because he appeared to be hiding so much internal distress and conflict. Much of this perception came from the knowledge that Gawain was half Briton and half Saxon and had spent long periods of time as a spy, living amongst Vortigern's army and feeding information to his allies in the British rebellion. A man would have to be made of stone in order to avoid being affected by such an experience, especially one whose cultural identity was already so muddled. However, on a few occasions, Gareth did notice Gawain's demeanor growing markedly brighter whenever he spied Rowena, a feisty young Saxon girl who had joined Arthur's cause, as she passed through the chamber assisting with their meal.

At Arthur's left and right hand sat Bedivere and Lancelot, respectively, who were clearly the king's most trusted friends and advisors. Throughout the feast, Bedivere mainly played the role of host and facilitator, staying seated only to eat and spending the remainder of his time roaming around the table, introducing himself to everyone, making small talk, and ensuring that each man had all he needed. *He really should have been a merchant,* Gareth mused, *because this man could easily sell a pail of water to a fish.* Lancelot, however, remained by Arthur's side, locked in conversation. It was a conversation punctuated by laughter, seamlessly shifting from serious matters to levity without a single awkward pause. And though he was certainly never rude or dismissive to anyone present, it became apparent that Lancelot shared a bond with Arthur far beyond that of king and consul.

There was one remaining vacant place at the table, the seat formerly belonging to the now departed anarchist, Maleagant, and its blatant emptiness loomed like a dark shadow as King Arthur finally rose up to speak.

"Brethren," he began, "I have called you here on Pentecost, for today is a day of rebirth. The old ways are dead and gone; all things will be made new. You see, although I stand before you now as king of these lands, many of you know that I was raised not in palaces or great halls, but in a humble monastery, tending a small garden with my nose buried in books. Friends, this great stone table is round for a reason. It has no head or foot, that no man may be first or last – *even the king*. This has been my dream since Vortigern's fall, and I have gathered you together in hopes that it may soon be realized."

Gareth was a bit surprised to have had detected a hint of apprehension in Arthur's demeanor as he first began to speak, but as the king continued, his self-assurance and fervor slowly increased until all trepidation seemed to fall away like chaff from harvested wheat on a hot summer morning.

"No longer will a sovereign rule over his people with an iron fist, but instead he will serve them with open hands," Arthur declared in a voice growing in both resolution and defiance, "In this new order of knighthood, strength will not be abused for plunder and subjugation, but harnessed to free others from oppression. For those of you without lands, today lands will be given to you – not to dominate, but to protect from harm. I charge you to give of yourselves in order to provide aid to all those in need. I charge you never to kill for material gain or vengeance, but only in defense of the innocent."

Arthur then paused for a moment and glanced over at Maleagant's unoccupied seat, clearly still shocked and hurt by the strong, silent warrior's abrupt desertion.

"Sadly, not all those who were once among us share this dream. There is now a vacant place at our table, and I fear that gazing upon it day by day may cause some of us to lose faith and wonder whether the ideals Camelot was built upon represent nothing more than misplaced arrogance and naïve, wide-eyed optimism. Truly, there are those who call our laws tyranny, wishing to live by their own rules based on a corrupted notion of freedom. But I tell you now, this fragile dream we hold dear and these principles by which we live and govern must either be righteous and true for all mankind, or else righteous and true for none. After all, is a Briton more worthy of liberty than a Pict or Saxon? As it is written in the scriptures, *there is neither Jew nor Greek, there is neither slave nor free, there is neither male nor female; for you are all one in Christ Jesus*."

* * * * *

They all took a solemn vow on that bright spring morning in Camelot, gathered together around the Round Table. Just as Arthur had entreated, the members of his council promised to protect and defend, to use their might for right, and to love others as themselves, no matter their rank, lineage, or station in life. And while all were earnest, some were certainly more affected than others. Gareth, in particular, felt as if he might explode as a deep sense of pride and gravitas swelled within his breast. But as much as it moved him to be entrusted with Arthur's wonderful dream, his attention kept drifting back to the empty seat at the table, which seemed to stare back at him with a mysterious, threatening gaze.

A Lily Among Thorns

Rowena pulled her heavy woolen cloak tightly around her shivering body as she peered out of the tower window at the icy rain falling gently in the late night air. There was just something about the monotonous, almost musical sound of rainfall that she always found soothing, and when coupled with a goblet of warm milk, like the one she was now enjoying, it became a natural sedative nearly potent enough to put her to sleep right where she stood.

Thinking back on the past few years, which seemed to have blown by like a raging whirlwind, Rowena could scarcely believe how dramatically her world had changed in such a short period of time. Following the initial gathering of Arthur's council on Pentecost, the newly-knighted warriors had scoured the land with a seemingly inhuman vigilance, making peace accords with tribal chieftains in the north, suppressing insurrections by rogue warlords and foreign antagonists – including an attempted invasion by the Roman usurper Lucius Tiberius, and driving any remaining Saxon raiders back to their settlements near the sea. However, by Arthur's order, any Saxons who agreed to yield to his rule and live in peace were permitted to stay on their lands, much to the chagrin of some of his knights, Tristan in particular, who had still not forgiven the pagan interlopers for their unholy alliance with Vortigern. Thankfully, even if some questioned the decisions of the King, they never lost faith in the man himself.

Legends quickly spread far and wide heralding the nobility and fearlessness in battle of King Arthur and his Knights of the

Round Table. Bedivere's even-handed diplomatic prowess and inspiring oratory led to him being known by friend and foe alike as the *Voice of the King*, a title he wore with pride; the strength and dexterity displayed by Gareth on the battlefield had turned the young knight into a national hero among the Picts of Caledonia, even among his own kith and kin; Percival's unrivaled generosity, selflessness, and concern for his fellow man rendered him an ideal ambassador for the fragile dream that was Camelot; and even Kay, despite his perpetual boorishness, had displayed a proclivity for financial administration and was named court *seneschal*, earning the esteem of his fellow knights as well as Ector, his proud father.

But no man's acclamation rivaled that of Lancelot, the King's Champion, matchless in courage, chivalry, and devotion. His heroic exploits as Arthur's mightiest warrior and closest friend had made his name nearly synonymous with knighthood.

Of course, Rowena had no intention of dismissing the accomplishments of Gawain, her own husband, the man who was currently snoring loudly in the bed directly behind her. A tribute to the Saxon race, his loyalty and fervor knew no bounds, though he was certainly not without his imperfections. But Rowena saw past his fierce facade to the pensive, tender soul beneath. They had only been married for a few short weeks now, following a lengthy courtship, and most who had witnessed their constant flirtatious interactions around the castle had begun to wonder why on earth it had taken them so long to finally tie the knot. Their common heritage made them an ideal match, along with the joyful camaraderie they shared as partners in battle. Indeed, Rowena was deeply and happily in love, although as the dull roar of Gawain's noisy breathing began to drown out the pattering rainfall, she thanked God for making her a heavy sleeper.

As for the deserter Maleagant, his seat at the Round Table thus far remained empty. It was said that he retreated to his ancestral home in the land of Gorre, and most assumed he would be neither seen nor heard from again.

Memories flooded Rowena's mind like river waters gushing through a broken dam, as thunder rumbled through the night sky like immense celestial drums. A flash of lightning behind the billowing clouds caught her eye as it briefly illuminated the pitch black landscape, and in that moment, Rowena noticed a frail, cloaked figure leading an injured horse by its reigns and begging for shelter from the storm. With another flash, she saw the figure's tightly clenched fists hammering against the castle doors in beleaguered desperation as the exhausted hackney gingerly lowered itself down onto the mud-covered ground in an act of weary surrender. Sensing the urgency with which the figure pleaded, Rowena bolted from the window and roused a groggy Gawain, who reluctantly and sleepily stumbled down the hallway after his wife toward the western gate.

* * * * *

The visitor sat in silence before the roaring fire, bundled up in blankets and wearing a clean, dry set of clothes that had been generously donated to her upon her arrival. Her own torn and tattered garments, soaking wet and yet still reeking of sweat and cheap perfume, had been promptly discarded. She held a bowl of hot broth, motionless, mere inches from her face, temporarily content to simply feel its radiated warmth in her numb, shaking hands and to allow the comforting aroma to lift her battered spirit. A few paces away on a small wooden bench sat her rescuers, a man and a woman, both blonde with striking Germanic features, and still somewhat awkwardly dressed in their nightclothes. The woman, Rowena, had tried fruitlessly to engage her in casual conversation, or at least obtain her identity, but after several failed attempts, she seemed to have resigned herself to tending the fire and intermittently poking her husband in the ribs to keep him from nodding off.

"Um... your pack horse should be just fine," Rowena began, apparently hoping to find a safe topic to breach.

"That's wonderful to hear. Thank you," the visitor replied in a quiet voice, not much more than a whisper.

"Yes, she's certainly cold and exhausted, but her ankle wound is far from serious. After a good night's rest, she'll be tended to by our dear friend Sagramore. He's an experienced Numidian horseman, you know."

But the visitor said nothing more.

Long before even arriving at the castle, she had made the determination to speak as little as possible. Despite the kindness and hospitality of these strangers, the visitor knew she would be turned away if ever they discovered the truth about who she was, or rather, *what* she was. Of course, part of her still longed to throw herself on the mercy of the new king, for she had heard that Arthur was a compassionate man. However, having already been cast out and disowned by her own father, she could ill afford for her sins to be unearthed and dragged once again into the unforgiving light of day. There was safety in the darkness. There was comfort in the darkness.

At that moment she was reminded of the Prodigal Son, a wayward young man who was welcomed back by his father with open, loving arms after years of wallowing in debauchery and excess. It was a lovely story, to be sure, but also terribly naïve. After all, how could such profound love exist in this fallen world? Despite her pitiable circumstances, she felt no anger toward her father, nor toward God – only guilt, shame, and sadness, for she now reaped what she had sown.

After silently swallowing the last few mouthfuls of her broth, which by now was only lukewarm, the visitor noticed that the heavy rainstorm had subsided and the pale light of dawn was already beginning to stretch its delicate fingers over the nearby windowsill. Unable and unwilling to speak further, she simply whimpered, "I'm so tired," and Rowena dutifully led the young woman to a warm bed.

* * * * *

Lancelot was in love. Hopelessly, desperately, breathlessly in love. At least that's what he thought. In truth, his feelings were probably more akin to infatuation or even basic, carnal lust, but their arrival was so intense, so overpowering, so all-consuming after his chance encounter with the beautiful stranger that he scarcely could tell the difference and was now teetering on the edge of madness.

It all began innocently enough.

At Arthur's behest, he had been searching high and low for Gawain, who had not yet arrived at the Great Hall to join the remaining members of the council as they held court following the midday meal. Gawain knew the king's schedule and he was never late, but Lancelot felt far more annoyance than concern, having convinced himself that his friend was simply neglecting his duties in order to steal a few more moments alone with that *new wife* of his. Now, it wasn't that Lancelot *disliked* Rowena – far from it, actually. She was kind, engaging, and surprisingly familiar with battlefield tactics. But he also firmly believed that women inevitably led to weakness.

Just look at Tristan! That love-struck fool scampers off to Lyonesse at least twice a week to visit his wife, Isolde, who's sufficiently pleasant to look at, of course, but what good is she in a world of blood and steel? Come now! At least Rowena knows how to swing a sword! Isolde spends every waking moment baking and sewing clothes and badgering Tristan about having a baby! If you ask me, he's already been unmanned, and at this rate, Gawain will follow soon enough!

Grumbling under his breath, Lancelot approached the door to Gawain and Rowena's chamber and barged in abruptly, sure to find his fellow knight gazing reverently at his wife and writing her flowery love poems or other such nonsense. The thought of it made him nauseous. But instead, Lancelot was greeted with a vision that would change his life forever.

A large, iron bathing tub sat in the middle of the floor, filled with steaming water obscured by islands of soapy residue. And emerging from the tub, like Venus rising from the foamy sea, was the most beautiful woman he had ever seen. She stood with her back to him as waves of dark brown curls cascaded over her supple shoulders and tiny droplets of water flowed gracefully down her womanly curves. Naturally, she was naked, as is typical when one bathes. Yet before his sense of propriety took control, Lancelot silently prayed that this angelic creature would turn around so that he might glimpse the fullness of her glory. It wasn't a conscious thought; it was merely an impulse, but its potency was such that Lancelot's wits abandoned him and he simply stood there, frozen in awe.

"Oh, Rowena, you're back," he heard the young woman say, "Would you mind handing me a towel?"

At the mellifluous sound of her voice, Lancelot suddenly found himself plunged back into reality, and he immediately realized how dishonorable it would look if he were found here, gawking at an unclothed stranger after having blundered into someone else's room without consent. And now the woman, still facing the opposite wall, had apparently mistaken him for Rowena, thus leaving two viable options at this juncture. He could turn and flee, hoping to remain unseen by the woman and anyone else roaming the hallways, but such an act would likely arouse suspicion. Alternatively, he could pose as Rowena for the moment, produce the towel the woman requested, and escape before she turned around.

After a short deliberation, he chose the latter.

Lancelot crept slowly toward the iron bathing tub, careful to step lightly in the way Rowena might, as opposed to his own typical oafish lumbering. He uttered not a word, but hastily retrieved a towel from a small wooden chest near the bed, then cautiously approached the young woman, still stark naked and as breathtaking as a mountain sunrise. *Dear God, she was incredible*. His face flushed with heat as he grew closer to her, yet he maintained enough composure to reach out and gently drape the towel over her right shoulder. *He had done it!* As she began to dry herself, Lancelot turned toward the door, smiling at the apparent success of his little ruse.

"Thank you," the woman called out.

And without a second thought, Lancelot casually answered back, "Oh, you're welcome!" in his own rich baritone, having neglected to even attempt feigning a higher register.

For a moment, there was silence. The young woman turned toward Lancelot and time slowed to a crawl as their eyes locked in panic and astonishment. They stood motionless, studying one another's blank expressions, until something within Lancelot snapped and he sprinted for the door, with frantic shouts of "I'm sorry! Wrong room!" following in his wake.

* * * * *

By the time Lancelot arrived at the Great Hall, Arthur had already begun holding court, and Gawain had taken his seat at the Round Table. He looked exhausted. His brown eyes were only half open, his tunic was wrinkled, and his thick blonde hair was littered with tiny bits of straw.

"Where have you been?" Lancelot whispered as he sat down next to his disheveled friend, "I've spent half the morning looking for you."

"I slept in the *stable,*" answered Gawain with more than a hint of disdain in his voice, "Rowena took in a vagrant girl who came banging at the castle gates in the middle of the night, and she determined that the two of them would share our bed while I found lodging elsewhere. I tried to protest, but Rowena argued that it would have been inappropriate for me to sleep in the same quarters as a young, unmarried woman."

Lancelot began to grow flustered, unsure of how to respond after his decidedly scandalous encounter. Gawain obviously did not yet know what had happened, but had the girl told Rowena? More importantly, *would she tell Arthur?* As a precaution, he quickly decided to wear the mask of ignorance.

"Oh... a vagrant girl, eh? Did she give you her name?"

"No, she refused," Gawain sighed, his prickly demeanor beginning to soften, "Obviously the young woman has been through something traumatic, and there are clearly ghosts in her past that she is either unable or unwilling to face. She does, however, look slightly familiar. Perhaps we've met her father before. Ah, here she comes now."

A chill of terror crept down his spine, and Lancelot turned to see Rowena leading the beautiful stranger into the Great Hall, now clothed in a simple yellow dress with her wild, brown curls pulled back in ribbons. Of course, she could be wearing a burlap sack and still look like an angel. As they passed by, Lancelot felt a powerful inclination to avoid eye contact at all cost, but her loveliness forbade him to look away and he stared unabashedly. Every rational instinct within him told him to either drop to his knees and beg for forgiveness or to flee in humiliation, but his muscles refused to obey his mind, and within moments the young woman was before him. However, much to Lancelot's surprise, she met his gaze and simply smiled knowingly, and he began to suspect that the details of their initial liaison still remained secret. Moreover, Rowena wore no expression of outrage or distress, but simply took notice of Gawain's unkempt status and kissed him lightly on the forehead as a sign of both thanks and apology.

* * * * *

The visitor grinned and barely stopped herself from giggling as she studied the fearful, embarrassed, enamored expression worn by the brawny, sandy-haired knight who had intruded upon her bath earlier. She really should have felt embarrassed as well, but honestly, this was not the first man to have seen her in a state of undress, and thus she was barely fazed by his sudden invasion of her privacy. In fact, she was actually a bit flattered by his nervous gawking.

As she strode past her anxious admirer, Gawain looked up and nodded at her in greeting, and she silently hoped that he hadn't been too inconvenienced by the previous evening's sleeping arrangements. In truth, she would not have minded bedding down in a pile of straw herself, but Rowena had been insistent. *A stable is no place for a lady*, she had said, although the visitor hardly felt that "lady" was a fitting epithet. As she followed Rowena around the table, they eventually came to a man, not much older than she, with stringy brown hair and a short beard. He was not as handsome as the sandy-haired knight, but he had kind eyes and a warm smile.

"Ah, good day, my lady!" the man said, "Rowena mentioned that you would be joining us today. Please make yourself at home, for you are most welcome. I am Arthur."

The visitor's eyes popped open wide. *Him? This was the High King? This was the great warrior who had vanquished Vortigern and crushed the stranglehold of the Saxons? He was hardly an imposing figure.* Still, he had shown her charity and welcomed her into his home, so she quickly remembered her place and bowed deeply.

"I'm honored, sire," she said with reverence.

"Oh, never mind all that," the king replied, taking her by the hand and lifting up so that her eyes met his own, "You're our *guest*, not a servant. Feel free to call me Arthur. Should you require anything during your stay in Camelot, you need only ask and it will be provided."

"Thank you... *Arthur*," the visitor answered, "The rumors of your kindness were certainly not embellished."

The king smiled and bowed his head, and then she walked with Rowena to a row of chairs near the hearth where they could sit and watch the proceedings. As the visitor promptly learned, Arthur and his knights now spent most of their days tending to smaller, local matters, having already dispensed with many of the larger problems facing the kingdom, such as rebellious warlords and leftover Saxon raiders. In the years that had passed, chaos had given way to peace and justice, though there was always work to be done. At the moment, Sagramore and Percival were away in Astolat, dealing with a company of roving bandits who had been causing trouble for the villagers, and Kay had just ridden out to the countryside to ensure that an aging widow was fairly compensated for a field of land stolen from her years ago during Vortigern's reign. Many people came and went, asking dutifully for the king's favor, which he always gave freely, showing no favoritism and turning none away. Needless to say, the visitor was duly impressed. But there was one favor granted that day which went far beyond inspiring and left her both astounded and speechless.

A middle-aged woman approached the Round Table, though she did not attempt to bow or kneel as so many others had done. Instead she stood firm, her head held high and her gaze cold, hard, and steady. Her long, grey hair looked frazzled, and her clothing, obviously once costly and beautiful, was now dingy, fraying, and torn. She carried a man's tunic draped over her shoulder. It was stained with blood.

"My name is Bellicent," she said stoically, "and I was once the wife of your enemy, Lot of Orkney. My husband was a powerful baron in the lands to the north, and he fiercely opposed your coronation, though for what reasons I know not. Nevertheless, I faithfully stood by his side then as I do now, and his hatred became my own. But his war against Camelot ended when he was slain by your own hand, and while you and your men rejoiced in victory, I was left to bury his body and watch our realm fall into ruin. With my husband dead and gone, his cruel brother has ravaged our lands and carried off my only son, Agravain, dooming him to a life of imprisonment and torture. And so, as recompense for your offenses, I demand that you send one of your knights to do battle for me, kill the treacherous thief, and return my son to his rightful place at my side. If you refuse, may you be damned to the fires of Hell."

The woman then removed the tunic from her shoulder, the Orkney emblem torn and bloodstained, and tossed in to the floor at Arthur's feet, her jaw set and her stare unwavering. A hush fell over the Great Hall, and as the visitor looked on in disbelief, she was certain she could hear her own quickening heartbeat over the deathly silence. At last, Gawain was the first to speak, rising from his seat with righteous indignation and glaring at the impertinent woman, sword drawn and ready.

"Blasphemy!" he shouted, "How dare this wench mock the High King with such barefaced insolence! Arthur, merely give the word and I will dispatch her where she stands!"

"Hold, Gawain," the king answered, "Sheath your sword and be seated. I will ensure she is answered rightly."

As Arthur stood and approached the woman, it seemed at first as if he would strike her down. However, one look into his eyes revealed that he bore no anger or resentment, but instead was overtaken with sorrow. The harsh realities of war had never sat well with Arthur, and since rising to the throne, he had made it his life's work to somehow strike a balance between peace and justice in these dark times. Indeed, fighting wars against insurgence had brought peace to Britannia – but at what cost? A single tear rolled down his cheek, and a collective gasp echoed throughout the chamber as the king dropped to one knee and lowered his head in submission.

"Bellicent of Orkney," he began, "I have grievously wronged you. It is apparent that you loved and supported your husband, and in that I can find no fault. Though he and I were enemies once, let not such hatred follow us all to our graves, and allow me the chance to mend that which is broken. I now beg your forgiveness and wholeheartedly grant your request. All that you ask and more will be given to you, with hopes that this meager offering may, in some small way, bridge the chasm that has been opened between us."

After a seemingly endless silence, the woman's icy stare eventually began to soften, if only slightly, and she hesitantly muttered, "I thank you, sir, and accept your offer."

"Gawain," the king called out, rising again to his feet and turning to face the outspoken knight, "Since you appear so eager to serve, I ask that you grant your assistance to this woman and rescue her son from his captivity."

"But Arthur, she is the wife of your enemy!" Gawain replied, still bewildered by the king's unorthodox reaction.

"That she is, yet is it not written that we are to love our enemies? Be mindful, Gawain, that though her heart is heavy, this woman did not come with threats of violence, but with an honest plea for help. We have sworn ourselves to defend the defenseless. She is no less worthy than any other."

The realization soon dawned on Gawain that he had failed in his incensed response to the woman's petition, and he briefly hung his head in shame before humbly kneeling before her and proclaiming loudly, "Madam, I offer you my sword."

As the visitor beheld these acts of selfless benevolence, a warm sensation began to swell within her chest, and her soft, green eyes welled up with tears. Hurriedly she wiped them dry, desperately hoping that no one in the room had noticed her sudden emotional outburst, yet she remained unable to wipe Arthur from her heart, for a blossoming sense of admiration and devotion had taken root and was steadily growing. *Who was this man, so strange and different than any other she had ever known? How could a king so effortlessly show favor to his enemies? Furthermore, how could anyone, royalty or not, respond to unveiled hatred with such mercy and compassion?* The more she turned it over and over in her mind, the more she began to wonder if perhaps such profound love as shown to the Prodigal Son could exist in this fallen world after all.

"Rowena?" the visitor whispered softly to the young woman seated next to her.

"Yes?" the fair-haired Saxon answered.

"When next you speak with the king, you may tell him that my name is *Gwenivere*."

Gareth and Lunette

A misty, summer rain had fallen throughout the grey morning, further saturating the dew-soaked ground and darkening the already gloomy atmosphere as Gawain and Gareth rode their weary coursers back toward Camelot. It had been raining for nearly a week now, and they began to wonder if their unhappy moods might be reflections of the miserable weather, or if somehow it was the other way around. Their horses trotted slowly, exhausted from the long journey and from the increasingly difficult terrain, which their hooves sank into with every step. A third horse trudged through the mud several paces behind them, carrying Agravain, Bellicent's son, whom they both now regretted rescuing.

At Arthur's urging, Gawain had offered to free the young man from imprisonment by his malicious uncle, and Gareth soon extended his services as well, having been deeply touched by the plight of his grieving mother. However, it soon became clear that Agravain was the kind of person that only a mother could *ever* love, and even then begrudgingly.

Apparently, after the death of Lot of Orkney, Agravain had been abducted by his uncle so that the greedy old man could pilfer the family's lands and wealth without having to worry about some vengeful whelp attempting to claim his birthright. The young man was at first kept in relative comfort, always fed well and locked in a bedroom rather than a prison cell, but he eventually became so demanding and obnoxious that his uncle tossed him shackled into the dungeon simply to avoid his bothersome bellyaching. So when Gawain and Gareth arrived, threatening to lay siege to the castle unless the captive was immediately released, they stood waiting for only a matter of minutes until Agravain was delivered to them without dispute, bound and gagged with a note pinned to his collar reading simply: "Good riddance!"

Agravain was like a spoiled toddler trapped in a man's body. He was a self-centered, narcissistic, ungrateful little dung pile who had somehow managed to survive into adulthood without having his head severed merely for talking too much. Whatever pity Gawain and Gareth may have once felt for him had now dissipated into barely restrained revulsion, and much of the latter half of their journey had been spent fantasizing about ways to somehow "lose track" of him without disappointing either Bellicent or Arthur. Currently, they were both wishing that they had just kept him bound and gagged.

"I don't know what manner of *rescue* this was supposed to be," Agravain grumbled, "but thus far it has been perfectly dreadful! This old nag you have me riding is hardly proper, and the food is atrocious! Honestly! Nothing but water, dry bread, and a few mouthfuls of salted pork for the entire journey? For goodness sake, I'm Agravain of Orkney! With treatment like this, you might as well have left me in the dungeon!"

"Perhaps we *should* have," muttered Gawain.

"And moreover, my mother may have somehow forgiven or reconciled with your pitiful excuse for a king after he murdered my father, but she does *not* speak for *me*, and I swear to you that I will still have my vengeance."

"Shhh! Quiet!" Gareth snapped.

"How dare you give me orders!" replied Agravain, "Why, if I had my sword about me, and if I had even the slightest idea of our location in this godforsaken country, I would dispatch the both of you and journey on alone..."

"Quit your incessant moaning right now or we'll tie you up and drag you behind that horse all the way to Camelot!" Gareth shouted, more than a little pleased with his not-so-empty threat, "Now give me a few seconds of silence. I think I heard something rustling around beyond the tree line."

As Gareth perked his ears to listen, the rustling sound grew louder and more frantic until a young girl finally emerged from the nearby forest, dashing into the clearing in full sprint and hollering for help as if her long, brown hair were engulfed in flames. She appeared to be uninjured, and no one seemed to be following her, but the moment she saw the mounted knights she began waving her arms in the air hysterically, pleading for assistance with some unspoken dilemma.

"Now what's this all about?" Gawain mused.

"I'll handle it," said Gareth, "Go ahead and take our... *guest* back to Camelot to meet his mother. This little one is probably just playing a game, or perhaps she has misplaced her pet kitten. Either way, I'd wager her company is far superior to *his*. Good luck. I should be back with you before long."

Gawain soon disappeared over the horizon followed closely by Agravain, who was probably still squawking like a chicken with a head injury, as Gareth descended from the pathway and led his courser into a grassy basin where the panic-stricken little girl stood anxiously waiting. He wondered where she had come from, since the nearest village was at least half a day's walk, and she was not nearly old enough to be out in the wilderness alone. Then as Gareth approached, before he could even utter a word of greeting, she rushed up to him and nimbly hoisted herself onto the back of his horse, wrapping her delicate arms around his waist and showering him with tears of supplication.

"Oh, sir!" she cried, "Thank you, thank you! You must help me! They have my sister, and they're going to kill her!"

"Whoa now, hold on a moment," Gareth replied, stuttering slightly with surprise and bewilderment, while also noticing the frayed pieces of rope tied to her wrists, "Slow down a bit and tell me what happened. First tell me your name."

"My name is Lunette," the girl said, "Last night the bad men came while we were sleeping. They took me and my older sister Lenorre and they tied us up and tossed us in the back of a cart, and I could hear them saying that we would both make *worthy offerings*. In the dark time before sunrise I managed to chew through my ropes, so I ran away to get help. But they still have Lenorre! We have to save her!"

"All right, child. All right. Don't be afraid. Who were these bad men? Where did they take her?"

"I don't know who they were. But they kept saying they were taking us to the *Great Stone Circle*..."

Gareth did not wait for the girl to finish. He knew the place of which she spoke, and the mere thought of it flooded his veins with ice. It was a place of savagery and murder, where the pagan Celts still honored the old gods, whose favorite sacrifice was blood. Yes, he knew it well. Without another thought he shouted, "Hold on tight!" then spurred his courser into a gallop and sped off into the waking dawn.

* * * * *

Meanwhile, Camelot was absolutely rife with gossip, most of which centered on the lady Gwenivere, whose identity had been simple to ascertain once she finally admitted her true name. She was the estranged daughter of Leodegrance, Baron of Lyonesse, who had been one of the first nobles to step forward in support of Arthur being crowned king. It was rumored that his daughter had fallen in love with a young Saxon soldier while Vortigern still sat on the throne, and Leodegrance naturally disapproved, resulting in her subsequent withdrawal from his household. Gwenivere still refused to tell anyone what had happened during her years in self-imposed exile, other than the fact that her love affair with the Saxon boy was short lived, but it soon became common knowledge that she had been officially disowned by her father and could never return to Lyonesse.

Thus, whispers of scandal and indecency began to circulate around Camelot when the people discovered her burgeoning relationship with the king.

Ever since that first day at court, she and Arthur had been almost inseparable. And although many thought it improper, since Gwenivere had been dishonored and there were shameful mutterings about her mysterious, sordid past, Arthur refused to yield his love and attention, answering each and every word of condemnation with a stern rebuke. *Her past be damned.* She needed him as the flower needs the sun, and he gave his love freely, not for her beauty or her charm, but because he knew deep within that he was somehow *meant* to love her. While not the torrid, passionate romance often written about in myth and legend, their love was strong and steadfast, like a current beneath the ocean's waves. They would often be seen strolling through the gardens talking and laughing, or huddled by the fireplace while Arthur read to her from one of the many books in Ector's extensive library, which the old monk had left to his adopted son before retiring to his humble home in Dinan. They ate their meals together, they walked the marketplace together, they gazed up at the stars together, and it nearly made Lancelot sick with jealousy.

Weeks had passed since Lancelot barged in on the young woman bathing, but his obsession had burned the image into his mind like a branding iron, and he felt completely powerless in its grasp. She was the most beautiful creature he had ever beheld, and he wanted her desperately. Grace was in her steps, Heaven in her eyes, and every curve of her flawless body was permanently etched on his memory. Her scent was like a drug, and he hungered for her touch more than food or drink, even more than breathing. He barely slept, and whenever he did, her angelic face haunted his dreams. Knowing full-well he could never betray Arthur, not only his king but his oldest friend, he did all he could to push the thoughts away, busying himself by taking long rides through the wilderness, offering his sword for each and every quest that was offered, or even sitting alone with old Pellinore, as he did now, listening for hours on end to his peculiar war stories and confused ramblings.

"...and that is why the Pellinores were always entrusted with the secrets of the White Dragon, having been obligated to hunt for the blasted thing each time it shows itself. It is the perpetual destiny of our bloodline, you know."

"Of course," Lancelot retorted sarcastically, certain that the lovable old fellow had lost his wits again, "It makes perfect sense. Now, what did you say it looked like?"

"But I've already told you, lad," whispered the aging knight, "It is a *wyrm*. A *basilisk*. A monstrous serpent spawned by the Devil himself, who thrives on darkness and chaos and whose gaze alone has the power to kill. In ancient times it was known as *Leviathan*. You see, the appearance of the White Dragon marks the coming of great disaster. I last saw it myself on the eve of Vortigern's arrival in the court of King Uther, and we all know what came of *that* so-called alliance, don't we?"

"Yes, sir. Certainly."

"Indeed! I chased that serpent back and forth three times across the entire known world, in *total* darkness, finally tracking it to the waters of *Loch Ness* in Caledonia. I lost nine horses and one of my legs on that quest. It took nearly 107 years, Lancelot, yet the beast still evaded my capture."

Lancelot badly wanted to laugh, mostly because he knew that the old man's legs were both still attached and in perfect working order, but instead he just smiled and nodded, listening respectfully to Pellinore's tall tales while trying with great diligence not to nod off during one of his lengthy asides. Listening to the old man prattle on for ages may not have been the most glamorous of activities, as he recounted ludicrous adventures and made fantastical claims about his own family history, but it kept Lancelot's mind off of Gwenivere, which had become the mark of a successful day. But as Pellinore quickly began a new story, which involved some nonsense about a tower collapsing due to a pair of monstrous creatures fighting beneath it, Percival suddenly burst into the room with a look of great eagerness and amazement on his face.

"Father!" he exclaimed, "The White Dragon has returned! It was spotted by villagers less than a mile from the castle! Come on, Lancelot. Hurry and gather your arms. A hunting party is being summoned as we speak!"

Lancelot bounded from his chair and followed after Percival in shock and disbelief, while Pellinore simply smiled knowingly, continuing to tell his story to no one in particular.

* * * * *

Lunette had fallen into a deep sleep as she lay huddled against Gareth on his dapple grey courser, galloping urgently toward the Great Stone Circle. Feeling the child's tender frame resting against his back, Gareth could not help but think of his own sister, Cailyn, who was about the same age as Lunette when he left home for Camelot. The very idea of one of these innocents being used for so ghastly a purpose as human sacrifice filled him with rage, but with every second that passed, another portion of Gareth's hope faded, and he feared that his efforts would be all for naught. Having spent most of his youth in the foggy highlands of Caledonia, Gareth was familiar with pagan ceremonies and altar sites, for there were still members of his own Pictish family that practiced them in secret, although the old ways were no longer considered acceptable, even in their society. Still, the screams and cries he had heard as a boy echoed though his memory, and he determined that as long as a heart still beat within his breast, neither Lunette nor her captive sister would suffer the same gruesome fate.

The child finally awoke in Gareth's arms as she was being placed in the tall grass under the shade of a large oak tree. In his haste, the young knight had pushed his horse to such lengths that the poor animal finally dropped dead of exhaustion, and so he carried Lunette for the last few miles, preparing to leave her side only because their destination was now in sight.

"Wait for me here and stay hidden," Gareth whispered. Then he kissed her gently on the forehead and drew his sword, creeping stealthily toward a nearby clearing surrounded by an imposing ring of oblong stone pillars.

As he approached the Great Stone Circle, Gareth suddenly found it difficult to breathe. Evil hung upon this accursed place like a thick blanket of fog, and its forbidding presence was nearly suffocating. Peering out from behind one of the large pillars, he could see a series of bonfires carefully placed in regular intervals around a massive stone slab that was stained black with blood. Gareth shuddered as he imagined how many innocent victims had been put to death on that pagan altar. Within the circle, eight figures dressed in long, black cloaks stood armed but as still as statues, while a ninth figure pulled along a terrified young woman, fully disrobed and bound at the hands and feet, and lashed her to the altar with her tearful face turned skyward. *Surely this was Lenorre*. Unlike the other shadowy participants in this festival of darkness, the ninth figure was not clad in black, but instead wore an iron helmet and shoulder guards over a chainmail hauberk, all of the deepest crimson. At first Gareth thought this discoloration might be a layer of rust, but he quickly realized that the armor had actually been coated with blood from head to toe. This one was obviously the leader or some kind of high priest. Gareth would take *him* alive.

Enraged and resolute, Gareth leapt into the circle of stones shrieking like a man possessed, and with a flash of steel the two cloaked figures nearest to him fell to the ground dead. At the sound of his war cry, the others turned to engage their attacker, but Gareth managed to slay two more before they had a chance to draw their swords, plus another whose initial strike flew wide right, causing him to lose balance and topple over directly in the path of Gareth's blade. Three enemies now remained, not including that high priest in the red armor, and the Pictish knight rapidly shifted to a defensive stance as this dark trio gradually descended upon him.

Had his emotional response to the situation not been so powerful, Gareth would have planned his attack a bit differently. He certainly would have relied more on stealth, and may have even attempted to steal a black cloak and infiltrate this sinister gang of zealots, methodically destroying them from within. However, as it stood he was now trapped in an enclosed area and outnumbered three-to-one, with no reinforcements and no clear strategy of how to proceed. Mouthing a silent prayer, he prepared himself to charge the cloaked warriors, hoping the tactic would catch them slightly off guard, when suddenly a small figure flew screaming onto the back of the man to his left, pummeling him in the head with a broken tree branch.

Gareth's heart sank when he realized it was Lunette.

Fearful for the girl's safety yet conscious of his opportunity to better the odds, Gareth took advantage of the distraction and moved swiftly to his right, kicking at the nearest bonfire and sending a shower of hot ash and burning cinders into the face of one of his attackers. With the hood of his cloak now swallowed by flames, the dark swordsman fell to the earth in agony, and Gareth turned to parry a strike from the second warrior before severing his head with a single blow.

Gareth then spun around to face the third cloaked figure, who had pulled Lunette down from his back and was smiling devilishly while holding a jagged knife to her throat. The game was clear. Either Gareth withdrew, or this monster would kill the girl, dispassionately spilling her blood onto the grassy earth as one might pour water from a basin. But looking down into Lunette's clear blue eyes, the Pictish knight saw courage shining through her fear, and before he could react she reared back and stomped on her captor's foot with such force that he dropped the knife and doubled over, giving Gareth more than enough time to thrust his sword into the fiend's heart.

During this whole incident, the crimson-clad priest had been gazing fixedly at the sky and grasping an ancient *grimoire*, his book of black magic, as he patiently waited for nightfall and the proper hour to invoke the power of some unknown pagan god. He had mostly ignored Gareth, as the lives of his followers meant little to him. They were far less important than the successful completion of this dark ceremony. Even his own life paled in the face of the task assigned to him by his mistress. So he remained in place, standing over Lenorre's supine, naked body, preparing to offer up this spotless virgin in depraved worship.

As the sun finally dipped beneath the horizon, the priest opened his grimoire and began to utter some unholy incantation. Lenorre closed her eyes tightly and cried to the heavens for salvation, trying desperately to drown out his cryptic words, which seemed to reach inside and pull her soul into darkness.

And then the priest abruptly fell silent.

She held her breath in morbid anticipation, but after a few moments that felt like an eternity, she heard a familiar voice whisper, "It's all right now, Lenorre. It's over."

The young woman timidly opened her eyes and saw the sweet face of her sister, weeping with joy as she loosened the ropes. In the distance, the bodies of the eight men in long black cloaks lay crumpled and lifeless near the weakening bonfires. More accurately, there were only six men in black cloaks, since Lunette had appropriated one of them to cover her sister's nakedness, and another had been totally consumed in flame. And at the foot of the altar, flat on his back, lay the priest in the blood-stained armor, with Gareth's boot on his chest and a sword at his throat. Gareth glared at him with righteous anger as the priest shook with panic and begged to be set free.

"No! No!" wailed the priest, "The ritual must continue! The White Dragon must be appeased!"

"Who are you?" Gareth growled, "And who is this White Dragon? *Answer me, you worm!*"

"I am Ironside, the Red Knight of Astolat, Lord of Blood and Fire. Behold, the day of the White Dragon is nigh, and we, his servants, shall soon taste immortality! His shadow will cover this land, plunging all unbelievers into darkness. You *must* set me free! The ceremony must be completed before nightfall! If I fail to deliver this maiden to my lady the High Priestess, I will suffer an end more painful than death."

"Well then," retorted Gareth, "allow me to save you from such a lamentable fate."

Then Gareth's blade silenced him forever.

Curse of the White Dragon

When Gawain returned to Camelot with Agravain in tow, he was greeted by scenes of anxiety and mayhem. Six of the knights, Lancelot, Palamedes, Kay, and the three sons of Pellinore, had ventured out to hunt *Leviathan*, the legendary White Dragon, and two had already returned with debilitating injuries. So Gawain happily left Agravain in the care of his doting mother and rushed to the infirmary, where the court physician was scurrying back and forth tending to Lamorack and Kay, the latter of whom was lying face-down on a table.

"What happened?" Gawain asked Lamorack, who appeared to be nursing a bruised sternum and several broken ribs.

"We tracked the White Dragon to a cavern in a nearby quarry," he replied, his voice straining against the pain, "And at *my* foolish suggestion, we ventured into the blackness after it. Of course, our torches did provide *some* illumination, but the cave was deep and branched into several tunnels – all perfect hiding places for an enormous serpent."

"So the monster was hunting *you* instead?"

"Aye, it was lying in wait for us. We could barely *see* the blasted creature, and its tail caught me in the torso, sending me sprawling onto a bank of jagged rocks. Palamedes took a blow to the shoulder as well, but he remained well enough to stay with the hunt."

"And what about Kay? He barely looks alive!"

"Ha ha!" Lamorack chuckled, "Not to worry. He'll be up and about in a few days' time. The old buffoon slipped on some wet stones and fell on his own quiver, and a stray arrow somehow got lodged in his buttocks! He's only lying on his face like that because it hurts too much to sit!"

"Keep it up, Lamorack!" Kay shouted furiously, "And the moment I can stand again, I'll knock your teeth in!"

"Please, no more!" Lamorack groaned, now quaking with laughter, "You're making my ribs hurt!"

Kay began to utter what he believed to be a scathing retort, but before he could get a word out, the rest of their hunting party stumbled into the room led by Lancelot, who entered with an injured Palamedes slung over his shoulder.

"Good physician!" the brawny knight called out joyously, "Come and tend to this man, for he has won the day!" Then he flung the dark-eyed Sarmatian off his back and onto a nearby table, where he winced briefly and then broke into laughter. Lancelot was clearly drunk on mead, as was Palamedes, whose infirmed state had more to do with the time spent in the local tavern than his mildly injured shoulder.

"For goodness sake, you're all inebriated!" bellowed the physician, "Get out of here right now! Out! Let your friend rest and I'll deal with him once he's sobered up!"

Feigning embarrassment, Lancelot tried to muffle his own snickering and then hoisted Palamedes back onto his shoulder, almost dropping him twice, and wobbled into the Great Hall singing victory songs with an equally drunken Aglovale following closely behind.

"It's shameful, really," lamented Percival, who had clearly chosen to abstain from spirits, "We finally defeat that infernal beast, and *they* carry on like a bunch of children."

Gawain smiled and rolled his eyes, as he was all too familiar with Percival's often over-the-top moralizing, but then quickly pulled up a chair next to Lamorack as they both implored the young knight to tell them all about the hunt.

"Ah, you see, when Lamorack was injured he dropped his torch," Percival began, "and it rolled toward the White Dragon and burned a portion of its scaly hide. Although the fire did not appear to cause it pain, the creature seemed to fear the light, as it backed away and made a terrible sound, something between a growl and a scream, then slithered off into one of the tunnels. We added more pitch-soaked rags to our torches so they burned bigger and brighter, and decided to split up into different tunnels and drive the great serpent into the base of the cavern. Sure enough, it fled from the light, and we finally cornered it in a shallow, subterranean pond."

"So you were able to see the beast up close, in full view?" Lamorack questioned excitedly.

"Aye, we saw it. Horrible, *ghastly* creature. Just as father always said, it was akin to an enormous snake with white, pallid skin – like that of a corpse. The horrendous thing shrieked like a demon from Hell, and its breath reeked of sulfur. Naturally, none of us dared look it directly in the face for fear of its lethal stare, so Lancelot, Aglovale, and I rushed around the cavern splashing in the pond and throwing rocks as a distraction, while Palamedes crept up from behind and severed its slimy head with that massive scimitar he carries around."

"Astounding!" Gawain interjected, "So it's dead then?"

"Well, the others seem to think so, but I'm a bit skeptical," answered Percival, "I mean, yes, we defeated the beast and drove it away from Camelot, and yes, Palamedes did lop off its head. But instead of sinking in the pond, the rest of its body seemed to slither off into one of the tunnels. Granted, I *have* seen ordinary snakes wriggle around a bit after being chopped in two. Then again, if it truly is the great *Leviathan* described in scripture, perhaps it *cannot* be killed. Father did tell us that it was spawned by the Devil."

"Come now, Percival," Lamorack replied dismissively, "You and I both know that Father says a great many things, and very few of them have any basis in reality."

"Oh? And I suppose you don't believe in the omen either? That the monstrous beast only appears on the eve of great chaos and misfortune?"

"My dear brother, what could possibly happen?" countered Lamorack with a smug sense of confidence, "There's no one left to challenge Arthur's reign, the Saxon raiders have been driven out, even the harvests have been plentiful! Over the past few years, the state of this country has shifted from turmoil and despotism to a peace so stable and constant that it borders on tedium! If you ask me, the arrival of that *basilisk* was the first *real* excitement we've had in some time."

"For all our sakes," Percival said, "I hope you're right."

* * * * *

Gwenivere was in Heaven. For the first time in her life, or more accurately, for the first time she could *remember*, she felt totally and completely loved. And whether she deserved it or not, Arthur always treated her like a princess, which went a long way toward making the vulgar comments and roving hands of the drunken men in the taverns sink into the abyss of distant memory. Often times she awoke at dawn expecting this new life to have been nothing more than a pleasant dream; after all, who would believe that a woman such as she, one who had been so damaged by the world, one with such dark secrets, one whose transgressions felt near unforgivable, could possibly earn the love of a king? Of course, she *hadn't* earned it, had she? That was the part that puzzled her the most. Indeed, what had she ever said or done to gain such favor in Arthur's eyes? *Perhaps he was insane*. Deep within, she felt no better than any common guttersnipe, and yet this noble, faithful, kindhearted man willingly held her in his arms each night, gazing into her stormy green eyes with untainted adoration. *But why?* Surely this was a gift from God, and Gwenivere spent each waking hour reveling in the joys that greeted her anew each morning. That is, until one day, when the world around her began to collapse.

The nightmare began in the early hours of morning when most residents of the castle still slumbered securely in their beds. Gwenivere had been dreaming peacefully when she was awoken by a great commotion outside her chamber, and she hastily dressed and emerged to find Bedivere helping a gravely wounded man make his way toward Arthur's quarters. Having first assumed that it was simply a farmer who had been injured in some accident with his tools or livestock, Gwenivere nearly fainted with shock when the man turned and revealed his face. It was Balian, a resident of Lyonesse who had been her father's personal servant since she was a child. Though his clothes were singed and tattered and his beard had gone white, she would recognize this man's gentle eyes anywhere. He had been like a grandfather, serving as her family when she had no other, as Leodegrance was often too preoccupied with the affairs of governance to spend time with his only child. And now the genial old man came before Arthur, his aging, wounded body slumped over in Bedivere's arms, bearing a message that would soon shake Camelot to its very core.

"Sire, I bring grave news from Lyonesse," he wheezed, "Two nights ago the city was attacked. Many have fallen."

The messenger's words were choppy and disjointed, and his breathlessness seemed to be caused by an affliction far more severe than exhaustion from travel. *He had been badly hurt*. Anxious and frightened, Gwenivere rushed to his side, cradling the old man's head in her slender arms and stroking his white hair gently. Their eyes met, and after a few moments Balian smiled with recognition, simply whispering, "Gwenivere..." before his body fell limp and she noticed the growing patch of blood seeping onto her nightgown.

"Balian!" she sobbed, "Oh dear God... Balian!"

For the next several minutes, time stopped for Gwenivere, and every agonizing second felt like an eternity. Bedivere stood by silently while Arthur knelt down in the middle of the stone hallway to hold her tightly as she wept. The only real family she had ever known was slumped over lifeless in her arms, and no amount of tears could wash away her heartache.

"Bedivere," the king finally whispered, "go and wake the court physician. Ask that the messenger's wounds be cleaned and dressed and his body prepared for burial in the churchyard at Saint Stephen's."

"Of course, Arthur," Bedivere replied.

"And please rouse Lancelot as well. We three will ride for Lyonesse at first light."

"You mean we *four*," interjected Gwenivere, as she wiped her eyes and slowly regained her composure.

"Please, my dear," Arthur replied, "You've just endured a terrible loss, and the road ahead may be fraught with danger. There is no need for you to travel in your condition."

"There is *every* need for me to travel!" she cried, "Banished or not, I am loath to stand idly by while my home is destroyed and all those I love put to the sword!"

"Even so, I still fear for your safety. Dry your tears and rest a while, Gwenivere. We will speak of this later."

But despite Arthur's pleas, the resolute young woman could not be dissuaded from her chosen path. By sunrise she had emerged from her chamber with fury in her eyes and fire in her belly. All softhearted concern for her father and the innocent townspeople was buried by her thirst for retribution, and she was quite vocal in charging Arthur to make those responsible pay for what they had done. With great reluctance he ordered that a fresh palfrey be selected from the stables and saddled for her, and along with Lancelot and Bedivere, they set out for Lyonesse to survey the devastation.

* * * * *

It was the smell that reached them before anything else. The acrid scent of ash and smoke lingered above the charred remains of flame-ravaged cottages and barns, and livestock lay slaughtered in the fields, swarmed with black flies and gradually decomposing. But none of these compared to the unmistakable stench of burning human flesh, which haunted the now gutted landscape with traumatic memories of the lost.

The once vibrant city of Lyonesse now lay decimated and nearly uninhabited. Many of the survivors had already fled to find shelter elsewhere, and those poor souls who remained either tended to the wounded or gathered together to dig mass graves for the deceased. The mere sight was almost sickening. It seemed that nothing had been left untouched by this vicious attack, for even the grey stones of the baron's castle were now stained with blood and soot.

Once those castle walls were within eyesight, Gwenivere spurred her chestnut palfrey into a gallop and rushed to the gates, desperately hoping to find her estranged father among the survivors. The others followed, and upon entering, they discovered that the Great Hall was being used as a makeshift infirmary, with beds, chairs, and tables all filled with burned and bleeding victims of the terrible onslaught. The townspeople, seemingly numb to the abject chaos surrounding them, barely flinched when Arthur and his knights came barging through the gates, and none took much notice of them other than a small boy who studied the king curiously for a moment and then grabbed his hand and began leading him hurriedly through the injured masses. When at last they came to a halt, Arthur gazed upon a body that now seemed barely human. Had the chest not been rising and falling with every breath, he would surely have presumed the man to be long dead. His clothes were blackened and torn, and his right arm was missing below the elbow. The chainmail chausses that once covered his legs had been shredded open, exposing peeling layers of burnt flesh, much of which was now painfully melded to the iron mail itself. The right half of his face was burned beyond recognition, leaving Arthur unable to discern his identity until he noticed the gold, lion-crested signet ring on his left hand. Alas, here lay what was left of Leodegrance, Baron of Lyonesse.

Arthur turned and glanced at Gwenivere, fully expecting her to fall weeping upon her father's broken body, begging him to cling to life just long enough for her to say goodbye. But instead she stood still and silent, apparently frozen in shock at the sight of the powerful man she had once known, now gruesomely transformed into a mangled lump of immobile flesh and bones. Then slowly she stepped forward, and Arthur could see fear hiding behind her eyes. However, what remained a mystery was whether she feared the sight of her father's grisly physical state, or whether his judgment and rejection still weighed so heavily on her soul.

"Father?" said Gwenivere meekly.

But there was no response.

"Father?" she said again, slightly louder this time.

And the once great man opened his single, remaining eye.

At that moment, the room seemed to fall silent, rendering the labored breathing of a dying man and the heartbeat of his long-lost daughter the only audible sounds. Leodegrance was clearly unable to speak, and Arthur found it exceptionally difficult to read the expressions of a man whose face was so badly disfigured, but then again, the stream of tears falling from his eye said more than words ever could. With what must have been his last ounce of strength, Leodegrance gingerly raised his left arm and grasped Gwenivere's hand, squeezing it as tightly as he could while sorrow and remorse poured from his gaze. Gwenivere wept as well, sensing her father's unspoken apology and allowing the warm, soothing waters of catharsis to flood her wounded spirit, washing away years of heartbreak and lost love. She then nodded her head softly as a sign of forgiveness and gently set her father's hand down on his own chest, finally stepping back into Arthur's comforting embrace.

Now, Arthur was never sure, but as he looked down at the malformed face of Leodegrance, for one brief second he could swear that he detected a hint of a smile. Yet the image faded as quickly as it had come, and the mortally wounded man soon caught the king's eye, subtly motioning him to come forward. Then with great difficulty, Leodegrance strained and reached out his hand, curiously brushing bloody fingertips back and forth against Arthur's shield.

"Look!" gasped Gwenivere, "He was writing..."

And as her words trailed off into silence, an intrigued Arthur turned his shield around and saw two small words scrawled in blood upon the crest: *KILL ME.*

"He is in pain," Gwenivere said softly, "He is *suffering*."

Arthur nodded anxiously and looked back at Leodegrance, eyes filling with tears as he reluctantly drew his knife. *This was not in his nature. Of course, he had done as much for horses fatally wounded on the field of battle. Was this really so different?* Naturally, Arthur understood the value of euthanasia, but if taking the lives of evil men had always been difficult for him, then taking the life of an innocent man would be nearly impossible. With agony in his stare, Leodegrance wordlessly pleaded with Arthur for mercy, and so he gathered his resolve and gently pressed his knife to the baron's throat.

"Don't fear, my friend," he whispered solemnly, "Soon there will be no more pain or sorrow."

Then Arthur mouthed a silent prayer of benediction and applied pressure. The knife cut effortlessly through the frail, burned skin at the dying man's neck, quickly finding its place, and within moments the flow of blood and oxygen ceased, releasing Leodegrance into the peaceful sleep of death.

"God save him," said Arthur.

"God save him," the others repeated.

After a few moments of silence, Arthur furrowed his brow as if in deep thought, and then his eyes popped open wide and he abruptly turned to his companions. *Tristan was here!* He had taken leave from Camelot nearly a week ago to be in Lyonesse with his wife. *Was he injured as well? Was he even alive?*

The anxious, frantic expression Arthur wore revealed his thoughts to the others before he could even speak a single word. So with minds spinning and nerves frayed, he and Lancelot turned and bolted for the open doorway, hurriedly making their way through the ruined city toward the humble home where Isolde and her family once dwelled.

It took them only minutes to reach their destination, as the cottage was not at all far from the castle gates, and much to their amazement, the home still stood, seemingly free from damage. Thanking the Lord for small blessings, Arthur leaned toward the front door and knocked.

"Isolde? Tristan? Is anyone here?" he called.

After failing to receive an answer, Arthur pushed the door open and cautiously stepped inside.

There he found Tristan, sitting motionless on the dirt floor, his sunken, bloodshot eyes only half open within a face as pale as death. His dark brown hair hung past his shoulders and was littered with dust and straw, as if he had been sleeping in that very spot for several days. Then Arthur saw Isolde's pretty blonde head resting in his lap, with her lifeless body stretched out on the floor alongside him. Dry blood stained the ground beneath her, traced back to a large wound in her torso, and blood covered Tristan's right arm as well, though it was at first unclear from whose body it had come.

"Hello, Arthur," said Tristan. Stoic. Emotionless.

"Oh dear God," Arthur cried as he dropped to his knees, "Tristan, what happened here? Who did this?"

"I couldn't save her, Arthur," he replied, his voice eerily soft and cold, "I tried, but I couldn't save her. There were too many. I... I couldn't save either *one* of them."

Arthur's heart stopped.

"Isolde was with child. She told me only a few days ago."

Then his frozen heart broke in two. For an instant Arthur wished for the earth to open up and swallow him whole, ending his life and saving him from the misery of this moment. *What manner of evil had befallen this place? What had these poor people done to deserve such tragedy?* Behind him he could hear Gwenivere's nimble footsteps as she arrived at the cottage, then her gasps of horror and gentle sobbing as she became aware of the gruesome scene before her. Yet the tears Arthur now wiped from his own eyes were not of sorrow, but of rage.

"I'm so sorry, Tristan," Arthur seethed, "I'm so terribly sorry. But you *must* tell us who did this."

"They came in the night," he answered quietly, "They were dressed in black hooded cloaks, and they kept on demanding... *something*. I don't remember what they called it. Some kind of artifact, I think. They called themselves the Order of the White Dragon. Certain we were hiding this... *thing* from them, they began burning everything in sight, starting with the church. The castle guards tried to resist, but then a woman came. She had pitch-black hair and hollow eyes, and this strange, guttural voice like a demon from Hell. With only a few words and a wave of her hand she sent every one of them flailing to the earth in agony, and the townspeople were left powerless. I don't know why they left me alive. I don't know why..."

"It is not a mere artifact they seek," said a familiar voice.

Arthur looked up to see an old man with a long, grey beard suddenly standing behind Tristan, his large, gentle hands resting upon the grieving knight's shoulders. *Merlyn*.

"They were searching for the Holy Grail," Merlyn continued, "and you must *not* allow them to succeed."

Quest for the Holy Grail

Arthur and his knights sat at the Round Table in somber silence, unenthusiastically picking at their meals and contemplating the strange tales of horror that had just been recounted. The king himself had spoken first, informing the others of the calamity that had befallen Lyonesse, including the tragic deaths of both Leodegrance and Isolde. Each man looked upon Tristan with empathy at the mention of his deceased wife and unborn child, yet the reticent Celt displayed no outward signs of pain or sadness. In the short time that had passed since Isolde's burial, the lost, dispirited lover who had been found cradling his wife on the floor of their cottage had all but disappeared, leaving behind naught but the warrior – a cold man of single purpose, driven solely by vengeance.

Gareth had been the next to speak, filling the room with gasps of amazement as he described his own bloody encounter with the Order of the White Dragon and his subsequent rescue of two young maidens from ritual sacrifice. He had escorted the girls back to their home village, where their grateful father offered him Lenorre's hand in marriage. But Gareth graciously declined, citing his duties at Camelot, when in truth he simply did not wish to hurt little Lunette, whom he was certain had developed a youthful infatuation with him.

Pellinore was also in attendance, seated by the hearth along with Gwenivere and Rowena, impolitely interjecting every now and then to insist he had been correct in predicting that tragedy would befall the land soon after the appearance of the White

Dragon. Everyone endured his unwelcome comments until he began some lunatic rant about how his goblet of wine was haunted and Rowena ushered him off to bed.

Merlyn stood near the hearth as well and paced back and forth before the crackling fire, at times listening with great interest to all that was being said, and at other times staring awkwardly at the ceiling with a distant, inquisitive look on his wrinkled face, almost as if he were mystically communicating with some unseen counselor or confidant. *What a puzzling fellow*, thought Lancelot, his mind harkening back to their first meeting when he was but an eager blacksmith's apprentice filled with dreams of war and glory. *What would Camelot have been without his wisdom and guidance?* Of course, it felt rather strange to have the old man here after such a long time away. He had always been one to come and go when he pleased, but once Arthur had taken the throne, Merlyn began appearing far less frequently, until finally, when the last war had been fought and won, he vanished from Camelot altogether. Prior to his unexpected arrival in Lyonesse, it had been at least a year since Merlyn was seen by anyone, and this fact alone filled Lancelot with dread, as he wondered what crisis could be so dire as to lure the old man back to these hallowed halls.

"The tales you have told are more closely linked than you know," Merlyn finally began, "Just as Tristan discovered, the cruel forces behind this *Order of the White Dragon* are seeking the Holy Grail, and they will destroy all those who stand in their path. I also believe that the ceremony interrupted by young Gareth was not merely some profane virgin sacrifice. Rather, it was something far more sinister. It seems to me that the Order intends to perform a Black Mass before their god, and the Grail itself is meant to be the centerpiece."

"But the White Dragon is dead, Merlyn," Gawain interjected impatiently, "Palamedes slew the serpent himself. Moreover, what makes this *grail* so special, anyway? And why do these foul devils would want it so badly?"

"In the same manner also he took the cup," replied Merlyn, *"saying, this cup is the New Testament in my blood. This do ye, as oft as ye drink it, in remembrance of me."*

He stood silently for a moment, waiting for the truth to sink in, and then seeing bewilderment on the faces of Arthur and his knights, mercifully offered a clearer explanation.

"The White Dragon lives, my friends. Did you truly believe that an ancient hellbeast such as Leviathan could be killed with weapons forged by man? Those who serve him seek the cup of Christ, *the Holy Grail*, blessed at the Last Supper and endowed with the power to heal by innocent blood that was shed for the guilty. It was brought to this land more than 400 years ago by Joseph of Arimathea, who became the first Christian missionary to the pagan peoples of Britannia. In those days, the cup was kept safe in Lyonesse by Joseph and his son Josephus, which is why it was initially sought there by the cloaked riders."

"But the Grail is *not* in Lyonesse," growled Tristan, "Those cowards destroyed our homes and murdered our loved ones for nothing! *For absolutely nothing!"*

"Aye, it was moved long ago to a forgotten place. I know not where it lies, nor have I been given the sight to locate it on my own. Such a task may only be undertaken by mortals. I only know that Josephus was last known to reside on an island to the distant north, a faraway place named *Ultima Thule* by the Romans – the end of the known world. You must make haste, for if the Priestess of the White Dragon obtains the Grail, she will corrupt its powers through dark sorcery, granting herself and her followers unnatural immortal life."

"But Merlyn, how is that possible?" Arthur inquired, "How can men corrupt into evil that which God himself has made?"

"Did God not make Man? And did Man not likewise fall into corruption? Truly, nothing that dwells in this sinful world for long can retain perfection. Remember your Augustine, my boy. *For evil has no positive nature; but the loss of good has received the name evil.* Just as darkness is merely the absence of light, that which we call evil is merely the absence of good. Wherever goodness is absent, corruption takes root, and it is fed by selfishness and pride. Yes, the Grail was a gift to Man, but even a good gift may still be misused..."

Lancelot tried to listen as Merlyn continued his theological discourse on the Holy Grail and its potential uses, both wise and wicked, but he found himself unable to focus on anything but Gwenivere. *She was intoxicating.* Although he had first been attracted by her physical beauty, of which he had inadvertently gained fairly intimate knowledge, Lancelot now found himself drawn to her other qualities, particularly her feistiness and wit. Having initially attempted to avoid the young woman, hoping that her stay in Camelot would be short lived, Lancelot's heart both leapt and sank as she and Arthur grew ever more inseparable and she was offered permanent lodgings. Of course, part of him rejoiced at the thought of seeing her lovely face each morning, but another part of him, still humiliated by their first encounter, dreaded the idea of even saying *hello*. Eventually, Lancelot found himself confronted by Gwenivere in the stables, where she laughingly forgave him for his awkward intrusion and, with a wink, vowed to keep the messy details to herself. Thus began a close friendship that gave the sandy-haired knight immeasurable joy, while also driving him mad.

At times he had no idea what to do with himself. Just being in her presence caused his blood to boil with passion, so on occasion, he would simply make up false excuses and escape to the tilting fields or the tavern, desperately attempting to drown his obsession through swordplay and flagons of mead. But the effect never lasted long, and he always found himself back where he started: hopelessly enamored with a woman who was being officially courted by his king.

No! It was near unthinkable! How could I possibly betray Arthur? If ever I were to attempt stealing Gwenivere away, it would be a knife in the back of our friendship and a black eye for the kingdom itself. Then what of the moral cost? True, she and

Arthur are not yet married. Would it still be immoral? While not technically adultery, God would certainly not look kindly on such underhandedness and disloyalty.

Lancelot scolded himself for even considering such things. Though in recent days, he had begun to suspect that Gwenivere was aware of his poorly-suppressed feelings for her, as he frequently noticed her blushing or giggling whenever he made one of his hasty exits or caught himself gazing at her for longer than necessary. *Surely she had noticed. Yet she never objected, did she? Perhaps she enjoyed the attention. Perhaps she shared his feelings! Or perhaps she just liked toying with him. No, such an angel could never be so cruel, with her shining brown curls and bottomless green eyes like pools of...*

"Lancelot!" a booming voice called.

Suddenly, he snapped out of his love-induced trance like one waking from a dream. He sat up quickly, startled, and in his disoriented state, accidentally plunged his right hand into a nearby bowl of mushroom gravy.

"Yes! Yes! I'm here!" Lancelot shouted.

"Ah, that's *lovely* to know," smirked Merlyn, "For a moment there it seemed you had been bewitched. Now, if you would please indulge us and offer your reply."

"My reply? I'm sorry, sir. What was the question?"

"Honestly, my boy, you must learn to pay closer attention," Merlyn said with a heavy tone of exasperation, "In fact, I recall telling you that very thing many years ago, but it seems the idea never fully took root. No matter. You see, Arthur has decided to send seven knights to seek out the Holy Grail and return it to Camelot, hopefully locating it before the Order of the White Dragon. You were asked to join that fellowship."

"Oh, yes, *of course*," Lancelot replied with mock confidence, while hastily wiping the gravy from his hand, "I definitely heard *that* question. I thought you were talking about... something else. Naturally, I would be *honored*, Arthur. Now remind me again who else is going?"

Merlyn let out a soft chuckle, giving the former blacksmith a sly look out of the corner of his eye, then turned and bid the other volunteers to stand. Lancelot looked about the chamber and saw that Gawain and Tristan had risen to their feet, along with the three sons of Pellinore, though including himself, he counted only six men.

"Pardon me, Merlyn, but who is the seventh?"

"Oh, he'll be arriving shortly," the old man answered.

"Wait a moment," Arthur abruptly interjected, "Merlyn, you never mentioned *this*. Are we to blindly add another member to our Council of the Round Table?"

"Didn't I tell you, my boy? I could have *sworn* I did. Oh dear, I've done it again. You see, dwelling on multiple planes of existence can be so *confusing* sometimes."

"Confound it all, Merlyn! Have we even *met* the man in question? That final seat has remained empty these many years for a *reason*, you know. Indeed, I made a grave error with my judgment of Maleagant, and I determined long ago that I would not make such a mistake twice. But since that time, all those who have come here with noble hearts have been useless with a blade, and all those skilled in battle have been louts and drunkards! *None* have been found worthy."

"Fear not, for he who comes will prove his worth," said Merlyn, immediately followed by a loud knock on the outside door, "Ah ha! There he is now!"

Bedivere swiftly rose from his seat and hurried toward the entrance, turning the lock and swinging the oaken door wide to reveal a young man clad all in white, with a sword slung on his back and a shining helmet bundled under his left arm. The tiny rings of his chainmail hauberk glittered in the firelight, as if they had never before been scarred by the blood and grit of battle, and his snowy tunic was without spot or blemish but for the large, red cross adorning his chest. Thick, tawny hair fell to his shoulders in waves, and his clear blue eyes, both fierce and childlike, sparkled like sunlight on the water. But most remarkably, his very presence seemed to lift the suffocating pallor of death that had fallen over the room.

"Hail, King Arthur!" the young knight proclaimed, "Behold your faithful servant, Galahad. I have traveled far, seeking only to find an honorable king who merits my respect and devotion, and the hand of God has led me here."

"You are most welcome," Arthur responded, "Tell me, what is your business in Camelot?"

"Sire, I have long heard legends of the courage and nobility of your Knights of the Round Table, and though I am a stranger to you, I wish to pledge my sword to your cause."

As the man in white spoke, Lancelot studied his face with great curiosity. He was *young* – even more so than Percival, yet the bravery and candor he displayed in every word seemed to paint him with a maturity far beyond his years. But there was something else. Something in his eyes that was demanding Lancelot's attention. Something oddly familiar.

"We are truly honored by your boldness and kind words," Arthur continued, "but you are still very young, and the cleanliness of your garments and untarnished armor would indicate that you remain untested in battle. The quest upon which these men soon embark will be fraught with peril, and I could not possibly guarantee your safety."

"Then I implore you, sire," Galahad replied, "Please allow me to cross swords with your finest warrior. If given the chance, I will gladly prove my mettle."

"Very well, Galahad. You may rest here with us tonight, and on the morrow you will face Lancelot on the tilting fields."

"Sire, if it is all the same to you, I am ready *now*."

"Now?" said Arthur, with great astonishment and a hint of admiration in his voice, "You wish to take to the fields right away, even after such a long journey? God bless you, Galahad! If nothing else, we know you have the heart of a lion!"

* * * * *

The tilting fields were situated on the far end of the castle, directly behind the stables, and were mainly used for training, battle preparation, and breaking in new horses. A long, grassy valley stretched out from east to west, allowing for mounted cavalry to practice charging with lances or spears; an elaborate archery range with targets of varying size and shape had been constructed immediately to the south; and a smaller arena, bordered by an octagonal wooden fence, was typically used for swordplay. Lancelot stood waiting in the center of this arena, carefully inspecting the blade of his mighty sword, Arondight, and grinning with confidence as this youthful upstart named Galahad strode forward to meet him.

"It will be an honor to do battle with you today, Lancelot," said the young knight humbly.

"I have no desire to do you harm," Lancelot replied, still intrigued by the relaxed gaze and striking visage of the boy who stood before him, respectful and unassuming yet strangely confidant, "So do not hesitate to yield if my attacks should become unbearable."

"I am not one to yield so easily," Galahad answered with a lighthearted wink, "But perhaps each of us can learn something from the other."

And wearing a sly grin, Galahad brandished his own sword, a curved, iron blade not unlike a long sickle, with a series of indecipherable engravings just above the hilt. It looked ancient, maybe Egyptian or Hebrew, with an inherently regal quality that Lancelot found difficult to place. Having armed themselves, the two men stood motionless at first, eying one another guardedly until Arthur gave the word to begin.

Iron and steel, sword and shield crashed noisily against one another like claps of thunder, as the combatants came together to test the limits of their strength and skill. Yet mere moments into the friendly match, it became overwhelmingly clear to Lancelot that his young opponent was far from ordinary. Most of those who excelled in armed combat tended to have their own particular techniques, be they learned or invented, and a standard set of movements utilized when first meeting an enemy, which could always be altered or adapted as the battle wore on. However, the very best warriors would study their opponents and learn how they fought, which enabled them to predict the actions of their adversaries and thus gain a distinct advantage. But somehow, young Galahad had managed to become startlingly familiar with Lancelot's fighting style almost immediately, and was using this knowledge to either avoid or deflect every blow he tried to land.

And so, Lancelot began to improvise. He promptly recalled certain thrusts and maneuvers used by their Pictish allies to the north, others by the Saxons, and started integrating them into his own manner of swordplay. Soon the tide had turned and he caught Galahad with a blow to the left shoulder, knocking him off balance and sending him tumbling to the ground. But the young knight was quick and resilient, and he soon rolled out of danger and leapt to his feet, then found a flaw in Lancelot's stance and struck him firmly in the right thigh, causing him to briefly drop to one knee before bounding forward in retaliation. On and on they fought, until it seemed to both combatants and their observers that the duel would end in a stalemate.

And then it happened.

The voice was unmistakable, calling out amidst the din, innocently offering a few words of support and encouragement to her loyal friend who had seemingly met his match.

"Hurrah, Lancelot!" Gwenivere shouted, "The day is yours!"

Of course, she was certainly not the only one cheering. Arthur, Merlyn, Gawain, and all the rest had surrounded the arena, rapping their fists against the wooden fence, applauding every successful blow, and hollering their approval as these two titans clashed before them. But Gwenivere's soft, lilting voice was the only one he heard, and the only sound on earth that could cause him to lose his concentration, if only briefly. In that moment of distraction, Galahad spied an opening and struck a powerful blow to his chest, loosing Arondight from his grip and sending him crashing to the earth like a falling tree.

When he opened his eyes, Lancelot was lying flat on his back with Galahad's sword at his throat, and he groaned at the realization that he had been beaten. The crowd of onlookers had fallen silent, rendered speechless with disbelief that their great champion had been bested by this young novice, though Merlyn simply smiled knowingly, as if he had, by some unknown means, orchestrated the entire event.

"Do you yield?" asked Galahad.

"Aye," Lancelot grudgingly answered, "I yield."

The younger knight laughed and offered Lancelot his hand, both to help him to his feet and as a sign of truce, as Arthur hurried into the arena and began heaping mountains of praise on this curious visitor in white.

"Bravo!" said Arthur, "Well done, Galahad!"

"Thank you, sire," he replied, dropping to one knee and bowing his head in reverence.

"Arise, young man! Arise! You are the first swordsman to ever best Lancelot, our finest warrior, and though I'm sure his pride is a bit wounded, he will recover soon enough, eh?"

"Of course, Arthur," said Lancelot, masking his shame with an over-the-top display of indifference and swagger, "After all, the sun *was* in my eyes."

Lancelot winced and cursed silently when he looked up and realized that the sky was overcast; then he dutifully followed Arthur and the other knights back into the Great Hall, where, with much fanfare and enthusiasm, Galahad was offered the final seat at the Round Table. Wine was poured and all rejoiced, through the celebration was bittersweet, and not only because of Lancelot's wounded pride. Truly, each man who laughed with joy that day also cringed with fear, for all knew that they would soon embark on a perilous quest upon whose success or failure rested the fate of all Britannia.

The Witching Hour

A frigid gust of wind howled through the trees, whose bare branches reached up from the earth like black, skeletal hands bathed in ghostly moonlight. The rocky terrain was largely void of vegetation, as the rough, dry grasses and patches of thorny thistles seemed to have choked out all other life, with even water becoming scarce as the elevation increased. Agravain rode his snorting hackney up the hazardous slopes, determined to reach his destination, yet conscious of only the cold, the darkness, and the ominous cawing of crows as they kept a constant vigil, waiting patiently for something to die. Unseen by mortal eyes, Naberius the Deceiver crept like a shadow over the layers of jagged stone, following alongside his charge and clandestinely guiding the angry young man toward a crumbling castle perched atop a cliff overlooking the sea.

The Romans had called it *Castorum Sepulcris*, the Fortress of Tombs, for in the centuries after its siege, destruction, and abandonment, the old stronghold had become little more than a burial site, housing the interred bodies of the soldiers and rebels who had met a violent end within its walls. Subsequent generations saw various kings and chieftains attempt to restore the castle to greatness, but all eventually renounced their efforts, primarily due to mysterious and bloody circumstances. Few had visited the fortress in recent years, for it was widely believed that the spirits of the dead walked its silent halls each evening, eternally seeking rest for their weary souls. But as of late, the red glow of torchlight could be seen atop the haunted hill, for it had finally become home to a sinister assembly who had no reason to fear the night.

As Agravain slowly approached the black gates of Castorum Sepulcris, an arrow whistled past his ear and plunged into the gravelly soil to his right, and a large silhouette appeared atop the ramparts, calling out to him in a loud, raspy voice.

"Halt! Move a step closer and the next one splits your skull! Who goes there? State your business!"

"I am Agravain of Orkney!" he responded, "And I seek an audience with the Priestess of the White Dragon! Now lower your bow and let me pass."

"You appear to be lost, Agravain of Orkney," shouted the guard, "There is no one here by that title. But all are permitted to make mistakes, so return from whence you came and I may be persuaded to spare your life."

Naberius slithered up beside Agravain and sunk his claws deep within the young man's brain, whispering a few words of suggestion in his ear and then slinking back into the shadows. At that moment, the insolence and hostility shown by the castle guard became too much for Agravain to withstand, and he swiftly drew his own bow and fired a screaming arrow into the silhouette that peered at him from the walls. Seconds later, the guard began to wobble and then tumbled down from his post onto the rocky earth below, an iron-tipped shaft protruding from his eye socket.

Smirking with satisfaction at his accomplishment, Agravain rode onward, dismounting just outside the gates and banging loudly with both fists, all the while demanding admittance with highly exaggerated threats of violence.

"Open up, you impertinent fools! Do you know who I am? How dare you treat me like a common vagrant! Now grant me entrance immediately or I will have your heads, but not before you are slowly and painfully disemboweled! It is Agravain of Orkney who knocks! Let me in, I say!"

Before long the huge doors creaked open and there stood a young boy, no more than nine or ten years old. His hair and eyes were both dark, drawing a stark contrast with his pale, almost translucent skin, and he stared up at Agravain with an empty, unsettling gaze.

"Have you come to see the White Dragon?" the boy asked.

"Uhh... *yes*. Of course," Agravain answered nervously, now growing increasingly unsure of himself as he finally set foot in this infamous lair of iniquity. The eroding stones that made up the castle walls, hopelessly fractured and on the verge of collapse, were still stained black with the ancient blood of fallen soldiers, and the dim torchlight bathed the halls in long, eerie shadows. Moreover, the child who stared up at him was unlike any he had ever met. Neither carefree and playful nor shy and morose, he simply appeared detached, unaffected by the horrors that surrounded him, as if such a disturbing atmosphere was all he had ever known.

"Come along then," said the boy nonchalantly, "Follow me. The ceremony will have already begun."

As Agravain apprehensively entered the vestibule, the boy looked past him through the doorway and saw the crumpled body of the castle guard lying motionless in a shallow pool of blood. Expecting him to cry out and sound an alarm, Agravain began hastily searching his mind for an acceptable explanation, but before he could open his mouth, the boy simply flashed him a disquieting smile and motioned for him to follow.

They wandered through a maze of passageways, each one more dilapidated and poorly lit than the next, without passing a single living soul. For a moment, Agravain began to wonder if this place might still be abandoned and that the strange boy might only be a homeless orphan or a runaway. But his theory was quickly dashed when they finally emerged into a large, open courtyard filled with a throng of worshipers, kneeling with hands outstretched toward a woman in white who stood regally on the edge of the cliff. A single glance at the raven-haired priestess told

Agravain that she was the child's mother. The two shared the same dark eyes and porcelain skin, and the boy seemed to swell with pride the very moment she came into view. Then with a firm tug at his arm, Agravain was aggressively beckoned to kneel amongst the others, most of whom appeared to be Saxons, though a sizable minority of Britons and other Celts had clearly joined their ranks as well.

When Agravain dropped to his knees, he noticed that the priestess had begun chanting in some indecipherable language, and her legions of followers repeated obediently. Thinking that it may have been Latin, he attempted to make out the words of her rhythmic refrain, but since he had never bothered learning to *speak* Latin to begin with, the whole endeavor was rather futile. As the chanting continued, an icy wind rose up and started swirling about them with such fury that the light of every torch was soon extinguished, and the crowd quickly fell silent in breathless anticipation.

"Don't look away," the boy whispered to him, "Not even for a second. *This* is the best part."

The eyes of the priestess had turned black as coal, and the growling voice that rumbled from within her gradually began to sound more bestial than human. A murder of crows ascended from the putrid mist below the cliff, screeching wildly and surrounding her with a cloak of living darkness, and her white linen gown billowed wildly in the wake of the raging tempest until the winds lifted her off the ground and into the frosty night air. Then she raised her arms high, and as her bare feet hovered a few inches above the rocky earth, she uttered one last incantation.

"Nos vocare te, o magnifica Albus Draconis!"

A flash of lightning illuminated the all-consuming night, and Agravain watched as the mist rose up and began to coalesce into a single entity whose serpentine form and enormous, bat-like wingspan suddenly blanketed the starless skies. The creature writhed and twisted, bursting forth from the womb of Hell into this mortal world, and Agravain shook with horror as layers of sallow, cadaverous skin began to stretch across its reptilian body. Finally two eyes opened, filled not with light but with darkness visible, and the monster shook the earth with a thunderous, bone-chilling roar.

The White Dragon had come.

"Don't look into its eyes," warned the boy, and Agravain obediently averted his gaze as the priestess began to speak.

"My servants, you have failed me!" she snarled in a deep, terrible voice, her mortal body now merely a vessel for some other demonic entity, "I have given you power and knowledge, yet you remain fruitless in your attempts to locate the Grail! Do not provoke the wrath of Leviathan!"

Agravain's instinctive reaction was to turn and run from this accursed place and to never look back. Prior to his arrival at Castorum Sepulcris, he had assumed that the Order of the White Dragon was nothing more than a name for some occultist religious sect, never once considering that these disciples of darkness bowed in worship before *an actual, living, breathing dragon*. But Naberius had crept back into his mind, and although the demon lacked the power to alleviate his sense of dread, it was easy to make the petrified young man fear the thought of leaving and being alone in the blackness of night far more than he feared the monstrous dragon. Reluctantly, Agravain decided to stay until the ceremony had been completed and hopefully gain audience with the priestess. Then he looked down at the boy, who was smiling from ear to ear.

"Men from Camelot have already slain our brother Ironside, the Red Knight of Astolat," the priestess continued as the White Dragon soared above the reverent congregation, "and they now seek the Grail as well with guidance from our old enemy, Ambrosius, a messenger of Avalon. They must be stopped at all costs! Find them, kill them, and bring me the Grail!"

In that moment, Agravain saw his chance. *He had visited Camelot*. After being forcibly taken there by that insolent fool Gawain, he now knew its layout, its entrances, its halls and passageways. He had met those insufferable knights, and even Arthur himself! Furthermore, his mother was still in Camelot, having been offered lodging in the castle as an act of hospitality by a king in search of forgiveness. *Treacherous whore*. She was dead to him now. Perhaps that feeble woman had succumbed to Arthur's charms, but Agravain would never forget who had murdered his father. *He would have vengeance*.

"I can do it!" he abruptly shouted, "I can find out where Arthur's knights are headed!"

Suddenly the priestess grew silent. The icy wind ceased and she stood upon solid ground once again as the White Dragon let out a deafening roar and then disappeared back into the waiting Hellmouth. Agravain surveyed the crowd and saw that every eye was now on him, including the priestess, and they all leered at him in astonishment as she descended from the cliff to meet this stranger who had so boldly disturbed their ritual.

Although the dragon had vanished, Agravain found that he was nearly as afraid of the priestess as he was of that winged monster, though he was deeply enchanted as well. When she finally approached, slowly and gracefully like a wolf on the hunt, her dark eyes studied him with great interest, and she wore a mysterious, bewitching expression, which drove Agravain to wonder whether she was searching for a sign of weakness or engaging in some form of seduction. *In either case, she was the predator and he was the prey*. Agravain had always taken pride in his appearance, and despite his fear, he made sure to stand up straight and puff out his chest as this intimidating, yet strikingly beautiful woman looked him over. His beardless face, long and angular, was framed by a smooth, neatly-trimmed head of reddish-blonde hair, much like his father before him. He was solidly built and well-armed, with a large dagger hanging loosely from his belt and a bow and quiver slung over his right shoulder. Atop his chainmail hauberk he wore a deep blue tunic bearing the family emblem, and he flushed with heat as the long, slender fingers of the priestess brushed against his chest, tracing the outlines of the yellow griffin rampant that signified the Orkney clan. She held his gaze for what seemed like an eternity, but then knelt down and spoke to the boy.

"My son, who is this man who dared to cry out?"

"He is Agravain of Orkney, Mother," the boy replied, "He has demanded to see you. And he killed a castle guard."

"Oh, *did* he?" the priestess hissed.

"I... I was only defending myself, my lady," said Agravain, his knees rattling with cowardice, all but certain that he would soon be unceremoniously run through.

"So Agravain of Orkney, your first action upon arriving at my home was to murder one of my servants, likely in cold blood, and then you had the gall to interrupt our most sacred ritual? What audacity! What hubris! What blatant disregard for pious, *Christian* virtue..."

At the time, Agravain was far too rapt with anxiety to notice the heavy coat of cynicism dripping from every word uttered by the dark priestess. But as she trailed off, her demeanor shifted from restrained anger into devilish glee, and a wicked smile stretched across her full, red lips. The priestess grasped his shoulder, gently pulling him down toward her so their faces were only inches apart, and Agravain shivered as she breathed into his ear with a warm, impish whisper.

"How utterly delightful," she sighed.

* * * * *

After the crowds were dismissed, Agravain was escorted into a private chamber by a pair of unsmiling mercenaries. The one called Cynric was a Saxon, blonde and heavy set with a long beard bound up in braids, and the other was a Celt, a gangly, one-eyed weasel named Urien, who smelled of old cabbage and prodded incessantly at Agravain with the tip of his sword. The jabs were not firm enough to break the skin, but were certainly sufficient to annoy him needlessly.

The room they left him in was rather curiously decorated, with dozens of dripping, wax candles lining the walls rather than the typical torch-filled sconces, and stacks of ancient books piled haphazardly on the stone floor. A single chair was set beneath a wooden table covered in crudely drawn maps, and a brass goblet lay on its side in a small puddle of spilled wine. Along the far wall were cluttered shelves occupied by odd, ancient-looking artifacts as well as glass jars and clay pots of various sizes, some filled with unidentified liquids, some with the tiny bones or the severed appendages of small animals, and even some with live creatures desperately trying to escape. However, Agravain was most fascinated by the massive, iron cauldron that stood alone within a circle of ash, surrounded by a large pentangle and several hand-scrawled symbols of some unknown origin. The cauldron was empty with the exception of a long, wooden stirring rod that rested within the gaping mouth, yet the pungent, metallic smell of blood still seemed to emanate from its depths. Horrified but still intrigued, Agravain stepped toward the cauldron and began to study it with morbid curiosity.

"So what do you think?" said a voice from behind him.

Agravain turned and saw the priestess leaning against the open doorway, her lithe, feminine frame bent into an alluring posture as the plunging neckline of her gown rested delicately upon her ivory flesh. *Good lord. What did he think?* Well, any man with a pulse knew *exactly* what he thought. Of course, even if Agravain *was* a conceited, self-entitled little wretch, he was also intelligent enough to realize when he was being manipulated. And he was *obviously* being manipulated. Still, never one to deny himself the pleasures of a beautiful, willing woman, he decided to play along.

"I find you more captivating every moment, my lady."

The priestess glanced up at Agravain from beneath her eyelashes and flashed him a mischievous smile, sauntering over to his side and allowing her fingers to lightly caress the rim of the enormous iron vessel.

"You may call me Morgana," she said sweetly, "and when I asked for your thoughts, I was actually referring to the cauldron. You seem to have taken an interest in it."

"Yes I have," Agravain replied, "It's quite... *peculiar*."

"Indeed. As you may have gathered, Agravain of Orkney, this is the chamber in which I store all of my most prized possessions. And naturally, that's why *you're* here."

The aroused young man grinned at Morgana's flirtatious banter and she winked back at him playfully, gently drawing the wooden stirring rod out of the cauldron. However, as its full length came into view, Agravain realized that it was actually an old Roman *pilum*. The antique spear was roughly two meters long, tipped with a heavy, leaf-shaped, iron shank, and the entire shaft was stained black with blood. After closer inspection, Agravain stumbled backward in astonishment.

"Your eyes do not deceive you," Morgana began, "This is the legendary Spear of Longinus, named for the unsung Roman soldier who thrust it into the flesh of that delusional carpenter as he hung dead on a cross. Hmm... rather ironic, wouldn't you say? A man who spent much of his early life shaping things out of wood finally met his end nailed to a tree."

Agravain chuckled uncomfortably.

"It has long been rumored that possession of the spear, first obtained by Emperor Claudius, renders its bearer invincible on the field of battle. Of course, you may judge for yourself whether those rumors are true, but the facts are undeniable: Claudius was able to expand Rome into the most dominant empire this world has ever seen, and Roman supremacy endured for nearly 400 years after his death. When Rome was sacked by the Visigoths, Emperor Honorius lost the spear to the barbarian leader Alaric, who carried it back to Gaul. Vortigern then managed to obtain it during the Saxon invasions, and he used the spear's power to rule Britannia with an iron fist for many years... that is, until I pried it from his charred, lifeless fingers. Now here it rests, ready to be wielded by one who would rule the known world."

At the conclusion of her tale, Agravain's lust began bubbling up within him, first for Morgana, and now for this weapon of power that allowed its master to reign over all mankind. *He could ask for no greater form of vengeance against Arthur!* The tyrant would be deposed, and he would claim the throne himself, with this raven-haired goddess by his side as queen. Agravain licked his lips. His initial fear had given way to a flood of carnal desire. In truth, he *coveted* both the priestess and the spear, and from that moment on he knew that he would do anything in his power to attain them.

"I am in awe, my lady," Agravain finally replied, struggling to hold back the fire of his own ambition, "But even with all you possess, I sense that you desire more."

"Your shrewdness matches your determination, Agravain of Orkney," Morgana whispered coyly as she pressed her warm body against his, sliding her delicate fingers gradually up his thighs, "In truth, I seek only what mankind has sought since the dawn of time, and what our Dark Father sought when he was so cruelly cast out of Heaven. But I must have the Grail to complete the Black Mass. When the time comes, the blood of an innocent who has been sacrificed to the White Dragon will be consecrated within the Grail. And once that blood is imbibed, *once we partake in that dark communion*, unlimited power will be within our grasp. Just think of it – invincibility *and* immortality! How would you like to be lord of all you survey? How would you like to live forever?"

Overcome with passion, Agravain nodded furiously, having found himself temporarily incapable of speech.

"Mmm... didn't I say you were delightful? Now go and find out where Arthur's knights are headed. Follow them to the end of the earth if necessary. Bring me the Grail and you shall have *everything* you desire. Oh, and Agravain?"

"Yes, Morgana?"

"*Do not fail*. I have ways of dealing with those who fail me."

"Oh, do you now?" he replied with a smile.

"Well, what do you think happened to Urien's other eye?"

* * * * *

Lord Astaroth, demon prince of the land called Britannia, stood waiting on the barren cliffs of *Castorum Sepulcris*. Thus far, his plan had been a resounding success. Teaching his human apprentice to summon the hellbeast Leviathan had been a stroke of genius, as that infernal serpent was a perfect choice to play on the superstitions of the pagan Saxons and Celts. They feared the dragon... nay, they *worshiped* him, and in that reverence they would obey every command of his priestess without question. *It was no wonder that the Enemy enjoyed this so much.*

Morgana was a fine pupil. Her descent into the darkness had taken much longer and had been far more difficult than the relatively effortless seduction of Agravain, but her skills of persuasion and manipulation rivaled even many of his allies in the Unseen Realm. *It was a pity she was human*.

Before long his servant, Naberius the Deceiver, arrived and knelt obediently at the feet of his master, his ghastly visage gleaming with malevolent pleasure. *The little imp did well this time*. Lust and Pride had always been two of his favorite sins, and that shameless, narcissistic imbecile had been as malleable as clay in Naberius' gnarled, leathery hands.

"Agravain has taken the bait, my lord," Naberius reported, "He will soon infiltrate Camelot and attempt to kill Arthur."

"No," replied Lord Astaroth, "I want Arthur incapacitated, but left alive. Let him watch what horrors befall his kingdom. Tell the pawn that I want him to *suffer*."

The Dolorous Stroke

Rowena missed Gawain already. Only a few weeks had passed since he and six other knights rode out from Camelot in search of the Holy Grail, yet their short time apart felt like an eternity. Naturally, Gawain had been called away from her before on numerous occasions, often for days or weeks at a time, but this was different. For the first time she could remember, Rowena was truly frightened that her husband might never return. The cruelty of her Saxon kinfolk and the military might of the Roman army were nothing in comparison to the enemy they now faced. *Such heartless savagery; such fervent, unwavering devotion; such wanton destruction and disregard for human life.* The mere thought of it sent ice through her veins.

So on this night, just as she had done every night following Gawain's departure, Rowena dropped to her knees and poured out her heart to God, drawing strength from the comforting words of Christ as she uttered each supplication: *Come unto me, all ye that labor and are heavy laden, and I will give you rest. Take my yoke upon you, and learn of me; for I am meek and lowly in heart, and ye shall find rest unto your souls. For my yoke is easy, and my burden is light.*

If she were honest with herself, Rowena would admit that she often wondered whether God heard her requests, or if He even had time for someone so small and insignificant. Surely the Creator of the universe had better things to do than listen to *her* trivial hopes and fears. In the greater scheme of things, was she really so important? Of what value was her life when mankind still suffered the ravages of war, famine, and disease? But in those moments of doubt and confusion, Rowena breathed deeply and remembered that God was big enough to hold all of these things in the palm of His hand – that the very hairs of her head were numbered. *And a sparrow shall not fall to the ground outside your Father's care...*

Therefore, she prayed for Gawain, whose loving face she longed to see again; for Tristan, who had already endured more than his share of tragedy; for Percival, an avatar of innocence amidst a world of horrors; for Lancelot, whose infatuation with Gwenivere had not escaped her notice. And though her prayers frequently centered on the brave men who journeyed out to face the unknown, she also made sure to always remember those few who had stayed behind.

Both former Roman soldiers, Sagramore and Palamedes had always been the eldest of Arthur's knights, and with the ongoing march of time, the years were beginning to take their toll. Their knees creaked and their backs ached after decades of battle and bloodshed, though both still proved useful in the occasional skirmish and invaluable as sources of experience and wisdom. Willing but unable to endure the physical strain of such an arduous journey, Sagramore had declined to join the Grail quest, instead choosing to remain at Camelot, tending to his beloved horses and offering his counsel. Palamedes, while still a bit more spry than his Numidian counterpart, had declined as well, partially because he was still nursing the shoulder injury he sustained in his clash with the White Dragon, and partially because he felt it improper for a pagan such as himself to take part in seeking an artifact so sacred to the followers of Christ. Indeed, while Rowena prayed daily for Palamedes' conversion, his unassuming nobility had forever earned her respect.

As Arthur's marshal, Bedivere chose to stay behind as well, having deemed it his responsibility to ensure the safety and security of Camelot in the days and weeks ahead. And with Lancelot away, Arthur had handpicked Gareth to act as personal guardian for Gwenivere, a duty that was typically granted to the kingdom's most valiant and reliable warrior, and an honor that Gareth bore with great humility. Finally, Kay had also opted to forego the quest and remain in Camelot, citing his obligations as court seneschal and the lingering limp that resulted from the arrow wound in his posterior, though Rowena suspected that the boorish redhead was either too fearful or too indolent to embark on such a challenging venture. Her less-than-flattering opinion of Kay stemmed from his often crass behavior, along with the widespread rumor that he held his place at court only because of his kinship with Arthur, but such qualms were of no consequence. She prayed for him all the same.

No sooner had Rowena invoked the name of the Father, the Son, and the Holy Spirit, than a loud knock sounded at the castle door. And since Bedivere was currently elsewhere making his nightly rounds, she rose from her kneeling position and hurried down the long, stone hallway toward the main entrance. She groaned audibly upon opening the door.

It was Bellicent's son Agravain, that petulant waste of skin whom Gawain and Gareth had saved from imprisonment. After returning from their mission, Gawain had been quite animated in telling her all about the long journey back, made even longer by the conceited young man's ungrateful attitude and incessant caterwauling. Truthfully, Rowena found it difficult to believe that Bellicent, who turned out to be rather pleasant once she renounced her feud with Arthur, could have possibly raised such a rotten human being. But on this cool summer evening, he did not have the look of one intent on starting trouble. Rather, as Agravain stood waiting patiently in the open doorway, unarmed and weary from his journey, he looked penitent and even a bit sad. *And his chin was quivering*. Suddenly feeling ashamed by her hasty judgment of a fellow child of God, Rowena silently scolded herself and confessed her sin while graciously beckoning the young man to enter.

"Oh, thank you so much," he began, still breathing heavily, "I was afraid you would turn me away, and to be honest, considering my discourteous behavior during my initial visit, I wouldn't have blamed you."

Rowena stared at Agravain, her brow furrowed with shock and bewilderment. *Was that an apology? Did he actually say thank you? Had the fool been brainwashed?* Somehow, this man who now stood before her was nothing like the arrogant whelp she had met previously. It was as if a refined, respectful doppelganger of Agravain had arrived in his stead.

"Umm... you're welcome," Rowena stammered, "Please, make yourself at home. Did you come to see your mother?"

"Actually, I would like to speak with the king, if possible. I think perhaps we got off on the wrong foot before, and I would be grateful for the opportunity to make things right."

A beaming smile full of joy and hope spread across her face as Rowena led the seemingly remorseful young man toward the library, where Arthur often spent an hour or two alone in the evenings, reading and collecting his thoughts. Her spirit soared as she pondered the abrupt shift in Agravain's disposition, as his conversion from selfish scoundrel to gracious gentleman had been like night and day. *But nothing was beyond God's power*. If one so lost as him could find redemption, surely there was hope for all. So enthused was she with this pleasant turn of events that she failed to notice how Agravain left the castle door unlocked after pulling it closed behind him.

* * * * *

Arthur ran his fingers through his stringy brown hair as he sat unaccompanied in the library, pouring over his well-worn copy of Augustine's *Confessions*. He had read the same passage over and over at least ten times, struggling to wrap his mind around the apparent paradox of human nature.

"I became evil for no reason," he read once again, this time out loud, *"I had no motive for my wickedness except wickedness itself. It was foul, and I loved it. I loved the self-destruction, I loved my fall, not the object for which I had fallen but my fall*

itself. My depraved soul leaped down from Your firmament to ruin. I was seeking not to gain anything by shameful means, but shame for its own sake."

What a mind-numbing mystery. It had always been quite easy for Arthur to understand or even sympathize with those who turned to evil out of poverty, or jealousy, or ambition. Of course, any reasons given could not justify the resultant actions, as sin was still sin regardless of the motive, but they *did* provide a logical explanation for the occurrence of evil. However, he was constantly baffled by the notion that humanity, in its corrupted, fallen state, actually *longed* to wallow in sin purely for the sake of rebellion. And such struggles were not isolated to Augustine, either! The Apostle Paul himself had lamented the same malady in his letter to the Romans: *For the good that I would I do not, but the evil which I would not, that I do.* Was this gross distortion of mankind's original righteousness so full and complete that even the holiest person yearned to stray from God's graces? *Oh, how the mighty have fallen.*

Eventually, Arthur gave up trying to comprehend the innate mysteries of the universe and set the thick, leather-bound tome back in its place on the shelf, when Rowena suddenly burst through the door, grinning like a child at play, with a repentant Agravain following close behind.

"I'm sorry to disturb you, Arthur," she said, "I trust that you remember Agravain?"

The king nodded and forced himself to smile, with the bitter memory of this unpleasant young man all too fresh on his mind. But then, much to his surprise, Agravain stepped in front of Rowena and bowed extravagantly, kneeling low with his face flat on the floor in submission.

"Sire, I beg your forgiveness," he said loudly, "for I have been spiteful and coldhearted. Despite your unsavory dealings with our household in the past, you have shown kindness and deference to my mother, and your knights have rescued me from bondage. I am truly in your debt."

"Stand up, friend," Arthur replied, his smile no longer forced but genuine, "You owe me nothing, though I am humbled by your gratitude. Ever since our first meeting, I have prayed for peace between us, and now it seems that prayer has been answered. Rowena, go and fetch Bellicent. A mother and her son should be together for such a celebration."

* * * * *

Agravain wanted to vomit. He had actually *bowed* before the villainous usurper who murdered his father, and it caused the fury within him to burn hotter than a blacksmith's furnace. *But his plan was working.* These gullible fools had bought into his charade so easily that he almost laughed out loud. But now was not the time to break character. *Not yet.*

He swallowed his disgust and engaged in meaningless, friendly banter with Arthur at agonizing length, until Rowena finally returned with his mother in tow. She smiled and embraced him, asking how he had been and telling him of the great kindness shown to her in Camelot, and he soon realized that this woman sickened him as well. In Agravain's twisted mind, Bellicent had betrayed their family by freely associating with the enemy, and she now bore equal responsibility for his father's death. She too would feel the brunt of his scorn and hatred. *She too would taste his wrath.*

The old woman was laughing now, prattling on with Arthur and Rowena about various subjects in which he had no interest. Agravain wasn't paying attention to their conversation anyway. He was listening for the signal.

"...and perhaps you could *both* stay in Camelot," Arthur was saying with great excitement, "Who knows, Agravain? Maybe one day you could be considered for the Counsel of the Round Table. I've heard that you're very skilled in archery."

Agravain was about to offer his heartfelt thanks in the most convincing way possible, when he heard three short knocks on the library door. *They were here. The time had come.*

"Do you honestly think I would be even remotely interested in joining your little club, Arthur?" said Agravain, his demeanor suddenly dark and combative, "You people are so wonderfully naïve. My heartless witch of a mother may have forgiven you for murdering her husband, Lot of Orkney, but my hatred is not quenched so easily. I *will* have my revenge!"

And at that moment, Cynric and Urien exploded through the door, shouting and brandishing their weapons ominously. With the element of surprise decidedly on their side, the two mercenaries quickly subdued Bellicent and Rowena, holding razor sharp blades firmly against their throats, while Agravain stared down the king with a wicked grin upon his face. Realizing that he had been duped, Arthur began to reach for Excalibur, but the women squealed in terror as cold iron grazed against their necks, and he lowered his hands in defeat.

"Surely it can't be this easy," Agravain said with a laugh as he retrieved a long dagger from Urien's belt.

"No!" cried Arthur, "Don't hurt them! But how..."

"How did my friends here get into the castle, you ask? Well, it's very simple, really. *I let them in*. Yes, Arthur, I left the gate unlocked when I entered, and that foolish little Saxon girl was far too lost in stupid euphoria to notice. Personally, I'm shocked that she believed my little masquerade. It was *hardly* one of my best performances."

"I'm the one you want, Agravain. Please... just leave the women alone. Do what you want with me."

"Oh, don't worry. *I intend to*."

And then several things happened in rapid succession.

First, Agravain began striding resolutely toward Arthur with dagger in hand. At the same time, Bellicent shifted her weight back and stomped hard on Cynric's right foot, causing him to cry out in pain and then loosen his grip on her, dropping the knife he had been holding. Moments later, as Bellicent rushed toward her son in a desperate attempt to prevent the shedding of blood, Agravain turned to face her approach, sneered with contempt, and plunged the dagger deep into her belly.

Bellicent gasped. Her eyes popped open wide, filled with distress and terror, and her son stared back without a hint of emotion in his cold, hateful gaze. She groaned in agony as the iron blade cut through flesh and bone, exiting swiftly from her lower back, and then exhaled for the last time just after hearing Agravain's final whispered words.

"Treacherous whore," he hissed as his mother's lifeless body crumpled onto the hard, stone floor.

Apparently having overheard the commotion, Kay then barged clumsily into the crowded library only to be met by Cynric, who had recovered from the vicious foot-stomping and was now hungry for retribution. Before Kay even had a chance to ask what was happening, he also found himself disarmed and restrained, propped up next to Rowena with a burly Saxon arm around his chest and a sharp knife at his throat.

"Well!" laughed Agravain, "This is becoming quite the little gathering, isn't it? More fresh meat for the grinder!"

"What is it that you want, Agravain?" Arthur interrupted with tears of misery in his eyes, "You've already slain your own mother. Will you now slay us all? Where will it stop? I tell you now, if taking my life will end this madness then come and take it. Enact your vengeance."

"Oh, come now, Arthur. Don't you see? This is about so much more than *vengeance*. On one hand, it's about power. I want it, and the Priestess of the White Dragon is willing to give it to me… as well as other, far more *desirable* rewards. And on the other hand, this is about punishment. Indeed, killing you would bring me great satisfaction, but not as much as watching you writhe and squirm while I take *everything* you've gained, including your throne."

Then gasps of horror filled the room as Agravain reached out for Excalibur. At first he nearly doubled over, surprised by its immense weight, but with a second effort he gripped the mighty sword with both hands and strenuously lifted it on high, laughing with maniacal glee as he lunged forward and drove the blade into Arthur's thigh. The king cried out in anguish as Agravain twisted the sword over and over, creating a massive, circular wound that would not easily heal.

"Where is the Grail?" he demanded, "What path have your knights taken? You *will* tell me where they've gone!"

Arthur wept. And in the moments before he blacked out from the pain, the words of Augustine flashed through his mind: *I became evil for no reason. I had no motive for my wickedness except wickedness itself. It was foul, and I loved it.*

* * * * *

Rowena was mortified. *This was her fault*. She was the one who had allowed Agravain into the castle. She was the one who led him happily to Arthur. How could she have possibly let that brutal miscreant fool her so handily? Perhaps he was right. Perhaps she *was* naïve. Clearly her faith had been misguided, but did the fault lie with her faith in God's power to redeem, or her faith in humanity? *No.* None of that mattered now. All that mattered was stopping this reign of terror before it went any further and all of Camelot was drowning in blood.

"Stop!" she screamed, "Stop, I'm begging you!"

Hearing her outcry, Agravain hurriedly approached Rowena, flashing a cruel smile as wrapped his fingers around her slender throat and began to squeeze.

"You wish me to stop? Certainly! But I do still have a task to complete, so I'll leave you and be on my way as soon as I'm told where the other knights are headed."

"But... I don't know!" Rowena wheezed, gasping for air.

"Maybe not," Agravain responded, motioning toward Kay with his dagger, "but I'm betting that *he* does. Of course, a big, strong, loyal knight like him could probably *handle* a little pain. Maybe even a little torture. However, if I were to start cutting off little pieces of *you*, I imagine he would tell me what I want to know in no time at all."

Rowena looked over at Kay and saw fear behind his eyes. *He would talk*. Not to betray Arthur or his fellow knights, but to save her from agony and disfigurement. Beneath that coarse exterior, he really was a good man – maybe not the bravest or the most selfless, but honorable and kind. *Yes, he would talk*.

"Kay," she shouted, "don't tell this devil anything!"

"Well, how very heroic of you! I didn't realize you had such fortitude, my dear. Let's see how long *that* lasts, shall we? Perhaps I should begin by cutting out your eyes..."

"Wait!" Kay shouted reluctantly, "Please... don't hurt her. They are riding north to Ultima Thule. I swear that's everything I know. God forgive me."

"Kay, no!"

"Ah, you see?" Agravain chuckled, "Never underestimate a man's instinct to protect a damsel in distress. Thank you for your help, Kay. Your services are no longer required."

Then he nodded to Cynric, who struck Kay hard on the back of the head with the pommel of his sword, knocking him unconscious and causing him to tumble flaccidly to the ground like a rag doll. Agravain signaled to Urien as well, and the lanky, brutish Celt freed Rowena from his vice-like grip and shoved her backward, sending her sprawling into a bookshelf, whose contents toppled down upon her, trapping her beneath a massive pile of leather-bound manuscripts. Rowena looked on helplessly as Agravain stepped over to Arthur's wounded body and gruffly withdrew Excalibur from the wound in his thigh, finally hoisting the heavy sword upon his shoulders and hurrying out of the library with his mercenaries close behind. She tried in vain to call out for help, but no sound would come. And then everything went black.

PANDÆMONIUM

Nearly an hour passed before Bedivere completed his rounds and finally stumbled upon the gruesome scene in the library, his attention caught by the puddle of blood slowly seeping from beneath the doorframe. Upon entering the room, he was shocked to find Kay gradually regaining consciousness next to the murdered body of Bellicent, Rowena lying immobile beneath a huge pile of books, and Arthur, pale and comatose, bleeding profusely from a gaping wound in his thigh. Moreover, Excalibur was missing. After rousing Rowena and learning of Agravain's treachery, Bedivere summoned the court physician to tend to the wounded and then met solemnly at the Round Table with Gareth, Sagramore, and Palamedes.

"I feel responsible," Bedivere lamented, "As the king's marshal, the security of this castle should be my first priority. Obviously I have failed in my post."

"Nonsense!" Palamedes replied.

"Agreed," said Sagramore, "Agravain was unarmed, and he entered Camelot under the guise of friendship. Neither you nor Rowena could have predicted his deception."

"Well, I *knew* from the beginning that that scoundrel would be trouble," muttered Gareth.

"And what is *that* supposed to mean?" Palamedes snapped.

"It means Agravain should never have been permitted to even come within *eyesight* of Camelot before being driven away like a stray dog! Gawain and I both told everyone long ago that he had sworn revenge on Arthur!"

"Oh, so I suppose things would have turned out differently if *you* had been in charge?"

"I didn't say that! I just mean..."

"I've already claimed fault!" Bedivere wailed, "What more do you demand from me?"

Sagramore unsuccessfully attempted to keep the peace as Bedivere grew increasingly despondent and Palamedes shouted at Gareth in anger and confusion. Tempers flared, voices grew louder, and conflicts escalated until it seemed as if the initially somber meeting might erupt into a fist fight. But then a strong, familiar voice broke through the uproar and everyone suddenly grew silent, as if a raging storm had just been calmed.

"What's done is done," said Merlyn, having materialized in one of the empty seats at the Round Table, "There is no use in self-pity or assigning blame. Now is a time for *action*. Agravain does not know what horrors he has unleashed."

"What do you mean? What horrors?" asked Gareth.

"All of you should know by now that Excalibur is more than just a sword. It is a divine weapon, forged at the dawn of time in the white mountains of Avalon. By stealing it, Agravain hoped only to humiliate Arthur and gain a treasure for himself, but he could not have realized that its presence in Camelot served as a powerful instrument of protection to ward off dark forces in the Unseen Realm – the same forces that have been hunting Arthur since his birth."

"But Merlyn, Arthur is gravely wounded," Sagramore replied, "He has bled far too much to be fully revived. He cannot even walk, much less defend himself."

"Indeed. Our only chance is to take shelter in the cathedral. Holy ground will provide us with some defense, but I fear that the evil spirits who stalk this land now smell fresh blood. They will not be easily deterred."

"Is there no other hope?" inquired Bedivere.

"My boy, there is *always* hope," said Merlyn, "But only the divine healing powers of the Grail can revive Arthur now and ward off the encroaching night. So we must not lose heart. We must hold out for as long as we can. And we must pray that your brethren can reach the Grail before the Order of the White Dragon, or Camelot will surely fall."

* * * * *

The weary traveler trudged ever onward through stagnant swamps and pits of sticky, reeking mud, often stumbling to a crawl whenever his aching legs gave out beneath him. Exhausted and emaciated, his parched throat begged for even the smallest taste of water, though the ancient bog surrounding him spewed forth naught but a bitter poison. His blonde hair and beard were littered with dirt, leaves, and nettles, and he had long ago discarded his heavy, iron armor, which had become weighted down with layers of rust and filth. The blade of his axe had grown dull with overuse, yet he still clung tightly to the weapon, his only tool for hacking a path through the soggy underbrush and tangled vines of the marshlands, and his only defense against the dark creatures who so relentlessly pursued him.

The thunder of horses pounded in the distance, and the traveler cringed with the knowledge that these... *things*, be they ghosts or demons, *certainly not men*, would soon be upon him. They were living shadows – armored servants of the darkness, unleashed upon a cursed land to usher in the end of all things. Perhaps Merlyn had been wrong. Perhaps man was too weak and fallen to stand against such evil. Despair clawed at his heart and mind, and he could feel himself being dragged downward, deeper and deeper into the abyss of desolation.

At last the final remnants of his resolve abandoned him, followed shortly by his consciousness, and the traveler collapsed face-first into the murky swamp, longing only for the sweet release of death. As his breathing slowed and his vision faded to black, the last blurry image he beheld was the shape of a massive knight clad in green, reaching toward him with a pair of brawny hands and calling out in a gravelly yet familiar voice.

"Hello, Gawain."

The distinct feeling of being pulled from the mud and tossed haphazardly onto the back of a large horse was the only coherent memory Gawain could grasp before his subconscious took control. From then on, his enfeebled mind was haunted by nightmares and hallucinations, frightening images of the huge Green Knight towering over him, spouting obscene threats and whispering secrets to the darkness. In his dreams he fought with great savagery, though when Gawain finally struck with his axe and severed the Green Knight's head, his fearsome adversary simply picked it up and placed it back upon his shoulders, raging back with a war cry like the howls of a thousand wolves. Gawain was overcome by terror, but still he battled on endlessly, until reality slowly began to draw him back.

He awoke in a bed. In truth, it wasn't as much a bed as it was a pile of dry straw next to a horse trough, but even these meager accommodations felt like the foothills of Heaven after such chilling visions. With dry, cracked lips and an aching head, he anxiously crawled to the edge of the trough and plunged his head inside, lapping and slurping at the cold water like a dog. Once Gawain had drunk until he felt that he would burst, he heard a restrained, wheezing laugh just behind him, and he turned in awe to see the terrifying figure from his dreams. The Green Knight was seated in a simple wooden chair with his helmet in his lap and an immense war hammer leaning against the wall to his right. With large, dirty fingers he motioned toward a nearby table that had been set with a plate of crusty bread, a bowl of lamb stew, and a large flagon of wine.

"I think you might prefer *this* instead," the knight muttered, "Especially since you won't have to share with the horses."

Maleagant.

Gawain blinked several times and wiped the water from his face, then stared in disbelief at the image before him. As unlikely as it seemed, there sat his former ally, his ancient bronze armor tarnished green with age and neglect, leaning back in his chair and grinning like the cat that ate the canary.

"Go on and eat. Make yourself at home."

"Maleagant?" he replied in astonishment, while ravenously devouring a large hunk of bread, "Where am I? What on earth are you doing here?"

"You are in Gorre, my homeland – in my own house, in fact. And as for your second question, honestly, it is I who should be asking that of you. What are *you* doing here, Gawain?"

As he filled his empty belly and gradually began to regain some measure of strength, Gawain quietly recounted the tale of his predicament. He told Maleagant how he had ventured out on a quest with six companions, though they were eventually separated while escaping from the hordes of dark creatures who had descended upon Britannia and covered the land in pestilence and famine. After a vicious battle with these servants of Hell, Gawain had found himself alone, without adequate supplies, and being tirelessly pursued by his vengeful attackers. His only chance of evading capture was to journey through the deep marshlands, where food was scarce and the water was polluted and toxic. He could not remember how long or far he traveled, but only knew that he had been at the precipice of death when Maleagant found him.

"You saved my life," he concluded solemnly, "I would be lying dead in a putrid swamp if it weren't for your intervention and hospitality. It's odd, you know. Not long ago I felt ready for the grave to take me – for blackness to overwhelm my senses and swallow me into oblivion, shutting out the horrors of this world once and for all. But now, here I am alive and safe, and the very idea seems so utterly alien. Just the thought of never seeing my wife again breaks my heart in two, and I know now that my deepest desire is to return to her loving embrace. Maleagant, whatever bad blood existed between us after your desertion is now washed away. I am forever in you debt."

"Oh, come off it, Gawain," the Green Knight grumbled, "You know as well as any that I was never one for sentimentality. Now just calm yourself and have some wine. You still look like Hell, after all. There's plenty here to go around, and you're welcome to stay as long as you like while you recover."

"Thank you, but no," Gawain replied diplomatically, "Again, I am eternally grateful for your generosity and all that you've done for me, and as much as I wish to go home to Camelot, I must return to my quest soon – this very night, in fact, if the conditions are favorable enough."

"Don't be daft! You were inches from death not long ago, and your wounds are far from healed," shouted Maleagant, suddenly erupting with anger, "Besides, have you not given *enough* already? Gawain, you've devoted your entire life to Arthur and his preposterous dream, and where has it left you? Lying face-down in some rancid bog! Don't you deserve a bit of rest? Christ! When will you begin to serve *yourself?"*

"I appreciate your concerns, Maleagant. But this quest is far too important for me to walk away now. Although I would be honored to eat, drink, and be merry here with you... well... I really should try to find my companions..."

"Why?" Maleagant retorted, "It appears no one has tried to find *you*. Perhaps they think you're dead. Or perhaps they don't care. In any case, why don't you just stay here for now? My stores are plentiful. Just think of it, Gawain. We can live like kings, feasting all day and drinking all night... and Arthur will be none the wiser."

"I don't know..." said Gawain hesitantly, licking his lips at the prospect of such unbridled hedonism as a sinister, unseen spirit clawed away at his mind, "...but I do suppose I could use a break from all this madness. Pour me another cup of wine, will you? It couldn't hurt to stay just *one* more day."

So the day passed, followed by another. And then another. And then another. And before long Gawain had forgotten all about the Holy Grail, Camelot, and even Rowena as he guzzled fine wine and dined each night on opulent meals that would have made the king himself green with envy. Now and again he felt the guilt of his broken promises pulling him back toward his abandoned quest, but each time he did so, Maleagant would conveniently appear with some new delicacy to sample – exotic food or exotic women, and those feelings would fade away like the morning mist. Gawain sometimes felt as if he had been bewitched, but then again, the fairer sex *did* have that power, didn't they? As time passed, his thirst for pleasure swelled into an unconquerable giant within, and eventually he grew weary of fighting back. His life in Camelot soon became little more than a distant memory as he and Maleagant spent night after night together in uninterrupted, epicurean revelry.

Late one night, after an extraordinary evening of drunken debauchery, Gawain had passed out on the floor of the great hall with one arm clutching an empty bottle and the other wrapped around the waist of naked harlot whose name he couldn't even remember. But despite the relaxing influence of wine and women, his sleep was far from peaceful, as vivid nightmares continued to torture his heart and mind, just as they had each night since he had been in Maleagant's household. Gawain tossed and turned as he found himself tormented by terrifying images – childhood memories of his mother as she slowly wasted away from the black fever; his beloved Rowena being viciously ravaged in Vortigern's bed chamber; the gruesome murder of that poor Saxon boy who he had so callously allowed to take the blame for his own duplicity. Moreover, the fearsome Green Knight stalked him through his dreams, calling out his name over and over in a deep, lingering growl, and no matter how fast Gawain ran he could never break free of that colossal shadow. Fear gripped his soul like an iron vice, crushing his spirit and weighing him down as if his boots were filled with lead. He tried to cry out for help but no sound escaped his lips, until he finally found himself cornered and the monster's massive war hammer came crashing down upon him.

Usually that was the moment when he awoke.

But not tonight. Still lost within his dream, Gawain opened his eyes and noticed that the Green Knight had disappeared, and in his place stood an old man with a long grey beard.

"What has become of you, my boy?" the old man asked.

"Merlyn?" muttered Gawain in shock, "What are you doing here? How did you find me?"

"At this point, I think the question you *should* be asking is how you can find *yourself* again."

"This quest is hopeless, Merlyn," he snapped back, "What power do mere men have to stand against such darkness? The way I see it, we're all just food for worms in the end, so we may as well enjoy the time we have left in this world. Besides, I have spent most of my life serving king and country. Now I've finally taken the time to tend to my own desires."

"Oh have you, now?" Merlyn retorted, "And at what cost? Yes, a veil of evil is indeed falling over this land. The Priestess of the White Dragon has gathered dark spirits from every corner of the Unseen Realm, seeking out only the most skilled demons to serve her in the war against Camelot. You were neither the first nor the last to fall away, and you were certainly not the easiest. The fellowship of the Round Table is close to breaking, Gawain. Come now. Touch the sleeve of my cloak and witness the lamentable fate of your friends."

Gawain sighed and reluctantly reached out for Merlyn, and as soon as the tips of his fingers brushed against the old man's cloak, the skies flashed and he found himself in a small grove of trees, with the hazy light of late afternoon pouring through the leaves and branches, and the two elder sons of Pellinore standing nearby conversing loudly.

"The servants of the White Dragon had been stalking these two since the moment they embarked from Camelot," Merlyn explained quietly, "Lamorack and Aglovale are both noble men and brave warriors, but their greatest weakness has always been their brotherly spirit of competition. Earlier on this day, they came across a young maiden being assaulted by a band of thieves and naturally rushed to her rescue, swiftly dispatching her attackers and preserving her womanly virtue. Lamorack then chose to make camp for the night while Aglovale returned the maiden to her home village, and as it turned out, her wealthy father rewarded him with two small sacks of gold. Now then, watch and see what evil unfolds."

"Two sacks of gold, eh? What a haul!" they heard Lamorack exclaim, "One for me and one for you!"

"One for you?" Aglovale laughed, "Come off it! Her father gave them both to *me*. After all, I'm the one who brought his daughter home safe and sound."

"Yes, but we both rescued her. As a matter of fact, I fought off more of the bandits than you did! If anything, I deserve *both* sacks of gold for my additional effort!"

"Ha! Don't make me laugh, you arrogant buffoon! Besides, you would probably waste every last ounce of this gold on flagons of mead, anyway!"

As he looked on, Gawain could barely make out the faint outline of a hideous creature with pitch-black fur, beady emerald eyes, and bristly mane crawling with mealworms as it held tightly onto Aglovale's back, digging jagged fangs into his brain and imbuing him with the deepest avarice. In the same way, Gawain saw that Lamorack's ear was being filled with dark whispers and tongues of fire by a frightening beast who appeared to be entirely composed of ash and burning embers. The demons howled with laughter, immensely satisfied with their success as they watched the two brothers curse and fight with one another as if they were bitter enemies, until both men finally became so consumed with the desire for riches that they drew their swords and threw themselves into furious combat. Then after a few minor injuries, Lamorack and Aglovale grew so enraged that they crashed into one another and began rolling in the mud, wrestling, biting, and throwing punches like a pair of overgrown children.

"By all the stars in Heaven!" Gawain said to Merlyn, "I've never seen them like this before."

"Aye. Envy is known for bringing out the worst in all of us," said the old man, "Of course, malicious spirits are unable wield absolute control over the men and woman they torment, no more so than I have the power to force righteousness upon you. We simply work with what we are given. Temptations to sin are not implanted within the hearts and minds of mankind. Such a feat would be contrary to Free Will. Instead, natural impulses are poked and prodded, and the flames of corruption, which burn within all men to varying degrees, are carefully fanned in hopes that they might erupt into infernos. Some time ago, the servants of the White Dragon detected this sort of a flame inside Tristan, so intense that only a little provocation would be required before it consumed and incinerated him."

At that moment the skies flashed again, and they were suddenly transported to the wild northern highlands, standing amidst green, rolling hills that crested into thick layers of mist. In the fields below them rode Tristan, still venturing northward toward Ultima Thule and faithfully seeking out the resting place of the legendary Holy Grail. And although the Celtic Knight was still committed to the quest, Gawain knew that his heart remained in Lyonesse, dead and buried along with his murdered wife and all he had once called home. Service to the king had been his duty, but *Isolde* had been his *life*. Still, despair had not yet overtaken him. While far from cheerful, Tristan did his best to remain stoic and even-tempered, struggling to suppress the unquenched fury that hung like an ominous shadow over his soul. He was strong, but he was not invincible.

As Tristan rode on, seemingly oblivious to the darkness that stalked him, Gawain watched in horror as a monstrous figure hovered overhead on black, fibrous wings. He blinked and rubbed his eyes in disbelief, but when he looked again the image was as clear as day. Soon Gawain began to panic as he watched the menacing spirit reach down with scaly hands and dig his claws into Tristan's eyes.

It was obviously the smell that reached Tristan first – smoke mingled with burning flesh, the metallic stench of blood, sweat pouring from pagan bodies as they danced around their slain sacrifice. Gawain could see his friend recoil in horror as his mind flashed back to the slaughter at Lyonesse. *No. Not again. Never again!* The painful memories boiled over until something deep within Tristan snapped, and his anger erupted into a terrifying, murderous rage. He spurred his charger into a gallop and raced frantically for the black plumes billowing into the afternoon sky. Tears of hatred and retribution clouded his vision, and he screamed like a devil of Hell upon entering the altar site, swinging and thrusting his razor-sharp falcatas with reckless abandon, slashing heartlessly into the bodies of the cruel pagan worshipers who now fled from the mangled body of their human offering. *She had been someone's daughter. Maybe even someone's wife*. And now, her precious life had been poured out onto the earth and burned in honor of some cruel, primitive deity. Tristan roared. He left none alive.

Finally, having exhausted his wrath with the soothing balm of vengeance, Tristan caught his breath and dismounted, eager to survey the scene and revel in the fact that justice had been done. But when at last he looked around with unveiled eyes, the horrifying scene before him tore his soul to ribbons. *This was not an altar site*. The burnt carcass that he once believed to be a slaughtered young woman was nothing but a wild boar, roasting slowly on an open fire pit. And the pagans he had slain were not a clan of vicious savages, but a small family, innocently preparing their midday meal. Tristan gagged and staggered backward in revulsion. There they were, lying motionless on the blood-soaked ground: a father, a mother, grandparents, two children, all callously taken before their time by a man too unhinged and blinded by rage to stop himself.

"OH DEAR GOD, NO!"

Gawain cried out in horror at the ghastly sight before him, suddenly immobilized by the crushing weight of guilt, shame, and remorse. His heart screamed from within, pounding like thunder and threatening to burst, while the image of that massacred family took root in the recesses of his mind. *What a selfish, ignorant fool he had been! He should have been there at Tristan's side. He should have returned to his quest long ago. None of this had to happen!* As Merlyn turned to him with tear-filled eyes and the enchanted images began to fade from view, Gawain was given one last vision of Tristan, now wholly broken, staring out at his handiwork and pressing a knife to his own throat for a few agonizing moments before the blade dropped from his shaking hand and he fell to the earth weeping.

"Why, Merlyn?" Gawain wailed in anguish, "Why did you wait so long to appear before me? Why did you not speak to me sooner, when there was still a chance to *stop* this madness? Where were you when I lost my faith?"

"I *did* speak to you, my boy," Merlyn whispered, "But you were neither willing nor ready to hear my voice. *They will indeed hear but never understand, and they will indeed see but never perceive.* Come back to the light, Gawain. You have wallowed in darkness, but no man is beyond the reach of God's love and forgiveness. Hope is not yet lost. As a great man once said, *hope has two beautiful daughters, and their names are anger and courage; anger at the way things are, and courage to see that they do not remain that way.*"

Gawain suddenly snapped awake. He rubbed his eyes and searched the room, but naturally, Merlyn was nowhere to be found. Regardless, Gawain knew the old man had been there in his own way, guiding him back toward the path of virtue with a firm but loving hand. With his wits finally restored, Gawain quickly began to dress himself while gathering up his weapons and armor. He became repulsed by his own wantonness, noticing the naked girl sleeping next to him and the empty wine bottles strewn haphazardly around the room. But now was not the time for shame or mourning. Truly, a day would come for Gawain to atone for his sins and make his peace with God, but now was a time for *action*, not reflection.

Once he had finished arming himself, Gawain hurried toward Maleagant's chamber, eager to learn the role that his former ally may have played in this self-imposed captivity. As he quietly approached the door, Gawain noticed that it had been left open a crack, and after thanking God for such a rare opportunity he stepped closer and peered inside. Maleagant was seated directly in front of the hearth fire, which was writhing and flowing with serpentine fingers, and an eerie, female voice was emanating from within the enchanted flames. If Gawain listened carefully, he could overhear bits and pieces of the hushed conversation between Maleagant and the unidentified voice, whose tone was both seductive and terrifying.

"And what of Gawain, the king's... *faithful* servant?" purred the voice, "Do the spirits of gluttony and sloth still hold him tightly in their grasp? After all, keeping that fool under control was your *only* task. I've already dealt with most of the others. As a matter of fact, the two elder sons of Pellinore may be close to killing each other over a few measly coins, and the Celtic knight has nearly lost his sanity in the throes of grief and rage."

"If nothing else," sneered Maleagant, "you certainly have a gift when it comes to manipulation of the weak-minded."

"Mmm... you have no idea," the voice cackled back, "Arthur is now teetering near death, his kingdom is in disarray, and his knights have been scattered to the four winds. Naturally, the White Dragon is quite pleased. He *delights* in chaos."

"Oh, enough nonsense, Morgana," Maleagant replied, "I'm not one of your brainwashed minions! You know I don't buy into that ridiculous 'Great White Dragon' nonsense. I agreed to help you because of the gold you promised me and because I want to make Arthur and his idiot followers suffer – *nothing more*. Yes, I've done my part. Now speak plainly!"

"Fair enough, Maleagant. Fair enough. Just have patience, and you'll get everything that's coming to you in due time. Now as I was saying, with Gawain... *indisposed*, only three of Arthur's knights remain on their futile quest for the Grail. May I assume that Agravain and my men will be overtaking them shortly?"

"I have no reason to suspect otherwise. When they arrived here I provided them with lodging and replenished their supplies, then they resumed their journey northward shortly before I stumbled upon Arthur's pathetic lapdog."

Gawain began to feel sick to his stomach. How could he have been so blind? What madness had overcome him that he would ever put his trust in one such as Maleagant? *No matter now*. He had to find Lancelot and the others. He had to warn them that the enemy lies in wait. With renewed vigor, Gawain took hold of his axe and the bundle of supplies he had gathered and turned to run for the stables, mentally adding horse theft to his long list of sins. But as he spun around his bundle fell open and the hunting knife, bridle, water skin, and apples he had packed for his journey spilled out into the hallway with a series of unwelcome thumps. Gawain drew his axe and froze, certain that he had been discovered, but when no one came through the chamber door he breathed a sigh of relief and anxiously dropped to his hands and knees to collect the fallen supplies.

Moments later Gawain felt a large boot slam into his side.

The pain was excruciating, like being kicked by a horse. Instinctively placing a hand on his cracked ribs, he groaned in agony and doubled over onto the cold stone floor.

"You know, Gawain," a gravelly voice sneered from above, "it's not polite to eavesdrop on private conversations."

Gawain opened his eyes to the sight of a huge, armored figure towering above him in the doorway, a wicked grin upon his scarred, weathered face. The fire that once blazed in the hearth had gone out, the mysterious voice was silent, and Maleagant, a man he had once called friend, had vanished as well. In his place stood the terrifying creature Gawain saw in his nightmares.

So this is how it all ends, he thought. *I'm so sorry, Rowena*.

"Don't worry," the Green Knight boomed, "I won't kill you. It's far more entertaining to watch you *squirm*. But surely you know that I can't simply let you *walk* out of here."

Gawain closed his weary eyes and mouthed a quick prayer for forgiveness and protection, while the Green Knight laughed menacingly and raised his massive war hammer high into the air. The last sound Gawain heard before his world went dark was the ear-splitting crack of his own bones.

* * * * *

A shroud of darkness had fallen over Britannia, and as Merlyn stood at the cathedral window keeping watch over the massive throng of evil spirits that had infested the skies like a swarm of giant locusts, Gwenivere sat devotedly at Arthur's side, holding his hand as he momentarily slipped in and out of consciousness.

There had been no word from the seven knights who had set out in search of the Holy Grail, and no way of knowing if they were alive or dead. Those who remained behind offered prayers for their safety and took turns keeping watch, but they soon grew restless, frustrated at their inability to assist their brethren in staving off the rising shadows. None felt the pangs of failure more than Bedivere and Kay, who walked the grounds in dejected sorrow, one blaming himself for Agravain's incursion into the castle, and the other for betraying the sacred trust of his fellow knights. Palamedes spent his time alone and away from the cathedral, praying to his Sarmatian gods for salvation, while

Sagramore took comfort in tending to the horses, deeply convinced that animals were far more trustworthy than men. After recovering from her injuries, poor Rowena had become overwhelmed with grief and now spent hours at a time staring out at the desolate landscape, patiently waiting for Gawain to return. Lastly, young Gareth found solace in his duty, patrolling the castle walls each night before sunset, ever standing armed and ready at Gwenivere's beckon call.

"Why is this happening, Merlyn?" she asked after Gareth left to secure the western gate, "What has Arthur done that such crushing evil should befall his kingdom?"

"The light shines in darkness," Merlyn replied cryptically, *"and the darkness comprehends it not."*

"Please, Merlyn, no more riddles."

"Camelot is a light in a dark world," the old man continued, "It is a beacon of hope for all those seeking peace and justice, and it succeeds in this endeavor not because of what Arthur has done, but because of what the Almighty has done *through* him. Although he is far from perfect, Arthur has made himself a vessel to be used by God for the good of many, rather than for the glorification of few. But the Enemy does not understand such humility and sacrifice. He was cast down upon deeming himself greater than his Maker, and in retaliation, he now seeks to drag all of mankind with him into the Abyss. So you see, it is because of no wrongdoing that Arthur is besieged, but because of the threat presented by his obedience."

"But shouldn't such holiness be rewarded?" Gwenivere responded, "Shouldn't life become *easier*, not more difficult, for those who walk with God?"

"The true reward lies in the next world. It is *eternal*, not temporal. And no, this life will not grow easier. Christ warned his disciples that they would be hated, imprisoned, and even killed for following Him. This is a world at war, Gwenivere. Do you think that the armies of Hell will simply throw down their weapons when the righteous arrive to lay siege to their gates? *Never*. In this fallen world, resistance only *increases* when the darkness is threatened."

Gwenivere turned back toward Arthur and squeezed his hand lovingly, her eyes welling up with tears.

"I understand, Merlyn," she whimpered, "At least... I *think* that I do. But why must it all seem so hopeless? I feel as if God has abandoned us. Daily I implore Him for answers, for some path out of this nightmare, yet He remains *silent*. In all honesty, I am on the verge of losing faith."

Then Merlyn smiled and his clear blue eyes twinkled.

"But He is not silent, my dear. Oh no, He is *never* silent. Far too often, those who wish to hear have made themselves deaf to His voice. However, in reality, His pursuit is *unyielding*. The Great Romance goes on, though mankind often runs and hides from the only true source of hope. And so, before crying out to the Most High for guidance or understanding, that self-imposed deafness must be shattered, that blindness must be put to flight, the light of His radiance must be permitted to shine down and wash over you like cleansing waters. Now, I do not claim to know His will in all things, but He understands your needs far better than anyone, including yourself. And though trials and tribulations may come, in His love is found the strength to look upon tempests and not be shaken."

Pride Before the Fall

Lancelot cupped his hands and knelt down at the edge of the calm, sparkling pond, lifting handfuls of cool water to his lips and drinking deeply until he was satisfied. The midday sun was bright and felt warm upon his back, and the carefree twittering of birds filled the crisp, summer air with a soothing serenity. With a song in his heart, the sandy-haired knight removed his boots and his armor and reclined in the shade of a large beech tree, his body sinking comfortably into the soft green grass. *Truly, this was paradise.* And as he looked out upon the water, he saw a figure in the distance standing waist deep a few yards from the shore and bathing, her dark brown curls tumbling like a waterfall over her delicate, ivory shoulders. *Gwenivere.* She turned and smiled at him, her green eyes warm and inviting, and then slowly began to emerge from the pond, gradually revealing every glorious inch of her curvy, feminine physique. Lancelot was awestruck. Heat began to ripple through his body as she approached him, saying not a word but simply gazing at him longingly until she finally lowered herself into his waiting arms. Her scent was exhilarating and evoked a cornucopia of memories and emotions, like flowers at springtime, like spiced apples and cream, like the air after a summer rain. As his strong hands gently caressed her smooth, bare skin, Lancelot felt Gwenivere's breath upon his neck, balmy and sweet, just before she pressed her soft lips to his. In that moment, he felt his body floating among the clouds, drowning in a sea of delight, for this was his own personal heaven. Waves of bliss spilled over him, and he took joy in the realization that he now had all he had ever wanted. Then he awoke.

The campfire had gone out, allowing the frigid autumn air to stir him from his slumber. Lancelot shivered and rubbed his eyes, rising up with weary, aching joints to gather more dry wood for the fire, stepping lightly so as not to disturb Percival, who had somehow managed to keep on sleeping.

Lancelot's dreams were becoming more frequent. At first he felt guilty and tried to push away such lustful thoughts, but as the nights grew colder and lonelier, he began to welcome them, believing that the vivid, sensual visions of his beloved Gwenivere, though forbidden, kept him from sinking into the dark waters of despair. He hungered for her, and these dreams sustained him like manna in the desert. She was now his only goal, consuming both heart and mind and driving him onward, not toward the Holy Grail itself, but toward any end that might bring him back into her presence. At times he even considered abandoning the quest and returning to Camelot just to be close to her, but his dedication to Arthur and his sense of honor held him to his duty, if only by a thread.

Percival, of course, was another story. Prior to the outset of their search for the Grail, Lancelot had spent very little time alone with the youngest son of Pellinore, and his assessment of the inexperienced knight had been based almost entirely on gossip and hearsay. Gawain, for instance, thought he was preachy and irritating, frequently put off by his calm, introspective nature and strict code of morality. Sagramore and Palamedes, the eldest members of the council, were impressed by his gift for diplomacy but skeptical of his ability to keep up with the more seasoned warriors on the battlefield. And naturally, his older brothers jested with him tirelessly, but Percival mostly took their mocking in stride, preferring to remain above such foolishness.

For his part, Lancelot had grown rather fond of the young man during their journey together, mainly because he reminded him of Arthur in many ways. Earnest, temperate, and rather bookish, Percival was almost a spitting image of the king in his youth, before the harsh realities of war and death had begun to dampen his spirits. Moreover, Percival had proven to be both an excellent companion and a surprisingly capable fighter, though his faith and hope for humanity never seemed to dwindle in the face of so much bloodshed and chaos.

Upon returning to their campsite with a heaping armful of dry branches and kindling, Lancelot noticed that Percival was now wide awake. He was sitting perfectly still with his sword drawn and ready, staring intently at something in the darkness. Instinctively, Lancelot froze as well, following the younger knight's gaze until at last he spied four sets of glowing eyes patiently watching from a nearby grove of trees. *Wolves*.

The campfire, which the beasts must have noticed during the night, had been extinguished by the wind, and with it, the only obstacle keeping them at bay. *The wolves were stalking their prey*. Lancelot cursed himself for neglecting to bring Arondight along as he gathered firewood, especially since the mighty weapon now lay dangerously out of reach atop his saddlebags. Percival was armed, of course, but being on foot, even if both of them had swords they could probably only handle one wolf each, leaving two more to finish the job once their hungry cohorts had been dispatched. *Checkmate*.

This was it. They were going to die, cold and alone, here in this frozen wasteland. The Fates had finished spinning their yarn, and the time had come to finally meet their Maker. At such a realization, most men would look back on their lives and beg absolution for any unspoken sins; however, in those few fearful moments, Lancelot silently cried out to God not to spare his life, but for the chance to see Gwenivere, the object of his affection, just one more time.

But the time for fear had passed. The wolves growled ravenously as Percival slowly lifted his head and glanced up at Lancelot, the fierce, determined look in his eyes indicating that he did not intend to go down without a fight. *If we are to die this night, we will die like men*. Lancelot nodded and quietly placed his pile of kindling on the frost-covered ground, drawing a small dagger from his boot in preparation for what would surely be their last stand. Then the two men turned and faced their ferocious opponents, jaws set, hands steady, and blades unsheathed. Time seemed to stand still as they simply waited in silence in the clearing, gazing at those eerie, glowing eyes that stared back from beyond the tree line. Finally, with a surge of fortitude, Lancelot let out a savage war cry as he and Percival leapt boldly toward certain doom.

But the wolves never touched them.

Within seconds, the pack of hungry predators had scattered into the night, frightened away by the thunder of horseshoes on frozen earth. And when Lancelot looked up in astonishment to learn the identity of their mounted savior, the first thing he saw in the waning moonlight was the red cross on Galahad's snow white tunic.

"Greeting, friends!" the young knight shouted happily, "It would appear that I've arrived just in time."

"Indeed you have! God be praised!" shouted Percival.

"You have our deepest thanks," Lancelot added.

"Where have you been all this time?" Percival inquired excitedly, "We have seen neither hide nor hair of the others since we were separated long ago. But we must surely be on the right track if your travels have led you here as well!"

The fire was soon rekindled, and in the hours left between darkness and daybreak, Galahad regaled them with stories of his journey northward, battling against servants of the White Dragon, both mortal and wraith, defending innocents from the demonic hordes that had besieged Britannia, and following divine guidance with every step toward the resting place of the Holy Grail. It made Lancelot want to scream.

Ever since they first met, there was just something about Galahad that rubbed him the wrong way. He did not hate the young man, nor did he feel jealousy or bitterness toward him. But being near him, hearing him speak, and especially watching him fight reminded Lancelot of something within himself. It was like a distant, repressed memory from childhood that was trying to break into his consciousness, or a long sought-after ambition that he had never found the strength to achieve. He did not feel angry or resentful, but simply sad and filled with regret, for even at such a young age, Galahad was already the knight that Lancelot always wished he had been.

"...and then I finally came upon you two almost completely by accident," Galahad was saying as the sun peeked over the horizon, "Then again, there *are* no accidents, are there?"

"No, I suppose there aren't," replied Lancelot.

And he meant every word.

Following a short breakfast of roasted fish – which Galahad caught, of course – the three knights led their horses to a nearby stream to drink their fill in preparation for what would hopefully be the final leg of a long and arduous quest. But as the weary animals eagerly lapped at the cold, clear water, a series of large ripples began to appear in the stream, almost as if a strong wind were rushing over the surface. *But there was no wind.* Lancelot looked about and saw no men or animals splashing about in the water, yet the swells quickly increased in size until they felt more like waves on the ocean than ripples in a stream. Curiously, the horses continued to drink, entirely unfazed, as if nature just behaved this way normally. Percival gasped and leapt back when a brilliant white light began to shine from beneath the water, though Lancelot knew at once... it was *her*. He glanced over at Galahad, who winked at him knowingly.

As the light grew steadily brighter, the waves began to congregate around it, building upon themselves until they took the shape of a feminine form, lithe and strong, delicately walking on the surface of the stream. Colors and textures soon appeared on this creature of living water, adding detail to her fiery red hair and the shimmering gown of green samite that hung perfectly about her slender frame. Nimue's eyes sparkled as she approached the captivated knights, only one afraid but all three amazed, and began to speak in a melodic voice more beautiful and enchanting than a mother's lullaby.

"Your quest is nearing its end," she said, "Follow the stream toward the sea and you will find a boat waiting on the shoreline, ready to bear you away to the island at the world's end. You must make haste, for Arthur has been wounded, and his life now hangs in the balance. But beware, and do not allow your souls to be burdened, for you will need every last reserve of strength to face the darkness that lies ahead. Remember, brave ones, that your battle is not against flesh and blood..."

Her final words trailed off into silence as Nimue turned her brilliant green eyes toward Lancelot, smiling at him knowingly and gazing through to his innermost self. *She knew.* In that moment, he had been stripped of all protection, and the secrets of his heart and mind were now laid bare before her. Lancelot dropped to his knees and cowered, unable to hide from the penetrating stare of this Lady of Avalon, but then she vanished almost as quickly as she had arrived, dissipating into mist and floating away on a gentle breeze.

"Who... or *what* was that?" begged Percival.

"She is the Lady of the Lake," Galahad answered, "and we would be wise to heed her warning. Come, let us each take a moment alone to atone with our Maker. It would be wise to make ourselves ready for the challenge at hand."

As he and Percival wandered off into the forest to pray, Lancelot remained behind, still on his knees on the banks of the little stream. *How had Galahad known her?* It seemed unlikely for the lady's legends to have spread far beyond the little town of Dinan. Although... Galahad *was* a traveler. Maybe he had even been to Brocéliande Forest himself. *How curious.* Finally noticing the icy water as it soaked through his chainmail and breeches,

Lancelot abruptly stood up and found a dry, grassy spot to sit and collect his thoughts.

Why did Nimue have to single me out, anyway? What have I done? I've done nothing, that's what! Is it so terrible to love someone, even if you cannot have her? I mean, it's not as if I am guilty of murder or thievery! Is it obsession? Is it lust? Yes, it's true that I often dream of lying with Gwenivere, but these are only thoughts, and thoughts are harmless, eh? I am certainly not hurting anyone. As a matter of fact, dreaming of her is all that has kept me from going mad during this hopeless quest! There is no reason for me to be ashamed.

Before long, Lancelot's thoughts shifted from introspection to indignation, and a seed of pride took root within his soul. With it grew the blossoms of vanity and anger as he compared himself with Arthur, scoffing at the idea that a shorter, weaker, less attractive man could ever truly compete with him for the affections of such a splendid woman. *After all, if Arthur were not the High King, this would not even be a competition*. But perhaps there was still hope. Perhaps he could steal away Gwenivere, the prize of all prizes, with the glory and honor that came from finding the Grail. *Ah, yes!* With Arthur at death's door, Lancelot could return to Camelot as a conquering hero, the legendary Grail in his sole possession, and ride a wave of acclamation into the upper echelons of power, even to the throne itself! Truly, *he* had been the right man all along, and the ramblings of Merlyn and Nimue were nothing more than naïve, idealistic drivel.

Greatly pleased with his newfound sense of purpose, Lancelot leaned back against a nearby tree and relaxed while he waited patiently for Galahad and Percival to return from their penitent prayers. On the frozen ground next to him sat Naberius the Deceiver, cloaked in shadow and invisible to human eyes as he threw back his wolfish head and laughed with delight.

* * * * *

The darkness that lies ahead. Those were the words Nimue had used to describe the next leg of their journey. But the three remaining Grail knights were not fully aware of what she meant until they began following the stream northward and realized that hungry wolves were not the only creatures that had been stalking them throughout the night.

It all began with a quiet rustling noise off in the distance. At first they shrugged it off as the typical morning wanderings of forest animals, but as time wore on, the sound grew gradually louder, building in both volume and intensity until their ears were filled with the unmistakable rumble of mounted warriors, charging through the trees with swords in hand. The clamor eventually became so pronounced that it could no longer be ignored, and Percival warily glanced backward, astonished to see that the servants of evil were nearly upon them. There were seven by his count. Onward they came, formidable and unyielding, with heavy plate armor covering their torsos and masked helmets concealing not faces but gruesome, living shadows. These were *wraiths*, not men – sinister heralds of death summoned by the Priestess of the White Dragon to bring terror and destruction to Britannia. And though the northern shore was now in sight, the black knights were gaining.

"They're much too fast!" shouted Percival, "We will never be able to outrun them!"

"Then we stand here and fight," Galahad replied with steel in his gaze, pulling his white coarser to a halt and turning to face the coming onslaught.

Percival turned as well and drew his Celtic longsword, then watched as the wraiths bore down upon them, snarling with hatred and brandishing their own jagged blades, already dripping with blood. He and Galahad were clearly outnumbered and lacked the advantage of higher ground, but since delusions of fairness rarely had a place in armed combat, he simply grit his teeth, spurred his charger into a gallop, and rode out to meet the enemy with fire in his eyes and a prayer on his lips.

Lancelot, however, was nowhere to be found. For when his fellow knights rode back to engage the dark horsemen, he had silently continued toward the shoreline, eager to disembark with the boat and reach Ultima Thule before any other. A part of him felt guilty for leaving his companions to their fates, but Naberius' fiendish influence had cultivated that tiny seed of pride into sprawling garden, and its branches now permeated Lancelot's consciousness and consumed him from within. *He alone would possess the Grail. He alone would have Gwenivere. He alone would claim the throne*.

Hurriedly approaching the icy North Sea, Lancelot surveyed the landscape until he eventually spied a small boat tied to a stake, bobbing up and down in the shallow waves. *This was his chance*. By now the plight faced by Galahad and Percival had become a distant memory, so he swiftly dismounted and knelt down to untie the ropes, enthusiastically preparing to cast off and secure his requisite glory. But before he managed to loosen the knots, Lancelot noticed a long shadow hanging overhead and heard a deep, raspy voice groaning out his name.

"Laaaaancelot..."

Cold fingers of terror crept up his spine when he looked up to see a fearsome black knight, clearly the captain of those foul horsemen, looming ominously over him and clutching an enormous, blood-stained broadsword in its armored hand. The creature possessed neither eyes nor face, but merely a visage of sentient darkness, which seemed to steal away all surrounding light. A thick, black fog emanated from the exposed portions of its vaporous body and billowed into dense clouds of ash and smoke that followed in its wake.

"Your final hour is niiiiiigh," the wraith droned in a slow, protracted growl, *"Look upon meeeee and despair..."*

Frightened but furious, Lancelot withdrew Arondight from its scabbard and hastily swung for the creature's head, hoping to end this threat with a single, devastating blow. But his strike flew wide left, and the wraith raised its own blade and brought it crashing down on Lancelot's shoulder, slicing through muscles and tendons and leaving behind a bloody, gaping wound that cut him nearly in half. Lancelot dropped his sword and wailed in agony, grasping his cloven shoulder and stumbling awkwardly into the shallow waters of the North Sea. The rocky shoreline turned red with blood that had spilled out into the tide, and as strength and warmth fled from his body, Lancelot suddenly felt as if a veil of shadow had been lifted, opening his eyes and unshackling his spirit. Indeed, now that he was weakened and helpless, Naberius was abandoning him, freeing his heart and mind but also condemning him to suffer the full disgrace of his arrogant, selfish choices.

What had he done?

In that moment of clarity, the searing pain of his injury paled in comparison to the shame and anguish that now surged through his conscience. *He had failed*. He had given in to lust and pride and allowed impulses of the flesh to dominate his soul. More importantly, he had deserted both his friends and his sacred quest to seek his own vainglory. Lancelot moaned. He was disgusted with himself. *He deserved to die*. So as he watched the wraith lift its sword on high, preparing to sever his worthless head there on the frozen shores, he sat motionless, calmly waiting for the end while mouthing a silent prayer.

"God, forgive me..."

Then a bloodcurdling shriek filled the skies as an ancient blade burst through the chest of the dark creature. Its massive body began to convulse and shake while rivers of smoke poured from the wound, until finally it exploded into nothingness, leaving behind naught but a pile of empty, iron armor and a smoldering mound of ash. When the black fog cleared, the first thing Lancelot saw was a red cross on a white tunic.

"God *always* forgives," said Galahad, "Never forget that."

Smiling tenderly, he knelt down in the icy water and hefted Lancelot's wounded body onto his shoulders with ease, carrying him across the beach and draping him atop his own horse.

"There is a monastery a few miles south of here. My mount knows the way. The kindly monks there will gladly care for you and tend to your wounds. Fear not, Lancelot, for your time on this earth has not yet reached its end."

Lancelot opened his eyes and smiled weakly, humbled by the unwarranted compassion being shown by one whom he had so recently betrayed. *How had this man even survived such a lopsided battle?* Galahad was certainly a skilled warrior, but the strength and power of those dark creatures stood far beyond that of *any* man. *Had Percival survived as well?* As if somehow privy to his thoughts, Galahad laughed and pointed to a spot in the distance where the young knight stood, uninjured amidst a chaotic mass of black ash and six newly vacant suits of armor. *Percival had bested them all.*

Confusion clouded his mind until Galahad spoke again.

"I know what you're thinking, Lancelot. *How did he succeed when I could not?* Truly, you are a more experienced warrior than Percival – taller and stronger as well. But the answer is a simple one. It is an age-old proverb that I'm certain you have heard before: Not by might, nor by power, but by the spirit of the Lord are great deeds accomplished."

"Who... who *are* you?" Lancelot whispered.

"Honestly, do you still not recognize me?" replied Galahad, "Even now? Come, blacksmith. Look again."

And then he saw it, like the light on the road to Damascus, and he wondered how he could have possibly been so blind. The same sandy-brown hair. The same bright, blue eyes. The same broad shoulders and mischievous grin. It was like gazing into a mirror to the past.

"I am *you*, Lancelot... or rather, one *version* of you. I am the man you could have been, and the man you still have it in you to become. My true identity was hidden from Arthur and the other knights from the very beginning, but the power to see has always been within your grasp. Perhaps you had strayed so far away that you no longer knew yourself. Perhaps you simply did not want to acknowledge the truth. Alas, I cannot see all things. But do not be afraid. Do not give up. You are destined to be Arthur's greatest champion if only you will cast away all that hinders, renew your faith, and run with perseverance the race that has been marked out for you."

Then Galahad winked again and swatted his courser lightly on its hindquarters. And as the snow white horse trotted away, bearing the wounded Lancelot southward through the forest and toward the old monastery, he felt a warm, comforting presence enter the saddle behind him. *It was Nimue*. She had returned, though in truth, she never left. For always she had been his silent guardian, ever watching, ever waiting. Lancelot soon noticed that the pain in his shoulder was beginning to numb as Nimue's long red hair fell gently over his broken body. Just before drifting into a dreamless sleep, he gathered his strength and looked back, wistfully watching as Galahad and Percival sailed off into the mist of the North Sea.

A Light Shines in the Darkness

Gareth winced and furrowed his freckled brow as he stepped outside the door of Saint Stephen's and breathed in the acrid scent of death. The midday air was stale, lifeless, and rotten, poisoned by the shade of evil that had overtaken Camelot, like hemlock seeds dropped into a goblet of wine. Still, it was almost a welcome variation from the dank, musty odor that permeated the cathedral, which had now been housing the injured king, two women, five knights, three monks, the court physician, and a handful of other castle residents for months on end with very few opportunities for bathing.

Merlyn had given specific instructions to remain indoors, locked within the safe haven of holy ground, but after endless days of suffocating sequestration, claustrophobia had taken its toll and the frustrated inhabitants had all begun to grow rather stir-crazy, with Gwenivere suffering the effects more outwardly than most. The emotional weight of Arthur's declining health along with the weariness of essentially being imprisoned for so long had affected the young woman markedly, and despite the monks' attempts at comfort, she often lashed out at God in anger. Sensing that Gwenivere's breaking point was rapidly approaching, Gareth had volunteered to accompany her outdoors to the small garden by the cathedral walls, if only for the chance to feel real soil beneath their feet.

Now standing barefoot in the center of the tiny garden, Gwenivere experienced a glimmer of joy as she began to wriggle her toes into the cold, dry earth. She closed her eyes and felt the icy wind biting at her cheek, yet she imagined bright, warm rays of sunlight breaking through the clouds like mighty horsemen charging past enemy lines. In her mind's eye, the sky was so blue that she squinted at its brilliance, and the grassy Camlann Fields beyond the castle gates were teeming with deer, squirrels, birds, and all other sorts of wildlife. The River Alen sparkled and danced throughout the green, rolling fields, and children splashed each other playfully as fishermen shooed them away in hopes of catching their evening meals. Farmers wandered about feeding and watering their livestock, and they smiled and waved whenever they caught Gwenivere's eye. As she waved back, a sturdy arm clutched her around the waist, and she looked up into Arthur's loving gaze as he pulled her affectionately to his side. A gentle sigh of contentment escaped her quivering lips. She was safe. She was *home*.

But Arthur was not standing by her side. He was lying on a makeshift bed at the brink of death, slipping in and out of consciousness as his weakened body struggled against a deep, festering wound that refused to heal. And there were no farmers or livestock or fishermen or playing children in the Camlann Fields. The land was now barren, and the veil of darkness that had descended upon Camelot had brought a pestilence that long ago drove away the native wildlife. Tears filled her eyes as Gwenivere beheld the grey, sunless sky, and her body shivered in response to a bitter cold that reached far beyond the weather. Her tender feet, inching slowly into the garden soil, were soon met with jagged rocks and thistles, and Gwenivere cried out in pain as she collapsed onto the cursed ground. Sobs of anguish echoed through the stale, poisoned air, for no physical pain could ever surpass the loss of hope.

Rushing to her side, Gareth knelt down and wrapped his arms around Gwenivere's trembling body, holding her close and simply letting her cry as she pressed her face against his chest. Neither said a word, as no words were needed. Desperation filled her every breath, and her soul-purging wails shook Gareth to his core as he struggled to maintain a facade of strength. With

Lancelot away and with Arthur incapacitated, Gareth had taken a vow before God and before his king to protect this young woman from danger, yet his prodigious skill with a sword was helpless against the onslaught of their most formidable enemy yet. Indeed, no opponent he had faced in his years of warfare could have prepared him for the battle he now waged against *despair*. As he gazed upward, Gareth was unable to see the writhing hordes of dark spirits that blanketed the skies, but he could almost hear their sinister laughter.

The encroaching gloom of inevitability grasped at Gareth's consciousness, tearing away at his fortitude and urging him to give in, to surrender, to accept the notion that this once great kingdom had seen its glory flicker and die like a candle in the wind. *Was it truly over? Had God finally abandoned them?*

Although he was not a learned theologian like Arthur, nor was he known to pray regularly like Rowena, Gareth reached into the reserves of his memory and recalled a passage from the Book of Psalms that seemed appropriate: *"Hear my cry, O God, listen to my prayer. From the ends of the earth will I cry unto thee. I call as my heart grows faint. Lead me to the rock that is higher than I. For thou hast been my refuge, a strong tower against the enemy. I long to dwell in thy tabernacle forever and take refuge in the shelter of thy wings."*

His simple prayer seemed to console Gwenivere, and he felt her trembling cease as she whispered a timid *amen*. Sensing that the time had now come to return to the safety and relative comfort of Saint Stephen's Cathedral, Gareth stood and offered his outstretched hand to the grieving young woman. But as Gwenivere slowly rose to her feet, she gasped and covered her mouth with both hands, prompting the wary Pictish knight to draw his sword and turn around rapidly in preparation to face whatever threat had startled her so. Yet what he saw caused him to drop his weapon in astonishment.

It was a solitary white dove, spotless and clean, perched atop a wooden fence post at the far end of the garden. The dove cooed softly but did not move, staring back at Gareth and Gwenivere completely unafraid, as if the bleak desolation that surrounded them were nothing more than the hour of darkness just before the dawn. In that instant, a feeling of peace and tranquility that surpassed all human understanding flooded their veins and warmed them like a roaring fire in winter. Then with a flutter of snowy wings, the dove soared into the sky and was gone, disappearing through a break in the clouds into a delicate finger of blazing sunlight.

* * * * *

The coarse, frost-covered grass crackled and crunched beneath Percival's boots as he and Galahad trudged through the bitter cold, their hooded cloaks pulled tightly around their faces in defiance of the arctic gales that had already ungraciously extinguished their torches. It had long been rumored that Ultima Thule was fated to dwell for half the year in daylight and half in perpetual darkness, and as luck would have it, they had arrived during those six months of endless night. At times, trying to find their way became an exercise in futility. The only respite from the stifling blackness was found in the full moon, beaming steadily down from the heavens, and the strange colored lights that intermittently lit up the dark skies like glowing clouds of fire. Gazing heavenward in amazement, Percival had mentioned that these must be what the old Romans called *auroras*.

The landscape itself was a nearly barren tundra, although they had noticed a race of diminutive Pictish people roaming about here and there, many of them fishing on docks near the shoreline, while others tended to herds of oxen, reindeer, and a breed of small, long-haired ponies. More often than not, the slight stature of these natives hid them from view beneath the heavy layer of mist that ebbed and flowed along the frozen ground like an endless grey ocean, and Percival frequently worried that he might trip and fall over one of them as he and Galahad plodded on faithfully through the darkness.

Percival had assumed that the Holy Grail would be hidden and fiercely guarded within a fortress of some kind, given its extraordinary supernatural value. So after struggling to converse with the local Picts in broken Latin, he was eventually able to obtain rudimentary directions to an ancient, dry stone *broch* somewhere near the southwestern coast. It certainly wasn't the strongest lead, but right now it was all they had.

By all accounts, Ultima Thule was a fairly small island, and Percival had been right to assume that the trip from one end to another was not terribly far. In truth, a healthy traveler with a clear sky could reasonably cover the same distance on foot in less than a day's time. However, the path that Percival and Galahad were forced to take was fraught with peril, even beyond the darkness, cold, and heavy mist, causing their journey to drag on endlessly and draining their spirits dry. Wolves and other nocturnal hunters stalked them through the unrelenting night, even more so as they lost sight of the small, torch lit cottages of the native Pictish settlements. Water was scarce farther inland, and the rocky, ice-covered hills that covered much of the frozen terrain slowed them down to a crawl.

As the two knights gradually made their way across the island, their extremities growing numb from the cold, Naberius the Deceiver lurked stealthily behind them, watching and waiting, careful to keep himself hidden within the thick mist that blanketed the frozen tundra. Normally he wouldn't bother hiding from his prey, since he, like all denizens of the Unseen Realm, had the innate ability to remain invisible to mortal eyes. But he had lately begun to suspect that the one who called himself Galahad was a bit more than human, so he made the decision to play it safe and remain out of sight, silently stalking Percival with a heart full of malevolent desires and cruel intentions. Both his hatred and his frustration had been mounting, as the young knight had thus far been all but impervious to his spiritual attacks. But Naberius still had a few tricks up his sleeve.

* * * * *

Percival coughed and rubbed his hands together vigorously as the freezing air gnawed at his skin like a pack of starving rats. It felt as if he and Galahad had been plodding through this arctic wasteland for an eternity, although any attempt to actually gauge the time had become futile. With no sunrise or sunset, and the moon often lost behind a sea of clouds, the minutes, hours, and even days faded into one another, drifting blindly through varying degrees of darkness. Waves of sleet began to fall from the sunless skies, and the grey mist that covered the ground had grown so thick that Percival soon lost sight of Galahad and could barely see his own hand in front of his face. He searched the ground for his companion's footprints, but saw nothing. He listened intently for his voice, but heard only the howling of the wind. Cold and alone, Percival could feel his bones creak as he plodded onward, his feet sinking into the deepening mud and slush with every aching step, and soon a pained, despondent voice buried deep within the recesses of his mind started whispering to him in the dead of night.

It's hopeless. The perils of this impossible quest have already claimed five of Arthur's best knights. Even the mighty Lancelot has fallen! Your brothers are lost and probably dead, and yet you still expect to succeed where they have failed? Why? Who are you? As the youngest and least experienced, logic dictates that your chances are slim to none. So why not turn back now? Are you really that arrogant? You're wandering around blind and without direction in some god-forsaken wasteland! Any more of this madness and you'll freeze to death. Turn back. Save yourself. After all, is Camelot truly worth dying for?

Naberius' words steadily clawed away at his resolve, and little by little, Percival began to give in to despair. His breathing slowed. His muscles tightened. His footsteps grew sluggish and more deliberate. And more than anything else in the world, he just wanted to sleep. Exhaustion and delirium played tricks on his mind, as images of his father and brothers appeared, pleading with him to join them – to let go and allow himself to be overtaken by the rising shadows. Finally dropping to his knees,

Percival noticed that the fierce bite of the icy air seemed to be waning, and a feeling of intense relaxation overtook his weary body as he collapsed face down on the frozen earth. The violent gales fell silent, and with his senses almost completely muted, he only maintained awareness of his own existence through the rhythmic throbbing of his heartbeat. He saw nothing. He felt nothing. And as the young knight's will drifted into oblivion, Naberius threw back his head and laughed with wicked glee.

And then he felt it – a still, small voice calling out to him from beyond the void. Not an audible voice, but rather, a supernatural presence that broke through the veil of cold and darkness and spoke directly to his weary heart. It was strong yet gentle, otherworldly yet all too familiar.

Get up, Percival.

Something began to stir within him. In the depths of despair, some measure of faith lived on, though it be smaller than a mustard seed, and Percival began to feel as if a spark had kindled the dormant reservoir of hope in his soul. Slowly the tiny flame grew, urging him to cling tightly to that beacon of light, until it burned strong enough to ignite his will to stand.

Get up and fight, my boy. This isn't over yet.

Slowly rising to his feet, muscles frozen and aching, Percival willed his eyes to open and was shocked to see an aurora, dim but steady, reaching toward him like a lighthouse beyond stormy seas. He took one step and then another, the numbness fading as blood began to pump to his extremities once again. The light grew steadily brighter as the grey mist began to recede, and Percival finally broke into a dead sprint, driven forward by some power far greater than himself.

The despondent voice in the back of his mind told him again and again that he was nothing, that his quest was doomed to failure, that he would never be strong enough to endure the trials that awaited him. But those lies were quickly cast aside by the knowledge that there was One who had conquered Death itself, and Percival's strength was found in Him alone.

"Get behind me, demon," the knight said softly.

Naberius screamed.

A surge of blazing white light exploded into him with the force of a charging destrier, and the malicious creature dug in his talons, trying desperately to cling on to Percival's wounded spirit. But it was no use. *The hunter had become the hunted*. As the light grew in both power and intensity, Naberius began to lose his grip until he found himself being thrown violently backward, tumbling and spiraling through the cold night sky until his gangly, fur-covered body disappeared over the horizon.

Percival felt as if he had been reborn. The faint light that drew him out of the darkness had swelled into a radiant sunrise, waking him from the living nightmare that tormented his spirit, and driving away the suffocating gloom that chilled him more deeply than any winter storm. With the burdensome weight of hopelessness finally lifted from his shoulders, his strength and vitality returned, his mind grew lucid, and the icy temperatures of Ultima Thule became little more than a mild nuisance. Still blinded by the overpowering brightness, Percival stumbled about on the rugged landscape until he felt a strong hand reach out to grasp his own, pulling him up toward the light and steadying his balance on the rocky ledge before him. With the grey mist finally fading away, he squinted as the light seemed to condense and recede. Images grew clearer and more defined, similar to when one's eyes adjust after stepping from a dark room into the midday sun. When at last his vision cleared, the first thing he saw was a red cross on a snow white tunic.

"Are you all right, Percival?" asked Galahad, "For a moment there I thought I'd lost you."

Finally surveying his new surroundings, Percival noticed that the skies were black again. The full moon beamed down steadily from above, bathing the landscape in an eerie glow, but the penetrating daylight that had led him onward was nowhere to be found. Had he imagined it all? Had it been a mere hallucination? Stepping up to join his companion, he rubbed his eyes and pulled back the hood of his cloak, allowing the cold air to whip furiously though his unkempt, ash-brown hair.

He and Galahad were standing near the base of a small hill, on top of which lay the crumbling ruins of a dry stone broch. *Their destination*. Yet this seemed no place to house and protect a sacred artifact. The ancient castle had clearly been abandoned long ago, while scavenging and erosion had left behind nothing more than a collapsed portion of the central tower and a few scattered stones.

"I... I don't believe it," stammered Percival, "There's nothing here! Has our quest has been nothing but a fool's errand?"

"Do not lose heart now, my friend," Galahad answered with a knowing smile, "I promise you, we are not merely tilting at windmills. Besides, you've come too far and endured too much to allow such a simple misunderstanding to weaken your resolve. Come, look down. *Here* is the treasure we seek."

Percival shifted his gaze downward and spied a cracked, weathered tombstone on the ground before them. The surface was covered with Latin inscriptions, most of which he was unable to discern, but he found it simple enough to read the name that had been emblazoned across the top: *Josephus, son of Joseph of Arimathea*. It had long been said that Joseph was the first man to bring the Gospel of Jesus Christ to Britannia, and according to Merlyn, he was also given the sacred responsibility of guarding the Holy Grail and keeping its power from falling into the wrong hands. When at last Joseph's soul departed from this world, that responsibility passed to his son, whose bones now lay interred on a frozen island at the far end of the world.

"Josephus!" Percival exclaimed, "So this *is* his final resting place after all! But where is the Grail, then? And what of the remaining inscriptions? I can make out a few letters, but most of them are far too worn to read."

"It is a passage from the Gospel of John," replied Galahad, *"But whosoever drinks of the water that I shall give him shall never thirst. It shall be in him a well of water springing up into everlasting life."*

"You don't think... the Grail... is *buried* with him?"

"Josephus guarded the Holy Grail with his life. Even in his death, he guards it still."

Percival opened his mouth in reply, but before he could utter a single word, a hard, heavy object slammed into the back of his head and he dropped to the ground like a felled tree, tumbling backward down the rocky, frozen ledge and grunting with pain as blackness once again began to overtake him. Just before he lost consciousness, Percival dazedly looked over to see Galahad lying face down, sprawled awkwardly across the jagged slope. And their assailant stood over him, casually cleaning blood off the hilt of his sword. The man wore a deep blue tunic with a yellow griffin rampant, and his face was long and angular, framed by a smooth, neatly-trimmed head of reddish-blonde hair.

"Chain them up and gag them," Agravain called out to one of his companions, "Cynric and I will get to work on digging up that grave. It seems the priestess will soon have her prize."

The Gaze of Leviathan

A ghostly wind howled through the bare, skeletal trees as they reached out toward the night sky like the hands of dead men rising from their graves, and the murder of crows who scavenged the desolate landscape surrounding *Castorum Sepulcris* still haunted the night with their menacing caw. Slowly but deliberately, a small caravan of men on horseback began to approach the towering black gates of the sinister fortress, while high atop the parapets stood Lord Astaroth, demon prince of Britannia, watching them closely and salivating with anticipation. As the riders grew closer, he spied Agravain in the lead position, head held high and chest puffed out like a strutting peacock, with the Saxon warrior Cynric following closely behind. Bringing up the rear was Urien, that ruthless, one-eyed Celt, leading two badly beaten men who had been bound at the wrists and made to walk behind the horses. *The last of Arthur's knights*. Astaroth sneered at Percival and Galahad with wicked delight as they stumbled forward, clearly exhausted and in great agony, eagerly awaiting the moment when he would finally claim their lives, the Grail, and victory over his enemy who lay dying in Camelot.

Lord Astaroth's black feathered cloak billowed in the wind as he left his perch and crawled along the ancient castle walls, finally dropping into an open courtyard bathed in the eerie red light of the rising blood moon. Grinning ear-to-ear with satisfaction, Astaroth paced back and forth unseen amidst the throng of kneeling worshipers, their hands raised on high as they chanted skyward in perfect unison. *These were his people. They belonged to him*. Ask one of them to kill, and he would do so gladly. Ask one to take his own life, and he would be equally compliant. Now *that* was power. Astaroth always found it far more gratifying when humans gave themselves over to the darkness willingly, rather than through torment or enticement, and he reveled in the fact that these deluded simpletons had been eating out of his hand since the beginning. Actually, they had been eating out of *Morgana's* hand, but since she had long been his vessel in this realm, he hardly saw any difference.

The raven-haired priestess stood at the edge of the cliff as always, her slender arms outstretched, beckoning gracefully to the reverential, submissive masses. Her thin, white gown was nearly translucent, and it clung to the gentle curves of her body like a second skin, frequently causing the illusion that she wore nothing at all. Of course, the alluring image did nothing for Lord Astaroth. All aspects of human sexuality repulsed him, yet he could still appreciate the fact that this was just another weapon in Morgana's arsenal used to seduce and deceive infatuated fools into willful servitude. *It was really quite a show*. Her dark, piercing eyes drew men to her presence, and her silken tongue captured them by extracting and inflaming their deepest desires. Those present tonight hung on her every word as she filled their waiting ears with promises of immortality and limitless power, proudly brandishing the Spear of Longinus as she stopped now and again to join the crowd in their echoed chants. Astaroth smiled again, congratulating himself for choosing an earthly mouthpiece whose skills of manipulation matched or even exceeded those of any demon from Hell.

Agravain and his barbaric companions soon emerged from the inner halls of the castle led by Morgana's son Mordred, who was quickly growing into the spitting image of his mother. At only ten years old, the boy was already well versed in the ways of their Dark Father, and Astaroth swelled with pride thinking of what they might accomplish together in his eventual adulthood. As Mordred stepped aside allowing the travelers to approach unhindered, the demon prince noticed that Cynric was hoisting that ancient relic of Avalon known as *Excalibur* upon his brawny shoulders to display as one of their spoils of victory. While the crowd of onlookers cheered at the sight of Arthur's stolen sword, Astaroth cringed briefly before spitting on the ground in disgust. Even without the hand of a king to wield it, the angelic weapon still held power, although the scorching white light that usually poured from the crystal blade was conspicuously absent in the possession of such brutish, evil men.

After Cynric passed by, straining under the massive weight as he held Excalibur aloft for all to see, Urien followed a few steps behind pulling along Galahad and Percival, who stumbled into the moonlit courtyard dragged by a long iron chain. The two men barely looked alive. Stripped of their armor and weapons, they staggered awkwardly through the mob of worshipers like a pair of marionettes on tangled strings. Their tunics were stained with blood, and their faces looked marred and sallow as if they both knew exactly what was coming yet were powerless to stop it. The crowd remained eerily quiet until a young Saxon woman finally cried out, "Villains! Infidels!" and began pelting the captured knights with stones. Soon the others joined in, hurling insults, spitting, and throwing anything they could find. Lord Astaroth laughed out loud, enraptured by the chaos and hatred on display before him. But the crowd soon fell silent again as Agravain knelt at Morgana's feet and stretched out his hands, revealing a simple chalice made of clay.

The Grail.

Despite its age and construction, the relic was surprisingly well preserved. It was not adorned with gold or jewels. It had no decorative embellishments or engravings. It was merely the cup of a poor carpenter, yet it still possessed a humble sort of beauty that captivated all who stood in its presence.

"My priestess!" Agravain exclaimed, smirking with hubris and a smug sense of superiority, "Here is your prize!"

The moment had arrived. Lord Astaroth could feel Morgana beckoning to him, and he eagerly possessed her, filling the young woman from head to toe with his power, malice, and wrath. The eyes of the priestess turned pitch black, like two gaping portals to Hell, and she hurriedly seized the Grail from Agravain as hundreds of ravenous crows rose up from below the cliff and began screeching and swarming around her. A fierce, icy wind rushed through the courtyard and lifted Morgana into the air, her bare feet hovering a few inches above the ground as the delicate gown she wore billowed violently against the blood red sky. With the Grail in one hand and the Spear of Longinus held tightly in the other, the priestess spread her arms wide, and then a rumbling, guttural, inhuman voice poured forth from somewhere within her body, uttering an unholy incantation that the gathered masses had heard so many times before.

"Nos vocare te, o magnifica Albus Draconis!"

Lightning flashed as waves of thick, putrid mist ascended from below the cliff and began to condense into a massive, serpentine entity whose bat-like wings blackened the night sky. Writhing and thrashing about like an enormous moth emerging from its cocoon, the White Dragon burst forth from the yawning Hellmouth into this mortal world. Colorless scales shrouded its twisted, reptilian hide, and the rotten stench of death filled the air as the monster looked down upon his human subjects and shook the earth with a terrible, deafening roar.

The crowd of worshipers fell on their faces out of reverence and terror, careful to avert their eyes from the White Dragon's deadly, penetrating gaze. It had long been rumored that the creature's stare alone had the power to kill, and no member of this dark congregation was brave or foolish enough to find out if the legends were true. So as the ancient serpent hovered imposingly in the night sky, hungrily awaiting his sacrifice, the priestess turned her focus to the two prisoners, who had finally dropped to their knees under the weight of their heavy chains. The cross emblazoned across Galahad's tunic was stained with blood, dirt, and sweat, yet the very sight of it still caused her to recoil with disgust as Lord Astaroth's rage consumed her.

"Where is your savior now?" Morgana growled as she reared back and drove the butt of the spear into Galahad's throat, crushing his windpipe and sending the wounded knight sprawling onto the stony ground. Galahad grunted with pain as she kicked him repeatedly in the chest and face, then he eventually fell silent, his eyes too swollen to see the priestess turn toward Percival and lick her lips with desire.

"Innocent blood," she hissed, "Yes, son of Pellinore, your life will be a worthy gift for the mighty Leviathan."

After lifting up the Grail to her Dark Master, the priestess began reciting a series of indecipherable words from her ancient grimoire, a book of spells written in blood and bound in human skin. She quickly glanced over and nodded at Urien, who pulled hard on the chains that bound Percival and dragged him onto a nearby stone altar encircled by a large pentangle and several demonic symbols scrawled in ash. The priestess placed the Grail at the base of the altar, and as she continued her wicked incantation, offering up Percival's body to the White Dragon and his soul to the realm of eternal night, tears began to stream down the young knight's face. *And he prayed.* Morgana cringed at the sound of Percival's cries for salvation, and as the hatred swelled within her, she raised the Spear of Longinus on high and snarled like a rabid beast, preparing to thrust the old Roman weapon into his still beating heart.

* * * * *

Agravain was beside himself.

It certainly wasn't the brutality that bothered him. After all, he had never found much practical use for mercy or compassion, and he thoroughly enjoyed every second of Morgana beating that sanctimonious fool Galahad to a bloody pulp. But as the priestess grasped the Spear of Longinus and readied herself to plunge its jagged blade into Percival's chest, Agravain became overcome with jealousy. She had promised the spear to *him*, hadn't she? It was to be *his* prize in return for obtaining the Grail. With the power of this supernatural weapon at his disposal, he was supposed to rule the known world with this raven-haired goddess at his side! He had trudged through rancid bogs, across precarious mountains, and through a barren land of ice and darkness following Arthur's knights to the end of the world and back! With all he had accomplished, shouldn't she be just a *little* bit grateful? Where was *his* acclaim? Why did the crowd of worshippers not cry out *his* name in awe? Trying desperately to hide his boiling anger, Agravain decided to intervene.

"Pardon me, my priestess," he interrupted, quickly stepping between Morgana and Percival as the latter continued his futile prayers for deliverance.

"How *dare* you disturb the Black Mass?" Morgana snarled in response, her eyes dark spheres of obsidian.

"I certainly don't mean to be disrespectful, but as I recall, you promised me the Spear of Longinus as a reward for bringing you the Holy Grail. I've obviously kept my end of the bargain. It only seems fair for you to do the same."

Morgana stood frozen in astonishment, staring daggers back at the ambitious young man with only the howl of the wind to break the silence. No one else dared to speak a single word, and tension hung in the air like a storm cloud ready to burst. But despite the fear and reverence the priestess inspired in her sheep-like followers, Agravain held his ground. Inside, he too was shaking with fear, but his lust for power overcame all other emotions, so his gaze remained like stone, strong and unyielding. Then little by little, Morgana's scowl began to soften until the faintest smile appeared on her blood-red lips. Noticing her apparent change in demeanor, Agravain smiled as well, now certain that she had recognized the veracity of his argument.

But the satisfied smile on his face soon transformed into a look of distress and horror, as a bout of strange, deep, maniacal laughter came rumbling from within Morgana's delicate body.

The sound of her demented amusement seemed to shake the foundations of the ancient castle, and Agravain nearly stumbled backward until she reached out grabbed him by the throat.

"You gullible little miscreant!" the priestess cackled, "Did you honestly think that I would bestow a gift of near limitless power on a pathetic worm such as *you*? How gloriously naïve! You were merely a *pawn*. You were a tool I used to accomplish a task and nothing more. Now be gone from my sight!"

And with one final look of disdain, Morgana tossed Agravain violently to the ground like a ragdoll, and he cried out in pain as the back of his head struck hard against the stone pavement. But the pain was hardly his primary concern, and he soon forgot all about the throbbing lump on his head. *He had been used. He had been cheated. That manipulative witch had strung him along all this time only to betray him publically and laugh in his face!* As Agravain slowly rose to his feet, he felt neither pain nor regret. Only rage. Blind, burning, rage.

Before Morgana could resume the Black Mass and complete her dark communion, Agravain screamed with the fury of a man possessed and plowed into her like a charging bull, sending the priestess sprawling onto the ground as the spear fell from her grasp and rolled down the pavement into his waiting hands. Sensing an opportunity, the ambitious young man quickly took hold of the spear and then rolled back toward the altar, snatching the Grail as well and lifting it on high for all to see.

"You treacherous harlot!" he shouted at Morgana, still lying flat on her back, "Behold the fruits of your deception! All you had to do was keep your promise! All you had to do was grant me what was rightfully mine! I would have gladly ruled with you, side-by-side in unmatched supremacy. Our children would have been giants among men, spreading our legacy over all the earth. But now? Ha! Fall to your knees and despair, for I now hold limitless power in my own hands! I alone hold the keys to life and death! You bow before this Great White Dragon? Now bow before *me*, for I am your new god!"

Then Agravain stood, reveling in the glory of his triumph, and waited for the cheers to begin. He waited for the crowd to sing his praises. He waited to hear their cries of mercy.

But the crowd remained silent.

After a few awkward moments, Agravain opened his eyes and gazed upon the gathered masses, enraged at their insolence as they refused to willfully acknowledge him as their lord and master. *Those brazen, impertinent dogs*. He opened his mouth to castigate them but quickly saw that their faces had gone deathly pale with terror. Agravain grinned haughtily, briefly convinced that the barefaced dread displayed by the crowd was directed at his own imposing presence. But before long he noticed that they were not looking at *him*. They were looking *beyond* him, into the snarling face of the White Dragon.

Agravain of Orkney, self-proclaimed ruler of all the known world, slowly turned to look upon the great hellbeast Leviathan, a massive, writhing, serpentine nightmare summoned forth from the realm of everlasting darkness. The monster had descended from the skies above and was now upon him, it's thick, sulfurous breath overwhelming his senses with its nauseating odor, its enormous talons scraping loudly against iron and stone, and its empty black eyes peering through flesh and bone into the murky shadows of his soul. *The rumors were true*. The gaze of the White Dragon did indeed possess the power to kill. But it did nothing so prosaic as turning men to stone, like the Gorgon Medusa from the old Greek myths. Rather, the creature's eyes were like mirrors, reflecting a man's deepest self back upon him. And as Agravain stood before Leviathan, awestruck, motionless, and terrified, he was finally confronted with the putrid blackness of his own heart, and he shrieked in revulsion.

Being presented with his true self was like a glimpse into Hell, and the harsh, hideous reality was far more than most any man could bear. The frightened crowd quickly disbursed and ran for shelter, scattering into the night like rats fleeing a sinking ship as the mountains surrounding the ancient fortress echoed with the sound of Agravain's bloodcurdling screams. With his sanity now hanging by a thread, Agravain cast both the spear and the Grail aside and began clawing at his own eyes, frantically trying to rip them from their sockets in a vain attempt to put an end to the horrors on display before him. Finally, his once handsome face torn into an unrecognizable, bloody mess, the young man gave out one last wail and threw himself over the parapets, plunging to his death in the rock-strewn valley hundreds of feet below.

* * * * *

Percival's eyes snapped open and he lifted his head from prayer at the jarring sound of Agravain's cries. As he began to survey the castle courtyard, nerves taut and senses acute, the wounded knight saw nothing but abject chaos, with Galahad lying face-down on the stone pavement dangerously close to death, the priestess staggering about in a bewildered daze, and a gaggle of terrified worshipers running in all directions in a desperate attempt to flee from the dragon's wrath. One figure in particular who caught Percival's interest was the brawny Saxon Cynric, who had fearfully cast Excalibur aside amidst the turmoil and then plowed over at least a dozen people, including several women, who were blocking his path to the exit.

King Arthur's mighty sword lay on the ground less than twenty paces away from the altar, but with his hands and feet still bound in chains, Percival was forced to roll off onto the pavement and crawl, inching along resolutely toward this newfound source of hope. Knowing that the blade was imbued with the power to protect its bearer from evil, Percival struggled and strained with all his might, his waning strength gradually being renewed by the promise of some escape from this living nightmare. But shortly after he began moving, he noticed that the priestess had regained her composure and was now moving toward the discarded sword as well. The two locked eyes for a brief moment and the priestess smirked at him mockingly, all but certain that she would reach the angelic weapon before her prisoner could even make it halfway. Percival's stomach turned and he helplessly watched his cruel captor approach Excalibur, her delicate fingers grasping the hilt as her scornful expression quickly transformed into a look of triumph.

Then the skies exploded with the light of a thousand suns.

The priestess shrieked and fell backward onto the ground as if struck by a powerful blast of wind, and for the very first time, Percival could see real fear behind her eyes. It quickly became clear that whatever demonic force possessed the priestess had now abandoned her, and as she crawled off toward the castle's inner halls, her few remaining followers leapt over the parapets in terror, following Agravain in a precipitous fall to their deaths. The White Dragon growled in thunderous anger and dropped below the outer walls of the castle, shielding himself with his wings in frantic struggle to hide from the blazing light. Percival watched in awe as the heavy chains wrapped around his hands and feet gradually dissolved into dust and then blew gently into the night sky like the florets of a dandelion. He finally turned his head toward the source of the light, and there he saw Galahad, alive and well, clothed not in a filthy, blood-stained tunic, but in garments of radiant white, shining into the darkness with supernatural glory.

"Pick up the sword," Galahad said, his gentle voice now infused with a familiar, commanding fire, "Remember Percival, not by might, nor by power..."

Now free from his chains, Percival dove toward Excalibur, grasping the handle tightly and lifting the mighty sword with ease. By all rights, such an endeavor should have been futile, as it had long been common knowledge that only Arthur could properly wield that blade. As the rightful king, he alone had been deemed worthy in wisdom, virtue, and faith; thus the sword was always light and nimble in his hands. But it became a heavy burden to all others, and great strength was required for a lesser man to brandish it. Many of the knights had tried, even Lancelot, the king's champion. Yet none prevailed – none, that is, until tonight. Any reasonable man may have expected Percival to be petrified with shock after achieving the near impossible, but the adrenaline flowing through his veins easily overruled his astonishment, and the blade gleamed like burning embers as he climbed atop the castle parapets and stood tall and defiant, daring Leviathan to return and face him.

As the brilliant white light faded from Galahad's face and garments, leaving the mysterious warrior dressed once again in his tattered tunic, Percival could see that the blood moon had finally passed, and heavy storm clouds now covered the moon and stars, cloaking the landscape in abject darkness. Gazing skyward, he watched a pair of immense, leathery wings rising up from beneath the walls of Castorum Sepulcris. *Showdown.* Now rabid with fury, the monstrous White Dragon hovered above the castle walls and let out a bone-chilling roar, glaring at Percival like a hungry wolf. The creature seemed to feed on the resurgent gloom, filling the blackened sky with its presence as the unholy embodiment of fear.

But Percival was no longer afraid.

The young knight's war cry echoed through the mountains, and as Leviathan bore down upon him with fangs bared and eyes blazing, he thrust Excalibur into the cruel, black heart of the hellbeast. A deafening shriek rang out in the night air as sulfurous smoke began pouring from the gaping wound and the surrounding skin crumbled and decayed. The creature's once pale, colorless hide quickly transformed into a cracking shell of ashen grey, until at last its massive body burst asunder, sending it screaming back to the Abyss and leaving behind nothing but a smoldering mound of reeking cinder.

"Well done, my friend," said Galahad, who had reclaimed the Holy Grail during the chaos and then taken possession of a pair of horses left behind by the departed worshipers, "Your faith is even stronger than I had imagined. But come now. Our journey is still far from over."

"What of the priestess?" Percival asked, still struggling to catch his breath, "Has she escaped?"

"She has taken the Spear of Longinus and fled into the night with her son, though I am certain you will meet again."

"And you... who *are* you?"

"Me? I am only a messenger," Galahad answered.

* * * * *

Lord Astaroth, fraught with envy and utterly humiliated, sat alone atop a nearby mountain, stewing in his own indignation and watching from afar as Percival and Galahad mounted their horses and rode like the wind southward toward Camelot. *How could this have happened? No mortal had ever stared down Leviathan alone and lived!* Unlimited, godlike power had been within his grasp, only to slip through his fingers like grains of sand. Now the Grail was gone, Morgana had fled, and his hordes of human followers were either dead or in hiding. But this was no time for self-pity. A legion of living shadows still swarmed through the skies above Arthur's castle, poisoning the land with famine and pestilence and suffocating all hope within the hearts of men. Despite the failure of his original plot, the unabashed, seething hatred flowing through his veins spurred the demon prince onward, and he took to the skies in the form of hundreds of ravenous crows, soaring off into the swamps of Gorre to plan his next move. *He had already lost his chance at victory; now vengeance would have to do.*

No Greater Love

It was just before dawn when Rowena heard several loud bangs on the heavy cathedral door. Rather, she only *assumed* that it was just before dawn, for it had been months since they had seen a real sunrise in Camelot.

There was still no word from the seven brave knights who set out so long ago on a quest for the Holy Grail, and most of those who remained huddled in Saint Stephen's Cathedral had already given up hope for their safe return. Palamedes and Sagramore, the two former Roman soldiers who had grown well accustomed to death and loss after a lifetime of war, were the first ones to fall away. While they never argued with anyone or mocked those who held on to the belief that their friends might yet return, Rowena often overheard them conversing together in private about where they might go after Arthur's passing. As for the king himself, he was alive only nominally, for though blood still flowed through his veins, his consciousness had finally abandoned him and he seemed locked forever in silent slumber. Gwenivere kept herself busy by selflessly doting on this man who had showered her with love and compassion when so many others saw her as nothing more than a wanton, undeserving guttersnipe, while Gareth doted on Gwenivere, faithful to the end in his oath to protect her. Kay, the king's half-brother, had become almost intolerable to bear, as he still blamed himself for giving up the destination of the Grail knights to Agravain and jeopardizing their quest. Though Rowena and the others had long ago offered him their forgiveness, his constant moaning and despondency did nothing to help boost morale after months of lonely sequestration. And lastly there was Bedivere, the king's appointed marshal and a man of such unwavering devotion that he still maintained his daily security inspections even in the tiny, clustered confines of the cathedral. Every morning he checked the door locks, and every evening he kept watch, surveying the desolate landscape for friend and foe alike. The casual observer might have found these rituals odd or even foolhardy, but Rowena knew that Bedivere was merely attempting to maintain a facade of strength and normalcy in a world that had fallen into chaos.

With the surrounding farmlands poisoned by disease and drought and their stores of food and clean water dwindling, it became easier with each passing day to give in to despair. Even Merlyn had left them, having come and gone for a time to offer what words of encouragement he could muster until he finally disappeared to places and ventures unknown. Yet somehow, Rowena managed to hold on to hope. Somehow her faith remained steadfast and unshaken in spite of the demonic onslaught that waited for them just outside the cathedral walls. Several of the others thought she had gone mad, and at times she even wondered herself. But the light within her refused to let her quit, and Rowena still believed with all her heart that Gawain was alive out there somewhere, doing everything in his power to return home to her loving embrace.

So when she heard that unexpected knocking on the outer door, her heart skipped a beat and she rushed to the nearest window, half expecting to see her husband's shaggy blonde hair and impish grin through the filthy stained-glass. But instead she saw an emaciated peasant – several, in fact – who wore not grins but scowls of despondency and anguish on their unkempt faces. One of them, a balding, middle-aged man who appeared to be the leader of the group, caught her gaze and stared back, a startling look of determination in his weary eyes.

Rowena studied the men and searched her memory, quickly confirming that she had never seen them before. Indeed, their presence alone seemed exceedingly odd, since most of the local farmers and merchants had long ago fled to other parts of the country, desperately searching for some sliver of land that remained unspoiled by the encroaching darkness. The few who chose to remain in Camelot had taken shelter in the cathedral as well, sharing in whatever food could be spared.

"We have come for the king!" the balding man shouted, "His reign has obviously cursed this land. Open the door and deliver him to us, and we will leave you in peace."

Overhearing the commotion, Bedivere hurried to Rowena's side and looked out upon the gathered mob in curiosity and bewilderment, anxious to quell this minor insurrection before it had the chance to escalate. *Where had these men come from?* They appeared to be unarmed, though a few of them bore random farm implements like trowels, sickles, or hayforks – hardly a match for sharpened steel. Of far greater concern was the thin-bearded youth in back who had started a small fire with a piece of flint and was now using it to light several wooden torches. As he distributed torches to the other peasants, they began to strategically position themselves around the cathedral with a threatening, unspoken message.

"Ho, there!" Bedivere called out to the strangers, "Who are you? What is your business here?"

"I am Caradoc the Elder," replied the balding man, who then gestured toward the younger man tending the fire, "I and my son here are all that remains of our family. The rest were lost to this pestilence, this famine, this wretched nightmare that hangs like a shadow over our once bountiful country. My loving wife Eurfron, her aged mother, our young children... the frailest among us are all dead and buried. I say yet again, this land is *cursed!* Look around you, for I am not the only man who has lost *everything*. On our long journey to this place we passed by withered farmlands, empty riverbeds, the rotting carcasses of dead livestock, and scores of unmarked graves. *Your* king has brought this evil upon us! Deliver him now, for we will never be free of it until he pays with his life!"

Rowena's eyes welled up with tears as she listened to the stranger's woeful tale. Her thoughts turned to Gawain, and she silently thanked the Lord that they had not yet conceived any children to be lost to starvation. No one deserved to endure such misfortune, and despite Caradoc's ill-advised vendetta against Arthur, she felt great pity for him.

"Peace, brethren!" Bedivere entreated, "We sympathize with your plight, for the same calamity has befallen *all* men in this kingdom, including the king himself! Here he lies in this humble cathedral, gravely wounded and teetering near death, as we anxiously await the return of seven valiant knights who ventured out many months ago on a perilous quest to lift this veil of darkness. Know that there are those among us who have lost loved ones as well..." he glanced empathetically over at Rowena before continuing, "...and we share in your suffering. We mean you no ill will. So come now. Extinguish your torches and enter these walls as friends. In truth, we cannot offer much beyond shelter and companionship, but you are welcome to share what we have left to give."

Despite the heartfelt eloquence of Bedivere's plea, Caradoc had grown deaf to all appeals for restraint or mercy. Unseen by human eyes, Naberius the Deceiver clung to him like a leech, digging long, black talons into his skull and filling his mind with lies. After his embarrassing failure on Ultima Thule, Naberius vowed to redeem himself and prove his worth to Lord Astaroth. He pondered long and hard before remembering that famous incident with the Hebrews and their ridiculous golden calf, then he realized how simple it would be to turn a frightened, grieving people against the one responsible for their salvation.

"Fie upon your lies and false promises!" barked an enraged Caradoc, "None of these disasters befell our countrymen while *Vortigern* held the throne! He may have been a scoundrel and a tyrant, but he never brought down the wrath of God upon us!

That snake you call Arthur *claims* to have given us freedom, but all we have received is judgment! Hell has been unleashed on earth as punishment for the insolence of this new king! I warn you one last time, marshal, release him to us at once or stay locked in that cathedral and meet your end in flames."

With Caradoc's menacing words still hanging in the air, the door to Saint Stephen's burst open and Bedivere stepped resolutely into the courtyard as Sagramore, Palamedes, and Rowena followed closely behind. They stood like statues, brandishing their weapons and positioning themselves between the peasants and the cathedral, ready and willing to defend their king at all costs – even to the death. Gareth and Kay remained at Arthur's side in the unlikely event that Caradoc and his venturesome companions somehow managed to overpower four armed warriors and storm their way into the sanctuary. Then Bedivere spoke, issuing one last call for reason.

"Gather your wits about you, Caradoc," he implored, "The darkness that covers this land has taken more than your family. It has poisoned your heart and mind as well. Again, we bear you no ill will. Surrender and no harm will come to you. But if you continue to threaten our lives and our king, we will be forced to stop your ingress by any means necessary."

"So be it," Caradoc responded indignantly, clearly resigned to whatever fate might await him.

For what seemed like ages, the knights and the peasants faced one another in motionless silence, neither side eager to be the first to strike. With torches aflame and swords drawn, each man instead endeavored to stare down his adversary, subtly maneuvering back and forth in the desolate courtyard as their hearts pounded like blacksmiths' hammers in their chests. This dispute had become a standoff, a chess match, a battle of wills, though every passing moment still bore the threat of Saint Stephen's exploding into a whirlwind of blood and fire.

And then, off in the distance, they heard the soft, muffled plodding of horseshoes on dry earth.

Momentarily distracted from their confrontation, all those present turned their heads in the direction of the far-off sound and noticed a lone rider, slumped awkwardly atop a scrawny, exhausted palfrey, just as he was emerging from beyond the withered tree line. Ever so slowly, the horse began to stagger toward the cathedral, and they were soon able to make out the rider's marred features. His blonde hair was long and dirty, his beard had grown ragged and was streaked with grey, and he wore no armor or heraldry that could be used for identification. But to those who knew him, his face was unmistakable.

Gawain.

Rowena nearly fainted. *Alive? He was alive!* She dropped her sword and flew into a dead sprint, ignoring Caradoc and his band of rebels as tears streamed down her face, running with wild abandon into the arms of her husband, home again at last. But when she approached him, Rowena noticed that Gawain's feet were not in the stirrups. Instead, his legs dangled in the air like the limbs of a ragdoll. They were warped and mangled and his breeches were stained with blood.

"Oh God," she whimpered, "Oh dear God... Gawain, what on earth has been done to you?"

"Nothing less than I deserved, my love," he replied.

His brown eyes were sad, forlorn, and full of regret, and as he rode past Rowena into the midst of the angry peasants, she could sense that Gawain's return to Camelot held no true joy for him. Yes, her husband was finally home. But what should have been a moment of celebration quickly descended into fear and uncertainty, for Gawain had the tranquil, submissive look of a man being led to the gallows.

"Which one of you is the leader of this rabble?" Gawain stuttered, wincing with pain every few words.

"Who the devil are *you* to ask?" Caradoc spat back.

"I am a Knight of the Round Table, one of seven charged by King Arthur to locate the legendary Holy Grail and put an end to the plague of evil that has corrupted and profaned our land. But more importantly... *I am one who failed."*

The fatigued palfrey then fell to the earth, practically dead after Gawain's relentless journey back to Camelot, and the crippled knight tumbled down as well. Rowena reached over to help him, but Gawain gently waved her off, pulling himself into a sitting position against the horse's scraggy hide.

"Listen to me well," he continued, "I know you have come here for Arthur – to slay him in retribution for the horrors that have befallen you and your family. I come to offer you my life in place of his. If spilling blood will satiate your thirst for justice, then I beg you to spill mine. It was my own selfishness and desire for carnal pleasures that led me astray from our sacred quest. Other knights have also fallen, though I might have saved them had I not been so lost in hedonistic revelry. I have betrayed all those who loved me, and I warrant neither pity nor compassion. Arthur is a good king and a better man. He does not deserve to pay for the sins of others."

Rowena could not speak. She could barely breathe. *Surely Gawain had gone mad! He had only just returned to her, and now he intended to leave again... forever? No! How could he possibly make such an offer? How could he simply lay down his life without a fight? After all, these wretched men were hardly a match for skilled, well-armed soldiers, so why negotiate with such a valuable bargaining piece?* Desperate, horrified, and heartbroken, she picked up her sword and prepared to rush to Gawain's defense, ready and willing to stand between him and Caradoc, alone if necessary. She would protect the man she loved even if he refused to protect himself.

And then, something happened that she did not expect.

Caradoc dropped his torch. As the flame fizzled and died on the dusty ground, his companions took notice and followed, and soon all the torches had been extinguished. Moreover, those carrying trowels, sickles, or hayforks released their grips on the meager weaponry and turned their hands outward, proving to all those who stood within the courtyard that they had chosen to renounce their threats of violence. And beyond human sight, Naberius the Deceiver suddenly found himself hurtling through the stratosphere, stripped of his influence and cast away by a power far greater than sorrow or fear.

"Never before have I witnessed such love," Caradoc said as he knelt on the earth next to Gawain, "I had eyes but did not see; I had ears but could not hear. Truly, I too have succumbed to my baser instincts. May God forgive us all."

"God *always* forgives," said a familiar voice.

They turned and saw a red cross on a white tunic.

* * * * *

Arthur awoke with the sun upon his face. He squinted and blinked a few times, for the light was far too radiant and overwhelming after nearly a year trapped in darkness.

He could not feel the festering wound in his thigh. In fact, he felt no pain at all, and as he breathed in the sweet air of spring, Arthur could tell that his once broken body had been restored and refreshed, just as when one awakens from a long, peaceful sleep. After his eyes finally had a chance to adjust, he grinned with delight as Gweinvere's loving smile came into view. She sighed with relief and kissed him gently while tears of joy glistened on her soft, rose-colored cheeks.

"Welcome back," her voice trembled, "I've missed you."

Arthur sat up straight and wrapped his arms around the angel before him, pulling her in close and holding her tightly to his chest as if he were afraid that she would vanish into the morning sunlight like the memory of a dream. The smell of her hair, the taste of her lips – they dazzled his senses and left him giddy and lightheaded as he allowed the world around him to fade away and lost himself in her embrace. This was more than comfort or affection. This was a *homecoming*.

After several minutes of silence, Arthur heard someone abruptly clearing his throat and realized that he and Gwenivere were not alone in the room. He lifted his eyes and spied Kay near the open cathedral window, disheveled and drenched in sweat after a long night of worrying, but with a resplendent smile stretched across his red, freckled face. Bedivere and Gareth stood waiting dutifully at the foot of his bed like a pair of good soldiers, while Rowena and Gawain sat together in the far corner, briefly looking up from their deep, tearful conversation to acknowledge that their king had awoken.

"What manner of sorcery is this?" gasped a white-faced Palamedes as he reentered Saint Stephen's, clearly in awe of Arthur's miraculous recovery. The bowl of hot broth he was carrying fell from his shaking hands and splattered all over the smooth, stone floor, and he grasped a nearby table in a frantic attempt to steady himself. Then before anyone else could offer the puzzled Sarmatian knight an explanation, a boisterous voice answered from outside in the courtyard.

"Peace, my brother," Galahad laughed, "There is no sorcery here. Now come. Look upon the fruits of God's grace."

Gwenivere helped Arthur to his feet, and all those within the cathedral hurried through the doorway, stepping eagerly into the blazing sunlight. The morning sky, no longer cold and grey as death, was so blue that they were forced to shield their eyes from its brilliance, and the abundant wildlife that had once frolicked throughout the grassy Camlann Fields was slowly returning, as squirrels, deer, badgers, foxes, and countless types of birds emerged from exile and set upon the lush countryside beyond the castle gates. The rippling sound of flowing water filled their ears as the renewed River Alen rushed and splashed along its sparkling, pebble-strewn banks, bringing back life to a previously dry, cracked, desolate earth.

Galahad was sitting atop a large tree stump, chuckling to himself softly and admiring a small patch of heather blossoms that had sprouted nearby. A warm breeze ruffled through his sandy-brown hair as he picked one of the flowers and raised it into the air, studying every detail of its pink and white petals under the soothing light of day. Then Arthur looked down and noticed something peculiar sitting on the stump beside him – it was a simple chalice made of clay.

"The Grail!" shouted Arthur, "You found it!"

"Aye," Galahad replied, "It was indeed the power of the Holy Grail that healed your wounds and lifted the dark shadow that had fallen over Camelot. But look not to me, friends, for I am merely a messenger. Rather, it is young Percival who deserves the gift of your gratitude. After all, it was he who vanquished a horde of black wraiths on the shores of the North Sea. It was he who summoned the courage and faith to wield Excalibur when all other hope seemed lost. And it was he who stood toe to toe with the monstrous White Dragon, banishing it back to the filth from whence it came."

"That reminds me," interjected a blushing Percival, who had been standing nearby, "I believe this is *yours*, sire."

He then knelt down before Arthur and presented him with Excalibur, its translucent, crystalline blade shining with ethereal fire. Grasping the angelic sword, the king could feel his strength returning, though he soon set it aside and bid Percival to rise, embracing him not as a subject, but as a brother.

"It is finished," Galahad announced with a knowing smile, "Long live the king."

Then he winked and lifted the Holy Grail on high, and all those gathered in the courtyard looked on in astonishment as a pillar of fire suddenly reached down from above and consumed him, whisking away the Cup of Christ and the mysterious young knight along with it. After both had ascended into the heavens, the flaming whirlwind vanished into thin air, leaving behind not a trace of its existence. The ground where Galahad once stood was not even singed, and all that remained was a single pink heather blossom resting atop the empty tree stump.

BOOK THREE: FALL

"GOD HAD ONE SON ON EARTH WITHOUT SIN, BUT NEVER ONE WITHOUT SUFFERING."

- AUGUSTINE OF HIPPO

The Wedding Feast

Golden fingers of sunlight reached through the ornate stained-glass windows of Saint Stephen's Cathedral, painting the stone floors and the smiling faces of the congregants with multi-colored images and filling the sanctuary with a warm, heavenly glow. The pews were packed to capacity, and the overflow of eager attendees spilled out into the narthex, all outfitted in their Sunday best. Gareth wore his finest court attire and stood near the altar with Arthur by his side, grinning resplendently, his palms sweating with anticipation. At long last, the priest beckoned to a pair of attendants with a subtle movement of his hand, and a band of trumpeters lifted their instruments to their lips, collectively blaring out a fanfare that echoed through the chamber as the oaken doors were opened wide.

Lunette entered the doorway wearing a blue silk gown with silver embroidery. Her shining, chestnut hair was adorned with wild flowers, and the intoxicating scent of herb-scented oils grew ever more intense with each of her delicate footsteps. The congregation rose together and gazed upon the spotless bride, a picture of fidelity and virtue, with her parents and elder sister Lenorre shedding joyful tears in the front row. On the other side of the aisle, Rowena stood arm-in-arm with Gawain, smiling with delight as she chose instead to watch the groom, his blushed red face beaming with pride and exhilaration to see the woman he loved approach the altar. Finally, at the behest of the priest, Rowena took her seat along with the rest of the gathered crowd, and she laughed silently to herself about the curious turn of events that brought these two together.

It had been nearly ten years since their dealings with the Order of the White Dragon and the search for the Holy Grail, and in that time, Lunette had grown from a precocious child filled with youthful infatuation into a charming, intelligent, feisty young woman who was still madly in love with the brave knight who had saved her life so long ago. Once she reached the proper marrying age, Lunette persuaded her father to ride with her to Camelot to speak to King Arthur about the auburn-haired Pictish warrior she remembered with such fondness. When at last the star-crossed couple was reacquainted, Gareth could scarcely believe his eyes, astonished that the stunning creature before him was the same little girl he once discovered dirty and weeping at the edge of a forest. Their love bloomed quickly, and the rest, as they say, is history.

Rowena smiled approvingly at Gareth as he repeated his vows, stammering nervously and squeezing his bride's hand in an endearing attempt to keep his own from shaking. Thinking back on the couple's relatively brief courtship, Rowena silently reflected on how much the now well-seasoned knight had grown in both rank and honor since the day they first met on Pentecost. Not only was he finally getting married, but Arthur had also named him the King's Champion, owing to the fact that his skills with a sword were unmatched by any man in the kingdom. There had been a grand ceremony, with Gwenivere personally bestowing the honor upon Gareth in recognition of his dutiful role as her protector during Arthur's debilitation. Of course, the position had remained vacant for many years, as Arthur patiently and sorrowfully waited for Lancelot to return. Eventually and with much consternation, he chose to move on, grudgingly accepting that his closest friend and greatest knight was likely dead. However, something within Arthur still refused to abandon all hope, thus he declined to fill Lancelot's seat at the Round Table, with his mighty sword Arondight marking his place to this day.

Nevertheless, Gareth quickly proved himself to be a capable and worthy champion, as he and the other remaining knights achieved remarkable success in rebuilding a kingdom struggling to recover from a precipitous plunge into darkness and chaos. Following Galahad's strange, otherworldly ascent into the heavens, the reunited Council of the Round Table scoured the countryside for remnants of the Order of the White Dragon; quelling insurrections; providing aid to the sick, wounded, and indigent; and restoring the shining light of hope that had once been found in Camelot. As such, they were greatly blessed by the wedding of Gareth and Lunette taking place during a time of peace, with Arthur's reign reaching a near utopian apex.

As the priest continued the Nuptial Mass, Rowena's mind began to wander and she harkened back to the last time such a ceremony was performed in this cathedral. *Ah, yes.* Without a doubt, Arthur and Gwenivere's simple exchange of vows still remained the most beautiful wedding she had ever seen. Only a matter of days after the king had been healed from his mortal wound by the power of the Holy Grail, while he was still walking tentatively and struggling to regain his full strength, Arthur managed to drop to one knee before the woman who had doted by his side throughout his infirmity and affectionately asked her to be his wife. Of course, Gwenivere said *yes* without hesitation. And since neither wanted to wait, the ceremony was held that very afternoon, with one of the cathedral monks officiating and a handful of haggard knights as witnesses. Arthur, ever the hopeless romantic, created his own vows – tender, heartfelt words that brought his bride to tears, although Rowena was certain she had caught a few of the men with misty eyes as well. When it was all over and the monk pronounced them man and wife, Gwenivere took Arthur's arm and they walked together through the Camlann Fields by moonlight. Indeed, it may have lacked the typical pageantry and regal grandeur one might expect from a royal wedding, but to this day, the understated simplicity and pure, honest love Rowena witnessed on that summer evening rang out more loud and clear than a thousand church bells.

The bells! Rowena's thoughts snapped back to the present when she heard them ring, joyfully announcing the marriage of Gareth and Lunette to all within earshot. She quickly stood with the rest of the congregation, cheering and applauding as the priest presented the blessed union to their friends, their family, their king, and their God. Once the priest dismissed everyone, Gawain took her hand and pulled her along through the crowd, evidently eager to reach the wedding feast in the Great Hall. Normally Rowena would have playfully chided her husband for thinking entirely with his stomach, but since she was famished as well, she followed along with enthusiasm.

The Great Hall was lavishly decorated with tapestries and bouquets of wild flowers, and the tables were filled with every sort of food one could imagine. Servants walked about carrying plates of roasted venison, quail with sage and onion stuffing, baked fresh-water fish, and steamed oysters in almond milk. Baskets full of hot wheaten bread were passed from guest to guest along with small dishes of butter and cheese, and pewter goblets of mead or mulled wine were refilled over and over again as the day wore on. In between each course, Arthur summoned jesters, jugglers, acrobats, and minstrels for the entertainment of the jubilant crowd. Everyone danced, sang, ate, drank, shouted, and laughed until they were all utterly exhausted, still wishing that the celebration would never end. They were all so caught up in the revelry, in fact, that no one seemed to notice the dark-haired young man who entered the Great Hall alone, carefully surveying the festive crowd until he located Arthur offering a toast at the head table.

* * * * *

Percival stood by himself near the hearth and peered out over the rim of his goblet as he finished off one last mouthful of wine. It was only his second glass of the evening, so unlike many of the other partygoers, he remained perfectly sober and still had his wits about him. Percival had never been overly fond of spirits in the first place, and his otherworldly encounter with the Holy Grail had only cemented his resolve to live a life of piety and virtue. But that same encounter also put him in a unique position on this night, as he was the only one alive who had seen that face before – the pale, stoic face of the dark-haired stranger who had just sauntered into the Great Hall. Ten long years had passed since they first met, but that face remained etched in his memory. The young man's appearance had grown slightly weathered by age and experience, and his hair was noticeably longer, falling past his shoulders in shining, black waves, but Percival would know him anywhere. After all, he was the spitting image of his mother. This was the boy who had led him in chains to the black mass atop *Castorum Sepulcris*. The son of the Priestess of the White Dragon.

* * * * *

As Arthur completed a rambling, jubilant toast to the bride and groom, he quickly emptied his goblet and slumped clumsily into his chair, knowing full well that the wine had gotten the best of him. He would undoubtedly pay for this overindulgence when morning came, but for now, the king had no other worldly concern than to enjoy the evening's festivities with gladness in his heart and his beautiful queen by his side.

Gwenivere sat quietly at the table to his left, nibbling on a fruit pastry and smiling broadly in a futile attempt to hide her exhaustion after their lengthy night of celebration. Arthur grasped her delicate hand and smiled back, still in awe after all these years that she had given herself to *him*. After all, he rarely viewed himself as a powerful king with the ability to ensnare any woman he desired with the greatest of ease. No, in Arthur's mind he was still that same awkward bookworm he had been in his youth – a lonely, studious orphan with stringy brown hair and no more status in the world than a common fishmonger. Yet here she was, his bride and his queen, the very image of nobility, beauty, and grace. Arthur *adored* her, though not in the cloying, worshipful way that often characterized romantic love and tended to border on unhealthy obsession. He simply loved her – body, soul, and spirit – with a depth that reached far beyond the surface, fervent and unwavering like an ocean current. In their private time together, he had been able to share his apprehensions and insecurities without fear of rejection, and she had finally confided in him about the difficult truths of her past, eventually breaking into redemptive tears of joy when she realized that he held no judgement and would gladly let those ghosts remain dead and buried. The two had formed a bond that became known and envied throughout the kingdom, and as Arthur watched Gareth and Lunette gleefully dance together in the waning candlelight, he prayed that they might find the same measure of happiness.

A few moments later, a yawning Gwenivere lightly touched Arthur's forearm, kissed him on the cheek, and announced that it was time for her to retire to bed. The king staggered to his feet and stood respectfully while she exited the room, and at his prompting, the other nearby guests stood as well, including old Pellinore, whose simultaneous drunkenness and senility had resulted in more than a few amusing conversations with other partygoers throughout the evening. But it was also Pellinore who finally noticed the dark-haired stranger standing a few feet in front of Arthur, waiting patiently to be granted audience with his king. As Gwenivere finally disappeared through a torch-lit stone corridor, the feeble old man leaned toward Arthur and mumbled something unintelligible, his breath smelling strongly of mead and baked fish, and then he promptly lost his balance and tumbled forward over the table, knocking dozens of plates and goblets to the floor before landing flat on his back directly in front of where the stranger stood.

"Someone here to see you, Arthur," Pellinore muttered incoherently before passing out in a drunken stupor.

Once they became aware of what had happened, Lamorack and Aglovale leapt from their seats and rushed to their father's aid, gingerly helping him to his feet before apologizing profusely to the gathered crowd and carrying the old man off to bed. As for the dark-haired stranger, he just stood there in a puddle of spilled wine with an expression of shock and confusion on his face. Surely he had expected a slightly more orderly and regal introduction to the famed court of Camelot.

The stranger's peculiar reception then continued on its disappointing descent when he shuddered to find the blade of Percival's sword pressed firmly against his throat.

"Sire, take heed and guard yourself," Percival shouted in warning, "for this youth means to slay you where you stand."

"I am unarmed!" the stranger answered with the palms of his hands outturned for all to see, "and I assure you that I come here in friendship. I mean no ill will to any man or woman who walks these hallowed halls."

"Your lies won't work with me, villain," replied Percival, "I know your face well. You are a child of the darkness – the only son of the Priestess of the White Dragon!"

"Aye... that I am," he said softly.

The crowd gasped in astonishment, and the other knights in attendance drew their swords, stepping resolutely between their king and the son of his notorious enemy. The dark-haired stranger neither moved nor spoke, but his eyes danced quickly around the room, apparently studying the positions of all who posed a threat to his safety. Tension hung in the air like a thick, suffocating fog, and the only audible sounds were staggered breaths and pounding heartbeats. Then after a few moments of deafening silence, Arthur emerged from behind the table flanked by Bedivere and Kay, but bid them both stand aside so he could speak to this daring young man face-to-face.

"Well, you're either incredibly brave or incredibly foolish," Arthur began, "If I were you, son, I would choose my next words carefully, for they very well may be your last."

"My name is Mordred, sire," said the stranger, "and yes, my mother was indeed the same dark priestess who brought such great calamity upon your kingdom."

"Was?" queried Arthur.

"I have neither seen nor heard from her in years, sire. At this point, I know not whether she is alive or dead. And though I hesitate to display animosity toward my own flesh and blood, I pray for the sake of Camelot that it is the latter."

"Why have you come here, Mordred?"

The young man slowly dropped to his knees in submission, and Percival withdrew his sword as he began to speak.

"My mother traveled a dark path in life. Long tormented by a painful past and a thirst for vengeance, she gave herself over to the hidden powers of this world, and she long endeavored to drag me down with her. But her ways are not my ways, sire. I have no desire to wallow in the same vile depths that finally drowned my mother and stole away her humanity. So after fleeing from her poisonous influence and scraping my way through life alone for a time, I found myself confronted with a simple choice: I could continue wandering this wide world on my own, aimlessly drifting like a ship lost at sea, or I could change my stars and seek out something to live for. And that, your majesty, is why I've come to Camelot."

"That's a very noble goal, young man," the king replied warily, his mind drawn back to Agravain's cruel deception, "that is, if you truly are sincere and not just attempting to beguile me with honeyed falsehoods."

"I have no impetus to lead you astray, sire," said Mordred, "especially when you are the only family I have left."

Arthur froze, and the Great Hall again fell silent.

"What... *what* did you say?"

"My mother's name was Morgana," Mordred continued, "She was the eldest child of Uther Pendragon, and until you emerged as leader of the British rebellion against Vortigern, she still believed that you had died shortly after childbirth. She was your sister, sire. And I am your nephew."

Arthur staggered backward and slumped into a nearby chair as his knees gave out beneath him. His palms began to sweat and he looked around the room frantically for answers, with the onset of panic causing his pulse to race. Spying a nearby pitcher of water, he filled a goblet and managed to drink a few sips before splashing the remainder in his face, with hopes that he would wake from some dream or hallucination brought on by the wine. *But it was not a dream*. As he scanned the shocked faces in the crowd with desperation, there was one in particular who caught his eye. And she was weeping.

* * * * *

Rowena wanted to disappear. She sank into her chair and cradled her face between her hands, wishing that the world would just fade away so she could escape from this nightmare. *It had finally happened*. Her deepest fears had at last been realized. What began as an evening of jubilation had turned to sorrow, and now she had no idea what to do. Rowena was the only member of the court who had ever known Arthur's sister, and the handful of stories she chose to tell over the years were filled with levity and joy, while she deftly skipped over the darker, more disturbing aspects of their shared past. For all Arthur knew, Morgana had simply left the country long ago in search of greener pastures, free from Vortigern's tyranny. But how would he react tonight, learning that his sister had allied herself with the servants of Hell? *There was only one rational course of action.* Honesty had not been her first choice, but it *would* be her last. When Rowena gathered the courage to look up at Arthur, her expression was not that of amazement or disbelief, but of devastation, like a child who was just told that her absent father had been killed in battle.

"Rowena," the king asked her tentatively, "is it true what Mordred has spoken? What have you not told me?"

Slowly rising to her feet, Rowena took a deep breath, wiped away her tears, and finally laid down the heavy burden that she had been carrying alone for these many years.

"I'm so sorry, Arthur," she replied softly, "I've long had my suspicions, but I never knew for sure until now. Morgana was once my closest friend, but as Mordred said, she traveled down a dark path. Long ago, I watched in horror as she conjured evil spirits at your mother's graveside, and it terrified me so that I fled from her presence. After that day, I never saw her again... not until I caught a glimpse of her at the Battle of Badon Hill, stealthily making her way through the Saxon barracks up to the keep of Vortigern's castle. *And we all know what became of him*. So when Gareth rescued Lunette and her sister from the Order of the White Dragon and we learned about the High Priestess, I prayed with all my heart that it wasn't *her*... that she hadn't fallen that far... that there was still hope for redemption. Alas, it seems I was naïve. Please forgive me, Arthur. I only wanted to spare you from the truth."

As she finished her cathartic confession, Rowena could feel Arthur staring back at her with pain behind his eyes. He spoke not a word but merely sat in silence for what seemed like an eternity, lost in deep, turbulent thought. She tried in vain to read his expressions, but his face was blank, oddly emotionless, and as hard as a slab of granite. The gathered crowd looked on in fearful anticipation, waiting with bated breath to hear how the king would respond to such earthshattering news. Finally he lifted his head and his countenance began to soften.

Rowena gasped.

Much to her astonishment, a wide smile stretched across the king's face and he began to laugh – not wildly and riotously like some unhinged madman, but with a genuine joy that easily spilled over and engulfed everyone in attendance. *It was contagious!* Before long the Great Hall was overflowing with laughter, and with glistening eyes Arthur reached for a bottle and filled two pewter goblets with wine, keeping one for himself and giving the other to the dark-haired stranger.

"Sheathe your swords, friends," Arthur commanded with a renewed confidence in his voice, "and raise your goblets in celebration. My nephew has come home."

Chevalier de la Charrette

Gwenivere yawned audibly with her arms outstretched as she slowly climbed the cold, stone staircase up to her bedchamber. The wedding feast had been absolutely enchanting, maybe the finest she had ever attended, but with exhaustion rapidly overtaking her senses, she only hoped to keep her eyes open long enough to undress and crawl into bed before collapsing on the hallway floor like a falling cherry blossom. After all, it would be a shame to ruin such a lovely dress. She was wearing an ornate, flowing silk gown, lavender with gold embroidery, and the delicate material swished around her feet as she walked, reminding her with every step that she truly was a queen. Nearly ten years had passed since she married Arthur, yet to this day she remained astounded and overwhelmed that he had somehow chosen *her*. The tawdry secrets of her past meant nothing to that strange, remarkable man, and when he looked at her, he only saw perfection.

Of course, Gwenivere knew that she was far from perfect. But Arthur loved her wholly and unconditionally, in spite of all her flaws and failings, thus she had grown to love him in return. Unlike most of her previous romantic relationships, her bond with Arthur was born not of fire and passion, but of selflessness, fellowship, and sacrifice. Whereas many men delighted in her physical beauty, Arthur also looked deeper – beyond her eyes and hair and smile – and saw the hurt, scared little girl behind that charming facade. Other men had measured her by what they could gain from her companionship, but from the very first day they met, Arthur instead displayed concern for her needs and gave of himself freely. He was a living contradiction – the complete antithesis of any man she had ever known. His face was round and remarkably common, his hair dull and stringy, and when he laughed he sometimes made an awkward snorting noise. Although he had been the victor in countless battles, Arthur looked more like a scribe than a soldier. Despite his crown, there was little in his outward appearance that a woman would normally desire. But she had always admired him, and she learned to love him because he first loved her, with a love that chased away doubt and fear.

After stepping into the darkened bedchamber, Gwenivere removed her slippers and began taking down her hair before fetching a taper to light the torch-filled sconces. She could still hear the joyful noises of the wedding feast resounding in the Great Hall below, and she smiled at the thought of Gareth and Lunette beginning their new life together. As the torches blazed to life and illuminated the room, familiar shadows danced upon the walls in the flickering firelight. However, there was one shadow that seemed oddly out of place. It was broad and tall, the shape of a massive man standing head and shoulders above the doorway, towering ominously over her as she immediately regretted her decision to leave the feast alone. Terrified, she turned to face the intruder, and a large hand clamped down over her mouth before she had a chance to scream.

* * * * *

The wedding festivities finally ended a just few minutes before sunrise, and Arthur drunkenly stumbled to his chamber and collapsed onto the large featherbed therein, falling into a deep sleep almost instantly. He had already overdone it by the time his nephew arrived, but the potent mixed emotions that stemmed from the ensuing revelations – sorrow, heartache, disillusionment, fear, incredulity, and finally jubilation – pushed him over the edge into an entirely new level of intoxication. As a normally temperate man, Arthur was hardly used to the effects of such deliberate excess, and his splitting head led him to dismiss his typical schedule and stay huddled under the blankets far longer than he would otherwise. Thus it was nearly midday before he realized that Gwenivere was missing.

When the persistent sunlight pouring through his chamber windows grew far too bright to be ignored any longer, Arthur rubbed his eyes and sat up slowly, splashing a handful of water on his face before dressing in a clean tunic and making his way downstairs to the kitchen. The Great Hall was deserted, and it seemed that most everyone else had already eaten and gone about their daily business, but he still managed to scrounge up some bread with butter and wild honey to sate his appetite. He was thirsty as well, but the mere thought of drinking more wine or mead after last night's overindulgence made Arthur sick to his stomach, so he decided to venture outside and draw a bit of cold water from the well instead.

After drinking his fill, Arthur began to feel rejuvenated, so he put off his regular schedule once again and casually strolled the grounds enjoying the warmth of the sun and the cool midday breeze. As he passed by the tilting fields, he spied Kay honing his skills on the archery range while Bedivere ambled past and bid him good morrow after completing one of his frequent daily patrols. A few moments later, Arthur noticed Sagramore scurrying around in a pasture near the stables, attempting to break in a young palomino stallion. The ravages of time had finally taken their toll on the old Numidian cavalryman, and with his days in the Roman army now decades behind him, Sagramore had finally chosen to put away his sword for good. Although he was still as tough as nails and his deep, booming voice had not yet abandoned him, the old soldier had certainly lost a step and often worried about being a liability on the battlefield. So now he spent most of his time tending to the horses, and as Arthur watched his faithful friend hard at work, he longed for the day when all men would at last beat their swords into plowshares.

In the small, octagonal arena just beyond the archery range, Arthur spotted his newly discovered relative, the dark-haired stranger who called himself Mordred, engaging in a friendly bout of swordplay with Palamedes, who was almost as old as Sagramore but still as spry as a man half his age. The Sarmatian knight brandished his fearsome scimitar and clashed against Mordred's own iron blade, a well-worn Saxon relic the eager young man had probably scavenged from the ruins of a barren battlefield. Arthur quickly made a mental note to ensure that his nephew was presented with a proper sword during his time in Camelot. Yet despite the drastic inferiority of his weaponry and the slightly awkward way in which he moved, Mordred was hardly outmatched as he somehow held his own against a vastly more experienced opponent. Arthur chuckled with pride as he leaned against the wooden fence enclosing the arena, and he began to scrutinize the battle intently, oblivious to the fact that someone else was watching as well.

"I still don't trust him," whispered an anxious voice.

Startled by the sudden interjection, Arthur swiftly turned to see Percival standing a few feet to his right, pensive and unsmiling, his sharp eyes focused on the two men circling one another in the center of the arena.

"Something on your mind, Percival?" Arthur answered.

"How can you welcome him so easily, sire? Forgive me, as I don't mean to appear insubordinate, but surely only a fool or a madman would allow the son of that dark priestess to walk freely among us, and I know that you are neither. He spent his childhood roaming the haunted halls of *Castorum Sepulcris* and stood happily by his mother's side as she performed an unholy Black Mass. He has denied none of this, and yet you greet him with open arms. I simply do not understand."

"Your rationale is not lost on me," the king sighed, "and I do not condemn you for questioning my own. Aye, the young man obviously carries the heavy burdens of a tumultuous life, and his surprising presence here does give me pause. He came to us in peace, although I am forced to admit that Agravain once came to me in peace as well, and his vicious treachery has left us all with scars both physical and spiritual. But even so, we must not succumb to fear or cynicism. I cannot allow myself to pass judgement on someone I barely know through the narrow lens of Agravain's betrayal. So yes, I welcome him. I will be wary, and I will not trust blindly, but for now I will take him at his word. He is family, after all. And if a checkered past is reason enough to withhold brotherly love, then we all deserve to live out our days alone in the wilderness."

"I pray that you're right, sire," Percival responded, nodding hesitantly before turning his attention back to the arena.

"As do I, Percival. As do I."

After greeting Palamades and Mordred, then offering the latter a hearty congratulation on his surprising performance, Arthur gradually made his way back toward the castle, struck with the recent realization that he had not seen his wife since last night's festivities. He hadn't expected to find her in bed when he first awoke, assuming that she had risen much earlier and had gone about her daily tasks without disturbing him. *But surely he should have come upon her by now.* After a brief deliberation, he decided to seek her in the small garden outside of Saint Stephen's. Gwenivere had been a frequent visitor ever since their temporary confinement in the cathedral ended many years ago, and tending to the flowers and wild herbs always seemed to nourish her soul.

The gentle, perfumed scent of violets, buttercups, bluebells, and orchids still lingered in the air after the previous day's ceremony, but when Arthur passed through the heavy, oaken doors of Saint Stephen's Cathedral, the first thing he saw was a kneeling Celtic monk with shoulder-length brown hair and a long scar just above his left eye. *Tristan.* After returning from his quest for the Holy Grail, the former knight had chosen to lay down his sword and dedicate himself to an ascetic life of prayer, devotion, and solitude. The tragic deaths of his wife and unborn child, coupled with his crippling guilt over murdering an innocent family while blinded by rage and sorrow had led him to reject violence of all kinds and spend his days desperately seeking forgiveness at the foot of the cross.

Upon Tristan's withdrawal and subsequent commitment to monasticism, Arthur lamented the loss of one of his most accomplished soldiers but also privately wondered whether he might be called to do the same. After all, far too much blood had been already been spilled on behalf of his ambitious, idealistic endeavor to create the *City of God* on earth. It was a romantic dream that may have truly been realized, as the luminous beacon of Camelot had finally ushered in a state of prosperity and hope in Britannia, though it remained a far cry from heavenly perfection. Still, the cost had been great, and it tugged on Arthur's conscience like a millstone around his neck as he attempted to weigh the greatness of his achievement against the lives lost and broken along the way. *What was it that Merlyn had once told him? Ah yes... the purpose of all wars is peace.* Over a decade had passed since the old man had walked by his side in Camelot, and the weary king often prayed for his return, eager for both wisdom and guidance.

Arthur warily stepped past the kneeling Tristan, careful not to disturb his ardent devotions, then he passed through the narrow back door of the cathedral and into the garden outside, where he found Gawain begrudgingly assisting Rowena as she tended to a patch of snow-white flowers.

"Well, well! Look who finally decided to join the land of the living!" Gawain playfully chided as he rooted around in the soil with a trowel, "How's your head, Arthur?"

"I've certainly had better days," the king replied.

"Arthur," Rowena interrupted, "before you speak further, I want to say again how deeply sorry I am for hiding the truth about Morgana until last night. It's just that... you've already lost so much, and I didn't want to add to your grief. But I realize now that I may have lost your trust instead. If only..."

"Peace, Rowena," he said, stopping the apologetic Saxon as she began to ramble, "All is forgiven. Now, I will freely admit that if you had told me the truth on another day, I may have reacted more harshly. But the heartbreaking tale relayed to me was thankfully sugar-coated by the numbing effects of wine as well as the unexpected joy of meeting a young man who may be my only surviving blood relative. Nevertheless, now that I've had the chance to consider all the facts with a sober mind, I understand why you chose to withhold the details of my sister's tragic fate. For your sake, I will always remember her as the clever, witty girl from the stories of your childhood."

"Thank you, Arthur," she replied, "Even after all these years, you never cease to surprise me. And as for Morgana, I will do my best to remember her that way as well."

"Not that I don't enjoy all of this friendly togetherness," said Gawain, clearly exasperated, "but can we finish the gardening, Rowena? I have more important things to do today."

"Oh, come off it, you big oaf. You would still be lying in bed snoring like a grizzly bear if I hadn't woken you."

"Well... *sleep* is important."

"Remember, Gawain, a happy wife yields a happy life," Arthur remarked with a knowing grin, "And speaking of wives, have you seen Gwenivere today? I assumed she had risen early, but I can't seem to find her anywhere."

"No, not since she left the wedding feast last night."

"I thought she was with you," answered a puzzled Rowena, "Usually *she* would be the one helping me plant flowers rather than Gawain, but when she didn't come down to breakfast this morning, I pulled *him* along instead."

"Lucky me," Gawain mumbled.

Before Rowena could offer a sharp retort to her husband's bellyaching, a troubled voice suddenly cried out from within the castle followed by the thunderous galloping of horses.

"ARTHUR! COME QUICKLY!"

The king was gone in an instant, with Gawain and Rowena trailing close behind after casting aside their gardening tools and rushing hurriedly in the direction of the voice. Percival, Palamedes, and Mordred spied them all running and followed along as well, anxious to know the reason for the uproar. When at last they approached the outer entrance to the Great Hall, fretful and out of breath, they noticed Bedivere running back and forth in the courtyard, hastily arming himself as a young squire saddled and prepared his mount. He was shouting incoherently with his hands in the air, waving a shredded piece of lavender cloth with gold embroidery.

* * * * *

Gwenivere awoke with a sharp, throbbing pain in the back of her head. A small patch of blood, which had already soaked through her soft brown curls, was now crawling leisurely down her cheek, and in the chaotic haze of her memory she could almost remember being knocked unconscious. She was bound and gagged, lying face down on the back end of a large black stallion, with the enormous, shadowy man who had invaded her bedchamber tightly gripping the reigns. The beautiful silk gown she had been wearing was torn to shreds, leaving her clad in nothing but her woolen underclothes, and a cold autumn rain fell steadily through the forest canopy, soaking through the humble garments and chilling her to the bone.

As her vision began to clear, Gwenivere frantically searched her surroundings, hoping to gain at least a rudimentary notion of where they were headed. Looking downward, she could see that the horse was following a narrow, pebble-strewn pathway that twisted through the densely wooded landscape and tangled undergrowth; however, the incessant rain, which was only growing heavier by the minute, would likely make any attempt to track them exceedingly difficult. Moreover, once they ventured into the reeking swamps that lay ahead, it would become nearly impossible.

She briefly considered attempting to signal someone for help, but as she caught a glimpse of the few bedraggled looking men meandering about amidst the ancient trees, it soon became clear that this particular forest was nothing but a den of bandits, thieves, and mercenaries. *She would not find help in this accursed place*. Gwenivere cursed under her breath, and then she closed her eyes and prayed for a miracle.

A few hundred yards south of the large black stallion that carried the queen and her captor, a makeshift wooden cart bumped and bounded unevenly down the same narrow path. The cart was being pulled by an irritated old donkey whose tail thrashed angrily back and forth, swatting the little black flies that were buzzing around nearby. He in turn was being driven onward by a bald, grey-bearded dwarf wearing a burlap tunic and brandishing a tattered leather whip, with tiny rolls of cloth shoved into his gaping nostrils to minimize the smell. Naturally, the old donkey gave off a rather pungent odor, and the dwarf was no prize himself, but the most prominent stench came from the mass of dead bodies piled on the back of the wooden cart. It was the dwarf's job to collect the corpses of all those who died of black fever and other illnesses and transport them to be buried or burned. He rather hated his lamentable profession, but dwarves were not always treated very well in these days, so opportunities were few and far between.

Having grown a bit parched during his journey, the dwarf pulled the donkey to a halt and dismounted, lifting a comically oversized jug of mead to his lips and drinking voraciously until the delightful honeyed spirit trickled messily down his beard. But no sooner had he lowered the vessel and wiped his dripping mouth than he saw a wild man, nearly naked with only a few dingy cloths covering his loins, emerge from the forest and leap atop the wooden cart. With a forceful shout, the wild man roused the old donkey into action, and before long the cart had rolled out of sight, speeding northward down the pebble-strewn path in pursuit of the black stallion. Shocked but surprisingly unagitated, the dwarf shrugged his shoulders and began to wander back home. Later that evening, when his friends asked him who had stolen his cart, he carefully described a tall, broad-shouldered man with sandy-brown hair – long, unkempt, and streaked with grey – who looked curiously similar to a famous knight he had come across many years ago.

The Nameless Knight

Gawain stood defiantly at the river's edge and stared daggers back at the well-armed warrior who was blocking his path to the narrow foot bridge. He was thin, lanky, and muscular, with a chainmail hauberk and a leather pauldron covering his scarred, battle-worn physique. He wore an old Corinthian helmet, likely scavenged decades ago from a fallen Roman soldier, which fully covered his head and face and rendered him unrecognizable to all passersby. His gnarled hands gripped a pair of Celtic short swords, each with an elaborate hilt carved from bone and shaped like a roaring dragon. As a cool gust of wind whistled hauntingly through the trees, the lone warrior remained still and silent, not speaking a word to either Gawain or Mordred, the latter of whom waited nearby tending to the horses and looking on with great anticipation.

After learning of the queen's abduction, Arthur had sent his knights out in pairs to search for her, and the most recent arrival to their court – the king's displaced nephew – had begged permission to come along and earn his keep. And while Gawain was not nearly as suspicious as Percival of Mordred's motives, the young man's questionable upbringing by the Priestess of the White Dragon still aroused his fears. Even so, Gawain was more inclined than most toward compassion and the offering of second chances. As Arthur often said, *he who is forgiven much loves much*, and Gawain would never forget his own multitude of sins and the great depths to which he himself had been forgiven.

Beyond the controversy surrounding his sudden arrival in Camelot, Mordred turned out to be an exceedingly worthy traveling companion. He was an accomplished rider, and he had obviously proven his skill with a blade against Palamedes that morning on the tilting fields. He did have a slight hitch in his step, which he attributed to an unspecified injury during childhood, but since the minor malady showed no ill effect on his performance in battle, it was easily ignored and remained nothing more than an insignificant yet easily recognizable characteristic. Gawain could relate, of course, as he suffered from a similar condition due to his bone-crushing encounter with the villainous Green Knight many years ago, with his left leg having been irreparably weakened below the knee. This point of connection sparked a series of lively conversations that had marked their journey thus far, eventually leading Gawain to determine that Mordred was probably the most intelligent young man he had ever met, with Arthur as the only notable exception. While not a bookworm or a theologian like the king was known to be, Mordred's deep knowledge of philosophy and his profound insight into human nature left the aging Saxon knight utterly dazzled. Thus, it was almost with a sense of relief that they came upon this lanky warrior standing boldly on the riverbank, as it provided Gawain with a clear opportunity to withdraw from their increasingly profound discussion without completely embarrassing himself.

"I say again, stand aside!" Gawain bellowed, "We travel on strict orders from the High King, and our mission must not be jeopardized by the selfish whims of some egotistical bridge keeper with delusions of grandeur!"

Yet the warrior stood his ground.

"Very well, you leave me no choice but to challenge you in open battle. Now prepare yourself, villain, for once we come to blows, I may quickly forget to be merciful."

"Gawain!" Mordred called out to his companion, his shabby iron sword already in hand, "Do you need my help?"

"Two men against one?" Gawain replied while drawing his axe, "Where is the honor in that? Besides, although I have seen many more winters than you, lad, there is still enough vigor left in these old bones to best a scoundrel such as *him*."

Mordred respectfully lowered his weapon as Gawain turned and slowly approached the stubborn bridge keeper. The light of the setting sun illuminated his aging but still powerful frame with an eerie orange glow, and his greying hair fluttered in the cool, autumn breeze like an open flame. Gawain's deep brown eyes sparkled with excitement as he let out a war cry and brandished his fearsome battle axe, for as much as he hated to admit it, some primal corner of his psyche actually reveled in the bloody exhilaration of warfare.

The bridge keeper raised his swords with blades crossed defensively in a clear attempt to divert the strike from Gawain's axe, and so as iron clashed violently upon iron, the two bold warriors fell into a bout of furious combat. Gawain remained on the offensive, hacking and slashing as if he intended to cleave his opponent in two, while the bridge keeper seemed strangely content to simply dodge and parry each attack, holding his initial footing and neglecting to levy any assaults of his own. Then suddenly, with their weapons interlocked after another thwarted blow, the bridge keeper nimbly moved to his right and drove his boot into a carefully selected spot just below Gawain's left knee. It was a very specific spot that was known only to a select few, and as Gawain fell to the ground in anguish, a single thought rose above the pain and consumed his troubled mind. Grasping his wounded leg, he began to wonder whether this stranger had simply been lucky, or if somehow, he had been instructed on precisely where to strike.

As Gawain wailed and writhed in agony in the tall grass by the riverbank, all but certain that he would soon be run through by the bridge keeper's blade, out of the corner of his eye he saw Mordred leaping into the fray with vengeance in his gaze. The dark-haired young man shouted forcefully as he bore into their opponent, knocking the lanky warrior off his feet and sending him sprawling into the icy river below. After a few moments of stillness, the next thing Gawain felt was a pair of strong, young arms wrapped around his shoulders, lifting him up and helping him limp his way back to his waiting courser.

"Have no fear, Gawain," Mordred said reassuringly, "I'll ensure that you return to Camelot in one piece."

"No, lad, you needn't worry about me. My leg hurts like hell, but I'm not crippled. I can make my way alone. Right now it's far more important that you continue the search for Queen Gwenivere. Go quickly. Do not let the trail go cold."

For a moment, Mordred stood in awkward silence, as if he were unsure whether to follow the orders of a superior or to shepherd a fallen comrade back to safety. But before long his sense of duty won out and he hurriedly mounted his steel grey palfrey, preparing to resume the desperate hunt.

"Oh, and Mordred..." Gawain called out.

The dark-haired young man tugged at the horse's leather reigns and turned back to face his companion.

"Know this day that you have earned my trust. I will never forget your loyalty or your courage."

"Thank you, sir," he replied.

Then Gawain watched as Mordred spurred his palfrey into a gallop, speeding over the narrow foot bridge and into the ancient forest beyond. However, the one thing Gawain failed to see as he clung to his mighty courser and plodded back toward Camelot was the anonymous bridge keeper emerging unharmed from the river, cold and dripping wet but no worse for wear. After clawing his way to dry land, the lanky warrior removed his Corinthian helmet to reveal a narrow, rat-like face with only one eye, and then he waved knowingly at Mordred, who nodded back before disappearing into the trees.

* * * * *

Gwenivere awoke shivering, sprawled out awkwardly on a cold stone floor. She was exhausted, her neck stiff and aching due to the uncomfortable accommodations, and as she slowly rose to her feet she began to survey her stark surroundings. The sun had long since set, and moonlight poured through the tiny tower window leaving splashes of illumination on the dingy, cobweb-covered walls. There was no bed or blanket to be found, only a small pile of damp straw on one side of the circular room, which was musty and infested with insects. On the ground near the heavy padlocked door she found an old waterskin, roughly half full, along with a clay bowl overflowing with some kind of foul-smelling stew. The grey lumps therein may have once been horsemeat, which Gwenivere already found distasteful, but someone had clearly left this portion sitting out for too long and it had turned rancid. *She was hungry, but not yet hungry enough*.

Ignoring her soreness, Gwenivere made her way over to the window and peered outside, trying desperately to find some way to escape from captivity. The tower was tall and the outer walls steep and featureless, with nothing to climb upon even if she could manage to squeeze through the tiny opening, which she quickly concluded to be impossible. And crying out for help would obviously be futile, especially since the only living soul in the courtyard below was an old donkey yoked to a wooden cart piled with corpses. Her only possible exit was through the main entryway. She tried kicking at the latch, but the door was made of solid oak and would not budge, and after nearly half an hour of fruitless pounding, the only thing broken was her spirit. Crying out in anguish from the hopelessness of her dilemma as well as the pain in her hands and feet, Gwenivere picked up the bowl of rotten stew and angrily hurled it against the stone wall, leaving the floor strewn with reeking horsemeat and small shards of clay. Overwhelmed with fatigue and frustration, she dropped to the ground and wept, curling up in a fetal position as she silently prayed for the hand of God to reach out and intervene for her deliverance.

Then the silence was broken by the unexpected sound of commotion outside the tower door. She heard muffled shouting, as if someone's mouth had been covered during a confrontation, followed by a deep grunt and the unmistakable crunch of metal cutting through bone. A lifeless body crumpled to the floor with a heavy thud, and through a tiny crack in the door frame, Gwenivere was shocked to see a half-naked man pulling the clothing and armor from the murdered guard and dressing himself in anything that wasn't covered in fresh blood.

Having previously determined that the land in which she found herself was teeming with thieves and brigands, her first thought was that some enterprising rogue had witnessed her abduction and wished to claim the ransom for himself – or worse yet, that he wished to claim *her body* instead. Gwenivere shuddered at the thought. As the intruder finished dressing and pulled on a pair of leather boots before stealthily approaching the door, the queen knew she had found her chance. Thinking quickly, she located the largest piece of the broken clay bowl and stood with her back against the wall by the entryway, ready and waiting to slash the throat of any man who entered. Once free, she would have to find a horse and somehow elude detection before making her way back to Camelot, but now was not the time to dwell on such things. *Now was the time to act*. As the padlock fell loose and the door began to open, she held her breath and gripped the clay shard tightly.

And then her heart skipped a beat.

Ten long years had passed, but she would know that face anywhere. His sandy-brown hair had grown long and unruly, and his beard was streaked with grey, but his clear blue eyes still sparkled with the mischief and boyish charm of his youth. His broad shoulders stretched the seams of the guard's pilfered tunic, making the muscular physique of this prodigal knight look all the more impressive. *Was this real?* Having finally come to terms with the idea that he was dead, Gwenivere was wholly unprepared to see the King's Champion standing right in front of her, alive and well. The shard of clay fell from her grasp as she felt her knees go weak, nearly collapsing in shock before a pair of thick, brawny arms caught her and lowered her gently to the floor. Then just before fainting, Gwenivere looked up at the familiar face of her rescuer and smiled.

"Hello, Lancelot..." she muttered before trailing off.

The next time Gwenivere awoke, it was under markedly more pleasant circumstances, though she still found herself on the floor of a dank tower in the middle of a swamp. But rather than lying on cold, hard stone or in a pile of moldy straw, her body was cradled in the arms of her friend and protector, the valiant knight who once was lost but had now been found. As she recovered her awareness, Gwenivere felt the waterskin being pressed to her lips and drank insatiably, as if she hadn't tasted water for days. Surprisingly enough, it was both cold and clean, and she finished off every last drop without bothering to ask Lancelot if he was thirsty as well.

"I'm sorry," she said, "I should have offered you some."

"Nonsense," he replied, flashing that endearing, impish grin, "After all, *you* are the one being rescued."

"Lancelot... but I thought... how did you..."

"There will be plenty of time for answers later. Right now we have to get moving. Can you walk?"

"Yes, I think so. But *please* tell me that you have a horse. I haven't any shoes, and my feet are *dreadfully* sore."

"I'm afraid not," Lancelot remarked with embarrassment as he pointed out the window, "That old donkey with the cart was my transport here, and I hardly think it's befitting of a woman to journey home amidst a heap of diseased corpses. Don't worry, though. I noticed some stables on my way in."

Then the former blacksmith stood and offered her his hand. It was rough and calloused, weathered by years of warfare and manual labor, but also strong and reliable like tempered steel. After helping Gwenivere to her feet, he reached down and took possession of the deceased guard's sword as the two moved quickly and quietly down the long, winding staircase and into the open courtyard below. Fortunately it was still dark outside, but a few rays of sunlight were already beginning to peek over the horizon, so they would have very little time if they wished to escape this God-forsaken country alive.

Lancelot hurriedly located the stables in a small, grassy field just south of the tower, and he broke into a dead sprint, hoping to find something stronger and faster than a donkey to carry them homeward. Gwenivere attempted to follow close behind, but she soon noticed that the ground was covered with sharp rocks and thistles, and she frequently stumbled, barely able to contain her cries as the terrain tore into her already tender feet. At the sound of her distressed whimpers, Lancelot turned back to offer his assistance, and before she knew it he had lifted her into his arms once again and carried her all the way until they reached a pair of black palfreys tied to a wooden post.

"Ride like the wind," Lancelot whispered as he assisted Gwenivere in mounting one of the horses, "Head straight into those woods to the southeast. I'll be right behind you. No matter what happens, don't slow down until the tallest tower disappears over the horizon."

"But wait... what are *you* going to do?"

"I'm going to ensure that your mysterious captor has far bigger things to worry about than following us."

Then Lancelot slapped the palfrey on its hindquarters, and with a jolt and a whinny, the little black horse galloped into the forest, carrying Gwenivere off toward the rising sun.

Deprived of both reigns and saddle in their haste to escape, the queen was forced to wrap her legs around her palfrey's torso and hold on tightly onto its mane, nearly tumbling over sideways before she eventually secured her grip and gained some small measure of control. After catching her breath, she rode onward under cover of the wooded canopy, successfully fighting the urge to look back until she sniffed the early morning air and caught the faintest scent of smoke. Anxiously turning her gaze back toward the site of her captivity, Gwenivere gasped as she witnessed the tower being engulfed in flames, with Lancelot charging through the trees on horseback and barreling toward her like a bat out of hell.

"Go! Keep riding!" he shouted, "They're gaining on us!"

"They?" Gwenivere called back as she swiftly spurred her palfrey into action, "What happened to your plan? I thought you were going to make sure we weren't followed!"

"Well, I assumed that setting the castle ablaze would draw away their attention. But apparently I grossly underestimated the value they placed on your imprisonment."

"What? I *am* the queen, after all! How could you think..."

"Now is *not* the time, Gwenivere! Let's *move*!"

The thunderous galloping of horses rumbled in the distance, growing steadily louder as their pursuers drew closer by the moment. Lancelot and Gwenivere drove their palfreys as hard as they could, but the lighter-weight horses were no match for the powerful destriers ridden by the men on their trail. Soon they could hear angry shouting and the familiar metallic ring of swords being drawn from their scabbards, and Gwenivere screamed with fright when an arrow flew past, just missing her left shoulder and plunging into a nearby tree.

"That was a warning shot!" a gravelly voice called out, "Stop now or the next one pierces your heart!"

Lancelot pulled his palfrey to a halt just before they reached a rickety wooden bridge stretched precipitously across a nearby river, and Gwenivere quickly followed suit, still shaking with fright after her near-death encounter. Ever so slowly, they both turned to face their pursuers, and the queen's jaw dropped in astonishment when she finally beheld the enormous man who had abducted her from her bedchamber. He was built like a mountain, taller than anyone she had ever met, with grizzled features and a thick, disheveled mane of greying hair. He wore a hodge-podge of ancient bronze armor, tarnished green with age and neglect, and he carried an enormous war hammer, the head of which was stained black with blood.

"Well, well... *Lancelot*. It's been a long time," the massive man said with a sadistic grin.

"Not nearly long enough, Maleagant," her rescuer replied, "Tell me, how many bags of gold did it take to convince you to kidnap Arthur's queen? You must be very rich by now."

"You have no idea. Of course, that woman *does* possess other assets that may be more *enticing* than gold."

"You diseased maniac. Mark my words, if you dare to defile the queen it will be over my dead body."

"Yes, that *was* the idea," Maleagant chided.

"Very well," Lancelot spat back, "How about telling your goons to back off so you and I can finish this like men?"

A profound, seething hatred filled Maleagant's icy gaze, and he chuckled softly to himself, motioning to the other riders in his retinue to lower their weapons and retreat a few paces. Gwenivere watched with great apprehension as Lancelot drew the battered sword he had pilfered from the tower guard and turned to face his enemy, jaw set in determination, ready and waiting for a confrontation that could only be satisfied through bloodshed. A haunting stillness fell over the lonesome forest clearing, and while the early morning sun had already begun to stretch her glowing fingers through the trees, coloring the dreary landscape with patches of pink and orange light, there was no chorus of songbirds to announce the new day, no comforting commotion made by fishermen or farmers hard at work in the fields – only the eerie quiet of inevitability and the foreboding promise of death that weighed heavily upon the waking dawn. At long last, Maleagant broke the silence, lifting his war hammer skyward and letting out a terrifying battlecry as he spurred his mighty destrier into a gallop and rushed toward Lancelot with a sneer upon his withered lips.

And so the two warring titans stormed into battle, weapons gleaming in the light of daybreak, and Gwenivere looked on warily, with the mingled emotions of hope and fear churning violently through her anguished psyche. She wanted nothing more than to turn away and hide her eyes from the brutality on display in the center of the clearing, but she forced herself to watch for Lancelot's sake, in faith that her support and devotion might somehow lift his spirits and provide him with even the slightest advantage against such a daunting adversary.

Charging on horseback, the combatants failed to injure one another on their first pass, with the blade of Lancelot's sword deflecting off of Maleagant's armor while he narrowly dodged a blow from that enormous war hammer. But on their second pass, Lancelot suffered a hard strike on his left side, dislocating his shoulder and nearly throwing him from his mount before the injured knight deftly managed to regain his balance. Maleagant looked back and began laughing haughtily at the sight of his opponent's left arm hanging limp and useless at his side, but Lancelot fearlessly turned back to reenter the fray, rushing back at Maleagant with defiance in his heart and conviction in his stare. Their tempers enflamed, the two warriors barreled toward each other with reckless abandon, and it first began to seem as if Lancelot and his small, black palfrey would be easily overtaken by the much larger man on his powerful destrier. But at the last moment, Lancelot leapt from his mount and rolled onto the muddy earth, rising to his knees and driving his sword through the flanks of Maleagant's horse as he rode past. The animal stumbled and fell, tossing the rider from his saddle and sending him flying into the trunk of a nearby tree.

Maleagant staggered to his feet in a daze, having lost his helmet during the fall, and he quickly noticed that blood was dripping from a large gash on his forehead. After wiping the dirt and blood from his face, the grizzled mercenary flew into a blind rage and began shouting like a man possessed as he hurtled toward Lancelot with war hammer in hand. But rather than charging back at his adversary, Lancelot stood still and waited, his sword drawn and ready to strike.

Watching the battle with morbid anticipation, Gwenivere shuddered and hurriedly averted her eyes when she heard the terrible, gruesome sound of flesh and bone being torn apart. An anguished cry rang out in the forest clearing, and when she finally chose to turn back and face the brutality, Gwenivere was relieved to see Lancelot standing over Maleagant's broken body, fatigued yet triumphant, the massive man's severed right arm still grasping his war hammer tightly.

"Idealistic fool," Maleagant wheezed, coughing up blood and struggling to breathe, "You still risk your life in service to that naïve dreamer you call a king? What a waste."

"I didn't do it for Arthur," replied Lancelot, "I did it for *her*."

Then with one final flash of steel, Maleagant's head left his neck and tumbled end over end down the muddy riverbank until it splashed into the rushing water and was lost forever.

Gwenivere gasped, and before she knew it Lancelot had remounted his little black palfrey and rushed to her side like a bolt from the blue, jolting her awake from her trance-like state of disbelief and leading her over the rickety wooden bridge and back into the ancient forest. The band of soldiers who had accompanied Maleagant attempted to give chase, but their heavy armor and powerful destriers proved to be far too much for the bridge to sustain, and it collapsed under their weight, sending the men and their horses hurtling down the river after the severed head of their master.

Betrayed With a Kiss

Lancelot cried out in pain as he drove his wounded shoulder into the trunk of an old oak tree again and again, frightening off the chirping birds and other nearby forest animals who quickly scampered, burrowed, or flew away in response to the abrupt, unsettling noise. Gwenivere cringed with every failed attempt until her companion finally succeeded in popping his dislocated joint back into socket, and she let out a prolonged sigh of relief as he wearily collapsed in the dewy morning grass.

Beyond human sight, a shadowy figure waited patiently just past the tree line, laughing quietly to himself and reveling in morbid delight at the sight of Lancelot's suffering. Naberius the Deceiver had always found the pain of mortals to be immensely entertaining, especially this *particular* mortal, who had at last revealed himself after years of hiding in the protection of a small country monastery in the northlands. And now, with his blackened heart set on retribution, the malevolent little imp pulled back the hood of his tattered cloak and crept closer to his prey, watching Gwenivere closely as she knelt down next to the injured knight to offer him the comfort of a woman's touch. An evil grin spread across Naberius' ghastly, lupine visage. *This was going to be easier than he thought*.

"Don't worry about me," Lancelot groaned, "It looks much worse than it actually is."

"Nonsense," Gwenivere quipped back with a knowing smile, "You've always been a terrible liar."

"Very well, then. My shoulder feels like it was trod upon by a team of horses... *fat* horses, in fact. Are you happy now?"

"Happy that you're in pain, or happy that I caught you trying to hide it in order to somehow prove your strength and virility to this frail little damsel in distress?"

"Mind your sarcasm, Gwenivere," he smirked, "Admittedly, I'm far from the quintessence of a proper, courtly gentleman, but it seems to me that mocking your rescuer is likely frowned upon in most circles."

"Oh, my *hero!*" the queen swooned jokingly before plopping down beside Lancelot in the tall woodland grass.

It was nearly midday already, but the ordeal had left them both too exhausted to continue their journey back to Camelot without at least a few hours of rest. Indeed, this was the first time they had stopped riding since vanquishing Maleagant and his men, as their intention had been to flee far enough from the wicked land of Gorre so that the murky swampland vanished from sight and the air was no longer stale and foul-smelling. Now thankfully surrounded with fresh, green vegetation and fragrant wildflowers, with plenty of clean drinking water in the small pond nearby, they reclined together in the shade of a large beech tree, its leafy, pendulous branches outstretched like a mother's arms across the forest grove, and they quickly fell into a deep, dream-filled slumber.

* * * * *

For the first time in what seemed like ages, Lancelot found himself resting comfortably in a forest clearing with warm rays of sunlight caressing his face and dancing joyously on the rippling water. The blissful twittering of birds filled the crisp autumn air with songs of serenity and contentment, which momentarily soothed the pain in Lancelot's shoulder and left his wandering heart satisfied. And yet a single, peculiar feeling still nagged at the back of his mind. Although he could not put his finger on it, there was something strangely familiar about his surroundings, almost as if he had lain in this same clearing dozens of times before, against the very same beech tree, near the very same glistening pond. Then with a flash of realization Lancelot opened his eyes and looked out upon the water, only to see a nude, feminine figure wading a few yards from the shoreline. Her dark brown curls fell gracefully over the shapely curves of her stunning, womanly physique, evoking a flood of emotions and calling to mind that fateful day when he first spied her emerging from a simple bathing tub like Venus rising from the ocean waves. Her deep green eyes beckoned to him seductively, arousing feelings long since abandoned and inviting the wayward knight to join her in the alluring depths of carnal pleasure.

Lancelot knew then that he was dreaming, and he briefly tried to fight back against the thoughts and memories that he had spent so many years learning to control during his stay in the monastery – thoughts he hoped were long dead and buried. Truly, the road he walked over this past decade had been long and arduous. *And lonely*. Once Lancelot's body was healed and his strength renewed after his confrontation with that fearsome black knight on the shores of the North Sea, the monks had shifted their attention to healing his soul. They counseled Lancelot with meditation, fasting, and prayer, and he willingly lived in solitude and isolation from the world, purposefully abandoning his home in order to stave off the impure desires that would only lead down the path to destruction.

But now that he and Gwenivere had been reunited, even under such perilous circumstances, Lancelot began to sense the tragic futility of his years in seclusion, for no matter how hard he tried, he could not extract this divine creature from his heart. There she stood before him, the sweetest forbidden fruit, and even with eyes shut tight her angelic face consumed his mind. Years of asceticism were tossed to the wind, and in an instant the brave knight was unmade. *He would not flee from her again. Their state could not be severed, for to lose her would be to lose himself*. Waves of heat began to ripple through Lancelot's body, and he suddenly felt as if he would burst into flame. He then looked upon his beloved standing waist deep in the sparkling water, her lithe arms outstretched and gesturing to him to come in and cool himself – to quench the rekindled fire that burned within him once more.

* * * * *

The raucous shouting of drunken farmers, merchants, and travelers resonated throughout the teeming tavern, as a bevy of buxom barmaids carried sloshing flagons of ale and mead to and fro between the oaken storage barrels in the cellar and the aggressively lecherous patrons cramped into the hall above. It was hard enough to avoid spilling drinks everywhere in such overcrowded conditions without intoxicated men constantly grabbing at their backsides, but most of the serving wenches took the unwarranted advances in stride, knowing full well that such concessions were part of the job. Many of them even accepted additional payment to render more *intimate* services in the sparsely furnished bedrooms upstairs, only to stagger back down afterwards and resume serving ale.

Gwenivere carefully counted the silver coins in her hand as she walked gingerly down the wooden staircase, dropping them into a small leather pouch tied around her neck before adjusting her dress and smoothing her tussled hair. It had been almost a year since her father had forbidden her to return to their home in Lyonesse, and after being abruptly abandoned by her Saxon lover, she was taken in by the owner of this rundown country tavern, first simply serving drinks, but later selling her body as well, with nothing on her troubled mind but survival.

Her initial reticence to provide the patrons with more than just flagons of ale was begrudgingly overcome by her decision to drink away the disgust, which remained her medication of choice for the first month or so. But eventually these dalliances became like any other menial, daily task, with no more meaning to her than sweeping the front porch or washing laundry. In fact, there was actually a part of Gwenivere that grew to enjoy her nocturnal liaisons. Having been callously dismissed by both her father and her lover, she craved the attention given to her by the eager young men who frequented the tavern, and she delighted in the sensual power she held over them. These men *wanted* her, they *pined* for her, and when she took them to bed Gwenivere finally felt like she mattered to someone.

Of course, not every patron was so benignly appreciative of her services. Those who were young and inexperienced always made the best customers, paying dependably and doing all that she asked of them out of sheer excitement alone. She even had a couple of regulars who brought her gifts now and again. But a few of the older men, mainly the rough-hewn travelers, were vicious and cruel, and it often seemed as if they only wanted to use her to exert their repressed frustrations. After a *good* evening with such a customer, it was difficult for her to stand the next morning. But after a *bad* evening, she might end up bedridden for several days, usually without a single silver coin to show for it. Fortunately such incidents were few and far between, but each time those nasty patrons reared their ugly, drunken heads, she seriously considered running away into the night, never to return to this accursed den of iniquity.

Tonight's last customer had been the mildly aggressive sort, more coarse and careless than downright violent. But still, he had paid her well and left her with only a lightly bruised cheek after a rather lengthy session, so Gwenivere chose to count her blessings and return to her regular duties as a barmaid until the tavern closed in the wee hours of the morning. It was then, as the last intoxicated patron staggered out into the moonlight, that a cloaked and hooded figure slipped quietly through the tavern door and asked for her by name.

"Sorry, love, we're closed," she said, "Come back tomorrow night. I may be able to find some time for you."

"Dear God. What has happened to you, child?" the man replied as he reached out and caressed the bruise on her cheek, "You are so much more than what you have become."

Shocked and anxious at the familiar sound of the visitor's voice, Gwenivere turned and pulled back the hood of his cloak to reveal the genial, weathered face of Balian, her father's personal servant and her own dear friend since she was a child. With Leodegrance frequently preoccupied with the duties of governance, Balian had been like a surrogate grandfather to her, serving as her family when it felt like she had no other. There was no one on earth she loved or respected more than this man, and if he had only appeared a few short months ago, Gwenivere might have been ashamed for him to find her in this ghastly place. But it was too late. A preponderance of sin had worn her conscience numb, and she now freely resigned herself to the lonesome, hollow life of a tavern harlot.

"I told you we're closed," she snapped back, "The owner will have my hide if I serve customers after hours."

"Gwenivere… my dear girl, please come back home with me. There is nothing for you here. Surely neither you nor your father can hold such a thoughtless grudge forever."

"I have no father."

Her voice was detached and her eyes were cold and lifeless. Gwenivere knew what she was worth now. She knew what she had become, and there was no going back. Besides, the lustful men she encountered each night made her feel sought after and desired, unlike the callous old fool who had given her life and then abandoned her to survive on her own.

"Please leave," Gwenivere whispered stoically.

Heartbroken and utterly defeated, Balian stood in helpless silence for a few moments before pulling up his hood and slowly making his way back toward the door. He briefly turned back as if to say something, and Gwenivere could see that his soft, grey eyes were glistening with tears. She caught his stare for a brief instant but quickly looked away and resumed wiping spilled ale from the tables with the edge of her ragged dress, wordlessly declaring the death of her old life as the one man whose love she had never doubted vanished into the night.

* * * * *

Gwenivere awoke with a start, sitting upright in the forest clearing and rubbing her eyes as she gradually reacquainted herself with reality. *She was a queen, not a barmaid... wasn't she?* The haunting image of a past that had nearly been forgotten clung to her like a leech, pulling at her conscience and relentlessly reminding her of the woman she once was. *It was a memory, nothing more. It had all happened so long ago...*

Looking about curiously, she quickly noticed that Lancelot had vacated their wooded resting place and was now kneeling in the shallow water near the edge of the nearby pond. He still wore his breeches but had removed his blood-stained tunic, attempting to wash the filth from the shabby garment as beads of sweat glistened upon his brawny shoulders. Gwenivere blushed slightly and could not help but stare, as she had long admired the burly knight's powerful physique from afar. *How could she not?* The years had been kind to Lancelot, and although his hair was greying and his flesh was scarred, he still gave the impression of a living statue inspired by the heroes of Roman myth. Moreover, Gwenivere was not unaware of his thinly veiled desire for her. In years past she had taken notice of his sideways glances and awkward demeanor while alone in her presence, never going so far as to acknowledge his attention but taking it as a compliment nonetheless. After all, her time in the country tavern had conditioned her to derive a great deal of self-worth from the lustful devotion of men, and at least a small measure of that mentality – that *need* – had never truly left her, having burrowed its way deep into her heart, still hungry and waiting to be fed.

"So what happened to you, then?" Gwenivere asked softly as she knelt down next to her rescuer in the cool, clear water. But the sweet sound of her voice startled Lancelot, who flinched and dropped his freshly cleaned tunic, and before he could grasp it again the garment casually drifted out of reach into the deep center of the pond. The two of them watched the tunic float away, then they looked back at one another and quickly burst into a fit of uproarious laughter.

"Well, so much for the laundry!" Lancelot smirked after catching his breath, "At least the tunic wasn't mine."

"It wasn't your color anyway," giggled Gwenivere.

But when the laughter finally died down, the wayward knight grew silent, somber, and still, and he turned toward the queen with both pain and longing in his gaze.

"What happened to me?" Lancelot began, "Why did I never return to Camelot? *Why indeed*. That, my queen, is a question I've been waiting to answer for a *very* long time."

"I… I think I know," she replied sheepishly.

"Do you? Well then you also know why I finally revealed myself after ten long, agonizing years in hiding. You know why I had no choice but to come to your rescue. And you know why these past few hours we have spent alone together have been both the most delightful and the most harrowing of my life. I love you, Gwenivere. *Desperately. Passionately*. I have loved you since the first moment I saw you, and I have not stopped loving you for a single moment since. Every fiber of my being yearns for your gentle touch. You are like air to me. There is no life for me without you, though I could blissfully endure a thousand deaths with you by my side."

The words gushed from his lips like water bursting through a broken dam, powerful and unyielding after being held at bay for so many years. Waves of adoration spilled forth relentlessly, and Lancelot felt like a drowning man struggling to breathe. Then when at last his reservoir of emotion was spent and he had spoken his piece, he turned away, an emptied vessel, and lowered his head in shame. Part of Lancelot was humiliated. He felt weak and defeated, for after a decade of ardent self-denial, he had allowed those old, hidden desires to overtake his will far too easily. But another part of him felt nothing but exhilaration and relief after finally admitting the truth, and it was this latter part that began to grow in vitality when he felt a delicate hand upon his shoulder.

"Lancelot," whispered the queen, "you know... I never properly thanked you for rescuing me."

At the sound of her voice, the wayward knight turned back to face his beloved, and before he could say a word she kissed him, lightly at first, with an innocent gratitude in her embrace. For a brief moment Lancelot stood frozen with astonishment, and he gazed back at Gwenivere in awe, just as one might look upon a breathtaking waterfall or a mountain sunrise. *She truly was a divine beauty*. Her shining hair cascaded gracefully over her shoulders, and the dingy, tattered gown that she still wore, once lavender with gold embroidery, was now soaking wet and clung tightly to her feminine curves like a second skin. Her soft green eyes looked sad and distant, and as Lancelot reached out hesitantly to wipe a tear from her cheek, he also noticed a hint of desperate urgency gradually bubbling up below the surface. Suddenly a look of yearning and barely restrained desire that he had never seen before overtook her countenance, and she fell into his arms and kissed him again, warmly and deeply this time, not as a friend but as a lover. At first they shared a sense of fear and trepidation, but within moments their misgivings melted away into a sea of unbridled passion.

And then they gave themselves to one another, there in the lush grass of the forest clearing.

Just beyond the tree line, two hidden figures looked on and smiled wickedly, overwhelmingly pleased that their plan had so effortlessly come to fruition. One was Naberius the Deceiver, a gangly, gruesome demon covered with bristly grey fur, eager to regale his dark master with the news of his success. And the other was a raven-haired young man, the spitting image of his mother, ostensibly tasked with seeking out the queen but imbued with other, far more sinister motives.

The Unkindest Cut

Gawain looked on as Arthur paced anxiously back and forth through the Great Hall, breathing rapidly and chewing his fingernails. He thought it was a rather childish for the High King of the Britons to be given to such tendencies, but he tactfully said nothing. In truth, Arthur seemed to share this sentiment, but every time the king caught himself and pulled his hands away, his apprehension quickly led them back. Old Pellinore sat nearby as well, lounging in a large, cushioned chair and laughing to himself intermittently as he reminded Arthur over and over again that his father once suffered from the same pesky habit. But Arthur paid no attention to the kindly old man's absent-minded commentary, for it was on this very night that his first child would soon be born. Every so often they would see Rowena or Lunette scurry past to fetch a towel or a steaming kettle from the kitchen, but they would always disappear back upstairs without uttering a single word of news. As such, Arthur went back to his fingernails, and Gawain began to reflect on the events that had led up to this moment.

Nearly a year had passed since Gwenivere's safe return to Camelot, an event rendered all the more joyous when Lancelot shockingly stepped forth and revealed himself as her rescuer. Arthur had been fittingly overcome with elation, weeping openly at the prospect of being reunited with both his wife and his closest friend after many long years apart. Gawain was astonished and delighted as well, greeting the wayward knight in turn with a strong, brotherly embrace and subsequently bombarding him with ceaseless questions late into the twilight hours. When asked why he had not returned to Camelot until now, Lancelot told of his disastrous confrontation with the sinister black knight and expressed shame and remorse at having failed in his quest for the Holy Grail. The years away had been penance, he said, for suffering defeat at a time when he was needed the most. Of course, no man knew such feelings of dishonor more than Gawain, who shared his own tragic fall from grace as well as his search for forgiveness. As the night wore on and the stories continued, Gwenivere interjected with her firsthand account of Lancelot's heroic battle with Maleagant. And though it may have been lightly embellished for dramatic effect, she still recounted his valiant stand more or less accurately, with the injured yet resourceful knight battling a vastly stronger enemy against incredible odds, equipped with nothing but an old, rusty sword and ill-fitting armor. Gawain could see Lancelot blush and squirm in his seat when they begged the queen to tell it again and again.

And so, with loved ones restored and the kingdom at peace once more, a jubilant celebration was ordered, lasting for seven days and seven nights and culminating with a massive feast to which every soul in Camelot was invited. On that final evening, after drinking to Lancelot and Gwenivere's safe homecoming, Gawain had lifted his goblet and offered a toast to Mordred, regaling Arthur with the tale his bravery in battle and steadfast devotion in their search for the queen. After all, the dark-haired young man had clearly shown his mettle by saving Gawain from almost certain death, so with the ringing endorsement of one of his oldest friends and most trusted knights, the king then chose to honor his nephew by formally offering him the final empty seat at the Round Table.

In the months that followed, Mordred proved to be better than his word, stepping with ease into his role as one of Arthur's knights and greatly impressing all those who dwelt within the kingdom with his wit, intelligence, and fearless honesty. He was cheerful and charismatic, and his magnetic personality enabled him to make fast friends with several of the younger denizens of Camelot with the notable exception of Percival, who remained cordial but cautious in his daily interactions. Nevertheless, Mordred soon managed to gain the favor of the king himself, as both were well-educated and quickly bonded over their lengthy discussions of philosophy and ancient history.

However, despite the young man's intellectual and familial connections to Arthur, it was Gawain to whom he eventually grew the closest. From his first day as a member of the Council of the Round Table, Mordred followed Gawain diligently like an apprentice studying under his master, and although he would be loath to admit it, the aging Saxon knight could not help but feel at least somewhat flattered. Moreover, since he and Rowena had been unable to conceive children of their own, Gawain often looked upon Mordred as the son he never had, doing his utmost to pass down his wealth of knowledge and train the boy in both combat and diplomacy. They soon became nearly inseparable – dining, drinking, and sparring together – to the point that Gawain grew to trust the young man even more so than he did Bedivere or Lancelot. Thus, it seemed more than fitting that it was none other than Mordred who rushed into the Great Hall on this momentous occasion to deliver the news that Gwenivere had at last given birth to a son.

As Arthur hurriedly stumbled up the castle stairs, elated to finally meet his child and heir, Mordred held back and privately pulled Gawain to the side, his countenance quickly shifting from excitement to a curious look of pensive disquiet.

"What the devil are you on about, Mordred?" asked Gawain in surprise and confusion, "This is a day of gladness."

"Something heavy weighs upon my conscience, and though I have held my tongue until now, I can do so no longer."

"Very well, out with it then. You know that your thoughts are always welcome in my presence. But please speak quickly. We are called to join Arthur in celebration."

"Aye, but that's the concern," Mordred replied, hesitating in silence before making his uneasy proclamation, "While I openly admit to knowing nothing for certain... I fear that this newborn child may not be of the king's bloodline."

"God's bones, boy... that is a *bold* accusation."

"I know it sounds slanderous, Gawain, but I swear on my life that this charge is merited. In truth, while I was still searching for Queen Gwenivere after her abduction, I happened to come upon her in a small forest clearing some ways north of Camelot. Lancelot was there with her, and though it pains me to say so, I witnessed them engage in... *adulterous acts*."

"Damn your tongue!" Gawain shot back, his voice quiet but teeming with rage, "How *dare* you make such an allegation?"

"Forgive me, sir," Mordred answered, "My desire was never to upset you. But you must believe that my intentions are just. Have you ever known me to be falsehearted?"

Gawain stepped back and scowled at the dark-haired young man, saying nothing, until he finally let out an exasperated sigh and began pacing back and forth across the room, muttering to himself angrily for a few moments before slumping into his seat at the Round Table and burying his face in his hands.

"Why did you wait so long to speak?" he asked softly.

"I was yet a stranger in this kingdom, Gawain. It was not my place. Moreover, why would anyone have believed me?"

"Most *still* will not," the Saxon knight mumbled.

"Even so, my words are as true as tempered steel."

"While I do lament your report, Mordred, I also value your candor. You need fear no reprisal from me. Now I charge you to speak no further until I have an opportunity to investigate these assertions myself. Do I have your word?"

"Of course, Gawain. *Always*."

* * * * *

They called the baby *Aurelius*. He was named for Marcus Aurelius, the last of the "Five Good Emperors" of Rome, whose philosophical writings on service and duty stood just behind those of Saint Augustine in influencing Arthur's thoughtful view of kingship. Derived from the Latin word for "gilded," the name was also well-suited for the child's appearance, as he was born with a full head of golden blonde hair.

Arthur couldn't have been happier. No one in the kingdom had ever met a prouder father, as the king could frequently be seen wandering around the castle hallways, the courtyards, and even the nearby village farmlands, joyfully displaying his newborn son for all to see. Once Gwenivere recovered from the ordeal she began to accompany him in his outings, and the two would walk hand in hand through the Camlann Fields, the baby peacefully sleeping on Arthur's shoulder, their royal family a perfect image of tenderness, devotion, and love.

Lancelot had done his best to share in their joy on the day of the child's christening, wearing the mask of a loyal friend and honorable knight, but since then he had chosen to keep his distance, tormented daily by the nagging thought his lustful transgressions might soon be unearthed. After all, the child's blonde locks *did* seem to betray his lineage, and a slew of vague rumors had begun to spread like a virus throughout the darkest corners of Camelot. Whether real or imagined, he could feel prying eyes upon him, voices taunting and accusing, denying him even a modicum of peace. For what it was worth, Lancelot already hated himself because of what he had done; however, he also knew he could *never* confess to Arthur. It wasn't the threat of retribution that held him back, for the guilt that tore away at his soul was far worse than either banishment or death. Rather, his only real motivation was to protect Gwenivere from whatever punishment might lie in store, for as much as his unrestrained passion had created the disorder and uncertainty that surrounded them, he still loved her and prayed that her days would be blessed. He also still loved Arthur, his king and childhood friend, and hoped beyond hope to spare him from the heartrending anguish that the truth would surely bring. Thus he kept it buried, suffering alone with a secret that hung like an anchor on his heart, constantly threatening to drag him down into the suffocating depths of oblivion.

For the most part, this happy facade had been enormously effective in keeping up the status quo, as his fellow knights had welcomed him back with open arms upon returning to Camelot, and their varied relationships had resumed as if not a single day had passed. Lancelot even managed to forge a casual rapport with the king's nephew Mordred, who, despite being a good twenty years his junior, was already one of the most skilled and learned knights on the council. Nevertheless, in recent weeks Gawain had begun to act a bit detached and standoffish, never saying anything overtly suspicious, but also seeming to have forgotten his normal self, as if he were holding back a discovery that was in imminent danger of escaping.

So it was with great trepidation that Lancelot begrudgingly made his way to join the Council of the Round Table as they held court according to the king's daily schedule. It promised to be an ordinary meeting, nothing odd or uncommon on the agenda, but merely business as usual on a grey, rainy morning in early winter. Still, Lancelot could sense that something was amiss, and the knot in his stomach only grew as he opened the heavy, oaken doors of the Great Hall.

Upon entering, he first noticed that Arthur and the eleven other knights were already seated and waiting for him. Every head turned in his direction as he slowly approached the table, their eyes openly tracing his movements, though no one spoke a single word. They simply glared at him stoically, cold and emotionless, as if each man were somehow gazing into his soul. *The silence was deafening.* Desperately Lancelot searched his thoughts, seeking some alternate explanation for their strange demeanor, but the truth was staring him in the face.

They knew.

No, this was not an ordinary meeting of the court. This was his prosecution. His judgement. *His fate.* Each blank stare told the sordid tale of his betrayal, and bitter disenchantment with the man they once called friend hung heavy in the air. What he had done was no mere indiscretion, no youthful dalliance, no common liaison between consenting adults. *He had committed the highest treason.* As Lancelot pondered his predicament, he glanced down at the Latin words that had been engraved in a circle around the center of the Round Table:

SANCTITAS • FIDELITAS • AEQVITAS • PIETAS • VERITAS

Virtue, Loyalty, Justice, Piety, and Truth. Together they formed the cornerstone upon which Camelot had been built. And with memories and emotions churning tumultuously through his tortured mind, Lancelot cringed and felt something break within him, like a massive crack had opened in the world. The tragic realization that he had violated every aspect of the sacred oath he took that fateful day on Pentecost tore his heart in two, and he was utterly devastated. *It was over.* His only hope now was to confess everything and fall on the mercy of the king.

"I don't know what to say, Arthur," he began, "other than to humbly beg for your forgiveness. While I know I don't deserve even a semblance of mercy, and I will obediently accept any punishment you deem appropriate for my litany of sins, I also beg you to spare the queen in this matter. She is truly innocent. It was I who pursued her, and it was I who took advantage of her weakness under such harrowing circumstances. So please, do what you will with me. You have been my truest ally since we were boys, and I am profoundly sorry to have betrayed that precious friendship. And as for you, my fellow knights, I beg your forgiveness as well, for the man you once laughed, cried, and bled with has dishonored the principles inscribed upon this very table and sullied the blessed name of Camelot. I entreat you, do not allow the failures of one feeble man to define this brotherhood, and finish the race that we began together so long ago. I ask only one thing before I am dragged away in chains. Tell me, when did you first know the truth?"

Lancelot looked on in morbid anticipation as Arthur slowly rose to his feet, eyes filled with tears and hands visibly shaking, then broke the suffocating silence with words that would haunt the penitent knight forevermore.

"I *didn't* know," the king said, "Not until now."

* * * * *

High among the rafters of the Great Hall stood a single crow, its feathers black as night and its beady little eyes ghostly and colorless. Having just overheard Lancelot's confession and Arthur's heartbroken response, he leapt from his perch and flew through a nearby window into the frosty morning air, soaring faster and faster until it became clear that this particular crow was something much more than an ordinary scavenger. Finally reaching his destination, the crow entered a small, tumbledown hovel deep in the forest to the north, unremarkable in every aspect with the exception of its occupant. She was a pale, thin, raven-haired woman dressed in white linen, and as she listened to the crow's account of what had transpired, she threw back her head and laughed with fiendish delight.

When Love Grows Cold

Gareth sat motionless and aghast, with tiny beads of sweat beginning to drip down his freckled forehead, as Lancelot boldly delivered his confession. *He didn't want to believe it.* After all, the affair had been nothing but a *rumor* until today. He had calmly and patiently listened to Mordred's damning account of the scandalous incident – relayed with great fervor by Gawain, of course – but lacking evidence, hope still remained that it had all been nothing but a tragic misunderstanding. *Mordred could have easily been mistaken, couldn't he? The boy had only seen Gwenivere briefly before her abduction, and Lancelot had been missing for ages. How could he have known them for certain?* But now there was no questioning reality. The facts of the case were incontrovertible, yet here Lancelot remained, apparently ready and willing to be condemned to death for his betrayal. So at the king's order, Gareth rose from his seat to assist Kay and Bedivere with the arrest, and their prisoner neglected to offer even the slightest resistance, willingly choosing to yield his mighty sword, Arondight, after having only recently reclaimed it upon his unexpected return to Camelot.

Despite Lancelot's obvious contrition, something had clearly changed within Arthur. Although he had first met the painful news with mourning, his tears soon dried and his countenance quickly grew cold, hard, and vengeful. The king began barking out his orders with stone-faced ruthlessness, and his normally gentle eyes seemed to burn with an unfamiliar fire. And while Gareth could hardly blame him for reacting to the confession with a surge of righteous anger, even as Christ had revealed his wrath to the money changers in the temple, the Pictish knight also cringed in fear, for the Arthur who now stood before him was someone he had never known until this day. Moreover, the next words spoken by the king seemed to linger in the air long after they were spoken, for it was those words that would alter the fragile dream of Camelot forever.

"Bring the queen to me as well," he scowled, "She too will answer for this treachery."

"Arthur, no!" Lancelot cried, suddenly defiant, "Gwenivere is innocent! I beseech you..."

"Peace, *brother*. Your mistress will join you soon enough."

And then Lancelot, who had not yet fully surrendered his weapon, tightened his grip and pulled the sword free, taking a defensive stance and brandishing the shining blade as the other knights hurried to arm themselves. His demeanor had visibly shifted from that of remorse and dishonor to bold opposition, for the penitent man had disappeared as the warrior emerged. Gareth knew that it was instinct that drew him toward battle, not blind aggression, but despite the circumstances, his knightly duty remained the same. *Had it really come to this?* Gareth hesitated to draw his own sword, torn between his loyalty to Arthur and his sacred oath to protect the queen from harm. A terrible sinking feeling came upon him, and he began to sense that this confrontation could only end in disaster.

"You don't want to do this, Kay," warned Lancelot, as the king's step-brother pressed cold steel to his neck.

"Stand down!" Kay snapped back, "You are outmaneuvered and outnumbered. There is no way out."

Then in an instant, Lancelot stepped back from the waiting blade and spun toward his captors with clenched fists, knocking Kay from his feet with hard blow to the side of his head, then deftly raising his sword to deflect Bedivere's ensuing strike. The fight soon erupted into chaos, as the close quarters provided little room for movement or counteraction, and any hope for civilized combat was lost in a flurry of flailing limbs and flashing steel. Gareth struggled to maintain his footing and ultimately became disoriented, unable to separate friend from foe, until suddenly he felt a sharp pain in his chest followed by an intense flood of cold, as if ice had filled his veins and the sun's fire had been extinguished. Time stood still as he looked down in shock to see a blade emerging from his body, pierced through his still-beating heart, and his eyes slowly moved along its bloody edge until he noticed Lancelot's horrified, shaking hand grasping the hilt. In that moment the skirmish stopped and every man stood frozen, locked in a ghastly daze, with all eyes upon Gareth and Lancelot as they stared back at one another, unblinking, their remorseful expressions imbued with sorrow and despair. As if he intended to turn back time, Lancelot quickly withdrew his sword, clinging to a fool's hope that the wound was somehow less serious than it seemed. *But it was wishful thinking, nothing more.* Arondight had found its target, and no measure of naïve optimism could possibly alter the fatal transgression. A tear ran down Gareth's cheek as he dropped to his knees, his final thoughts of his new bride, Lunette, while the life quickly fled from his earthly vessel. Lancelot swore and whispered a faint, "I'm sorry," before turning and rushing from the Great Hall, soon disappearing into the frigid winter morning.

* * * * *

An icy rain fell gently on the castle courtyard as the citizens of Camelot gathered close together in tight, huddled groups in a desperate attempt to weather the cold. Logic dictated that they should have been indoors, warming themselves by a hearth fire and filling their bellies with steaming bowls of hot broth. But instead they chose to stand shivering in a bitter, unwelcome drizzle, their collective attention turned toward a makeshift wooden platform where gallows had been hastily erected. The king was seated in the center, flanked by his remaining knights, while the queen stood nearby, her head lowered in shame, with her hands and feet bound by iron shackles. Word had spread that she had been charged with high treason, thus every man, woman, and child within the city walls had anxiously come to observe the public trial.

The crowd grew deathly quiet as Bedivere stepped forward and unrolled a scroll of parchment marked with the king's seal, then began to read the list of indictments that had been levied against the queen and her escaped paramour.

"By order of Arthur, High King of the Britons, son of Uther Pendragon, the accused Queen Gwenivere is hereby charged with treason against the Crown by way of adulterous actions, in defiance of both the laws of man and the laws of our Lord God. Furthermore, her accomplice in this matter, the disgraced knight Lancelot of the Lake, is charged with treason *in absentia*, as well as the most egregious murder of our comrade Gareth, son of Talorc, may his soul rest in peace."

Once the charges had been read aloud, the king's marshal returned to his post and let out a subtle, reluctant sigh. It was imperceptible to the multitude of onlookers, but those few who stood nearby noticed and said nothing, several sharing his feelings of unease with the grim ordeal that lay ahead. Arthur noticed as well and glanced disapprovingly over at Bedivere, but then he quickly turned back to the crowd, and with an awed hush, he stood and began to speak.

"Good citizens of Camelot," the king proclaimed, "I have invited you here today neither to celebrate these proceedings nor to humiliate those involved; but rather, to prove once and for all that *no* man stands above the law. Indeed, from the lowliest peasant all the way to the High King, the law remains steady and dispassionate, judging us not by our wealth or our station in life, but by our *actions*. Lancelot of the Lake, a man I once called friend, is already condemned to death based on his own confession and his murderous flight from justice, both of which may be confirmed by several reliable witnesses. And as you also know, my wife the queen is accused of betraying this kingdom by committing adultery with the same man, who had once taken an oath to defend it. Her complicity in this matter is not under contestation, as such facts have already been established. Instead, we come here today to ascertain the true level of her guilt; more specifically, whether she was an active, willing participant in this sordid affair, or whether she was somehow deceived and seduced by the illicit machinations of our former brother at arms, rendering her actions only foolish, weak, and sinful rather than overtly treasonous. In summation, this public trial will justly determine whether she will face execution or merely be banished from our presence. And as is customary, the truth will be established through single combat. He who has brought forth the accusations, our loyal servant Gawain, will cross swords with any man who chooses to defend the queen's honor. So I charge you now to stand and be known. Who will fight on behalf of Queen Gwenivere?"

The crowd of spectators waited in silent anticipation. Many looked to the horizon, thoroughly expecting Lancelot to arrive and take up the king's challenge, but as the minutes passed, it eventually became clear that he had truly fled and would not soon return. Then all eyes were drawn back to the makeshift platform as a single knight boldly stepped forward. He had a youthful complexion and unkempt ash-brown hair, and once he had approached the king, he knelt down with sword in hand and bowed his head in submission.

"Many years ago, sire," said Percival, "you made us swear a sacred oath to defend the defenseless. I come before you today to honor that vow."

Arthur nodded at Percival who then turned to face Gawain, the latter already armed and prepared for battle. Neither man wished to harm the other, but they also respected the hallowed tradition of trial by combat and would trust in God to grant victory to whoever was deemed worthy. The rain had turned from a drizzle to a downpour, and as the two opponents circled one another, the onlookers began to jeer and shout, having grown restless in the freezing courtyard and eager for the thrill of bloodshed. But before the men could come to blows, a shrill, mournful voice rang out among the din, commanding the attention of king and commoner alike.

"Stop!" cried Gwenivere, "I beg you, Arthur, do not allow these brave men to fight to the death on my account. I freely confess that I *did* betray our wedding vows, and that I did so of my own volition. If you wish to know the whole truth, I will answer anything you ask of me... but I will answer to *you* alone. Please, dismiss these people and speak with me privately. You are still my husband and I remain your wife."

Gazing upon his queen with the mingled emotions of anger and sorrow fighting for dominance within the fragments of his broken heart, Arthur deliberated for a few moments before sighing deeply and lifting his hand as a signal to end the trial by combat before it even began. Puzzled but thankful, Gawain and Percival sheathed their weapons and dutifully returned to their respective posts, while the king whispered something to Bedivere and retreated with his queen into the castle. Then as the spectators were dismissed, much to their chagrin, Bedivere turned back toward the other knights with sallow look upon his face and relayed their new orders.

"Ready your horses," he said with trepidation in his voice, "Arthur has commanded us to track Lancelot to wherever he has flown... and bring back his head."

* * * * *

The metallic *clang* of a heavy, cross-peen hammer pounding loudly against an iron anvil echoed through the twilight air, startling the horses in the stables nearby and causing anyone who passed to quicken his pace for fear of further provoking this dejected man whose rage had finally risen to the surface and exploded into the night like a spewing volcano. Wooden barrels were smashed to pieces, buckets filled with iron slag were strewn about the floor, and swords with broken blades were scattered everywhere as if this humble forge were a worn-torn battlefield. Arthur's right arm eventually grew numb from overexertion, so with one final, cathartic swing he hurled the hammer toward the bloomery furnace, sending a shower of sparks and flaming lumps of coal flying in every direction. Within moments, the entire blacksmith shop was consumed in flames, so Arthur retreated to a safe distance, then stood and watched it burn to the ground with perverse satisfaction.

After their private meeting, he had decided to temporarily confine Gwenivere to her bedchamber until he could decide exactly what to do with her. As promised, she had answered every question he asked with brutal honesty, often to the point that he could not bear to hear another word. She was contrite and apologetic, of course, offering no excuses for her betrayal but frequently making reference to the scars left on her heart during the tribulations of her youth. Despite their many years together, she said, she still had a difficult time understanding and accepting his love, because it was so markedly different than any version of love she had ever known before. It was calm, steady, and unwavering, yet seemingly unconcerned with exploiting her more *enticing* attributes. Right or wrong, she remained more comfortable and familiar with the unrestrained passion offered by Lancelot, and some small, wounded part of her still felt the need to be looked upon as a mere object of pleasure. Arthur had calmly listened as her words and emotions spilled forth like a rushing river, and while he knew that her intent was pure and without malice, the truth still pierced him deeply, like a dull knife being twisted in his back, and only served to fuel the fires of his anger. So when Gwenivere had finished speaking and pleaded hopefully for his forgiveness – after reaffirming her own love, of course – he simply stood up and left the room, too hurt by the simultaneous loss of his wife and his best friend to entertain any sort of rational thought. He began to ponder whether it would have been better if Lancelot had never returned home – if he had stayed dead and buried and left everyone blissfully unaware of the queen's latent feelings for this brawny, sandy-haired blacksmith.

What good was a king who was apparently unable to inspire loyalty, especially among those closest to him? Likewise, how could any man expect to gain the respect of others when he no longer respected himself? These questions and others haunted Arthur's restless mind as he watched the final remnants of the forge collapse into a heap of burning rubble.

"Damn you, Lancelot," he muttered under his breath.

And then, in that moment, a familiar voice from ages past seemed to miraculously emerge out of the cold night air.

"Feel better now, do you, my boy?"

Arthur quickly spun around to see an old man with a long, white beard. He wore a dingy, dark-green cloak and a wide-brimmed hat, and he carried a gnarled walking staff with a little geriatric owl perched precariously on top.

"Confound it, Merlyn!" Arthur exclaimed, "Why the devil do you always wait until the darkest hour to show yourself?"

"Darkest hour?" the old man replied, "Honestly, Arthur, if you can't bear to endure *this* meager indiscretion, how will you possibly withstand the trials yet to come?

"Merlyn, for just this once, can you at least *try* to remember your own lack of humanity? Being heartlessly betrayed by one's wife *and* closest friend is not merely an insignificant slight to us mortal men, you know. And curse your blasted apathy! You cannot simply disappear from Camelot without notice and then show up at a time like this expecting calm indifference from a man so grievously wronged! Aye, not just a man, but a *king*, rendering these sins all the more deplorable!"

No sooner had the words left his lips than Merlyn walloped Arthur over the head with the knob of his walking staff, leaving that ancient grey owl to abandon his perch and resume dozing atop the old man's pointed hat.

"Ow!" Arthur shouted, "What on earth was that for?"

"It was meant to knock a little sense into you, my boy," Merlyn answered, "Listen to yourself! Have you forgotten all I once taught you in the time I was away? What arrogance! Cast aside your foolish vainglory and remember that a good king is meant to be a *servant*, not a god among men. As a great thinker once said, '*Take heed not to be transformed into a Caesar, not to be dipped in the purple dye. But wrestle to be the man philosophy wished to make you.*'"

"More Augustine, Merlyn?"

"Actually, that little quotation was taken from the writings of Marcus Aurelius, your own son's namesake. Curious how even a pagan can offer a dose of divine wisdom, eh?"

"My own son..." the king said before trailing off, seemingly lost in another world, "Is he... is the child even mine?"

"Fatherhood is much more than blood, Arthur."

"But what of justice? What of the law? Surely such brazen infidelity cannot go unpunished. That which was once beautiful has now been trampled underfoot."

"Ah, yes. *Cast not thy pearls before swine.* Is that it?"

"Don't mock me, Merlyn," Arthur grumbled softly, his voice quivering with emotion, "I loved Gwenivere with all my heart. I gave her *everything*. I always looked upon her as a queen even when the rest of the world saw only an undeserving harlot. And yet *this* is how she repays me?"

The old man smiled and his clear blue eyes twinkled.

"Love is easy when it asks nothing of us," he said, "Any common rogue naturally loves those who show him kindness or charity. But to love the unlovable? To turn the other cheek? To sacrifice your pride, nay, even your life on behalf of another? This is the *true* measure of a man, Arthur. Now, I do not doubt the pain you feel because of what Gwenivere and Lancelot have done. But I also challenge you to ask yourself how this act of betrayal is any different than the near ceaseless rebellion, from the dawn of time, of mankind against their Maker. How many times have God's people turned away from Him, and how many times has He lovingly called them back? This is a love beyond reason – beyond *comprehension*. It is what an unbelieving world finds truly unbelievable. So as you wallow in self-pity, know that your anguish is only a dim reflection of what your own redeemer has felt in every waking moment since the loss of Eden."

Arthur felt his knees grow weak and he slumped down onto the muddy footpath below. Cold water quickly soaked through his woolen breeches, chilling him to the bone, though the mild discomfort caused by the wet, icy weather paled in comparison to the grief that now stung his heart. For a long time the king sat in thoughtful silence, mulling over Merlyn's words as the conflicting ideals of justice and mercy battled fiercely in his troubled mind, until all of a sudden the floodgates opened and he began to weep. The old man said nothing, but simply sat down in the mud at Arthur's side and wrapped him in his cloak, offering comfort as a father would his child.

* * * * *

When morning came, Gwenivere rubbed her weary eyes and walked to the window of her bedchamber, quickly noticing that a thick blanket of snow had fallen overnight. The skies had cleared, and the light of dawn reflecting off the frozen white fields made the countryside glow like an earthbound star. And although she had spent most of the previous evening in tears, there was something about the unblemished purity of fresh snowfall that made everything seem new, as if hope had been restored and was now just within reach. When she opened the shutters to feel the crisp morning air on her face, a gust of wind blew through the opening and lifted a small piece of parchment that had been slipped beneath the door, sending it fluttering across the room until it landed gently at her feet. Gwenivere could feel the fine vellum brushing against her toes, and as soon as she bent down to pick it up, she easily recognized Arthur's pristine, fluid handwriting:

"My dearest Gwenivere, I have been a fool blinded by anger. Please know that you have my love and my forgiveness, now as

always, though I must ask for your forgiveness as well. I had forgotten what it means to truly love someone. But then again, perhaps I never really knew until this night. I have ordered the locks removed from your chamber, and I have instructed those knights who remain that you are to be respected and obeyed as rightful regent during my absence. As for me, I have set out after Gawain and the others, hoping to intercept them before they can follow through with my lamentable orders. Pray for swiftness as I ride, my queen, for the life of Lancelot, our friend and champion, depends upon it."

Son of Perdition

Rowena stepped softly down the long, darkened corridor after leaving the chamber that once belonged to Gareth and Lunette and gently pulling the door closed behind her. The young bride was beside herself, having refused to dress, bathe, or eat for the past three days after receiving the news of Gareth's untimely demise, and Rowena had sought to console her in whatever way deemed possible. She brought fresh venison stew and a cup of hot cider to sate the girl's appetite and warm her grief-stricken spirit, but Lunette was still reticent, swallowing only a few small mouthfuls of stew before pushing the bowl away. On the morrow she would return to her family home, so after sitting attentively at her side as she mourned and offering a short prayer for peace and comfort, Rowena left the girl to sleep for the night and wandered pensively into the snowy, moonlit courtyard to collect her thoughts.

The castle had been eerily quiet since Arthur left, with most of the knights out hunting for Lancelot, and with Gwenivere at home mainly keeping to herself, trying not to ruffle any feathers in light of the awkward circumstances. Only Sagramore, Tristan, Kay, and Mordred remained behind, and the former two were *already* seldom seen – the aging Roman soldier keeping to his beloved horses and the Celtic knight refusing to vacate the safe haven of Saint Stephen's Cathedral.

As court seneschal, Kay had taken it upon himself to ensure that every aspect of life in Camelot continued to run efficiently in the king's absence, thriving in his role as royal administrator over daily affairs. His late father, Ector, would have been proud, for the years had worn away much of his former boorishness, and the care he displayed in overseeing finance and domestic arrangements had earned the garrulous redhead the respect of all those he encountered, from his fellow knights all the way down to the servant maids. Especially in a time such as this, Rowena thanked God for the stability Kay offered and prayed earnestly for his continued fruitfulness.

Mordred, however, was another story. Much like Percival, Rowena had never fully trusted the dark-haired young man, and his peculiar actions over the past few days only served to further arouse her lingering suspicions. He spent inordinate amounts of time roaming the castle, inspecting every outer gate and mode of defense, and though he claimed only to be performing security assessments in Bedivere's stead, it seemed more like he was searching for weaknesses. He also frequently went missing in the late night hours, set out for destinations unknown, and then always returned by early morning with his clothes smelling of smoke and peat moss. Of course, Rowena had expressed misgivings about Mordred long before the onset of his recent behavior, though whenever she chose to express such sentiments to Gawain, her wary admonitions were lovingly but summarily dismissed. And while she naturally understood her husband's great affection for the king's nephew, she also worried that his judgment had been clouded by the extravagant fawning of a shrewd young man whose wit and charisma might be masking something far more menacing.

He was, after all, Morgana's son.

Rowena shuddered at the memory of her departed friend, who had unfortunately left behind a legacy of pain and horror. A chill shivered up her spine as she harkened back to that final, frightening image of Morgana's eyes turning pitch black while dark spirits infested her body like a swarm of locusts. It was a nightmare Rowena would never forget.

Over the years, she had often wondered about the woman Morgana may have become had she not been so viciously wounded by Vortigern's boundless lust and cruelty. As a child she had been cheerful, clever, and mischievous, always playing silly games and chattering on endlessly about even the most delightfully nonsensical topics. Indeed, Morgana was a very different person before that malicious tyrant broke her spirit, but hatred and a thirst for vengeance eventually overwhelmed and destroyed the happy little girl that once was, leaving behind little more than an empty husk entirely consumed by evil. Even now, a tiny measure of hope still lingered within Rowena's heart that her friend may not be completely lost, and although Morgana's fate remained unknown, she still prayed for her redemption, however futile it seemed.

As her thoughts eventually turned to Gwenivere and the now uncertain patrimony of her child, Rowena overheard the snapping of twigs and turned to see a cloaked figure trudging through the snow near the tilting fields, apparently making his way toward the northern woods. Despite the distance and his head being covered, Rowena instantly recognized Mordred's awkward gait as he ambled gracelessly across the darkened winter landscape. *Where on earth are you headed, Mordred? What strange adventures do you seek in the moonlight?* Then before she could talk herself out of it, Rowena made up her mind to follow him, determined to discover where he had been disappearing each night under cover of shadow.

She kept her distance, moving only fast enough to maintain eye contact with his cloaked silhouette, occasionally ducking behind trees or large rocks in order to avoid detection. A fierce, icy wind howled through the pastureland, prompting Rowena to pull her woolen scarf closely to her face and wrap her tingling hands in the folds of her overcoat. As they entered the forest the air only seemed to grow colder, though it also became slightly easier to hide from sight in the midst of the towering oaks. Her primary concern then became avoiding the roots and fallen branches that were blocking her path; fortunately, Rowena had always been fairly nimble-footed and was able to successfully navigate through any impediments without much difficulty. She must have followed Mordred for miles before the dark-haired young man stepped into a small, moss-covered clearing, in the center of which stood a run-down hovel with plumes of black smoke billowing from the chimney.

Rowena waited until Mordred was indoors and out of sight before creeping along the perimeter of the clearing and slowly making her way toward the hovel from the rear. As she skulked through the thick undergrowth, briefly snagging her dress on the sharp edge of an unseen rock, she began to hear a female voice speaking fervently with the mysterious young man. Their conversation remained quiet despite the secluded location, so she moved closer to the open window in an effort to discern the substance of this clandestine meeting.

"Your plan seems to be coming together flawlessly," she heard Mordred remark, "Camelot has fallen into uncertainty, and the Council of the Round Table is fragmented."

"Arthur still suspects nothing?" the woman inquired.

"Ha! That pathetic old fool! His naïve insistence on always looking for the *best* in others has blinded him to the truth. He trusts me as if I were his own son. By now, I know everything there is to know about the castle defenses and how to exploit each weakness, so Cynric's army should have no trouble getting through the walls when they arrive."

"And what of the skeptics? Have they been... dealt with?"

"As I told you, Percival is off with the other sheep hunting for Lancelot, so he won't pose any immediate threat. Right now it's that Saxon woman we need to worry about. She grows ever more curious with each passing day. Her laughable attempts to turn Gawain against me failed before they could cause any real damage, but I fear that she may soon find an attentive ear with the queen, who *might* still hold enough sway in the kingdom to impede our coup in its infancy."

Rowena covered her mouth to keep from gasping audibly, shocked and dismayed to find that her worst suspicions had been realized. *Somehow, she had to get word to Arthur.* The pieces of the puzzle began to fall into place as she considered the totality of recent events, with Gwenivere conveniently being abducted on the very night of Mordred's arrival in Camelot, and the same dark-haired stranger stepping forward as the lone witness of the queen's infidelity with Lancelot. *It had all been carefully arranged. Even his relationship with Gawain was a calculated move solely meant to gain access to Arthur's council.* And now the kingdom was ripe for the taking, with most of the knights sent away to kill one of their own, the public losing their faith in the wake of Gwenivere's aborted public trial, and the king himself far beyond reach on a possibly futile quest to stop the acts of vengeance he had set in motion.

As the conversation continued, Rowena gradually began to recognize the devilish female voice. It was raspy, weathered, and slightly deeper than it once had been, but it was also a voice that had long haunted her dreams. Quaking in fear, she began inching ever closer in order to properly hear the details of this newly uncovered plot, when a sudden, boisterous noise caused her heart to skip a beat, breaking the silence and immediately giving away her hidden presence. Rowena glanced to her left and spied a large black crow perched atop a nearby fencepost, cawing incessantly while staring back at her with eerie, lifeless eyes. Moments later Mordred's head burst through the gaping window, a look of seething hatred on his face, and he grasped Rowena around her neck, pulling her violently through the small opening and into the hovel.

She now found herself lying motionless on the cold, earthen floor, with sharp pain shooting through her head and neck after being carelessly dropped like a sack of old turnips. The frigid air chilled her to the bone, and Rowena quickly realized that her overcoat had been taken, along with her scarf and winter boots. Her hands and feet were quickly growing numb, but she fought the urge to move, distressed to see Mordred standing over her imposingly with one hand clutching her coat and the other resting suggestively on the hilt of his sword.

"I see we have a visitor," she heard the woman say, "Let her stand, Mordred. I want to look my old friend in the eye."

Half-dressed and shivering, Rowena slowly rose to her feet and stood face to face with Morgana, her beloved childhood companion, though now primarily known as the Priestess of the White Dragon. Despite the lengthy passage of time, she still boasted the same slender frame and long, jet-black hair, but her once beautiful face seemed to have aged disproportionately in comparison with the rest of her body, looking worn and sickly, as if wallowing in darkness had finally taken its tragic toll. With a wicked smile, the priestess reached out toward Rowena and snatched away the small iron cross that always hung around her neck, studying it carefully and rolling it over in her fingers for a few moments before speaking again.

"You still cling to this useless relic?" Morgana chided before angrily throwing the cross into the roaring hearth fire.

"As I recall, *you* once did as well," Rowena replied.

"Ah, yes. My ridiculous, youthful ignorance. *When I was a child, I spoke and thought and reasoned as a child. But when I grew up, I put away childish things."*

"Nothing like a bit of blasphemy to set the mood, eh, Morgana? Perhaps you'd like to burn another prayer book?"

"Your memory serves you well," the priestess sneered, "but the answer to your question is *no*. I've moved well beyond such banality. Besides, I'd much rather see Arthur's kingdom burned to the ground instead."

And with those words, she walked to the far corner of the hovel and retrieved a long, thin object wrapped in a woolen blanket and bound with thick cords of hemp. As the priestess carefully removed the covering, Rowena could see that it was an old Roman pilum, roughly two yards long and tipped with a heavy, leaf-shaped, iron shank, the entire shaft stained black with blood. She then presented the ancient weapon to her son, who dropped his own sword and gaped in awe before hesitantly reaching out and grasping it with both hands.

"Behold the legendary Spear of Longinus," she announced, "thrust centuries ago into the side of that deranged carpenter as he hung dead on a Roman cross, and fated to be possessed by one who would rule the known world."

As Mordred studied the spear, feeling a surge of dark power course through him, his mother stepped close and held his face in her hands, commanding his respect and attention.

"This weapon was wielded by your father, King Vortigern, once the most powerful warlord in all Britannia. He ruled the land with an iron fist until his reign was prematurely ended by that churlish commoner who now sits on the throne. The time has come, my son. Go now and claim your destiny."

The dark-haired young man then retrieved his heavy cloak and stepped into the frosty winter night with the ancient spear in his hand and hatred swelling within his heart. Moonlight poured through the woodland canopy, leaving behind intricate patterns of light that filled the clearing with a soft, ethereal glow. But despite the superficial beauty of their surroundings, the cold had rendered dormant all of the sweet-smelling flowers and shrubs, leaving behind nothing but the stale scent of death. Mordred turned and glared viciously at Rowena before closing the hovel door, and then she watched in silence until he disappeared into the blackness of the forest.

"You ought to be proud, Rowena," the priestess finally said in a stoic monotone, "for you are a witness to history. Here we stand at the beginning of a new world, and all that was once taken from me will soon be reclaimed."

"Have you lost your mind?" Rowena asked in amazement, "You praise your cruel abuser and condemn your own blood?

Arthur has done *nothing* to deserve this, Morgana. Are there no depths left to which you will not sink?"

"A means to an end, my dear. Just a means to an end."

"Did you bother telling your son that Vortigern was a brutal, cowardly, narcissistic despot? That he is a bastard child born of incestuous lust and violence?"

"...and that his father, sniveling worm that he was, died by my own hand?" Morgana interrupted, her gruff tone masking a hint of deep melancholy, "Don't be so infantile. Mordred needs to *believe* he is the rightful king."

"Heaven help you, Morgana!" Rowena cried, "You have raised that poor, troubled, *angry* boy on a diet of hatred and lies, purely in order to satisfy your own twisted need for... for *what* exactly? Power? Validation? Some unresolved vendetta? Or simply to stand upon the mountaintop with fists clenched and curse the God who made you?"

"*There is no God!*" Morgana screamed with a frightening, inhuman ferocity, "*You* are the one who feeds on lies, Rowena! The merciful, loving father that was promised to us as children does not exist! Mercy is a *myth*. Love is an *illusion*. In this life, there is only suffering and pain, and if we are to endure it, then we must *become* suffering! We must *become* pain!"

Then the door to the hovel abruptly flew open and a burst of icy wind rushed through and extinguished the hearth fire, leaving the two women in near total darkness with only the dim light of the moon providing the slightest illumination. Even in the dead of winter, Rowena began to feel uncommonly cold, as if the oppressive weight of some dark presence had suddenly filled the surrounding air. Terror enveloped her mind and she mouthed a silent prayer as Morgana slowly stepped toward her with eyes like spheres of obsidian, brandishing a small knife and speaking in a guttural, animalistic growl.

"Farewell to your *precious* light, where false hope springs eternal! *Oh, you deluded, misbegotten wretch*. Can't you see that the one you worship has forgotten and abandoned this world? Now here you stand – fearful, shivering, and weak – while *my* master imbues me with power beyond measure! *What a pity.* You may be willingly blind to the inborn desolation that defines all human life, but now you will *truly* know how it feels to dwell alone in darkness. Hail, horrors... hail!"

Gales of demonic laughter defiled the peaceful midnight air, and the last thing Rowena ever saw was the blade of Morgana's knife gleaming ominously in the moonlight.

The Scattered Flock

It was nearly midday in the tiny, hillside village of Dinan, and as the conspicuous team of armed horsemen crossed the rickety, wooden footbridge that spanned over a narrow segment of the River Rance, their mounts began to noticeably slow their pace. The melting snow had transformed the well-trodden roads into a quagmire of slush and mud, and so the horses trudged along, their hooves sinking deeper with every step.

A few fishermen sat in the tall, frost-covered grass along the shoreline, their hopes of catching fish in the icy river dwindling by the hour, while farmers grazed their cattle on soggy fields of ryegrass and oats. It was Sunday, and the weekly chapel service had just been dismissed, leaving the village priest to stand patiently outside his modest stone chapel offering blessings to each of his congregants as they ambled homeward to fill their hungry bellies. Most of the local merchants had closed up shop for the day, of course, with the notable exception of the portly, jovial tavern owner, who would likely stay open for business even if a cyclone had buried the town in waist-deep flood waters. Pleased to finally be free from the mud, the mounted knights plodded down a crumbling, cobblestone pathway past the darkened storefronts of carpenters, butchers, and tailors, as well as a boarded-up and seemingly abandoned apothecary's potion dispensary. They eventually arrived at their destination on the far side of town, where a stone-built blacksmith shop stood midway up the hillside on the western shore of the river. The front door was closed, but the forge was clearly occupied, with firelight glowing through the windows and black smoke pouring from the furnace chimney.

"What makes you think he's here?" asked Percival.

"He has nowhere else to go," Gawain replied.

* * * * *

Lancelot stood alone in his elderly uncle's shop, mindlessly hammering away at a set of horseshoes. Sparks flew here and there like tiny shooting stars as he pounded upon the iron anvil, the red-hot metal slowly being formed into the proper shape. His muscles burned from overuse, but as soon as he finished one horseshoe, he tossed it carelessly into a large pile to his left and started on another. Despite the grueling nature of his work, it was meant only as a distraction, especially since the old blacksmith had long since retired, instead deciding to offer the forge for lease by a young apprentice who lived on the opposite side of the river. This being Sunday, the shop was closed, which provided Lancelot with ample opportunity to blow off steam while pondering his lamentable situation.

If he had not been condemned before, he most assuredly would be now. Not only had his infidelity with the queen been counted as high treason, but he had also slaughtered Gareth, a friend and fellow knight, in cold blood before fleeing like a coward from captivity. Lancelot wanted to believe the killing had been an accident, and perhaps it had been; nevertheless, a nagging voice in the back of his mind still whispered *murderer* firmly and relentlessly. *How many lives had he destroyed?* As he thought of the slain Pictish knight and his lovely new bride, Lancelot became overwhelmed with sorrow and began to curse his very existence, struck by the realization that the innocent, sacred love between Gareth and Lunette had been lead to the grave by his reprehensible lust for Gwenivere. *It wasn't fair.* He should have remained in Camelot and accepted his punishment, justified as it was. But it was panic that prompted his flight, for although he had at first been ready and willing to humbly face judgement, fear quickly proved to be a much more powerful motivator than his meager sense of honor.

As he tossed yet another finished horseshoe into the pile, Lancelot began to wonder why Nimue had bothered to watch over him all these years; why she felt compelled to heal his wounds after his encounter with the ghostly black knight on the shores of the North Sea; why she had promised him a heroic destiny so long ago in Brocéliande Forest. *He was no hero. He was a scoundrel and a traitor who had brought nothing but pain to the people he loved.* Thoroughly dejected, Lancelot dropped his hammer and tongs to the floor and stood up to leave the shop, intent to wander without direction, when he suddenly heard the sound of a familiar voice calling out to him loudly from just outside the front door.

"Come forth, Lancelot!" Gawain shouted, "We know that you have taken refuge here, and armed horsemen stand ready at every exit. There will be no escape this time."

They had found him. *Of course they had found him.* It was only a matter of time, really. All of his friends had been sent to kill him, and his only family lived here in this tiny fishing village. The sole alternative was going back to the wilderness, but in truth, part of Lancelot *wanted* to be discovered. *This was how it had to end*. He peered through the nearest window and saw Bedivere and Percival waiting on one side of the forge, swords drawn and ready. The opposite window revealed the presence of Lamorack and Aglovale, both silent and expressionless, riding shoulder-to-shoulder and often bumping into one another as they approached from the east. And at the back door he spied Palamedes, the sinewy Sarmatian swordsman, mounted atop his jet black courser with that massive scimitar resting against his right shoulder. *Lancelot almost smiled.* Although Palamedes was the eldest of any man present by far, he looked ten or even twenty years younger than most men his age, and he could still probably best the majority of Arthur's knights in hand-to-hand combat. For the briefest moment their eyes met, and although Palamedes struck an imposing figure, Lancelot could still sense a heavy reluctance from the aging warrior as he straddled the uncomfortable line between duty and friendship.

Lancelot took a deep breath and stepped slowly toward the front door. As he lifted the latch, he noticed Arondight propped up against a slag barrel in the corner of the room and reached for it, hoping to find some measure of comfort with his mighty sword in hand. But as his fingers brushed against the ornate, bone-crafted hilt, dredging up the blood-soaked memories of years upon years of battle, Lancelot suddenly stopped short and backed away as a strange sense of peace and acceptance fell over him. *No more fighting. No more bloodshed. The time had come to meet his fate.* Rather than bursting through the doorway with sword in hand, leaving this life in a blaze of glory, the great warrior instead chose to lay down his weapon and face justice with a heart of contrition, and he began to feel a calm that he had not known since boyhood. It was a sign of utter submission – a heavy burden finally laid to rest.

"Here I am," Lancelot said softly as he stepped out of the blacksmith shop and into the daylight.

There Gawain sat, tall atop his buckskin charger, its golden coat shimmering in the sun, with a sharpened battle axe in his hand and an unforgiving scowl on his face. His armor was dull and damaged, revealing its long history on the battlefield, though the well-worn steel was not so blemished as his own wounded spirit. Indeed, while the other knights had journeyed to Dinan in the name of duty and justice, Gawain had taken Lancelot's betrayal far more personally. Ever since the uprising against Vortigern many years ago, when his own duplicity resulted in the horrific murder of an innocent Saxon boy, even the smallest acts of falseness or treachery were particularly abhorrent to Gawain. Thus he became famous for his intense loyalty and fervor, even more so than the other members of Arthur's council, although that same passion was also known to render him overly zealous and myopic from time to time. This fiery demeanor made Gawain an ideal asset to have on one's side during battle, but when circumstances arose that required tact, nuance, or diplomacy, he became – as Rowena lovingly called him – a crass, lumbering ogre.

"Arm yourself, traitor," Gawain sneered, his teeth clenched with hate, "Arthur has ordered us to bring back your head, but I refuse to kill a man in cold blood. I will not be like *you*."

"Gareth's death was an accident," the disgraced champion replied, "While I accept full responsibility for what I've done, you must know that I *never* intended to harm him."

"Save it for when you meet your Maker, Lancelot! We have no more patience for your lies! No matter what pathetic excuses you attempt to offer, the fact remains that a good man is dead by your hand… a man you once called *brother*. Now go on. Draw your sword. We two will meet in trial by combat, and the wages for your sins will be decided once and for all. If you deny guilt, then prepare to stake your life on it!"

"I bear no desire to cross swords with you. Remember that I once called *you* brother as well."

"Arm yourself!" Gawain growled in anger.

"I will not," replied Lancelot, his empty hands outstretched in resignation, "Do what you must."

"Hold, Gawain," Bedivere interrupted as the enraged Saxon began to charge forward with axe drawn, quickly placing himself in between the two former friends, "While justice must be done, there is also room for *mercy*. Despite Arthur's ruthless decree, issued when his mind was obviously clouded by heartbreak and rage, remember that we *never* leave a fallen man behind – even one who has fallen from grace. Give him the night to think things over, and we will return in the morning."

"And provide this scoundrel with yet another opportunity to flee? God's bones, Bedivere! Have you lost your mind?"

"Come off it, Gawain," Percival added, "You said yourself that he has nowhere else to go."

"He's right," said Bedivere, "After all, Lancelot *did* come out to face us willingly, unarmed and seemingly penitent. Whether or not that remorse is genuine has yet to been seen, but still, thus far he has given us no reason to anticipate another escape attempt. Now lower your weapon."

For a moment Gawain remained frozen, silently seething as his irate gaze alternated between Bedivere and Lancelot, until at last he yielded and resentfully tossed his battle axe onto the muddy walkway nearby, narrowly missing an unsuspecting Lamorack and Aglovale as they galloped over from the other side of the forge. After offering a meager nod of apology to his comrades, Gawain let out a loud, frustrated grunt and shouted, "Tomorrow, then!" before riding off toward the village tavern, obviously intent on drinking away his wrath.

"Let him go," Bedivere muttered to Percival, who had begun to follow behind, "Perhaps a bit of ale will calm his temper. Come, we will try to find an inn for the night."

Then Lancelot watched as his former companions, men he had once fought and bled with, turned their mounts and rode somberly back toward the town square, their deafening silence only broken by the familiar sound of horseshoes plodding along down the crumbling, cobblestone pathway. Percival, humble and obedient as always, was the first to go, followed by his two quarrelsome brothers, with grizzled old Palamedes bringing up the rear on the back of his swift black courser. Bedivere waited until the others had gone, squinting up at the bright midday sun as it rose higher in the sky, then turned back to Lancelot and issued one final ultimatum before riding away.

"We will return tomorrow at sunrise," he said solemnly, wincing with each word as if the very thought of carrying out his orders caused him pain, "Although I hope to spare your life, I still advise you make your peace with God... and I also *beg* you not to run. I have placed my faith in you, Lancelot, and whatever honor you have left. Don't make me out to be a fool."

No one slept that night, save for Gawain, who passed out drunk in the tavern and had to be dragged into bed by Lamorack and Aglovale, much to their vexation. But it hardly mattered anyway. Whatever rest might have been gained had they not been beset with insomnia would have surely been interrupted when the inn was unexpectedly visited overnight by a solitary, mysterious traveler wearing a hooded cloak. As for Lancelot, he tried desperately to sleep but only tossed and turned fruitlessly, unable to calm his weary mind with the prospect of swift, merciless death waiting for him on the morrow.

* * * * *

Meanwhile, old Pellinore slept deeply and soundly in his darkened bed chamber, which was located on the top floor of the highest tower in Arthur's castle at Camelot. A lumpy heap of furs and blankets was piled atop his wool-stuffed mattress, keeping him safely insulated from the cold as he dreamed of the valiant quests and glorious battles that filled his younger days. No one ever bothered him up here, and that was the way he liked it. Despite his fondness for memories of the past, the old soldier preferred a quiet life nowadays, keeping adventure relegated to the stories he told and retold in the Great Hall over goblets of fine wine. Pellinore had also made the choice to keep to himself more in recent months, with the poignant realization that he was becoming a burden on his sons as well as the others who cared for him, although he knew they would never be so bold as to tell him so. Time was taking its toll, as it eventually does for all men, and the confusion that marked his senility had grown so severe that he frequently found himself unable to recognize otherwise familiar people he had known and loved for decades, including members of his own family. He had also begun to see and hear things that weren't there, having once caused a minor panic among the women in the castle after mistaking a discarded pair of stockings that was accidentally left by a wash basin in the lavatory for a large, poisonous serpent. Such embarrassments made him wonder whether it was better for a man to know that he was slowly losing his senses or to live out his days remaining blissfully unaware.

In his dream, Pellinore was still an idealistic young soldier in the service of the Roman general Uther Pendragon, taking arms against a contingent of Saxon raiders who had stormed a small outpost on the southeastern coast. But just as he was about to leap into the fray, a sudden noise woke him from his slumber. Pellinore sat up in bed and rubbed his eyes, then wrapped one of the heavy blankets around his shoulders and shuffled over to the tower window in hopes of identifying the commotion. As he peered outside, with the courtyard illuminated by moonlight, the feeble old man saw what appeared to be a battalion of warriors stealthily scaling the castle walls. Most of them were using Saxon armor and weapons, notably similar to the raiders in his dream, and oddly enough, their points of incursion were at very specific locations where blind spots existed in the defenses and where the stone walls were not so thick. It would have been impossible for an invading force to identify those weaknesses from the exterior of the castle, so it stood to reason that they must have received assistance from someone within. *But who?* Pellinore threw off his blanket and began to get dressed so he could rush downstairs to warn Gwenivere, Kay, and the others, but then another thought came upon him and he stopped, cursing Father Time for callously ravaging his brain. *Surely none of this was real.* Once again, the senile old man was confused and seeing things that weren't there, and he would *not* be the cause of yet another unwarranted panic.

And so, having decided that the Saxon soldiers scaling the castle walls were nothing more than an extension of his dream – a figment of his age-addled mind – Pellinore crawled back into bed, pulled the heap of blankets and furs over his frail, tired body, and quickly fell back into a peaceful sleep.

* * * * *

Exhaustion finally overtook Lancelot just before sunrise, and by the time he awoke it was already early afternoon. He had spent the entire night in his uncle's blacksmith shop, propped uncomfortably against the side of a large slag barrel waiting for the inevitable. So standing up proved to be extremely difficult, as his back was sore and his neck was as stiff as a board. After stretching and groaning for a few moments, he looked over and noticed the young blacksmith apprentice from across the river, who had arrived that morning to work but was now sitting atop the anvil eating a plate of fried fish and watching this sleeping stranger who had somewhat unceremoniously invaded his place of business. After finishing his meal, the apprentice stood up, cleared his throat, and opened the nearest window, preparing for the smoke and soot that would soon fill the room as he returned to his daily tasks. Sunlight poured through the open shutters, and it was then that Lancelot began to wonder exactly how much time had passed while he dozed.

"What hour is it?" he asked the bemused apprentice, "How long have I slept? Is it long past sunrise?"

"Sunrise?" the apprentice laughed, "That was nearly seven hours ago! What the devil did you do last night? Oh, and by the way, would you terribly mind, um... *leaving* for a while? I realize your uncle owns this place, but I *do* have work to do."

The young apprentice must have been pleasantly surprised to see Lancelot quickly gather his belongings and bolt through the front door of the blacksmith shop. He hurried down the shabby cobblestone road toward the town square, passing by carpenters, butchers, tailors, and other merchants as they peddled their wares, until at last he reached the village inn. Lancelot bent over briefly to catch his breath and then began pounding on the door, calling loudly for the innkeeper after noticing that there were no horses tied up in the guest stables nearby. Eventually a plump, grey-haired woman wearing an ill-fitting brown frock and a dirty apron opened the door, clearly annoyed by the incessant knocking.

"Oy! Stop all that, ye daft little miscreant! Such terrible racket is likely to wake the dead!"

"Tell me, madam," Lancelot implored, "Where are the men who lodged here last night?"

"Ye mean them five soldiers and the drunkard? Left here hours ago, they did. Rode off early this morning with another fellow who showed up in the middle of the night."

"Another fellow?"

"Aye, a man of some importance, it seemed. When he took off his cloak I saw a fancy gold crest on his tunic. Looked like an eagle with a cross in the center. Ye know him?"

"Know him?" Lancelot smiled, his voice beginning to crack with emotion, "He's my oldest friend."

To Reign In Hell

In the dim light of early morning, Lord Astaroth smiled wickedly as he strolled among the mangled corpses of night sentries and castle guards who had been quickly and quietly slaughtered by the invading Saxon forces. Steam rose from gaping wounds in the bitter cold of winter, and crimson footprints besmirched the shimmering, white limestone of the parapets, creating a series of gruesome trails that led from the shallow pools of blood beneath the soldiers' bodies and into the depths of Camelot. Most of the residents still slumbered unsuspectingly with this clandestine assault well underway, and Astaroth began to swell with hubris at the thought of Arthur's imminent downfall. Ten agonizing years had passed as he awaited the perfect moment to exact his vengeance, and it pleased him to see his long-gestating plan finally come to fruition.

Of course, the preliminary success of this elaborate revenge scheme could not have been achieved without help. Maleagant of Gorre, for instance, had played a crucial role in the abduction of Gwenivere. *But he was never really one of them.* In the end, Maleagant was merely pawn, a blunt instrument, a voracious brute whose loyalty was easily bought with the promise of a queen's ransom. Astaroth laughed to himself at the memory of the big warrior's scarred, severed head floating lazily down that little river on the edge of the forest. *His death hardly mattered anyway.* In fact, the trauma may actually have been useful in pushing Gwenivere into the arms of her rescuer. But despite it all, the most integral and advantageous assistance had come from Morgana's son Mordred. As a trusted Knight of the Round Table, his unfettered access to the castle defenses had enabled him to provide inside information regarding their subtle yet important flaws to Cynric and his Saxon brethren. Moreover, the industrious young man had taken it upon himself to lace the evening meals of the castle guards with nightshade – not quite enough to kill, but enough to render them delirious and highly vulnerable shortly after taking their posts.

It was no great secret among the demonic hordes that Lord Astaroth had grown *extremely* fond of Mordred. The boy was intelligent, deceitful, ruthless, manipulative, and highly adept at twisting the truth just enough to fool even the wariest of skeptics. Unlike their previous servant Agravain – *that spoiled, thin-skinned little narcissist* – Mordred was not beholden to his emotions, nor did he flout responsibility in the service of his massive ego. He was calm and even-tempered, with an innate affability that enabled him to easily ingratiate himself to either friend or foe, whichever was necessary. And unlike Morgana, he never actually had to be seduced or tempted to embrace his own inner darkness. Rather, malevolence seemed to come to Mordred naturally, like swimming to a fish or scavenging for corpses to a vulture.

Astaroth puffed out his chest with pride as he surveyed the rampant destruction that now descended upon Camelot. *It was beautiful.* Dawn was breaking, and the world was cast in an eerie silver glow that revealed the lifeless bodies of Arthur's men, slowly freezing as they lay strewn about the bloodied castle walls. Scattered screams began to echo through the courtyard, with women and children waking to find their loved ones slain as Mordred dispassionately came forth to greet his Saxon allies. Naberius waited nearby, of course, a sadistic smile stretched across his gruesome, lupine visage. Although he hated to share the glory, Astaroth was forced to admit that the devious little imp had done exceedingly well in guiding the boy for all these years and deftly leading him toward this moment. But the powerful demon prince had already claimed the coming victory for himself. *This would be his finest hour.*

* * * * *

Kay stood aghast as the wooden gate to the stables slowly creaked open, revealing Sagramore's broken, mangled body lying motionless in a pile of blood-soaked hay. Wild dogs licked at his wounds while his beloved horses whinnied nervously in their pens, woefully unable to comprehend the fate of their master but still aware that *something* had gone terribly wrong. A pair of armed Saxon soldiers lay dead nearby as well, proving that the aging cavalryman had refused to go quietly, though the mass of muddy footprints leading back toward the castle indicated that he had been ambushed by at least a dozen men. Kay had been out hunting just before dawn, called back from the forest by the distant sound of anguished cries, which ultimately led to the grisly sight that now appeared before him. The red-haired seneschal dropped to his knees as sorrow, anger, and fear threatened to overwhelm his senses. His spirit grew heavy, almost too burdensome to endure, but then his sense of duty began screaming at him through the blackness, urging him to stand until he grudgingly crawled to his feet and ran like wildfire toward Saint Stephen's Cathedral.

The ornate stained-glass windows shook in their panes as the heavy doors to the cathedral flew open and Kay stumbled into the narthex with sword in hand, agitated and out of breath. Alarmed by the sudden noise, Tristan hurriedly rose from his morning prayers and lowered the cowl of his robe, turning back to see his fellow knight with terror in his eyes and a face as pale as death. The Celtic monk cringed with vexation. Long ago he had taken a solemn vow to renounce violence and live out his days as a man of peace, and after all this time, he would not allow what he assumed to be some routine skirmish between one of Arthur's warriors and a handful of disgruntled peasants to draw him back into the life he once knew.

"Sheath your sword, Kay!" warned Tristan, "I will not abide bloodshed in this house of worship."

"Sagramore is dead," Kay responded, his frantic expression making it clear that this was *not* just an ordinary scuffle.

"Dead? God rest his soul. What happened?"

"There are Saxon soldiers within the castle walls, Tristan. Maybe hundreds of them. I don't know how they managed to breach our defenses, but with Arthur and most of the other knights far away from Camelot, we may soon be overwhelmed. Now come, you and I must protect the queen."

"What about Mordred? Is he not with you?"

Kay opened his mouth to reply, but before he could utter a single word, the iron shank of an ancient Roman spear came bursting through his chest, leaving a cavernous hole where his heart had been. The seneschal's eyes rolled back in his head as he collapsed onto the stone floor of the cathedral, his features already marred by the unmistakable pallor of death, revealing a familiar silhouette standing behind him in the golden light of daybreak. As the figure slowly stepped into the narthex, with fresh blood dripping down the shaft of his spear, he brushed a shock of long, black hair from his eyes and smiled menacingly at Tristan before sadistically spitting onto Kay's corpse.

"Did someone call for me?" Mordred smirked.

Tristan could feel it – that same seething rage that once led him to blindly slaughter an innocent family who he mistakenly believed to be engaged in pagan sacrifice. *Their lifeless faces, eternally frozen in shock and disbelief, still haunted his dreams.* These long, lonely years spent in an ascetic life of prayer and solitude were supposed to have freed him from such wanton bloodlust and absolved him from his sins, unforgivable as they seemed. But as the anger swelled within him, Tristan began to realize that it was neither hatred nor savagery that now urged him onward. Unlike before, grief and sorrow had not left him teetering on the edge of sanity and pushed him toward reckless acts of vengeance. *No. This was a righteous anger.* With a renewed sense of determination, he slowly began to remove his monastic robe, bidding farewell to his vows before kneeling down to retrieve Kay's fallen sword. Surely God would forgive him just one last time.

"Why Tristan," sneered the traitor, "I thought you had sworn off violence. Whatever would your dead wife say?"

"For you, Mordred, I'll make an exception."

But as Tristan brandished the sword and stepped forward to meet his opponent, the cathedral doorway quickly filled with Saxon soldiers, all armed and ready to defend their devious ally. Mordred lowered his spear and grinned at the Celtic monk, then mockingly made the sign of the cross before slipping through the growing crowd of warriors and hastening back toward the castle. Tristan cursed. Before he knew it he was surrounded, with hostile Saxons standing guard at every door and window, eliminating even the slightest chance of escape. *This would be a fitting end. A noble end.* With an anguished war cry, Tristan leapt into the fray, determined to die a soldier's death as the enemy hordes bore down upon him.

* * * * *

Gwenivere cringed with fright as someone began frantically knocking on her chamber door, the startling sound interrupting the relentless roar of battle that had been echoing through the castle halls. Clutching little Aurelius tightly to her chest and wielding a small knife with her delicate, shaking hand, the queen attempted to remain as quiet as possible, hoping beyond hope that the enemy soldiers might somehow pass them by. She was not afraid to die, and in years past, she may even have tried to escape, more than willing to take her chances against an unsuspecting army that lacked knowledge of the castle's hidden passageways. *But not today.* Gwenivere knew that she must stay alive and unseen in order to protect this innocent child that slept peacefully in her arms, oblivious to the dangers that now encroached upon him like rising flood waters. As the knocking continued, she silently stepped toward the door and peered out through the keyhole, desperate to discover what fearsome threat waited for her on the other side. However, the moment that she recognized Rowena's long blonde braids, Gwenivere hurriedly removed the locks and pulled her visitor inside before slamming the door shut once more.

The ghastly sight before her made her stomach turn.

Rowena's bare feet were scratched and blistered, her filthy dress was torn nearly in two, and her extremities had become oddly discolored with the onset of frostbite. But those meager maladies paled in comparison to the gaping, bloody wounds that now stood in place of her once sparkling blue eyes.

"My God," Gwenivere exclaimed in horror, quickly wrapping her shivering friend in a heavy, woolen cloak and retrieving a length of clean linen to cover her vacant eye sockets, "Rowena, what have they done to you?"

"Not *they... she*," Rowena answered, her voice trembling with pain and exhaustion, "Morgana is *alive*. She and Mordred planned this insurrection from the beginning along with Cynric, the newly promoted Saxon general. And although that fallen priestess has taken my eyes, I have still *heard* enough to know that Camelot now teeters on the brink of oblivion."

Rowena winced as Gwenivere carefully cleaned and dressed her wounds, slowly regaining her composure while the roaring hearth fire warmed her frozen body.

"You and the child must flee," she continued, "The invading forces are boasting that Kay, Tristan, and Sagramore have all been slain, along with most of the castle guards. We are *alone*, Gwenivere, and now they will come for you and Aurelius. With Arthur away from his throne, his queen and heir will be their most valuable targets."

"That vile, loathsome traitor!" Gwenivere snapped, "And to think that we were foolish enough to trust him! Mordred will pay for his villainy when Arthur returns. But for now... I cannot leave.

As you said, the soldiers swarming the castle halls are looking for me, and I would never escape without their notice. Not *now*. How did *you* manage to evade them?"

"A dirty, disheveled, blind woman wearing a tattered dress hardly poses much of a threat. They barely took notice."

Gwenivere then grew eerily quiet, sitting down on the edge of the bed and holding her infant son tightly, as if she were afraid that he would somehow float away without her loving embrace. *This was not his fault. No child deserved to be born into such turmoil.* When at last the queen began to speak again, it was clear she was fighting back tears.

"Rowena, please take Aurelius away from here. Conceal him in your cloak and make haste to the hidden passage at the far end of this corridor. The rear staircase will lead you toward the stables, and you should be able to escape into the forest. I will remain behind to draw the attention of the Saxons. After all, they may not be concerned with a blind woman, but they will still want the heir to Arthur's throne."

"Don't do this, Gwenivere. They mean to *kill* you."

"No, I would wager that Mordred wants me alive to use as leverage. But even so, I do not fear death. If saving this child costs me my life, then that is a price I will gladly pay."

"Gwenivere, please..."

"I am asking you as a friend."

"Come with us..."

"I am ordering you as your queen."

"But it's suicide..."

"I am begging you as a mother with a broken heart."

Not another word was spoken. After a few moments of deafening silence, Rowena rose and stepped toward Gwenivere, her wounded body quaking with emotion, though she was physically unable to cry. Morgana may have taken her eyes, but she could never take her heart, and right now it was wailing within her like lost and dying animal. Rowena stood by as the crestfallen queen kissed her baby and bid him one last, tearful goodbye before entrusting the child to her waiting arms. Finally, as Gwenivere prepared to step through the chamber door and into the unknown, she turned back for an instant, her expression sad but resolute, and whispered, "Keep him safe," before disappearing into the depths of the castle.

* * * * *

The abrasive sound of metal pounding against stone echoed through the Great Hall as Cynric and several of his strongest warriors struck the Round Table over and over again with their heavy war hammers to seemingly no effect. Mordred stood waiting nearby with an incensed scowl on his face, his patience growing thinner with every second that this legendary symbol of Arthur's reign remained intact. But just as the dark-haired young man was about to let his indignation be made known, a group of Saxon warriors led by Urien, the brutish one-eyed Celt, marched into the room with the queen as their disdainful yet acquiescent captive, and Mordred began grinning from ear to ear with cruel satisfaction.

"Ah, Gwenivere, how nice of you to join us!" he said as the incessant pounding carried on behind him.

"How could you?" she demanded, "Ever since you arrived in Camelot, Arthur has shown you nothing but love, faithfulness, and brotherhood, yet *this* is how you repay him?"

"Spare me the needless sentimentality, *your highness*," he snapped back, "Arthur may have built his beloved kingdom around a handful of naïve, antiquated ideals – the very ideals enshrined by this *damned table*, in fact – but those rigid moral absolutes hold no value for men like myself who have, shall we say, *evolved* beyond such nonsense."

"You're a heartless monster with a diseased mind, Mordred. Nothing more. It's now clear that every moment of your service to this kingdom has been a lie. Have you no honor?"

"Honor, loyalty, compassion... *ha!* What use have I for such things? In the end, the only real virtue is *power.* Those who lack it desire it, and those who have it will always seek to obtain more. *This* is the only truth. What is it that your sacred book says... blessed are the weak? Humble yourselves before God? *Pathetic drivel.* Any god who requires his followers to *love their enemies* is a god of poor, enfeebled, hopeless people. Arthur's idiotic sense of *righteousness* has blinded him to reality, along with all the mindless sheep that cower before him begging for his table scraps. But I am no sheep. *Oh, no, my queen.* I am a prowling lion, and the time has come to *feast*."

As the thunderous hammering continued, Mordred grabbed Gwenivere by the wrist and dragged her forcefully to a nearby window that overlooked the main courtyard. The view was like something out of a nightmare. She saw the mangled bodies of dozens of castle guards that lay dead or dying in the streets, while common villagers trembled with fear as they watched the Saxon army tearing into anyone foolish enough to oppose them. Some gathered their families and fled toward the outer gates, while others offered support for the insurrection, with a few going so far as to join the enemy ranks and fight back against their own friends and neighbors. Gwenivere recoiled in horror. Whether these were the actions of genuine defectors or simply desperate men hoping to save themselves, the result was still a once great kingdom descending into chaos.

"Look around you, Gwenivere," Mordred whispered, "Your subjects have lost their faith. We both know that Camelot was only a *dream*. Now I have awakened these good people to the abject futility of it all. *They once were blind, but now they see.* Come now, do you understand what pandemonium arises when a king is loved rather than feared? When you offer them freedom and brotherhood instead of leadership and order?"

"And what would *you* offer them, Mordred?" the queen replied, "Oppression? Servitude? An iron fist?"

"What a simple-minded response. Of course, I should have expected something so traditionally moralistic. You still don't understand, do you? The greatest evil in this world is neither violence nor tyranny, but *compassion*. Your absurd pity for the weakest among you is harmful to life by preserving that which should rightfully be destroyed. So in answer to your question, I offer restoration of the natural order. Stronger, more evolved men are inherently meant to rule those beneath them, just as a wolf is meant to prey on sheep."

Gwenivere opened her mouth to offer a scathing retort to the dark-haired young man's blasphemous, amoral philosophy, but before she could utter single a word, a loud crack rang out in the Great Hall, so deafening that she instinctively covered her ears and cried out in alarm. When the dust finally cleared, the queen turned to see that the Round Table had been broken in half, leaving huge slabs of stone to crash onto the floor in a pile of misshapen rubble. Cynric, Urien, and the Saxons cheered and shouted, while Mordred stood in silent astonishment, grinning like an idiot at his unexpected triumph.

"Do you see?" he laughed, "Do you see it now? The strong survives while the weak is demolished! And now, Gwenivere, we will determine whether *you* wish to survive this culling. You see, I already know that your son, the child you believe to be Arthur's rightful heir, has been whisked away from here for his own protection. But in truth, the poor little bastard is of no great importance to me. I already have a formidable army at my command and a claim to the throne through royal bloodline. However, I still need help winning over those segments of the populace whose allegiance remains with Arthur – people who would likely remain loyal to *you* as well. So tell me, will you choose to stand by my side as queen? Will you kneel down and call me master? Will you lay with me and give me an heir? Or will you choose to be broken like this stone table?"

"What the devil do you think of me?" Gwenivere shouted, her fists clenched tightly and her lips quivering with emotion, "I am the bride of the High King, not some common whore willing to sell myself for worldly gain!"

"That's odd," smirked Mordred, "I've heard otherwise."

Haunting memories of her dark, sordid past in the country tavern began to flash through the queen's troubled mind, followed by vivid recollections of her affair with Lancelot. *After all these years, had anything truly changed? Perhaps Mordred was right after all. Perhaps she really was just a cheap harlot. A woman so damaged and filled with regret had no business being self-righteous anyway.* Gwenivere felt utterly exposed. She was lost and alone, separated from everyone she loved and trapped in a prison of her own making. Her mind turned to Arthur, the one man in her life who had dared to treat a disgraced runaway like royalty, and her eyes grew clouded with tears of sorrow. As the spirits of despair clawed away at her mind, Gwenivere dropped to her knees in defeat, having lost the will to go on fighting. She could hear Mordred snickering to himself, swelling with pride at his impending conquest, when suddenly another voice broke through the veil of misery that covered her like a newly interred corpse. It was a still, small voice – strong yet gentle, otherworldly yet all too familiar.

Who condemns you, child?

And when she opened her eyes, Gwenivere was no longer kneeling in the Great Hall at Camelot, but on a dusty hillside path surrounded by olive groves. The air was warm and sweet, and the crowd of strangers who had gathered nearby looked on with quiet anticipation, eager to hear how she would respond. Surveying her surroundings, Gwenivere was stunned to realize that Mordred and the Saxons were nowhere to be found. She waited to hear the voices of her father, of the tavern patrons, of the gossiping women of the village, but none stood before her in accusation. So she turned back toward the direction of the voice and quietly answered, "No one."

"Neither do I condemn you," the speaker replied, grasping her hand and gently helping her to her feet, "Now take heart, for you walk no more in darkness."

Then just as suddenly as it had come, the vision was gone, and Gwenivere once again found herself on the cold, stone floor of the Great Hall. *Yet something had changed within her.* The despair that formerly held her in its deathly grip seemed to melt away like snow in the springtime, and the sins of her past began to feel hazy and distant, like the grey, fading memories of a bad dream. With a renewed sense of confidence, the queen rose up and stood defiantly before Mordred, bold and courageous, and spoke words that shook him to his core.

"I'm not concerned with what you've *heard*, Mordred," she stated boldly, "Our pasts may shape us, but they do not have to *define* us. One day soon, whether in this life or the next, you will learn that there is a kind of strength that is made perfect in weakness, and that love and compassion are far more powerful than a thousand armies. You may try to frighten me with your threats of violence, you may tear down these castle walls, you may even destroy this earthly vessel, but you will *never* vanquish Camelot. For as long as good men like Arthur dare to stand strong against the darkness, their dream of a kingdom ruled through both justice *and* mercy will live on. So enjoy your Pyrrhic victory, you sniveling worm, because when the *true* king returns, you will know what it means to be afraid."

For a brief moment Mordred was speechless, struck with awe at the queen's conviction and resolve in the face of certain death. *He was almost impressed.* But the young man's stunned expression quickly transformed back into a vengeful scowl, and he motioned to Urien with a slight wave of his hand.

"It would seem she has made her choice," he announced.

Gwenivere then breathed deeply and closed her eyes one last time, her soul finally at peace, as the cruel Celtic mercenary lifted up a jagged fragment of stone from the collapsed Round Table and brought it crashing down upon her head.

Man of Sorrows

The old man's frail, haggard body lay almost frozen in the midst of the rising snow drifts, nearly imperceptible to the naked eye with the exception of a single outstretched hand emerging from the blanket of whiteness like a nascent sapling. A bitter wind howled through the tall, skeletal trees, their bare branches heavy with ice, while a red fox scurried past as it chased down a family of wild rabbits. Nearby, Arthur and his band of knights rode steadily northward, their horses' hooves leaving a series of deep imprints in the snow as they entered the final leg of their journey home from Dinan. With the king's last minute arrival, Lancelot's life had been spared, allowing mercy to triumph over vengeance. *Merlyn would have been proud,* Arthur thought to himself, still astounded by the strange peace that came from letting go of the rage that briefly consumed him and allowing himself to forgive, even in the face of the deepest betrayal. As contradictory as it appeared, there was freedom in choosing to love without condition. Most of the knights seemed relieved when their friend's death sentence was lifted, and even Gawain, with all his fire and passion, ended up softening a bit once he was sober. Now Arthur could think only of Gwenivere, his wife and queen, and longed for nothing more than to hold her in his arms once again. As such, his mind was elsewhere when they passed by the old man's blackened, frostbitten hand, which did indeed appear to be a lone sapling upon first glance. It wasn't until Aglovale looked back and recognized the family crest on his father's signet ring that they all realized it was Pellinore who lay before them dangerously close to death.

At the sight of the old man's near lifeless form, Percival and Lamorack leapt from their mounts in horror and then hurriedly joined Aglovale in rescuing their father from his icy tomb. He was dressed in only his nightclothes, with the exception of a single woolen blanket intended to shield him from the cold, and he had apparently armed himself with a dull kitchen knife that dangled from a thin leather strap around his waist. Without any viable shelter nearby, they wrapped the old man's body in as many cloaks and furs as could be spared and vigorously rubbed his frigid limbs in a desperate attempt to restore blood flow. After several agonizing minutes, Pellinore gradually opened his eyes and smiled weakly at his sons before turning toward the king with sadness in his trembling gaze. *The situation was dire.* At first the old man seemed to have lost the ability to speak, looking about erratically in torturous silence before he began to wheeze and gasp at the frigid air, exhausting every last ounce of strength to deliver one final message.

"I'm sorry, Arthur," he said shivering in the waning twilight, each labored breath a struggle against time as the old man's fragile, weakened body gradually succumbed to the bitter cold of winter, "I should have said something. I should have *warned* them, but I did not trust my own senses."

"Warned who?" Arthur asked, "What has happened?"

"They're *dead*. Tristan... Sagramore... even your brother Kay. All of them. All dead. The villain Mordred has betrayed us and usurped your throne; now he has infected the kingdom with chaos. The villagers have turned on one another and an army of Saxon warriors roams the hallowed halls of Camelot."

"Dear God... and what of the queen?"

"I couldn't save them, Arthur. I'm so sorry..."

"Pellinore, you must tell me! Is Gwenivere alive?"

"I can still see their faces..."

"Pellinore, please..."

"I barely escaped with my life, but I still found *you*, Arthur. Not bad for a crazy old man, eh? You know, I tend to forget most things these says, but I will always remember the first time we met. You were still just a boy, and I was roaming the countryside searching for adventure. Of course, *now* I'm just old and tired. So very tired. I need to sleep. But my sons are by my side, and in that, I am content. Goodbye, my friend. Here I embark on my last and greatest adventure..."

And in that moment, Arthur knew that his question would remain unanswered, for those hoarse, whispered words would be the old man's last. Pellinore's weary eyes rolled back in his head and he exhaled one final breath that quickly condensed into a tiny cloud as the life and warmth fled from his body. Percival, Lamorack, and Aglovale dropped to their knees and wept at their father's side, the tears freezing on their faces in the merciless winter evening, while Arthur rose to his feet with a steely gaze, both brokenhearted and resolute.

"God save him," the king prayed.

The snow-covered ground was far too hard for Pellinore to be properly buried, so Arthur and his knights scoured the frozen countryside for dry branches and kindling in order to build him a funeral pyre. Naturally, the small, rudimentary structure they eventually managed to construct was hardly up to standard for brave soldier and honored member of the royal household, but then again, the eccentric old man was not the sort who would have cared about such things. All that truly mattered was that he was loved and would be remembered. And so, the sons of Pellinore stood close to the blazing fire and mourned their father's passing, while Bedivere, Palamedes, and Gawain paid their respects and then began to sharpen their swords and gird their loins for battle. Meanwhile, Arthur meandered about the wintry landscape alone and in a grief-stricken daze, doubting himself, unsure of whether to feel sorrow, anger, regret, fear, indignation, or some unholy amalgam of them all. When at last he reached the edge of a nearby cliff, he knelt down in the snow and cried out to the heavens in despair, his strained, despondent voice echoing amongst the hilltops.

* * * * *

An ocean of thick grey clouds masked the light from the rising moon, leaving the snow-covered landscape bathed in a dim, mournful glow. As the king raged and wailed in lamentation, beseeching his Creator for some kind of guidance, two figures dressed in cloaks of emerald green appeared atop the white hills surrounding the Camlann Fields just outside of Camelot. They were taller than most mortal men, and their shining faces illuminated the nearby scenery with a heavenly brilliance more radiant than any star. The old man's pale blue eyes appeared sad yet thoughtful, and the young woman, whose wild red hair blazed like a roaring fire, wore of look of rugged determination.

"Will you not speak to him?" she asked.

"These are the trying times in which men are measured, Nimue," Merlyn replied, "If a baby bird is given help as he breaks free from the egg, he will remain weak and die. It is only through arduous struggle that he develops the strength to fly."

"Has Arthur not struggled enough?"

"The question we must instead ask is whether the Almighty is done *using* him. If nothing else, I believe Arthur has learned and now understands that his true purpose on this earth is to be an instrument wielded for a glory greater than his own. Thus far, he has remained strong and steadfast in the face of oppression, war, famine, illness, and betrayal, and he will not falter now. He will fight with honor through his pain, just as always. Lancelot, on the other hand…"

"You still don't believe in him, do you, Merlyn?"

"Ha! You say that as if I did not already know what is to come. We have both seen how this ends, Nimue. I know well the role that Lancelot is to play. I simply fail to understand how that lump of clay will be formed into the man he is meant to be."

"He is nearly there, Merlyn. All he needs is a little push."

"Since you have watched him more closely than I over these many years, I can only take you at your word. But if, as you say, Lancelot only needs a push, then the time to act is *now*. He is penitent, yes. But he is also apprehensive and disheartened. So if you want my opinion, it matters not whether I believe in him. What truly matters is whether he believes in himself."

The woman turned and vanished into the icy mist of twilight, and soon the evening winds pushed away the heavy clouds that had covered the unnerving luminescence of the crescent moon. Merlyn stood on the hilltop and waited, gazing downward at the bloodied and broken walls of Camelot. The night was quiet, and the firelight gleaming from the Saxons' torches flew through the city like a wave of falling stars. And then, unseen to human eyes, an ominous black vapor began creeping through the pastureland and along the cobblestone streets. *It had begun*.

* * * * *

In the cold light of early morning, Lancelot ambled slowly alongside the winding River Rance toward the ancient oaks and beeches of Brocéliande Forest. A smattering of snow had fallen overnight, but the skies were now bright and clear, and the warm sunlight peeking over the horizon had transformed the frosted landscape into a radiant field of orange and pink. The shallow water on the riverbanks was frozen solid, and the tall grass and bulrush reeds that lined Lancelot's path crackled and crunched under the weight of his boots. Upon awaking that morning from a restless sleep, Lancelot had no plans in mind to make such a journey, but after dragging himself out of bed and filling his belly with hot bread and honey fresh from his aunt's kitchen, he began to feel something pulling him toward the mythic wood. Whether it was fate, nostalgia, or merely boredom that led him from the relative comfort of the blacksmith shop and into the wilderness, Lancelot neither knew nor cared. In his mind, it would at least serve as a distraction from the guilt that weighed so heavily upon his troubled soul. After walking for an hour or so, he could see the forest up ahead, with the thick canopy formed by its immense, primordial trees now blanketed in white.

Once within the shelter of the forest, Lancelot found his surroundings cold yet surprisingly dry. Fortunately, the icy north winds that blew across the countryside were stifled by the dense foliage, allowing the interior clearing to feel slightly less frigid than the outside air. Grateful for the shift in climate, he sat and rested for a few moments atop a large, flat rock, reminiscing about his childhood when he and Arthur used to wander carelessly through these woods, before letting out a wistful sigh and pressing ahead toward the Lake of Diana.

Despite the desolation within his soul, Lancelot surveyed his surroundings and began to take notice of the simple beauty of God's creation. The few rays of dawn that broke through the trees lit up the forest and glittered upon the leaves and branches like a thousand fireflies. Ice crystals rested gently upon twigs, grass, and shrubs in tiny, intricate patterns, shimmering like diamonds whenever the daylight reached them. *He didn't deserve to walk in such splendor.* Arthur's mysterious mercy had given him a second lease on life, but it all still felt so hollow, for he knew that by all rights he deserved to die for his crimes. Part of him even wanted to. He had betrayed his king. He had killed a good man in cold blood. And he had done it all while wearing the mask of honor and friendship. The wrong man had been set free. *But the crowd shouted, "Give us Barabbas."*

When Lancelot finally reached the Lake of Diana, he dropped down on the nearest shoreline and – with nothing else to occupy his time – began casually searching the tall grass for a handful of small, smooth rocks to toss out onto the frozen surface. He eventually located five flawless specimens, drew back his right arm, and flung them with all his might into the center of the lake, obviously expecting to hear them scattering over the dark, shimmering ice within a few seconds. But instead, he heard only *plop, plop, plop, plop, plop* as the stones fell and sank into the deep. The sudden realization that the water was not frozen over struck Lancelot as exceptionally odd, especially considering that even certain portions of the River Rance had turned to ice in this unforgiving winter climate. Far more curiously, when he looked again there appeared to be steam rising from the surface, like a pot of soup on an open fire, as if the lake were actually generating heat from somewhere within its depths.

As Lancelot reached down and plunged his hand into the abnormally warm water, a low, rumbling sound began emanating from within. Moments later, a lithe, feminine shape slowly began to emerge from the ebullient froth, her long red hair ebbing and flowing like ocean waves and her emerald eyes sparkling with sunlight. A green samite gown hung gently from her shoulders, and her face glowed with an ethereal radiance as she silently beckoned Lancelot to step into the lake and join her. Lancelot's jaw dropped. Though he had encountered Nimue, the fabled Lady of the Lake, many times since childhood, her supernatural presence never ceased to take his breath away.

Tentatively he stepped into the balmy, bubbling water, and before he was even waist-deep, a sigh of relief had escaped his dry, cracked lips. The luxuriant warmth that enveloped him was comfortable and soothing, not only to his body, but to his mind and soul as well. With his spirits suddenly lifted, Lancelot made his way deeper and deeper into the lake until he stood face-to-face with Nimue, the dark water splashing near their shoulders, and simply basked in her intense, celestial glory.

"What are you doing here, Lancelot?" she asked in a soft, lilting voice that still rang out like a choir of angels.

"I thought you wanted me to come out here."

"In *Dinan*, Lancelot – wasting your life away banging out horseshoes and growing fat on your aunt's cooking? Come, now. Why haven't you returned to Camelot?"

"I couldn't possibly go back," he replied somberly, looking away to hide his shame, "I am a traitor and a murderer..."

"...who has been *forgiven*," Nimue interrupted, "Nothing can change the past, but you can *always* change the future. Don't let your sins haunt you forever."

"Forever? Nimue, I fled from Camelot a matter of *weeks* ago, not years. It's hardly a distant memory. And besides, despite my life being spared for some unfathomable reason, I could never show my face in those halls again. Arthur may have forgiven me, but I fear I may never be able to forgive myself."

"Do you think yourself to be special, blacksmith? Do you think you are the lone sinner amidst an ocean of saints? In truth, you are no different than any other mortal who has stumbled off the straight and narrow. But unlike some men, you still have the chance to make things right. Camelot needs you! And yet, you believe God cannot use someone so flawed and broken? Ha! Remember that Abraham was a coward who sold out his wife to save his own skin. Moses was a reluctant leader who was afraid to speak due to his stutter. David had an innocent man killed so he could marry his widow. Peter was reckless and impulsive. Mary Magdalene was possessed by demons. Paul hunted down the followers of Christ and had them executed. Need I go on? You don't have to be perfect to be an instrument of righteousness, Lancelot. You only have to be *willing*."

"Even so," he stammered nervously, "it would be unwise and improper for me to be near Gwenivere again."

"The queen is dead," replied Nimue, her voice powerful and unwavering, "Murdered alongside hundreds of your brethren by a once trusted ally who now sits on Arthur's throne."

Lancelot's heart broke within him. For a long time, he stood in pensive, mournful silence, feeling the warmth of the water against his skin and listening to the cold winter wind as it rustled through the ancient trees. He didn't know what to think. He didn't know much of *anything* anymore. The only thing he knew for certain was that he wanted to be free of this suffocating guilt that hung like a millstone around his neck, dragging him downward into hopelessness. If there truly were a chance for him to attain redemption and rededicate his life to keeping Arthur's fragile dream alive, he would latch onto it with both hands and hold on tight. For beyond the conquests and the glory, it was that solemn oath he took so many years ago on Pentecost that had given his life direction. So with a leap of faith, he closed his eyes, bowed his head, and spoke to the Lady of the Lake in an act of peaceful surrender.

"Here I am," he said, "What would you have me do?"

"Submerge yourself beneath these waters. Wash away the man you once were, then rise and become the man you were meant to be. A new beginning. A rebirth."

Lancelot did as he was told and ducked his head under the surface of the lake, and immediately a dissonant chorus of cruel, accusing voices began shouting at him from the darkness. Words of condemnation slithered over their wicked tongues, and their savage indictments echoed through his mind just as fiercely as ever. Then as the chorus grew into nothing but a muffled roar, a new voice suddenly pierced the din and started to drown out the others, like sunlight breaking through the clouds. It sounded all too familiar, like the voice of an old friend, and it spoke not in judgment but in words of profound, incomprehensible grace. Of course, if Lancelot had been asked to describe exactly what he heard in that moment, he would have found no words suitable for the task – at least, not in any mortal language. But as soon as he rose from the water and into the waking dawn, he breathed deeply of the fresh morning air and knew that he had been changed. And more importantly, he knew what he must do.

A Rider On a Pale Horse

"Is that it?" Mordred smirked as he peered out the castle window and into the expansive Camlann Fields, "Is *that* the army Arthur brings to challenge me? I ought to be insulted!"

"Your eyes do not deceive you, sire," answered Cynric, "Our scouts inform me that he has spent the past three days scouring every nearby town and village for any loyalists willing to come to his aid. However, since most of those who refused to surrender to us have already been imprisoned in the castle dungeons, the majority of Arthur's soldiers are either old men or young squires, presumably without any formal military training. His Pictish allies in Caledonia, while formidable, dwell too far away from Camelot to provide any immediate assistance in battle. Garrisons from Astolat and Lyonesse did arrive late last night, but their numbers are still less than half of our own."

Mordred grinned ear-to-ear with satisfaction upon hearing that his foolish uncle would be both numerically and strategically outmatched on the battlefield. He was sprawled out lazily atop Arthur's throne wearing a black silk tunic, flawless and clean, with a golden circlet resting regally upon his head. A bowl of candied fruit sat on a small table to his left, though he was careful to clean his hands meticulously after every bite, determined not to soil his fine, new garments. The cold stone floor was littered with books he had pilfered from the ousted king's extensive library, most of which were being periodically fed into the blazing hearth fire in order to stave off the harsh, winter chill. A few select volumes he had chosen to keep, of course, primarily the violent Greek tragedies that amused him so. But the large collection of works by Christian theologians such as Ignatius, Irenaeus, Ambrose, and Augustine had all been quickly transformed into mounds of black, crumbling ash. A young, nude servant girl danced provocatively near the fire, though Mordred barely paid her any attention. It was only when she attempted to gather up her clothing and flee from the room that he glanced sharply in her direction, ordering the frightened young women to resume her salacious duties or to have both legs broken. After all, he was far less interested in carnal indulgence than the intoxicating power he now held over all those beneath him.

“Are our men prepared for battle?” he inquired.

“Armed and ready, sire. The castle defenses are still in a state of disrepair after our siege of the city, so we plan to march out and meet Arthur’s forces in the fields at dawn.”

“Slaughter them all, Cynric. Leave none alive. Then after the last of these damned rebels are defeated, I want the dungeons emptied and the prisoners publically executed in the castle courtyard. All of my subjects must learn that defiance will not be tolerated. Now then, is there anything else?”

“Yes, sire. An emissary has delivered a message from Arthur. He demands that we release the queen and her child to his care by morning. How do you suggest we respond?”

Mordred lounged in his throne and pondered the request for a few moments, fully aware of the status of both Gwenivere and the boy. Naberius sat nearby, unseen to human eyes, with his sharp, black talons rooted in the young man’s skull and his acid tongue whispering to him in the shadows. Before long, Mordred began chuckling quietly to himself as a sadistically depraved idea entered into his shrewd, calculating, amoral mind.

“So Arthur wants his queen, eh?” he sneered, “Well, my dear general, we should probably deliver her to him.”

* * * * *

Before the sun had risen, Rowena was awoken by the sound of Aurelius' hungry cries. The tiny, abandoned farmhouse where she had brought the child for safekeeping was fairly secluded in relation to the towns and villages nearby, so she had not yet had the opportunity to locate a suitable wet nurse. Fortunately, the previous residents had left their winter food stores and livestock behind, thus Rowena was able break off bite-size pieces of the fresh bread she had baked from the grain provisions, soak them in a bowl of goat's milk, and feed them to the boy, who was already beginning to teethe.

Despite her blindness, Rowena was surprised to discover that she could maneuver around the farmhouse reasonably well by using her other senses. Moreover, her daily tasks, while more difficult than they once had been, were far from impossible. The simple act of baking bread, for instance, had become so firmly ingrained in her mind and in her skillful hands after decades of experience that she was able to do it successfully through smell and muscle memory alone. Aurelius, despite his constant curious exploration, was easy enough to keep track of by listening to the cooing noises he made as he crawled along the floor, and drawing water from the nearby well was no problem at all once she learned to avoid stepping in the bucket.

It helped to keep busy, for it was in those quiet, thoughtful hours that fear, grief, and anger reared their ugly heads and gradually began to whittle away at her resolve. Rowena cringed when she considered all that had been taken from her. Every so often she would lift up the strip of fabric covering her face and lightly touch the empty, mangled caverns where her eyes had once been, still incredulous with disbelief. *But she had to stay strong. For Aurelius. For Gwenivere.* She missed her dear friend, and she missed Gawain even more, praying often for both. In her weaker moments Rowena restlessly tried to sleep away the pain, but unfortunately, sleeping had become a significant problem since she lost her sight, as she understandably found it terribly challenging to tell night from day. But still, she was alive and so was the child. For now, that would be enough.

Rowena estimated that it was still very early, as she could not yet feel the sun's warmth upon her skin, so after feeding Aurelius she wrapped herself in a heavy cloak and stepped outside to gather a bit of kindling from the woodpile. The morning was cold and deathly quiet, with the fragrant smell of evergreens lingering in the icy winter air. In the neighboring hills a wolf howled, and then as Rowena listened for the distinctive call of the lark, she began to hear a faint tapping sound from somewhere off in the distance. Soon the peculiar noise grew louder, quickly increasing in strength until it became a powerful, rhythmic pulse, not unlike the fearsome drums of war.

"Mordred's armies are assembled," said a familiar voice from just beyond the woodpile, "And at dawn they will march out to meet Arthur and all that remains of his noble knights. The end is near. The last battle is at hand."

"Merlyn!" gasped Rowena, "Is that you?"

"Of course. Who else would I be if not myself?"

Rowena readily shrugged off the old man's unusual response and dropped the kindling she had gathered before rushing into the comfort of his warm embrace. His deep green cloak smelled of peat moss and pine needles, and she could hear the rustling of feathers as that elderly grey owl who always accompanied him shuffled around atop his wide-brimmed hat.

"Oh, thank God," Rowena sighed with relief, "I have so many questions, Merlyn. Tell me, is Gwenivere still..."

"Right now we face more pressing concerns," he interrupted, "I do apologize for my abruptness, but we haven't a moment to lose. Quickly, bundle up the child and follow me."

Without argument, Rowena scurried into the farmhouse and then emerged a few moments later with little Aurelius cradled in her arms, swaddled in linen and wrapped in a thick, wool blanket. Merlyn grasped her hand, and before she knew it they were off, walking at a brisk pace through the powdery snow drifts and into the mysterious depths of the northern woods. She was mildly comforted to know that Merlyn was leading the way, for if she had been moving along so swiftly on her own, she surely would have crashed into a tree within seconds. Then as glowing rays of sunlight began to peek over the horizon, the sound of distant war drums grew even louder, and Rowena tugged at the sleeve of her guide's dingy, threadbare cloak.

"What is happening, Merlyn? Where are we going?"

"The time has come for you and I to confront Morgana," the old man replied, "Even now, she is not beyond saving."

* * * * *

Gawain wasn't sure whether to cry out with rage or to vomit with disgust when Arthur opened the parcel that a young Saxon soldier delivered to the front lines just moments before dawn. It was medium-sized willow basket covered with a dirty, crumpled sheet of linen, and as the corner of the sheet was pulled back, he saw what appeared to be a lock a brown curls, caked with blood, peeking out just above the tightly woven rim. Horrified at the ghastly sight before him, Arthur dropped the basket into the snow and out tumbled a woman's head, severed at the neck, her lifeless green eyes now staring out into nothingness. *Gwenivere.* The king was speechless, and tears rolled down his cheeks as he struggled to maintain composure in front of his ragtag army of volunteers. Gawain instinctively averted his eyes, fearful that Rowena may have met a similar fate, and then off in the distance he spied Mordred sitting arrogantly atop Arthur's favorite white destrier, armed and ready for battle, with a cruel, scornful smile upon his lips. *How could he have been so blind?* Rowena was right to have been skeptical of Mordred's motives, but like a fool, he never listened to her. He had fallen for the clever young man's charm and sycophantic fawning, both of which in hindsight seemed maddeningly transparent. He had looked upon Mordred as his own son and had trusted him even more so than the older knights who had fought and bled alongside him for decades. *He had been oblivious to the devil at his doorstep.* And now the sharp, twisting knife of Mordred's betrayal wounded him more deeply than even the bitter sting of Lancelot's crimes, which now felt like minor indiscretions by comparison. But on this cold winter morning, in the stark, revealing light of dawn, there was no time to dwell on the past. Drums pounded and the trumpets blared, for the sun was rising on a day of war.

Last night's snow storm had long since ceased, leaving the landscape blanketed in fresh white powder, and the dark skies began to transform into a brilliant canvass of orange and pink, with patches of wispy clouds painted along the expanse in thick, purple brushstrokes. Soon the sprawling Camlann Fields were fully illuminated, and the sheer, staggering numbers of the Saxon army finally came into clear view. Gawain shuddered. The fact that they were badly outnumbered, coupled with witnessing the gruesome fate of Queen Gwenivere, struck fear in the hearts of Arthur's meager forces, and Gawain began to hear restless rumblings about surrendering to Mordred or simply packing up their belongings and fleeing to Armorica.

As he reached down and began messaging away the chronic pain in his bad leg, prayerful that he had one last fight left in him, Gawain watched Arthur slowly dismount from his horse and drop to one knee in the snow, gently brushing the tangled hair away from Gwenivere's face and closing her now vacant eyes. A few tender words were whispered, meant for her ears alone, before he carefully placed the remnants of his wife back into the willow basket and handed it off to one of the squires, instructing him to keep it safe until she could be suitably buried. A reverent hush fell over the crowd, and all those gathered looked on while their king bid farewell to his queen, empathetic with his loss but in awe of his bravery as he mustered the strength to stand. Then with his mournful expression shifting into a peculiar look of peace and acceptance, Arthur climbed atop his courser and turned back to address his frightened troops.

"The queen is dead," he said somberly before a reassuring smile stretched across his face, "But someday soon we will meet again... *perhaps today*. If indeed our Creator sees fit to call me home, reaching His loving hand down to this battleground and carrying me off to Avalon, I will step eagerly onto those golden shores with joy erupting from my heart. I will run like the mighty west wind to greet my wife, my mother and father, and the friends who have fallen before me, shedding tears of gladness at that happy reunion. Perhaps you too await such a day…"

Arthur trailed off for a moment, gazing silently heavenward before he began riding into the midst of the fretful soldiers with a flash of boldness in his stormy, sorrowful eyes.

"But if our time has not yet come, if our mission in this life has not yet been completed, then it is our sacred duty to meet the challenge before us with strength and courage! Now, I know that many of you are afraid. *So am I.* For these many years I have strived to be a godly man and a good king, though in dark times such as these – in days marked by war and death – living up to both personas has felt like an impossible contradiction. I am torn between Heaven and Earth. Although the theologian in me seeks peace with my fellow man, the king in me knows that sometimes there is a peace that only exists on the other side of war. Such is the paradox we face in a fallen world. Friends, our path ahead is obscured by shadow, and we are often powerless to stem the tide of fate. While we cannot always choose when we leave this world, we *can* choose how we *meet* that end, and I, for one, choose to stand and fight! *Look around you.* This kingdom we created together – this shining city on a hill – may have fallen into the hands of evil men, but remember that Camelot is not made up of stone and mortar, and it cannot be contained by walls, gates, or battlements. Camelot lives within each one of us, for it is the sacred belief that honor, justice, and liberty belong to *all* people, and that these ideals are worth dying for. So stand with me now, one last time on this hallowed ground, and we will show our enemies the true meaning of valor!"

Not a single man fled.

Every whispered notion of retreat ceased without exception as the gathered troops watched their king ride among them, his armor shining in the sunlight and his very presence inspiring faith as if a Greek god had stepped down from Mount Olympus to walk alongside mortals. Here was a man that they would surely follow to Hell and back. And then without warning, the Saxon army let fly a volley of arrows into the early morning sky, and it quickly became clear that Hell was now upon them.

Arthur's forces lifted their shields as the deathly hailstorm rained down from above, with iron-tipped bodkins finding their way through holes in their defenses to pierce armor and flesh. Many brave soldiers fell, each poor player having fretted his hour upon the stage until he was heard no more. No sooner had the harrowing wails of death gone silent than a second volley was upon them, catching several of the less seasoned men off guard and leading to yet another tragic slew of casualties. Gawain at last lifted his head to survey the mortality that surrounded him, and first he spied Arthur, standing with Excalibur drawn over his own fallen horse, who lay weak and motionless on the frozen ground. A few yards away there was old Palamedes, wincing as he gingerly pulled a broken arrow from his left shoulder, while Percival stepped through the field of battle helping the injured to their feet. And lastly, beneath the naked branches of a nearby dogwood tree, Lamorack knelt in the snow and cradled the body of his dying brother while Aglovale clutched at him with bloodied hands and took a few final, gasping breaths.

"Did you ever once foresee such a day?" inquired Bedivere, who now stood next to Gawain preparing to charge with him into battle, "When you and I were young men, and we began plotting our hopeless revolution in those abandoned Roman bath houses, did you ever think it would end like this?"

"You *know* what I thought," Gawain answered solemnly.

"Aye. You thought I was mad to believe that the Pendragon would actually return and lead us all to conquest and glory. Well, I guess you were wrong, Gawain."

Bedivere smiled weakly and turned his eyes to the east.

"Look there," he continued, his face grim and ashen, "Even now Arthur stands upon the front lines speaking words of hope, urging this small but loyal army onward against even the most insurmountable odds. These are not *soldiers* – they are farmers and fishermen! These poor, brave souls know nothing of war; some have never so much as picked up a sword before. And yet they fight for him gladly because for one glorious moment, he made them *believe*. He showed them the light in an ocean of darkness. It was a fine dream while it lasted, although I suppose every dream has to end someday."

"It's not over yet," said Gawain.

Then the two aging knights looked at one another, speaking more with a single glance than a thousand words could ever say, and brandished their weapons as they rushed into the fray, their fierce battlecry echoing among the white hills above.

* * * * *

As war raged on throughout the snow-covered Camlann Fields, the castle itself stood nearly deserted, with only a handful of Saxon sentries remaining behind to watch over the loyalists who were shackled in the underground dungeons. Despite their seclusion, the prisoners could hear the war drums and the cries of the fallen deep within their cells, and they pulled at their heavy chains in futile frustration, helpless as friends and family alike were crushed beneath Mordred's iron fist. One such prisoner was Caradoc the Younger, son of the grief-stricken villager who had threatened the king's life so many years ago, now willingly standing beside him in his darkest hour. While only a thin-bearded youth at the time, he had watched his father – *God rest his soul* – transform from an angry, desperate widower hell-bent on vengeance into a penitent man of peace after experiencing the sacrificial love of one of Arthur's knights. From that moment onward, young Caradoc vowed to honor both his father and his king by defending Camelot at all costs, against all enemies, even at the expense of his own life.

His vexation only increased as the ferocious sounds of battle grew ever louder, until he swore that he could hear the clashing of iron and steel from the catacombs above his cell. *He could not wait any longer.* Caradoc looked about frantically for anything he could possibly use to free himself, finding nothing, eventually resolving to break his own thumb in order to slide one hand free from his manacles. However, before he had the chance to do so, he saw the bodies of two Saxon guards come tumbling down the nearby stone staircase, quickly followed by a man he did not recognize wielding an ornate Celtic longsword. The man was tall and broad-shouldered, with sandy-brown hair streaked with grey and fire behind his sparkling blue eyes.

"How many of you are there?" the man asked as he pulled a cell key from the belt of one of the dead Saxons and proceeded to set Caradoc and his fellow prisoners free.

"Several dozen at least," Caradoc replied, "There may even be close to one hundred spread out among the dungeons, all of us faithful to the true king and ready to fight."

"Good. Quickly, grab that second set of keys from the other guard and help me open these cells. We haven't much time until Arthur's forces are overwhelmed."

Now unfettered by their chains, the loyalists fled hurriedly from captivity, rushing against the few remaining Saxon soldiers who had heard the commotion from the Great Hall and had come downstairs to investigate. Neither pain nor hunger constrained them. Despite being beaten, fatigued, and unarmed, they fought like lions against their captors, for they were driven to battle by the burden of honor and the cleansing flames of retribution. Caradoc looked on in amazement as a group of lowly prisoners became a company of warriors, and then he turned inquisitively toward the man responsible for their rescue.

"Wait, before we go on I must know... who are you?"

"My name is Lancelot," the man said, "Now tell the others to follow me upstairs. We have an armory to storm."

THE LAST TRUMPET

Mordred was delighted. Although the sun still hung low in the morning sky, the Battle of Camlann appeared to be all but over, as Cynric and his multitude of Saxon warriors easily decimated Arthur's meager, ill-equipped army. From his perch at the river's edge, the dark-haired young man surveyed the carnage before him with a perverse sense of satisfaction coursing through his icy veins. *How glorious it was to watch the mighty fall.* Shields were splintered and gleaming blades pierced through flesh and bone, leaving scores of bodies strewn about the winter landscape, their warm blood staining the snow a deep crimson. This motley crew of farmers, fishermen, merchants, and other commoners never stood a chance against experienced mercenaries, and despite the fortitude of Gawain, Percival, and Arthur's other knights, the Saxon soldiers would prove far too numerous for even the most skilled combatants to withstand much longer.

How in the world had such a gullible, insipid weakling ever managed to hold the throne for so many years? After all, as far as Mordred was concerned, there were only two kinds of people walking this earth: Either you were a slave, always subservient to stronger men, or you were a master, destined to rule over the poor and feeble. And whether a person was slave or a master would inevitably determine his or her morality. For a man such as Mordred, *a man of strength and ambition*, the idea of "good" was determined solely by consequence, specifically the impact of actions upon oneself. *That which benefits me is good, and that which harms me is not.* He cringed knowing that the weak turn this rationale on its head, placing value on *intentions* rather than consequences and ultimately vilifying the strong, who they come to view as *oppressors.* This was why the weak were susceptible to the trappings of religion, for the belief that adherence to some arbitrary code of conduct might influence their imagined, all-powerful deity to act as an advocate against perceived injustice remained all too appealing. *It was a morality of vindictiveness and resentment.* Cowardly men sought to redress grievances not by willing strength to power, *as he had done*, but by inventing a fantasy of spiritual vengeance in the afterlife. In the end, religion would always require *enemies* in order to sustain itself, thus the priests and theologians lived only to deceive pathetic, lesser humans into thinking that the poor and meek are *blessed* and will win everlasting life, thereby ultimately vanquishing the strong. Mordred absolutely deplored such farcical logic, primarily for its demonization of higher beings such as himself. *Truly, there was nothing so unhealthy to the progress of mankind as the pervasiveness of Christian pity*.

Consumed with rage and eager to reap the sweet rewards of victory, Mordred lifted the Spear of Longinus on high and spurred his warhorse into a gallop, riding out into the midst of ferocious battle and laughing like a man possessed as one-by-one, Arthur's soldiers fell before the ancient lance. With iron clashing loudly against steel and men on both sides crying out in anger, pain, or both, the noise on the battlefield had become almost deafening. It was so loud, in fact, that Mordred failed to notice Lancelot and the freed loyalists emerging from the castle and hurtling like a shower of comets into the Saxon ranks.

As the vengeful reinforcements unexpectedly stormed into battle, a swirling typhoon of death followed in their wake, taking Mordred's forces by surprise and quickly tightening the odds in this previously one-sided confrontation. Lancelot led his band of warriors onward like Alexander reborn, fighting more ferociously than any other and swinging his mighty sword Arondight with a strength and intensity unmatched since the days of Achilles.

Within moments, Mordred felt his powerful destrier tumbling to the ground beneath him and quickly noticed a cold, steel blade protruding from its side. Hurriedly he leaped from the back of the grievously wounded animal and rolled into the blood-stained snow, regaining his footing swiftly enough to turn and flee from immediate danger. Then as he turned and surveyed the field of battle from a safe distance, Mordred smiled. *Finally a real fight.* Now only one thing remained. He would locate Arthur and end this fateful conflict once and for all.

* * * * *

Merlyn finally began to slow his pace as they entered the outskirts of the northern woods. And although Rowena could not see, the sounds and smells of this dark forest had become all too familiar, dredging up memories of the fear and pain that haunted her still. Despite the rising sun, the air only seemed to grow colder as they drew ever closer to Morgana's hovel, with the suffocating fog of evil making it difficult for her to breathe and weighing heavily on her soul. Fortunately, Aurelius had fallen into a deep sleep, and while Rowena did not know whether he had done so naturally or if he was under some enchantment by Merlyn, she felt grateful that he would not have any memory of the impending encounter. Soon the mingled smells of moss and smoke told her they had arrived at their destination. Holding the child tightly, she mouthed a quick prayer for protection, for it was in this humble forest clearing that a witch practiced her craft and a demonic presence patiently waited.

The door to the hovel was already ajar, almost as if Morgana were expecting them, and the room was filled with an eerie red glow emanating from the ethereal fire that blazed in the hearth. As Merlyn and Rowena cautiously stepped inside they found her seated on a small wooden stool, gazing intently at the dancing flames. Her eternally slender frame was wrapped in a white linen gown, and her raven tresses, still long and silky, flew about wildly with the cold wind blowing through the open windows. After their previous meeting, Rowena remembered how Morgana's once beautiful face had grown worn and sickly – a ghastly visage that at last reflected the ugliness dwelling within her. But in her mind's eye, Rowena instead chose to picture her old friend as the cheerful, clever, and beautiful girl she had known as a child, not as the cruel monster she had become.

"Well here we are," Morgana announced, obviously aware of their company, "Welcome to Armageddon."

"This doesn't have to be the end," Rowena replied.

"Oh, but of *course* it does. I've been watching the Battle of Camlann unfold since the hour it began, and Arthur's army, while recently resurgent, will not hold out much longer. Soon my son will fulfill his destiny as the unchallenged High King, and all that was stolen from me will have been restored. Just look into the fire and see for yourself... wait, *you can't*."

Then the witch turned to face her visitors and smirked at them disdainfully, her blood-red lips twisted with hate.

"Your words cannot harm me, Morgana," said Rowena, "You may have taken my sight, but you will not take my spirit. Despite all that stands between us, I haven't come here for retribution or to dredge up the past. I've come to take you home."

"Home?" Morgana laughed, "What the devil do you know of *home*, Saxon? Your parents are dead, and your husband is likely to follow by sunset. You have no more home than I."

"Come back to the light, Morgana. We both know that the person you've become is not who you truly are inside. You felt joy once. And friendship. And *love*. But after years of wallowing in darkness, you have allowed anger to poison your heart. I beg you, step away from the brink of Hell and awake. Rise from this living death, and let hope shine on you again."

With those words, the scant rays of sunlight that had broken through the forest canopy disappeared altogether and the skies turned pitch dark. A raging tempest arose, blowing the door shut and prying the shutters from their hinges. Then the hearth fire exploded into a thousand tongues of flame, setting the hovel ablaze and filling the tiny room with thick, black smoke. In the midst of this chaotic nightmare, a sinister laugh burst forth from Morgana's mouth, deep and booming like the voice of some vile creature ascended from the deepest abyss. The witch's eyes grew black as night, and Rowena felt the same overpowering fear she had experienced long ago at the site of Igraine's burial. But this time she did not turn and flee.

"Tell me your name, spirit," Rowena demanded.

"*He* knows my name," the inhuman voice spat back, glaring at Merlyn with brazen malevolence, "Don't you, Ambrosius?"

"Aye, I know your name, Astaroth," the old man replied, his words booming like thunder and his garments aglow with white light, "And mark my words, before this day is over, that woman will be freed from your wicked clutches and you will be banished back into the filth from whence you came."

* * * * *

At long last, Lancelot felt like himself again. That old, familiar blend of fear and exhilaration surged through his veins, and he flew through the Saxon ranks wielding Arondight with proficiency and passion, leading his company of freed loyalists in one final, heroic stand that seemed destined to become the stuff of legend. Memories of the past came flooding back to him, and for the first time in ages, he felt the simple, joyful satisfaction of giving every last breath to a noble cause. His cold, steel blade flashed like lightning in the midday sun, vanquishing enemies left and right, and although he was exhausted from fighting, the thrill of battle seemed to drive him onward. *And yet something had changed.* Unlike so many other battles in times gone by, it was neither bloodlust nor retribution that fed his strength. Rather, it was the solemn vow he had taken long ago on Pentecost, and the selfless desire to defend a good man's dream.

After retreating for a moment to catch his breath, Lancelot began searching the battlefield for Arthur until he heard a single voice ringing out among the din – an old friend crying out in anguish. With a surge of adrenaline, he rushed through the chaos and bloodshed to find Gawain lying on his back in an ever growing patch of crimson, his left leg severed just above the knee. A thin, lanky warrior stood over him with a sword in each hand, wearing a chainmail hauberk and a leather pauldron over one arm. Upon spying Lancelot's rapid advance, he removed the old Corinthian helmet that he wore to reveal a scarred, weathered visage with only a single bloodshot eye. This was Urien, the ruthless Celtic mercenary who had long allied himself with the enemies of Camelot, and he sneered at Lancelot as the vengeful knight stepped between him and Gawain.

"This is my friend, villain," Lancelot growled, "and if you want his life you'll have to take mine first."

The two warriors circled one another methodically, each man studying the other's every movement while awaiting the perfect moment to strike. Urien sneered. Lancelot could hear his own heart beating over the noise of battle, but he quickly slowed his breathing and cleared his mind of every thought but the man who stood before him threatening the life of a fallen comrade. Then suddenly something snapped and Urien gave out a feral cry, thrusting violently with his pair of short swords in an aggressive attempt to gut his opponent with a single attack. Lancelot leapt to one side, narrowly avoiding the twin blood-stained blades and then bringing his own weapon crashing down against one of them, promptly knocking the additional sword from Urien's grip. But the mercenary recovered quickly, and as he spun around to regain his footing he caught Lancelot with a hard blow to the right shoulder, leaving a gruesome gash in his bicep and sending him stumbling to the ground in agony, with Arondight flying from his hand and into a snow bank far beyond his reach. As he lay prone next to Gawain, who was still alive but motionless, Lancelot held his wound tightly, applying pressure so as to slow the bleeding while fruitlessly reaching for his sword. Moments later, a quiet, weary voice caught his attention, and he turned his head to see Gawain struggling to call his name and feebly motioning to his left where his battle axe lay half buried in the snow.

"How very quaint," Urien laughed contemptuously, casually dangling his dragon-hilted shortsword a few inches above their faces, "It appears that you'll soon have the pleasure of dying right beside your friend here. But at least it will be a quick death. After I cracked your pretty queen's skull, she writhed and moaned for hours before I mercifully put her out of her misery."

Then as Urien lifted his blade on high and prepared to pierce Lancelot through the heart, the wounded knight quickly rolled over, pulled Gawain's axe from beneath the snow, and hurled it toward the one-eyed mercenary, who looked down in shock to see a heavy, frost-covered blade embedded in his chest. Within seconds, his stunned expression transformed into a blank, lifeless stare, and he fell to the ground dead.

"*That* was for Gwenivere," the blacksmith muttered.

As war continued to rage on around them, Lancelot cut a strip of fabric from his tunic and wrapped it around the grisly gash on his arm, and then he knelt down and hoisted Gawain onto his aching shoulders, deftly evading danger with every step while carrying his gravely injured comrade beyond the field of battle and into the relative safety of Arthur's camp. A pair of fatigued young squires who had been helping tend to the casualties scurried over bearing a heated axe blade to cauterize Gawain's wound, a roll of linen bandages, and a skin filled with strong wine intended to numb his senses. Despite guzzling down every last drop of the wine, Gawain let out an anguished wail and Lancelot had to hold him steady when red-hot steel met the bloody stump where his leg had once been. After the searing pain had passably subsided, the fading Saxon knight, too mangled to speak, reached out with quivering hands and grasped Lancelot about the neck, pulling him close until the two men were face-to-face. Not a single word was spoken, though none were needed. The contrite look in Gawain's eyes made evident both his gratitude for being pulled from the battlefield and his remorse for having previously lost all faith in his longtime friend.

"I couldn't leave a fallen man behind," said Lancelot, whose expression also spoke more deeply than his words.

In fulfillment of his vow, he had returned to defend Camelot without pretense, expecting to be greeted as a man condemned. But now, kneeling at Gawain's side while they bled together once more, he felt the nagging guilt of his litany of sins being washed away like sand in the morning tide. *At last he understood*. In the end, they were *all* fallen men just waiting to be rescued.

* * * * *

Morgana could feel the dark power surging through her body like a drug. While the phenomenon had been terribly frightening in the beginning, over the years it grew into a powerful addiction, easily supplanting her pathetic, human weaknesses and imbuing her with all the strength she would ever need to never again be victimized by anyone, be he god or man. Of course, allowing Lord Astaroth's spirit to consume her had resulted in a few unforeseen side effects, which she had ultimately taught herself to overlook. Aside from the obviously degraded state of her outward, physical appearance, the most noticeable shift concerned her connection with the demon prince himself. The strange sensation of being possessed, which in her younger years had felt like some foreign entity invading her persona, later became more of a symbiotic partnership, with Lord Astaroth taking more and more control until she began to feel like a guest in her own body. Instead of simply providing her with the power to reclaim what she had lost, the dark spirit was now harnessing her as an earthly vessel to breach the walls of this mortal world. Morgana felt lost within herself. She could hear the voices of Merlyn and Rowena as they cried out in desperation, but they sounded distant and muffled, as if she were listening from underwater.

What was that? The old man seemed to be speaking to her, begging her to cast Lord Astaroth away and free herself from his influence. *Ha! What utter nonsense! Why would she ever want to do such a thing?* Despite the cost, the demon prince had been there for her since childhood, always protecting and empowering her when no one else would. And while it was true that he had taken much from her as well, with a bit of humanity slipping away every time she tapped in to his infernal authority, the sacrifice had certainly been well worth it... *hadn't it?*

Morgana felt herself screaming at Rowena with indignation as the blind Saxon attempted to remind her of their childhood together. *But wait, had it been her voice or that of Lord Astaroth speaking through her?* She barely knew anymore. The fine line between the demon's tantalizing whispers and her own thoughts and choices had become blurred, and Morgana could no longer tell truth from lies, impulses from actions, or reality from fantasy. *Had she really gouged out Rowena's eyes out of spite? They had been friends once, after all. No, surely the wretch deserved it. As long as she clung tightly to her naïve belief in... in... Lord Astaroth wouldn't allow her to utter that name. And why not? What the hell was he so afraid of? Unless he had been lying to her all along. It certainly wouldn't be the first time...*

The blazing hellfire she had summoned would soon bring the hovel down around them, though Astaroth's presence within her had saved Morgana from being burned thus far. Of course, the same could not be said for poor Rowena, who had removed her thick, protective, outer garments and was now using them to keep the child she carried safe from the smoke and flames. But despite the danger, she stayed and pleaded as Merlyn continued speaking forcefully to the demon prince in a language she did not understand. Just before the raging inferno became too much to bear, the old man seemed to have gained the upper hand as he spread his arms wide, blasting a pulse of white light through the room that instantly extinguished the fire and sent the splintered front door flying into the wintry forest.

And then, for the briefest moment, reality broke through and Morgana was finally *afraid*. It was as if the darkness within her had been illuminated and she could finally see both the world and herself with utter clarity, if only for an instant. The flash of brilliant white light unearthed a long-buried memory from her subconscious, and she recalled that fateful night on the parapets of *Castorum Sepulcris* when Galahad and Percival stood tall in defiance of the Great White Dragon. It was that same light, that same sense of clarity that led her to flee from the ancient fortress in terror, and as the blackness faded from her eyes, she could see Rowena huddled on the floor, clutching the child to her chest and praying fervently for salvation. But curiously enough, it was not her *own* salvation for which she pleaded. Despite the lingering smoke that clouded the air, despite her blindness, despite all that had happened, Rowena still knelt before her God interceding on behalf of her wayward friend's soul.

Morgana was speechless. *What had she ever done to deserve such unrequited compassion, especially from one who had long been her enemy?* Ever since their ominous confrontation at her mother's graveside, she had brought only pain and suffering to Rowena and all those she cared about... and yet still she trusted, still she hoped, still she persevered. Rowena had been ready to die in those flames for an old friend who abandoned her. *So what cause was there to hate? Why could she feel nothing but wrath and revulsion?* Of course, Morgana knew the answer. She had *always* known, but her addiction to the vast power offered by the demon prince had grown so overwhelming that she became willfully blind to the incremental loss of her own humanity. She had spent a lifetime imprisoned by an unquenchable thirst for vengeance, intensified by the dark spirit that dwelled within her, yet only recently had she begun to question whether she had sold her soul for liberty or simply another far more insidious form of subjugation. Then her doubts and fears all came to a head in that fleeting instant when her eyes were opened by the flash of white light and she finally witnessed the true meaning of love.

"Leave me, Lord Astaroth," Morgana whispered timidly, her own voice eventually escaping from those blood-red lips.

The hovel fell deathly silent until a wave of cruel, disdainful laughter answered back, rumbling inside the delicate mortal shell that the fiendish monster had possessed. His claim had been staked, and Morgana knew he would *not* go quietly.

"Release me *now*," she shouted this time, her confidence slowly increasing as the fear of being without him was overcome by the greater fear of losing herself forever.

"How dare you!" the demon growled from deep within her, turning her eyes black as night once again, "You were *nothing* without me! Just a frightened little girl being violently mistreated and abused by powerful men! Is that what you want? Do you desire helplessness, victimhood, and humiliation?"

"I desire my freedom," Morgana answered, reaching with bare hands into the dying embers of the hearth fire and retrieving the small iron cross she had once pulled from Rowena's neck. As she turned it over between her charred fingers, she could feel the demon prince fighting against her will, filling her mind with lies and beseeching her to return to his devilish command. But it was too late. *She remembered and she believed.*

"You are no longer welcome here. I order you to leave in the name of One who has conquered Death itself."

Lord Astaroth screamed... and Merlyn smiled.

The old man now stepped forth fully transformed in glory, his emerald cloak changed into a radiant white, wielding a massive sword that burned with blinding, ethereal fire. Although the dark spirit dug in his claws, frantically attempting to keep his grip on Morgana's battered soul, he knew that he held no more power in this place. Now that Astaroth had been separated from his human vessel he was as vulnerable as a snail without its shell, so with a satisfied grin, Merlyn reared back and plunged the flaming sword into his black, merciless heart. The shrieking of crows rang out through the forest and bubbling rivers of tar and sulfur began flowing from the wound as the demon's pale, cadaverous skin began to crack and decay until nothing was left but a withered husk. Then with his final measure of strength, Astaroth reached into the earth and shook the foundations of Morgana's hovel, causing the weakened structure to begin crashing down as his scaly, corroding remains were finally ripped from this mortal world and thrown howling back into the Abyss.

As smoldering debris fell to the floor and the walls started to cave in around them, Morgana spied Rowena passed out in one corner of the room, the sleeping child still wrapped in her arms. Without a second thought, she rushed to Rowena's side and tried fruitlessly to wake her, then grabbed her by the ankles and began pulling her and the baby to safety. A loud cracking sound told Morgana that what was left of the falling structure was about to collapse, so with all her might she lifted her former friend and threw her over the threshold just as the roof gave way and she was buried under a mound of smoking rubble.

With clean air in her lungs once again, Rowena awoke to the feeling of snow melting through her underclothes and the touch of Merlyn's gentle hand upon her shoulder. She sat up quickly, first checking on little Aurelius, who was still sleeping peacefully, and then called out for Morgana, unsure of what had become of her. After a few moments, a faint whimper caught her attention and she crawled on her hands and knees toward the remains of the hovel until she felt thin, delicate fingers reaching out to her from beneath the ruins. Heartbroken by her discovery, Rowena grasped the shaking hand and then felt a small metal object being pressed into her palm. *It was the iron cross.*

"I'm so sorry, Rowena," Morgana gasped, "Please, tell Arthur I'm sorry. God forgive me."

"God *always* forgives," the blind Saxon replied, and then she sat in the snow and held her friend's hand tightly until the sound of Morgana's labored breathing finally stopped.

*****

Arthur could barely see or hear in the midst of the chaos that surrounded him. It was already afternoon, and as the sun began to dip into the western sky, shadows of the dead and dying men that lay strewn about the field of battle stretched out across the icy, frosted plains. The snow was melting now, turning the winter landscape into an unruly mess of slush, grime, and blood, and Arthur cursed himself for having lost count of the number of his men who had fallen. Gareth, Sagramore, Kay, and Tristan were already dead and buried. Palamedes still fought bravely, despite his injured shoulder, and Bedivere was doing his best to provide leadership and direction to the woefully depleted garrisons left under his command. Percival, the last living son of Pellinore, had been engaged in a rancorous duel with Cynric, the Saxon General, ever since Lamorack fell before his blade and joined their brother Aglovale in the hereafter. As for Gawain, rumors had spread that he was now teetering near death, while Lancelot – for all Arthur knew – was still back in Dinan after being driven away like a stray dog. The bitter loss of his knights was made all the more painful by the fact that Mordred, his own nephew, his own flesh and blood, had treacherously orchestrated everything.

A loud cracking sound resonated in the distance, and Arthur looked toward his beloved city to see the battlements suddenly crumble into ruins, the final remnants of Camelot's once robust defenses demolished by the horrors of war. Beyond the derelict walls, dark spirits roamed the abandoned cobblestone streets, and although they remained invisible to mortals, Arthur could feel their black, putrid malevolence as they filled the pastureland and courtyards with their rancid stench.

How had he let it come to this? What fatal flaw had caused the dream that was Camelot to come crashing down around him? At first Arthur wondered if he had not been faithful enough, or if maybe his pride and anger at Gwenivere's infidelity had been his undoing. As it was written, *pride goeth before destruction*. Or perhaps it had been unavoidable – *inevitable* even, for the ever-present evil of humanity ensured that there could be no idyllic kingdom, no shining city on a hill… not for *long*, anyway. As Merlyn had once told him, *nothing that dwells in this sinful world for long can retain perfection*. Arthur was reminded of the words of Saint Augustine in his magnum opus, *City of God*, explaining to a disbelieving world that "the evil will itself is not effective but *defective*. For to defect from Him who is the Supreme Existence, to something of less reality, *this* is to begin to have an evil will. To try to discover the causes of such defection is like trying to see darkness or to hear silence."

No sooner had the familiar passage run through his memory than Arthur noticed heavy footsteps approaching from behind, and he instantly recognized Mordred's awkward gait.

"This is how it *always* had to end," said the dark-haired young man with a satisfied grin, "You and I, all alone, facing one another on the field of battle. It's like poetry."

"Why are you doing this, Mordred?" Arthur pleaded, "We welcomed you as a brother! Even now, despite the betrayal and the bloodshed, know that you *still* have a choice. You do not have to walk the same dark path that your mother followed."

"Ah, the *priestess* Morgana?" he quipped scornfully, "*Please*. Yes, it's true that as a child I marveled at her powers of sorcery and necromancy. I stood in awe of her great white dragon. But eventually I realized that it was nothing but a farce, for bowing before the Devil was no different than bowing before God. In the end, both amounted to abject *servitude*. The idea of an ultimate good opposed by some ultimate evil is so prosaic and outdated anyway. These supernatural forces you call *God* and *the Devil* are both merely manifestations of the same spiritual power that flows throughout *all* sentient life and is there for the taking by those with the strength to claim it! I have *evolved*, Arthur. I have risen beyond your antiquated notions of right and wrong to give birth to my own morality – my own *truth*. So spare me the tired lecture about repentance and forgiveness. It's a tragic waste of what little breath you have left. You ask me why I am doing this? Because I *can*. We both know only the *strong* survive, Arthur. I have called the powers of this world into myself; now I am both God and Devil, savior and destroyer, and I serve no one!"

Arthur felt sick to his stomach at the painful realization that Mordred, his only family left in this world, appeared to be beyond redemption. The young man's heart had been hardened against the very foundation of all that he believed in... *but no, was this even a man anymore?* As Arthur looked upon his nephew, he saw before him a hollow form in which humanity had once resided, now wholly infested with evil. While his dark hair and pale skin still proclaimed to the world that this was *Mordred*, in another sense he was nearly unrecognizable, for the light of life no longer shone behind his eyes. He stood there like a walking corpse, and when Arthur blinked, he could almost see the dark, gruesome visage of the demon Naberius staring back at him.

The air fell silent as the two titans clashed, with Arthur lifting Excalibur to parry a strike from Mordred's spear, razor sharp and stained black with the blood of his victims. Then iron and steel, sword and shield crashed against one another like thunder, and jagged bolts of lightning began to fill the darkening skies. Arthur could now feel the ravages of time on his weathered body, and regardless of the additional strength derived from his heavenly blade, the aging king's reflexes were noticeably slower against a warrior nearly half his age. Set back on his heels, Arthur tried to mount an attack, but Mordred was fighting like a man possessed and gave him little to no opportunity to step off the defensive. Then with the setting sun to his back, Arthur drew upon the pain that had built up within him – Gwenivere's death, the loss of his oldest friend, the looming fall of his kingdom – and charged at his enemy with renewed vitality, channeling all his might into one passionate strike that knocked Mordred from his feet and sent him sprawling into the crimson snow.

"You're wrong, Mordred," the king bellowed, the tip of his shining sword resting against his enemy's throat, "You've *always* been wrong. Honor, forgiveness, and compassion are not signs of failure or weakness; rather, such acts of love should be the standards against which true strength is measured. Selfishness is easy. *Hatred* is easy. But mercy? Hope? A man sacrificing his pride or even his *life* on behalf of another? There is *nothing* more powerful in this world or the next."

Mordred was beaten, and for an instant Arthur saw humanity in his eyes once again. So with a weary smile he let Excalibur fall from his grip, and then, as an act of clemency, Arthur stretched out a bloodied hand to his opponent and whispered, "Come, let us end this. No one else need die today."

The warfare around them had ceased. Every soul on the field of battle stood frozen in awe, watching speechlessly as a man who had already lost everything dared to show mercy to the man who had taken it all away from him. Mordred dropped his spear in surrender, then rose to his knees and took Arthur's hand with head bowed and eyes focused downward.

"Thank you, Arthur," he murmured.

Then Mordred looked up with a wicked sneer on his lips and pulled Arthur toward him, picking up the Spear of Longinus with his other hand and plunging it into the king's belly. The onlookers gasped as the sharp, iron shank burst through Arthur's back and dark red blood began flowing from the wound.

"Just as I said," Mordred taunted, *"Weak."*

The king stared back at his enemy brokenhearted, wide-eyed with shock and disbelief. *This was the end.* The pain in his gut was excruciating, and it quickly became difficult to breathe as he started coughing up mouthfuls of blood and bile onto the melting snow. Excalibur lay out of reach near Mordred's feet, and before losing consciousness, Arthur looked at the angelic sword for a moment and then prayed to the Almighty for one final measure of strength. When he finally set his gaze upon Mordred again, a new fire was blazing behind his eyes, and he gripped the spear tightly as he began to slowly pull it through his broken body. Mordred was horrified to see the blackened shaft slide inch-by-inch through Arthur's gaping wound until he eventually pulled himself close enough to reach Excalibur.

"Camelot lives," the king wheezed. And then he lifted up his sword and thrust it into Mordred's side.

Time seemed to stand still as both warriors collapsed to the ground, each one mortally wounded. Not a word was spoken by the gawking soldiers gathered nearby, for no man on either side had ever witnessed anything quite like the scene that had just unfolded before them. Arthur's few remaining knights looked on in both sorrow and amazement, particularly Percival, who started when he felt a large, rough hand upon his shoulder.

"Both our lords have fallen," said Cynric, dropping his sword into the mud and extending an open hand of truce, "Let us shed no more blood today."

Percival rubbed the sweat and grime from his face before turning toward the place where Arthur lay and peering into his king's fading eyes. Moments later, with a long sigh of exhaustion, he dropped his sword as well and took Cynric's hand in his own, putting an end to the Battle of Camlann just as the setting sun disappeared over the horizon. A gentle dusting of snow began to fall in the waning twilight, gradually covering the patches of spilt blood with a fresh blanket of white that made the battle-scarred valley seem peaceful and renewed. But as both captains signaled their forces to retreat, a glint of steel appeared in their periphery. Mordred, still gasping for life, had pulled a small dagger from his boot and was now crawling toward Arthur, prepared to slit the dying king's throat like the cowardly serpent that he was.

Then before Percival could cry out in alarm, there was a flash of light and Mordred's head fell from his shoulders, tumbling to the ground and rolling toward his outstretched hand, which still held the gleaming dagger in its grip. Once the brightness finally faded, Percival looked again and saw Lancelot standing over the traitor's body wielding Excalibur, his body quaking with emotion, as well as Merlyn, who was kneeling at Arthur's side, idly stroking the tail feathers of his little grey owl.

Arthur's face looked pale and sallow, its color having faded as the last remnants of life quickly fled from his body, though his eyes were still red from weeping. Merlyn placed the owl atop his wide-brimmed hat and took the king's hand in his own, offering what little comfort he could while tiny snowflakes drifted down and came to rest upon his dingy green cloak.

"Dry your tears, Arthur," said the old man, "You were never meant to save the world. God assigned you a task, and nothing more. You have done all you can."

The king struggled to speak as the pool of blood beneath him spread, with streams of deep crimson trickling steadily through newly fallen snow. "Then I have failed Him," Arthur finally replied as he lowered his head in shame.

A wry grin spread across Merlyn's face as he placed his hand beneath Arthur's chin, lifting the dying king's face to meet his own. "Oh, *have* you, my boy?" he asked knowingly, "Do you think God was *wrong* to choose you? No, Arthur, you have not failed. Camelot may have fallen, but its *spirit* will live on. No man can see in his own lifetime the ways in which his actions will echo throughout the ages."

"But the battle is lost, Merlyn. Darkness has prevailed, and I am helpless to stand against it."

Merlyn's smile disappeared and a reverential hush fell over the war-torn fields. "Listen to me well, Arthur," he whispered, "A man's life is not measured by the battles he has won. No, my boy, God does not reward land or kingdoms or the spoils of war. God rewards *faithfulness*. In this mortal life, few things are ever certain. Some battles we may win and some we may lose, but what is truly important is that we *fight*. You may be a king, Arthur, but you are still only a man. A time will come when the *true* King returns, crowned in glory and shining like the sun. And on that day, the darkness will fall forever."

"I long to see that day, Merlyn."

"You will, my boy. You will."

Then the old man held Arthur in his arms like a father would his child, cradling the king's head and lifting his face toward the heavens. Arthur no longer spoke, and his breathing had become short and strained. With a knowing glance up at Percival, Merlyn leaned down to whisper something in the king's ear, and his eyes grew wide and flashed with light as if they had been opened for the very first time. Tears began to stream down his cheeks and his voice was heard once again, no longer faint and broken, but booming with joyous laughter. Finally, a look of perfect peace fell across his face and he spoke his final words.

"It's beautiful," Arthur said before he closed his eyes forever.

The few remaining knights who had survived the battle stood there in silence for what seemed like an eternity. Their king – *their friend* – lay dead in the winter snow, with Excalibur resting on his chest and his face turned toward the stars. After wiping away his own tears, Lancelot looked over at Merlyn, who smiled at him with a warmth that filled his soul.

"Merlyn, what did he see?" Lancelot asked.

"Hope, Lancelot," the old man replied, "He saw hope."

Epilogue

Lancelot cupped his hands and knelt down beside the Lake of Diana, lifting handfuls of cool, clear water to his lips and drinking deeply until he was satisfied. The bright morning sunlight that found its way through the woodland canopy felt warm upon his face, and the carefree twittering of birds filled Brocéliande Forest with an air of soothing serenity. He reclined in the shade of a large oak tree, his body sinking comfortably into the soft green grass, and proceeded to unwrap an oblong parcel bound with twine and enveloped in a bolt of silk. *Excalibur.* To this day, it remained the most magnificent sword he had ever seen. The hilt bore the shape of a screaming eagle, wings outstretched in flight and trimmed in pure gold, with a small cross fashioned from blood-red sapphire adorning its pommel. The translucent, crystalline blade was still blindingly bright, even after a lifetime of warfare, and it flashed with an ethereal fire that sent tremors through his memory of times gone by.

The crackling, windswept flames of the king's funeral pyre had permanently etched their image into his mind's eye, and Lancelot vividly remembered standing side-by-side on the icy banks of the River Alen with Palamedes, Bedivere, and Percival as they paid final tribute to the fallen and bid a tearful farewell to the friends and loved ones they had lost. It had taken days for them to bury all the dead, including Gawain, who eventually succumbed to his injuries on the morning after the Battle of Camlann. Thankfully, he somehow managed to hold on long enough for Rowena to return, much the worse for wear but still alive, and say her final goodbye. And while Lancelot had been somewhat dismayed when she declined to attend her husband's interment, preferring to remember Gawain as he was, part of him understood Rowena's need to cling tightly to life, with her heart newly focused on the cooing child she cradled in her arms.

After scattering Arthur's ashes to the sea, Lancelot stole away to pay his final respects to Gwenivere, who they had buried near her favorite garden outside the ruins of Saint Stephen's Cathedral. *She never deserved such a fate.* Despite his adulterous pursuit of the queen prior to the fall of Camelot, Lancelot truly did care for her, and as the surviving knights reluctantly broke ranks and went their separate ways, he knew that he always would.

The kingdom was in shambles, and although it was mutually accepted that the Saxons would soon develop into an entrenched ruling class as they gained further dominance throughout Britannia, the nobility and honor Cynric had shown on the field of battle provided them with hope that a light still shined in the darkness, however faint that it may be. For their part, Percival and Bedivere chose to stay behind and spread that light to all those with ears to hear and hearts to understand, guarding it watchfully like a candle flickering in the wind. Old Palamedes retired to his homeland of Sarmatia, happy to live amongst his own people for the first time since he was conscripted into the Roman army as a boy, nearly a lifetime ago. As for Lancelot, he returned to his childhood home in Dinan along with Rowena and little Aurelius, having taken a solemn vow to protect them both until his dying day. Uncle Bors and Aunt Vivienne had finally passed on – within a week of each other, in fact – and had left the house and blacksmith shop to the care of their beloved nephew. And so Lancelot ended his journey in the same place it began, sharpening tools and pounding out horseshoes for the local farmers and craftsmen, though he had since discovered something far greater to live for than vengeance or glory – something *beyond* himself.

When Aurelius grew older, perhaps he would take him fishing now and then, teach him to hunt and how to defend himself, and maybe even show him the proper way to handle a sword. *It was the least he could do, after all.* Whereas Rowena had proven to be a capable, loving guardian, quickly earning the respect and admiration of each new person she met in their tiny village, even without the use of her eyes, Lancelot felt responsible for teaching the boy what it truly meant to be a man. And after years of watching Arthur, he finally understood what that meant. So when Aurelius was old enough, Lancelot would tell him stories of knights and heroic courage, of love and sacrifice, of hope and redemption, but most importantly, he would tell him stories of his father, a great king and an even better friend.

A gentle breeze rustled through the leaves of the ancient oak that Lancelot had been sitting beneath as he reminisced, and he gazed heavenward and sighed with contentment, sweeping a few loose strands of greying hair from his eyes. Excalibur lay in the tall grass at his side, glimmering in the midday sunlight, and as he rose to his feet Lancelot lifted the angelic sword with ease and stepped resolutely toward the shoreline. Then with one final glimpse of its heavenly blade, he raised Excalibur on high and cast it into the center of the lake. The dark water was as still as glass, and the sword's reflection remained clear against the surface as it tumbled end over end through the air until at last it was caught by a delicate hand that suddenly emerged from the deep. The arm that followed was like porcelain, draped in a sleeve of sparkling green samite, and with a flash of brilliant white light she pulled Excalibur into the watery depths and was gone, vanishing as if neither one had ever existed.

"Goodbye, Nimue," Lancelot said softly, "and thank you."

Then the blacksmith casually brushed the grass from his tunic and turned to leave, but not before noticing something unusual near the edge of the lake. For when he stepped back and gazed into the crystal water, he did not see his own aging, weathered visage staring back at him. Rather, he saw a much younger face, with thick, sandy-brown hair and a pair of mischievous blue eyes, wholly unscarred by time or the ravages of war and death. It was like looking into a mirror to the past. *Surely,* he thought, *this was Galahad's face...* but nay, it was his own. In that one miraculous moment, when Lancelot beheld himself he saw the reflection of the man he was always meant to be.

The man he had finally become.

And then the vision passed away like a shadow at sunrise as a single pink heather blossom drifted lazily through the air and came to rest a few inches from the shoreline, leaving nothing behind but a gentle ripple on the surface of the water.

Some natural tears they dropped, but wiped them soon;
The world was all before them, where to choose
Their place of rest, and Providence their guide:
They hand in hand with wandering steps and slow
Through Eden took their solitary way....

- John Milton, *Paradise Lost*

Appendix: Rex Quondam, Rexque Futurus

The Heroic Role of King Arthur Throughout History

William Shakespeare once wrote that "cowards die many times before their deaths; the valiant never taste of death but once."[1] The deeper meaning, of course, is that the cowardly may experience many forms of moral, spiritual, and emotional death throughout their time on this earth, but a person who is heroic and honourable will only die physically. According to legend, the tomb of King Arthur is marked by the cryptic inscription, "Here lies Arthur, the Once and Future King." Although this epithet is meant to signify the promise of Arthur's prophesied messianic return, the phrase may also be adapted to the premise that the character of King Arthur is a changing, dynamic hero who serves as a touchstone for the ideals of the various times and cultures in which his tales have been recorded. Although the weak and craven may die a thousand times, it would seem that Arthur has instead lived a thousand times. Other larger-than-life literary characters such as Beowulf and Achilles serve as definitive champions, each exclusively for his own age and society; however, Arthur appears to be a more protean figure. The varying elements of his exploits, character, and principles reflect the qualities of the ideal hero valued by each successive generation. From his portrayal by Geoffrey of Monmouth as a nationalistic saviour battling the Saxons and Romans, to Malory's civil war-influenced portrait of the tragic leader of a fallen empire, to the king's depiction as a Victorian Christ-figure by

[1] Shakespeare, William, *Julius Caesar* (Act II, Scene II, lines 36-37).

Alfred Lord Tennyson, to his appearance in T.H. White's allegorical account of the warring political ideologies of Europe during the second World War, Arthur remains a blank slate. Rather than being defined by his own values, Arthur is instead defined by the predominant values of the age, as the embodiment of an evolving heroic paradigm.

In order to fully comprehend Arthur's unique role as the ideal hero for numerous societies and generations, we must first examine and contrast the cultural roles of other, comparable literary figures. The first such example comes from Homer's *Iliad*, which may be considered the most classic and enduring tale passed down from all of ancient Greece. Although the main narrative of the *Iliad* tells of the final days of a war between Greece and Troy, the thematic focus of the epic poem centres on the heroic protagonist, Achilles, and his disputes with the Greek general Agamemnon. However, for modern readers to understand the internal conflict faced by Achilles, we must first understand the opposing Greek ideals of κλέος (*kleos*) and νόστος (*nostos*). The word κλέος refers to honour and glory earned in battle. Dying valiantly and having one's name remembered was often viewed by the ancient Greeks as more important than νόστος, the ability to safely return to one's home and family.[2] It is for this reason that Achilles initially refuses to return to the fray alongside his countrymen. He has been shamed because his love-slave, his pride and glory and his plunder of war, has been taken from him, and he must be prodded and coerced to take up his sword again. A modern reader would likely call Achilles selfish, disloyal, and barbaric. He would hardly appear heroic. This is because Achilles is a hero for his own time, not all time, and he stands for a set of ancient ideals that are no longer prized in western society. Similarly, the Old

---

[2] For translation of the Greek terms, I utilized Liddell and Scott's *Greek-English Lexicon*, published by Oxford University Press in 1996. The thematic discussions of the *Iliad* come from my own reading of the text and lectures by Dr. Craig Kallendorf on Greek and Roman Epic in 2004 at Texas A&M University.

English poem *Beowulf*, one of the most important works of Anglo-Saxon literature, also features a protagonist who reflects a value system foreign to a modern reader. The hero Beowulf lives in a culture dominated by the principles of the pagan Germanic warrior society, which places great emphasis on personal reputation and the relationship between the warrior and his lord. For instance, Beowulf spends a considerable amount of time in the king's hall boasting about his heroic (and uncorroborated) exploits, and while modern readers may view such an act as vain, pompous, and arrogant, Beowulf's boasting actually increases his honour and renown among his own people.[3] Heroes like Beowulf and Achilles must be viewed through the lenses of their own cultural ideals. They are like words in another language that cannot be directly translated into our own.

Conversely, Arthur functions less like the one of these fabled heroes, and more like the abstract Platonic universal of the Hero, a recurrent entity which contains all that man may view as heroic throughout time and history. Whereas Achilles or Beowulf represents the specific, Arthur's universalism is far more wide-reaching. He is akin to the monomyth, as described by Joseph Campbell in his seminal work, *The Hero With a Thousand Faces*. As Campbell writes, "A hero ventures forth from the world of common day into a region of supernatural wonder: fabulous forces are there encountered and a decisive victory is won: the hero comes back from this mysterious adventure with the power to bestow boons on his fellow man."[4] Campbell initially uses well-known religious heroes as his examples, Prometheus, Moses, Buddha, and Christ, each one reflecting vastly different spiritual values, but all elevated to the universal heroic ideal. He goes on to explain the characteristics and plight of such figures:

---

[3] The referenced boasting by Beowulf of his exploits as well as the ensuing reaction by the king and court occurs between lines 407-641 of the poem.

[4] Campbell, Joseph, *The Hero With a Thousand Faces*, (Fontana Press: London, 1993), p.30.

> The composite hero of the monomyth is a personage of exceptional gifts. Frequently he is honoured by his society, frequently unrecognized or disdained. He and/or the world in which he finds himself suffers from a symbolical deficiency. In fairy tales this may be as slight as the lack of a certain golden ring, whereas in apocalyptic vision the physical and spiritual life of the whole earth can be represented as fallen, or falling, into ruin.[5]

In each of his various incarnations, Arthur is certainly a man of exceptional gifts. As a youth he is unrecognised and disdained, often by his own surrogate family, but he is greatly honoured when he rises to claim his rightful place as king. Regardless of time or culture, he always finds himself in a deficient world, on the brink of ruin and in great need of a hero. In this essay, I will examine and describe four specific types of heroes embodied by Arthur throughout history.

In the earliest, pseudo-historical Arthurian texts such as Lawman's *Brut* and *The History of the Kings of Britain* by Geoffrey of Monmouth, Arthur is a nationalistic hero during a time after the Norman conquest in which the people of England were searching for an identity. He then becomes a respected but tragic imperialist hero in Thomas Malory's *Le Morte d'Arthur,* influenced by the civil and political unrest stemming from the dynastic War of the Roses. As we move away from medieval tales and toward the modern era, we are presented with Arthur as a Christ-like hero, reflecting the strong moral values of Victorian England in *Idylls of the King* by Alfred Tennyson. Finally, during the chaos of World War II and the early days of the Cold War, T.H. White's classic *The Once and Future King* reveals Arthur as a politically idealist hero, struggling with the concepts of just war and proper government. Despite the shifting cultural roles, in

---

[5] Campbell, p. 37.

each manifestation the character of King Arthur serves to embody the great heroic archetype.

Geoffrey of Monmouth was born around 1100 AD, about 40 years after the Norman victory over the Anglo-Saxons at the Battle of Hastings.[6] The invasion of England by William the Conqueror and his armies had changed the island nation significantly, with a replaced ruling class, a stronger, more centralized government, and a an amalgamation of languages that would one day become modern English. Although we know almost nothing about Geoffrey's life, it seems evident that he utilized his skills as a writer in an attempt to provide a national identity to a people whose identity had been stolen away from them. The native Britons had been largely without a true face for close to 1,000 years, having been first colonized by the Roman Empire around 43 AD, then gradually invaded by the Anglo-Saxons throughout the fifth and sixth centuries, and finally conquered by the Normans in 1066 AD.[7] In their essay about the life and work of Geoffrey of Monmouth, John Perry and Robert Caldwell state that "he provided for the Britons, whom he found without a history, one that was not seriously challenged for four centuries, [and] established his greatest creation, Arthur."[8] This character of King Arthur, who previously existed either as a Romano-British military leader or a perhaps a mere legend of Welsh folklore, was now given a full narrative history and a literary persona. But more importantly, Arthur gave the Britons back their identity, and although modern scholars know that Geoffrey's *The History of the Kings of Britain* can hardly be called a true history by academic standards, it is likely that the citizens of twelfth century England would not have cared. When discussing human concepts of the past in his book *The Discarded Image*, C.S. Lewis wrote that those who studied supposedly

---

[6] Loomis, Roger Sherman, ed., *Arthurian Literature in the Middle Ages: A Collaborative History*, (Claredon Press: Oxford, 1959), p. 72.
[7] Morgan, Kenneth, ed., *The Oxford Illustrated History of Britain*, (Oxford University Press: Oxford, 1984).
[8] Loomis, p. 74-75.

historical works about Arthur during the Middle Ages probably "believed their matter to be in the main true," but more certainly that "they did not believe it to be false."[9] Lewis goes on to argue that the potential truth or fiction of Arthur was not of their concern; rather, their business was to learn the story. It was the story of a nationalistic hero who not only "adumbrated the ideals and practices of medieval kingship,"[10] but who gave the native Britons a newfound sense of pride and power.

Geoffrey begins his pseudo-history by claiming that the entire work is merely a Latin translation of "a certain very ancient book written in the British language,"[11] thereby giving some amount of credence to his tale with a simple, although largely inaccurate, assertion. After describing the founding of Britain (originally called *Albion*) by a Trojan exile named Brutus, Geoffrey goes on to list various kings and important events throughout the nation's timeline. However, the portion of the history dealing with Arthur and Merlin is easily the longest and most interesting. Merlin's role is primarily that of a prophet, cryptically foretelling the reign and conquests of Arthur, the great "Boar of Cornwall." The coming-of-age tales of Arthur's childhood with Sir Ector and the Sword in the Stone are not yet present in Geoffrey's version of the story; instead, Arthur simply becomes king upon the death of his father, Uther Pendragon, despite being only fifteen years old at the time of his coronation. The young ruler is immediately described in highly complimentary terms, as a man "of outstanding courage and generosity, [whose] inborn goodness gave him such a grace that he was loved by almost all the

---

[9] Lewis, C.S., *The Discarded Image: An Introduction to Medieval and Renaissance Literature*, (Cambridge University Press: Cambridge, 1964) p. 181.

[10] Turville-Petre, Thorlac, *England the Nation: Language, Literature, and National Identity, 1290-1340*, (Clarendon Press: Oxford, 1996), p. 81.

[11] Geoffrey of Monmouth, *The History of the Kings of Britain*, (Penguin Books: London, 1966), p. 51.

people."[12] Almost immediately after becoming king, Arthur is forced to continue his father's war against the treacherous Saxon invaders, who have been aided by the native Picts and Scots. Geoffrey purposely demonizes the Saxons, going so far as to have Arthur say that their "very name is an insult to heaven and detested by all men."[13] However, although they are foreign invaders and enemies of the Britons, the reasons for the intense villainization of the Saxons are far more complex. As previously mentioned, Geoffrey traces the lineage of the British people back to the Trojans through Brutus. Likewise, the Normans, who had fairly recently taken control of England during the time period this text was written, claimed descent from the Trojans themselves. In his book *England the Nation*, Thorlac Turville-Petre argues that the Norman conquerors were meant to see themselves in the place of Arthur as the divinely ordained British hero:

> Geoffrey's account encouraged a cyclical view of history which the Normans could manipulate to legitimize their own conquest. Just as the folly of the last of the Britons had resulted in the withdrawal of God's favour and their defeat by the Saxons, so in turn the wickedness of the Saxons justified their subjection to the Norman rulers.[14]

Arthur's war against the Saxons is similarly retold in Lawman's *Brut,* a thirteenth century narrative poem partially based on Geoffrey's work. In an essay on Lawman's antiquarian sentiments, E.G. Stanley stretches the cyclical history idea further in claiming that "by accepting the anti-English attitude inherent in an Arthurian account of the Anglo-Saxon settlement, [Lawman] has more than the parallel to the Norman Conquest...

---

[12] Geoffrey of Monmouth, p. 212.
[13] Geoffrey of Monmouth, p. 212.
[14] Turville-Petre, p. 81-82.

he found the moral cause of the Norman Conquest." This literary link serves a dual function: it first allows the invading Normans to see themselves as heroic and justified in overthrowing the seemingly barbaric Saxon traitors, and secondly, it allows native Britons to identify with their new rulers and make peace with the Norman occupation.

King Arthur's heroism is further cemented as he and his armies unite Britain and win a decisive victory against the Saxons, with Arthur single-handedly dispatching 470 enemy soldiers in a berserker rage during one blood-soaked battle. Lawman adds the story of the Round Table to Geoffrey's tale, with Arthur using the table to provide equality within his court and quell disputes among his barons.[15] The king and his now unified men go on to conquer the Picts and Scots as well as large portions of Western Europe, but no triumph would be as poignant and meaningful to the native Britons as Arthur's battle against the Roman emperor Lucius Hiberius. After his victories in Europe, Arthur returns home to fame, fortune, and happiness. Geoffrey writes that "Britain had reached such a standard of sophistication that it excelled all other kingdoms in its general affluence, the richness of its decorations, and the courteous behaviour of its inhabitants."[16] All remains well until Arthur receives a letter from the Roman emperor, insultingly calling the king an insane criminal and demanding that he pay tribute to Rome. Unwilling to go down without a fight, Arthur goes on the offensive and proceeds to defeat Lucius Hiberius in Gaul and then prepares to march on Rome itself. One can only imagine the feelings of nationalistic pride that must have swelled within the hearts of Geoffrey's twelfth-century audience. Not only had Arthur conquered his enemies at home, but he was now marching on

---

[15] The idea of King Arthur's legendary Round Table was first introduced by the Anglo-Norman poet Wace in his pseudo-historical *Roman de Brut*, the intermediary work between Geoffrey and Lawman.

[16] Geoffrey of Monmouth, p. 229.

Rome, the first invaders of Britain, and the most powerful empire the world had ever seen.

Historically speaking, it seems likely that both Geoffrey and his audience would have known that a powerful British king did not actually succeed in leading a siege on the Roman Empire. However, in order to retain Arthur's heroic image and the pleasurable sense of British superiority, Geoffrey allows Arthur to be betrayed, losing his kingdom due to sedition rather than pure defeat. Parry and Caldwell write that "a hero as great as Arthur could not be conceived as falling except by treachery, and so Geoffrey introduced Modred."[17] Thus the character of Arthur's treasonous nephew becomes a standard and almost indispensable part of the Arthurian legend. He is the usurper of the throne of the rightful king and the prime figure involved in Arthur's downfall and the subsequent subjugation of Britain by the Saxons. In the loss of Arthur, the Britons of Geoffrey's day would be able to see their own loss of identity; however, in his reign they would find the hero their people always needed. "Geoffrey's avowed purpose in composing his magnum opus was to provide the descendants of the Britons with a history of their own race from the earliest times," as well as a sense of pride in who they were. The historicity of the book may be questioned or criticised, but "if the account was not true, something like it was – or should have been."[18]

Following the works of Geoffrey and Lawman in the twelfth and thirteenth centuries, numerous Arthurian legends and romances were written throughout England and France, most focusing on Arthur's knights rather than the king himself. During this era, he became a secondary character, pushed aside in favour of the compelling tales of Lancelot and Gwenivere, Tristan and Isolde, Percival, Gawain, and Galahad. However, all this would change in the late fifteenth century with the composition of Sir Thomas Malory's *Le Morte d'Arthur*, possibly the most

---

[17] Loomis, p. 85.
[18] Loomis, p. 86.

important and seminal work in all of Arthurian literature. It has been said that Malory's account is like the narrow centre of an hourglass, with all previous Arthurian tradition flowing into it, and all subsequent literature flowing out.[19] Thomas Malory lived and composed his tale during the dynastic War of the Roses, as supporters of the rival houses of York and Lancaster vied for control of the throne of England, leaving the nation divided and torn. Any feelings of British nationalism in the face of foreign invasions would likely have given way to the fear and uncertainty that comes from such internal strife. Felicity Riddy argues in her essay on the historical context of *Le Morte d'Arthur* that "Arthur was not a people's hero in the later Middle Ages; he belonged to a past which was conceived of as the scene of chivalric activity, and was a way of representing the interests of a society whose function had been, traditionally, to fight."[20] Instead of Geoffrey's nationalistic hero of Britain, Arthur changes under Malory's pen into something else entirely. "Malory's Arthur is king of England, not of Britain... and the narrative is written from an English point of view."[21] Additionally, Arthur is no longer placed in the historical and generational sequence of British conquest and revolt; rather, his story is pulled out of the timeline entirely, and his fall becomes an entrance into aristocratic insecurity, providing a parallel to the intense civil war that marked England at the time. In short, Arthur becomes a tragic imperialist hero, not in the sense of one who strives to conquer as much territory as possible in order to construct an empire, but instead as a good and just king struggling to hold together his own *imperium* as it crumbles from within.

Sir Thomas Malory was born in Warwickshire in the early fifteenth century to John Malory, a member of parliament for his

---

[19] I attribute this metaphor to Dr. Robert Boenig, professor of Old English, Middle English, Tolkien, Lewis, and Arthurian literature at Texas A&M University.

[20] Archibald, Elizabeth, and Edwards, A.S.G., eds., *A Companion to Malory*, (D.S Brewer: Cambridge, 1996), p. 55.

[21] Archibald, p. 64.

county. Although Thomas was himself elected twice to a seat in parliament, he also accrued a lengthy list of criminal charges in the 1450s including burglary, assault on property, rape, and attempting to ambush the Duke of Buckingham.[22] He was arrested and imprisoned on multiple occasions, broke out of jail at least twice, and eventually died in prison for treason. In an essay on Malory's life and work, Eugene Vinaver argues that many of these charges may have been false or unfounded, that the "indictments were only accusations, not evidence, and that there is no record of a trial and conviction."[23] Regardless, Malory spent much of his life as a fugitive and a prisoner, possibly due to his political alliances during the dynastic civil war. As Vinaver explains, he probably followed standard Warwickshire policies and initially remained loyal to Edward IV, then later switched his allegiance to Henry VI when the Duke of Warwick joined the Lancastrians. Much of his masterwork was most likely composed during his time in prison, as evidenced by his final colophon:

> I pray you all, gentlemen and gentlewomen that readeth this book of Arthur and his knights, from the beginning to the ending, pray for me while I am alive, that God send me good deliverance, and when I am dead, I pray you all pray for my soul. For this book was ended the ninth year of the reign of King Edward the Fourth, by Sir Thomas Maleore, knight, as Jesu help him for His great might, as he is the servant of Jesu both day and night.[24]

Just as Geoffrey of Monmouth drew upon the cultural and political climate of his own era when writing of Arthur's exploits, it appears that Malory's own circumstances greatly influenced his

---

[22] Loomis, p. 541.
[23] Loomis, p. 542.
[24] Malory, Thomas, *Le Morte D'Arthur*, (The Modern Library: New York, 1994), p. 938.

personal spin on the Arthurian legend. Interestingly enough, much of this new vision of Arthur may be attributed to one seemingly simple change Malory made to the king's timeline. In Malory's version of the tale, Arthur's victorious battles against the emperor Lucius Hiberius occur much earlier in his reign, and his betrayal and downfall take place not while he valiantly marches against Rome, but while he pursues a civil war against one of his own knights after discovering an adulterous relationship with the queen. Thus the story no longer focuses on a powerful, ambitious king who strives to resurrect the British identity, but instead on a tragic ruler whose knights squabble amongst themselves, whose wife is unfaithful, and whose kingdom is destroyed due to broken alliances and treason. Of all the plot devices Malory appropriated from the French Arthurian romances, this one seems the most significant.

In *Arthurian Propaganda*, Elizabeth Pochoda's discourse on the "historical ideal of life" depicted in *Le Morte d'Arthur*, we are presented with two contrasting but equally valid views of the Arthurian legend as expressed by Sir Thomas Malory. The author argues that Malory's version of the tale arises out of "a cultural context specifically related to the contemporary aristocratic concern with reliving the ceremonies and traditions of the past."[25] From an age of turmoil and civil unrest, Malory looks back on the mythical age of Arthur as one of chivalric glory and knightly idealism, and yet at the same time, he reveals the tragic nature of the attempt to live up to such impossible standards. Pochoda expresses this sentiment in her essay on medieval political theory, stating that the underlying social concerns expressed by Malory are revealed when he takes the Arthurian myth "as a valid ideal of life, employs it initially as a realistic guide for his age, and then turns this idealization back on itself, exposing the very fundamental weaknesses of the Arthurian

---

[25] Pochoda, Elizabeth, *Arthurian Propaganda: Le Morte D'Arthur as an Historical Ideal of Life*, (The University of North Carolina Press: Chapel Hill, 1971), p. 23.

structure."[26] Malory's ennoblement of the values of Arthur's court are clearly expressed in the Pentecostal oath taken by the knights:

> Then the king stablished all his knights... and charged them never to do outrageousity nor murder, and always to flee treason; also, by no means to be cruel, but to give mercy unto him that asketh mercy... and always to do ladies, damosels, and gentlewomen succour, upon pain of death. Also, that no man take no battles in a wrongful quarrel for no law, nor for no world's goods. Unto this were all the knights sworn of the Table Round, both old and young.[27]

While the contemporary audience may have felt a wave of nostalgia and optimism upon reading this passage, Malory himself might have seen the oath as a jab of ironic foreshadowing, knowing full-well that each one of these righteous commands would eventually be broken by Arthur's knights by the end of the story.[28] These simultaneous sentiments of idealistic reminiscence and almost heart-breaking realism serve to mark the socio-political conditions of Malory's day and age.

Although thematic elements related to civil war are certainly present within Malory's text, to claim *Le Morte d'Arthur* as some sort of political allegory for the rupture of England during the War of the Roses would be to oversimplify a more complex issue. Instead, it seems that Malory is providing a cynical critique of the prevailing political value system in England during the fifteenth

---

[26] Pochoda, p. 25.

[27] Malory, p. 100-101.

[28] It is interesting to note that Arthur himself did not always keep the Pentecostal Oath. For instance, he clearly does not show mercy to Gwenivere, his own wife, when he attempts to have her burned at the stake.

century. The principles of Arthurian society were seen as the "historical ideal," and chivalry in the later Middle Ages was "valued, among other things, as the active expression of what we might call a political theory." As a man who experienced the civil war first-hand and spent large portions of his life in jail for treason, Malory "seems to have chosen to exploit the tragic possibilities inhering in the illusory nature of the 'ideal' civilization."[29] In other words, he saw in Arthur a valiant and idealistic hero striving to hold his society together under an honourable but doomed-to-fail chivalric code – the same code which was highly valued in Malory's day by the ruling classes, and the same code which ultimately failed to prevent England from declining into dynastic war.

Malory's apparent views on political failure are reflected in Arthur's downfall. Whereas Arthur loses his kingdom solely due to treachery in the pseudo-historical versions by Lawman and Geoffrey of Monmouth, Malory presents Arthur as more personally responsible due to his own shortcomings and, by extension, those of his knights. For instance, as Gawain lay dying in Arthur's arms after a fierce battle with Mordred's forces, he laments that the division of the kingdom is his own fault, spurred on because of his selfish pride and need for vengeance against Lancelot:

> Mine uncle King Arthur, said Sir Gawaine, wit you well my death-day is come, and all is through mine own hastiness and wilfulness... had Sir Launcelot been with you as he was, this unhappy war had never begun; and of all this I am causer, for Sir Launcelot and his blood, through their prowess, held all your cankered enemies in subjugation and daunger.[30]

---

[29] Pochoda, p. 31-33.
[30] Malory, p. 915.

Additionally, Arthur seems greatly disillusioned with his own kingship and system of values. After he is mortally wounded and prepares to be carried off to Avalon, Sir Bedivere cries out helplessly to the dying king, "Ah my lord, Arthur, what shall become of me, now ye go from me and leave me here along among mine enemies?" Arthur looks back at him and answers, "Comfort thyself... and do as well as thou mayst, for in me is no trust for to trust in."[31] These last words are hardly befitting such a legendary leader; however, after a lifetime of courageously striving to unite England under a banner of chivalry, Arthur appears to have lost faith in his quest and in himself. Instead of charging his last remaining knight to follow in his footsteps, Arthur advises Bedivere to simply do his best and not to place his trust in a monarch whose kingdom has crumbled. For Malory, this loss of faith may have acted as a parallel to his own misgivings about the state of England's precarious political system. However, we must remember that Malory's Arthur is a tragic figure, not a fool. Despite the ultimate failure of his chivalric dream, he is still shown to be a brave, visionary hero who lived and died defending a value system that, although impracticable, defined the fifteenth-century historical ideal.

Following the immense popularity of Thomas Malory's magnum opus,[32] public interest in the Arthurian legends began to wane, leading King Arthur into a literary drought that ended up lasting roughly 400 years.[33] However, with the rise of Romanticism and medievalism in the early nineteenth century, along with the Gothic Revival, the stories of Arthur and his knights regained a foothold in artistic and social culture. The most famous and important work from this era of Arthurian

---

[31] Malory, p. 924.

[32] It is no coincidence that William Caxton, one of the earliest publishers (1485) of *Le Morte d'Arthur*, chose Malory's text for one of his principal editions.

[33] John Milton actually planned on writing a national epic based on the history of King Arthur during the mid-1600s, but his goal never came to fruition.

restoration was Poet Laureate Alfred Tennyson's *Idylls of the King*. Tennyson lived during the reign of Queen Victoria, in an era that was marked by a lengthy period of prosperity for the British people, with the industrial revolution in the economy leading to the emergence of a large middle class.[34] The nineteenth century was also distinguished by period of relative peace in Great Britain, known as the *Pax Britannica,* which existed largely due to British naval superiority, imperialism, and the prevalence of overseas trade. However, one of the most influential aspects of Victorian England was the religious revival sparked by the Evangelical movement. According to Joseph Altholz in his essay on Victorian theology, the nineteenth century in Great Britain saw a resurgence of "religious activity unmatched since the days of the Puritans," which served to shape a system of morality that we now call *Victorianism*. During this period, Christianity played a vital role in the public consciousness, achieving a level of importance unmatched in the previous or following century.[35] The Evangelicals were favoured by Queen Victoria and Prince Albert and had significant influence in the aristocracy, but unlike the Catholics or Anglicans, they were not interested in rituals, synods, or political organization. Instead, they were very active in mission societies and sought to help the poor and fight against slavery. In addition to their humanitarian philosophy of active benevolence, the Evangelicals also imparted a sense of strict moral propriety on British society, as well as an emphasis on honesty and trustworthiness. Therefore, in Tennyson's account of the Arthurian legend, the king again transforms from the tragic defender of chivalry to a hero more attuned to the values of the Victorian era: a Christ-figure.

Rebecca Umland, in her essay on the religious and social allegories present in *Idylls of the King*, states that Tennyson "infused the Arthurian legend with Victorian standards of conduct," thereby creating a modern myth that embodies

---

[34] Morgan, p. 423-425.

[35] Parsons, Gerald, ed., *Religion in Victorian Britain*, (Manchester University Press: Manchester, 1989), p. 150.

distinctly nineteenth-century values rather than the nostalgic medieval principles emphasized in *Le Morte d'Arthur*.[36] Although the bulk of Tennyson's story is based on Malory's narrative framework, Arthur is shown in a different light as a divinely-inspired, visionary leader and as a paragon of Victorian dignity and morality. In an effort to complete Arthur's role as the perfect king, Tennyson removes all of the unsavoury elements of his character, such as his illegitimate birth and his incestuous adultery with his half-sister Morgause.[37] He also inserts numerous parallels with Jesus Christ, which surely would have resonated with his highly religious audience. For instance, when Arthur is first introduced, Gwenivere sees him approaching her father's castle without any heraldic or royal markings, riding as "a simple knight among his knights."[38] This image calls to mind the humble way in which Christ carried himself during his years of ministry, not crowned in glory but poor, dirty, and surrounded by fishermen. Furthermore, the barons initially doubt Arthur's claims to be king, crying out that he is not the son of Uther Pendragon but merely the son of Gorlois or Ector, [39] just as the Jews doubted Christ saying, "Is this not Jesus, the son of Joseph, whose father and mother we know? How does he now say, 'I have come down out of heaven'?"[40] However, Arthur's royalty and spiritual blessing are divinely confirmed when Gwenivere's father dreams of him being crowned in heaven.

---

[36] Shichtman, Martin, and Carley, James, eds., *Culture and the King: The Social Implications of the Arthurian Legend*, (State University of New York Press: New York, 1994), p. 274-275.

[37] In Malory's version, Arthur is conceived after Uther Pendragon deceives the wife of his enemy Gorlois through magic, and as a young man Arthur sleeps with Morgause, resulting in the birth of the traitor Mordred.

[38] Tennyson, Alfred, *Idylls of the King*, (Amereon House: New York, 1961), p. 16.

[39] In Tennyson's version, Sir Ector is called Sir Anton. I have used the more familiar name to avoid confusion.

[40] The Holy Bible, John 6:42, New American Standard Version.

The prevalent influence of Evangelical theology on Victorian England is clearly expressed in the first story Tennyson tells after the ascension of Arthur. In the tale of *Gareth and Lynette*, a young would-be knight named Gareth begs his mother's permission to join the court at Camelot, and in his pleading he describes what he considers to be a man's duty:

> How can ye keep me tether'd to you? – Shame.
> Man am I grown, a man's work I must do.
> Follow deer? Follow the Christ, the King,
> Live pure, speak true, right wrong, follow the King –
> Else, wherefore born?[41]

The knightly values conveyed by Gareth serve as a direct parallel to the Christian values encouraged by the Evangelicals. In both cases, a good man is expected to live a morally upright life, to be honest and trustworthy, to do acts of benevolence for those in need, and to follow the King, which in this instance refers both to Arthur and to Jesus Christ.

In addition to the moral elevation of Arthur, Tennyson relieves him of responsibility for the fall of his kingdom, placing the blame instead on the two women in his life. Gwenivere is held accountable for the collapse of the Round Table due to her adultery with Lancelot, and unlike the fiery execution she nearly receives in Malory's version, Tennyson instead allows Gwenivere to repent and flee to a convent where she is eventually forgiven by the merciful king. Despite her ultimate redemption, the queen's sexual promiscuity would have been viewed as one of the most detrimental and corrupting of all sins by Victorian society. Tennyson drives this point home with the character of Vivien, known in most other versions as Morgana le Fay. She is a seductress and a deceiver who attempts to beguile Arthur and succeeds in seducing Merlin in order to gain his knowledge of

[41] Tennyson, p. 30.

magic. Additionally, she informs Mordred and the other knights of the relationship between Gwenivere and Lancelot solely in an attempt to destroy the ideal kingdom Arthur has worked so hard to create. Often compared by the poet to a snake or serpent, Rebecca Umland argues that Vivien is the Satan to Arthur's Christ:

> Vivien's rebellion against Arthur, her antagonism towards his principles, and her use of her sexuality to achieve personal gain, have prompted readers to view her as a prototype of the archetypal temptress – Lilith, Eve, and Delilah – or even as a modernized version of Milton's Satan or Keat's Lamia.[42]

Just as Jesus resisted the temptation of Satan in the desert, Arthur resists Vivien's attempted seduction, revealing him as "the ideal Victorian man, who remains uncorrupted by the immorality around him."[43]

The most poignant reference to King Arthur as a Christ-figure comes just before he is fatally wounded in combat with Mordred. Prior to the climactic battle, as Sir Bedivere hears Arthur in his tent lamenting the tragic fate of his kingdom, the mournful king speaks of fighting God's wars and bemoans the fact that most men are unable to see the world through the eyes of God as he does. Finally he cries out, "My God, thou hast forgotten me in my death! Nay – God my Christ – I pass but shall not die."[44] This statement clearly mirrors the final words of Jesus on the cross, "My God, my God, why have you forsaken me?"[45] and also calls to mind the prophesied messianic return of both figures. Through such allegorical characterizations, Tennyson is able to transform King Arthur into the Victorian ideal: a faithful, morally

---

[42] Shichtman, p. 277.
[43] Shichtman, p. 283.
[44] Tennyson, p. 242.
[45] The Holy Bible, Mark 15:34, New American Standard Version.

upright leader seeking to create a better society in the vein of Evangelical philosophy, and a human reflection of Jesus Christ providing all men with a source of inspiration and hope.

Public interest in the Arthurian legend continued through the nineteenth and early twentieth centuries, with the stories of Arthur and his knights influencing writers such as T.S. Eliot and Mark Twain. The medieval romances branched into other media as well, appearing in everything from operas by Richard Wagner to the long-running comic strip *Prince Valiant*. However, in 1938, a young medieval scholar named T.H. White began to turn the Arthurian myth on its head, deconstructing the old legends and translating them into a thought-provoking political allegory entitled *The Once and Future King*. White published his masterpiece in four stages, beginning just prior to the outbreak of World War II and culminating during the height of the Cold War. By the time the first section was completed, Adolf Hitler had abolished democracy and rearmed Nazi Germany, Benito Mussolini had turned Italy into a fascist police state, and Joseph Stalin was on his way to creating a vast socialist empire. As Hitler's violent quest for power and new territory continued essentially unabated, war soon became inevitable and ignited intense debate between the largely pacifist British public and the unpopular fringe who supported military intervention.[46] Fittingly, it is this political dispute that White's King Arthur struggles with for the majority of the novel. In his attempt to contemporize the Arthurian legend, White removes all traces of the idealism that came before, from Geoffrey's idolization of military glory, to Malory's infatuation with the chivalric code, to Tennyson's emphasis on religious perfection. Rather than purely idealizing the hero himself, White instead turns Arthur into the idealist as he struggles to create a perfect society by searching for the balance between strength and justice.

Although he mainly follows the basic structure of Malory's narrative, White notably adds a great deal of new information on

[46] Morgan, p. 551-552.

Arthur's childhood in his first book, *The Sword In the Stone*. This whimsical fantasy tells of the years Arthur spent living as a commoner with his foster-father Sir Ector, as well as Merlin's attempts to educate the boy in ethics, proper government, and leadership. White's cynical view of war is illustrated by his treatment of the medieval knights, who are predominantly portrayed as oafish fools and whose chivalric principles are consistently mocked and parodied. For instance, the first example of knighthood that is introduced in the novel is the bumbling King Pellinore, a man obsessed with the endless, and often absurd, pursuit of the "Questing Beast." Additionally, during Kay's jousting lesson, Arthur informs Merlin that he would like to become a knight one day, and Merlin mocks the idea, referring to knights as "a lot of brainless unicorns swaggering about and calling themselves educated just because they can push each other off a horse with a bit of stick!"[47] Arthur is then allowed to watch a ridiculous joust between King Pellinore and another knight, which eventually ends with neither man hurting the other and both crashing into trees due to the weight of their armour.

The most significant addition White makes to the Arthurian legend is Merlin's use of magic to teach the young Arthur about various political philosophies. The old wizard first transforms Arthur into a fish so that he can meet a large pike named Old Jack, the King of the Moat, and learn the dangers of absolute tyranny. During their short conversation, the despotic pike lectures Arthur about power:

> Love is a trick played on us by the forces of evolution. Pleasure is the bait laid down by the same. There is only power. Power is of the individual mind, but the mind's power

[47] White, T.H., *The Once and Future King*, (G.P. Putnam's Sons: New York, 1958), p. 55.

is not enough. Power of the body decides everything in the end, and only Might is Right.[48]

This short statement, the barbaric claim that "only Might is Right," eventually becomes the driving force behind Arthur's noble quest to discover a fair and proper way to rule. The totalitarian dictatorship of the pike[49] may be comparable to the fascist governments of Hitler and Mussolini, which also placed great importance on militarism. In that vein, Merlin next turns Arthur into a falcon and allows him to spend the night talking with the other birds-of-prey, who refer to each other by military rank and speak mostly of hunting tactics and the glorious deeds of their ancestors. Through the falcons, Merlin reveals White's critique of militaristic societies, telling Arthur that while the birds "look on themselves as being dedicated to their profession, like an order of knighthood," they are really nothing more than prisoners being used by others.[50] The continued criticism of knighthood and the military in White's novel serves as a sharp contrast to Arthur's glorified wars against the Saxons and Romans in the pseudo-histories by Lawman and Geoffrey of Monmouth.

White proceeds in his campaign against unjust political philosophies through Arthur's experiences as an ant, thereby exposing the dangers of the so-called socialist utopia. The ant society is communal, but the tiny creatures do not freely work together for the common good. Instead, they give up all individuality, blindly and monotonously carrying out whatever mundane tasks they are assigned by an all-powerful central planner. They are nameless, faceless slaves, unable to think or ask questions, and unable to even perceive the notion of

---

[48] White, p. 47-48.

[49] It is interesting to note that the pike has a reputation as an overly voracious and vicious predator, which may serve as a parallel to Hitler's insatiable appetite for power.

[50] White, p. 71.

personal liberty. This uniform civilization of ants appears to be an allegory for the Marxist-Leninist collectivism that dominated Soviet Russia under Stalin.

Through Arthur's final transformation, we are shown White's vision of what constitutes a perfect society. After being turned into a goose, Arthur is introduced into a world of absolute freedom, a world without borders or boundaries, and a world without war:

> They [the geese] had no kings like Uther, no laws like the bitter Norman ones. They did not own things in common. Any goose who found something nice to eat considered it his own, and would peck any other one who tried to thieve it. At the same time, no goose claimed any exclusive territorial right in any part of the world – except its own nest, and that was private property.[51]

Young Arthur learns to love and appreciate the world of the geese, which might be politically labelled as either pure communism or as a form of democratic anarchy. However, White then spends the remainder of the novel exposing the tragic impossibility of such a society in this fallen, human world.

After *The Sword In the Stone,* White's novel moves into more familiar literary territory with the return to Malory's narrative prototype, and each successive book becomes darker and more mirthless than the last. Throughout the second book, *The Queen of Air and Darkness*, Arthur learns about the horrors of war and the justification of fighting in self-defence against wickedness. He creates the Round Table as a means of utilizing Might to achieve Right, but his noble experiment is plighted by obstacles and philosophical disagreements. For example, Sir Kay proposes that it would be justifiable for a king to start a war if he believed

---

[51] White, p. 173.

it necessary to force his beliefs on others for their own good. In response, Merlin again serves as a mouthpiece for the author and compares this view to Nazism, telling Kay of the charismatic Austrian who "tried to impose his reformation by the sword, and plunged the civilised world into misery and chaos."[52] Despite such setbacks, the king briefly succeeds in creating a more peaceful, civilised society, thereby allowing White to reveal his Arthur as a politically idealist hero whose lofty goals hold the answers for the problems of the twentieth century. However, as Europe began to be overcome by World War II, White must have seen the tragic impossibility of Arthur's dream, which is unveiled in the heart-breaking final chapter of *The Candle In the Wind*. With his queen imprisoned, his best knight banished, and his country broken in two by war, Arthur laments the loss of his youthful innocence and optimism. "He had been taught by Merlyn to believe that man was perfectible: that he was on the whole more decent than beastly: that good was worth trying," and he had struggled against the evils of Might in an attempt to make men happier, "but the whole structure depended on the first premise: that man was decent."[53] The tragedy is that White's Arthur lives in a world in which man isn't decent. At the core man is selfish, greedy, and vengeful, with no hope of achieving the perfect society illustrated by the geese. Therefore, Arthur remains the idealist, carefully shielding the flickering flame of his dream from the wind in hopes that one day it will be fulfilled.

Although T.H. White's characterisation of King Arthur as a pacifist political innovator differs greatly from his depiction by Thomas Malory as the tragic defender of chivalry, he is no less heroic in either retelling of the legend. And despite the vast thematic differences between Geoffrey of Monmouth's portrayal of Arthur as the redeemer of British identity and Alfred

---

[52] White, p. 274. For those unfamiliar with the text, Merlin is able to discuss Adolf Hitler and other elements of twentieth-century Europe because in this version, he lives backwards through time.
[53] White, p. 666.

Tennyson's exaltation of his reign to parallel the life of Christ, the mythic king remains a source of inspiration and pride. In recent years, there have been numerous further retellings of the Arthurian legend, each with its own distinct thematic tone and interpretation of the heroic ideal. The tales of King Arthur and his knights have been used to promote a wide range of ideas including anti-intellectualism, pagan revivalism, and even feminine empowerment, as seen in Marion Zimmer Bradley's *The Mists of Avalon*. Even modern attempts to strip away the fantasy and romance and portray Arthur as a genuine historical figure often showcase the predominant values of the day. For instance, a 2004 film version[54] posits Arthur as a Dark Age military leader of Romano-British descent protecting an outpost at Hadrian's Wall, but the primary conflict in the film emphasises traditionally American views on the inherent freedom and equality of all men. Regardless of the particular time or culture, the character of King Arthur continues to live on, repeatedly satisfying mankind's intrinsic need for a hero. He truly is *Rex Quondam, Rexque Futurus* – the Once and Future King, the ideal hero of legend, and the embodiment of our own evolving system of values. Throughout history he has changed and adapted to fit varying cultural standards for righteous kingship, and his reign has provided heroic inspiration for not just world leaders, but for the common man as well; therefore, we are able to project ourselves onto Arthur, drawing out the better angels of our nature. In a way he is a representative of the individual's desire to live up to his full potential, because as Joseph Campbell writes, "the mighty hero of extraordinary powers... is each of us: not the physical self-visible in the mirror, but the king within."[55]

---

[54] *King Arthur*, Dir. Antoine Fuqua, Writ. David Franzoni, Perf. Clive Owen, (Touchstone Pictures, 2004).

[55] Campbell, p. 365.

Bibliography

Archibald, Elizabeth, and Edwards, A.S.G., eds. *A Companion to Malory*. D.S Brewer: Cambridge, 1996.

Campbell, Joseph. *The Hero With a Thousand Faces*. Fontana Press: London, 1993.

Geoffrey of Monmouth. *The History of the Kings of Britain*. Trans. Lewis Thorpe. Penguin Books: London, 1966.

Lawman. *Brut*. Trans. Rosamund Allen. Everyman's Library: London, 1992.

Lewis, C.S. *The Discarded Image: An Introduction to Medieval and Renaissance Literature*. Cambridge University Press: Cambridge, 1964.

Loomis, Roger Sherman, ed. *Arthurian Literature in the Middle Ages: A Collaborative History*. Claredon Press: Oxford, 1959.

Malory, Thomas. *Le Morte D'Arthur*. The Modern Library: New York, 1994.

Morgan, Kenneth, ed. *The Oxford Illustrated History of Britain*. Oxford University Press: Oxford, 1984.

Parsons, Gerald, ed. *Religion in Victorian Britain: Interpretations*. Manchester University Press: Manchester, 1989.

Pochoda, Elizabeth. *Arthurian Propaganda: Le Morte D'Arthur as an Historical Ideal of Life*. The University of North Carolina Press: Chapel Hill, 1971.

Shichtman, Martin, and Carley, James, eds. *Culture and the King: The Social Implications of the Arthurian Legend*. State University of New York Press: New York, 1994.

Stanley, E.G. "Layamon's Antiquarian Sentiments." *Medium Aevum* Vol. 38, (1969) p. 23-34.

Tennyson, Alfred. *Idylls of the King*. Amereon House: New York, 1961.

Turville-Petre, Thorlac. *England the Nation: Language, Literature, and National Identity, 1290-1340.* Clarendon Press: Oxford, 1996.

White, T.H. *The Once and Future King*. G.P. Putnam's Sons: New York, 1958.

60837150R00274

Made in the USA
Charleston, SC
07 September 2016